Sew in Love

SEW IN LOVE

4 HISTORICAL STORIES

DEBBY LEE
JACQUOLYN MCMURRAY
DARLENE PANZERA
KIMBERLEY WOODHOUSE

THORNDIKE PRESS
A part of Gale, a Cengage Company

Fountaindale Public Library
Bolingbrook, IL
(630) 759-2102

Hearts Sewn with Love ©2019 by Darlene Panzera
Woven Hearts ©2019 by Jacquolyn McMurray
A Language of Love ©2019 by Kimberley Woodhouse
Tailored Sweethearts ©2019 by Debby Lee
All scripture quotations are taken from the King James Version of the Bible.
Thorndike Press, a part of Gale, a Cengage Company.

Thorndike Press® Large Print Christian Historical Fiction.
The text of this Large Print edition is unabridged.
Other aspects of the book may vary from the original edition.
Set in 16 pt. Plantin.

LIBRARY OF CONGRESS CIP DATA ON FILE.
CATALOGUING IN PUBLICATION FOR THIS BOOK
IS AVAILABLE FROM THE LIBRARY OF CONGRESS

ISBN-13: 978-1-4328-7808-5 (hardcover alk. paper)

Published in 2020 by arrangement with Barbour Publishing, Inc.

Printed in Mexico
Print Number: 01   Print Year: 2020

Sew in Love

■ ■ ■ ■

HEARTS SEWN WITH LOVE

BY DARLENE PANZERA

■ ■ ■ ■

With special thanks to
Krysteen Seelen and Kate Breslin,
for your friendship,
generosity of time, and compassion.
You are a true blessing
to those around you.

CHAPTER 1

April 16, 1850
Maggie McDermott leaned over the rail of the 226-foot sidewheel paddle steamer, her pulse quickening as she surveyed the Sacramento port where they would soon dock. "Almost there, Mother," she said, glancing at the beloved, gray-haired woman beside her. " 'Tis a long journey we've had, but within the hour we will step off this boat and into our new home."

"God willing," Clara McDermott muttered, a touch of a smile upon her lips.

"Yes," Maggie said, and drew in a deep breath. For she fully believed leaving New York City and journeying to Gold Bar, a small town outside Sacramento, must certainly be God's will for their lives. Even if it meant she must marry Lewis Parnell, her late father's second cousin, whom she barely knew.

"Surely," her mother said hesitantly,

"Cousin Lewis would have estimated the time of our ship's arrival?"

Maggie glanced toward the shore where several finely dressed men had gathered to greet the passengers. "I am certain he will be here."

It had taken their schooner, the *Cordova,* six and a half months to sail from Boston down around Cape Horn, the southernmost tip of South America, and then back up the other side of the continent to California. But they'd whisked through the mile-wide waterway known as the Golden Gate and into the San Francisco Bay on schedule. From there, they secured passage aboard the *Senator,* and it had only taken another six days for the paddle steamer to transport them upriver to Sacramento.

Maggie's mother clasped the folds of her gray cape tighter about her neck as they followed the other passengers off the boat. "I don't see him."

"He must be up there by the buildings." Maggie swept her gaze over the sparsely treed town perched on the hill. "And if he isn't, we can at least find something to eat while we wait for him."

Her mother nodded. "A good meal *would* be nice. I never want to eat another crust of moldy bread from the meager rationings of

12

a ship ever again."

"And you won't have to," Maggie reminded her. "Cousin Lewis assured us in his letter that we'll be living in luxury."

Her mother's face took on a wistful expression. "In a big house along the river, with an expansive green lawn and terraced gardens."

"And enough gold lining our pockets to make us richer than a leprechaun," Maggie said, smiling.

"At the moment, enough money to buy a meat pie would suit me just fine." Her mother's weary eyes suddenly brightened. "Or a bowl of Irish stew with savory beef and potatoes and carrots —"

Maggie pointed to a sign on one of the wooden buildings labeled EATERY and asked, "Shall we?"

Leaving their trunks in the care of the ship's porter, Maggie caught sight of the nine-year-old boy, Phillip Trescott, who had also sailed on the *Cordova* out of Boston then boarded the paddle steamer. He'd been unaccompanied, much to Maggie's disapproval. And now he stood off to the side, alone, with an aloof expression Maggie suspected was merely a brave attempt to appear unafraid.

Maggie extended her hand. "Phillip,

would you care to join us while you are waiting for your uncle to arrive?"

He gave her a vigorous nod. "I'd be honored, Maggie. Besides, you may need a chaperone."

The boy's polite, polished prose usually made her smile, but when she saw the clusters of men to whom he referred staring at her, she clamped her lips together tight and kept her head down as she ushered both him and her mother into the eatery.

Were there no other women in town? Maggie saw one, but she wore bright red feathers in her hair and a dress with a bodice cut too low to be called anything but indecent. The type of woman rumored to entertain men. The kind whom her mother had always warned her to stay away from so as not to tarnish her own reputation. Were there no other mothers, daughters, sisters, or even grandmothers of polite society to associate with, then?

Inside the eatery the eyes upon them only multiplied, until self-consciousness destroyed Maggie's hunger and all she wanted was to escape.

"Excuse me, sir?" she asked the man behind the counter. "Do you know where I might find a carriage to take us to Gold Bar?"

14

His eyes widened as he looked her up and down then gave her a toothy grin. "A *carriage*? You won't be findin' any carriage around here, miss, not even with a pound of gold in your satchel."

Maggie frowned. "How might one get to Gold Bar?"

"You might walk," he suggested. "Or go by mule."

"Did he just say *mule*?" Maggie's mother asked, her eyes wide. "Surely he doesn't expect a lady to sit her skirts upon one of those filthy animals!"

"I rode a horse once," young Phillip boasted.

"Horses will cost you," the man behind the counter told him.

Maggie's mother gestured toward the chalkboard on the wall. "Apparently, so will the food. Ten dollars for a dozen eggs? Whoever heard of such prices?"

Several men around them burst into laughter, and one shouted that he could buy her eight dozen eggs with the gold he found that morning. Maggie tried not to make eye contact with any of them. With her heart thumping in her ears, she leaned toward her mother and whispered, "Perhaps we should leave."

"They can eat, because everyone here has

money," her mother said, her attention clearly fixated only on the food. "Or at least it seems they do, for all their boasting. Did you hear the young man in the corner bet the others a full ounce of gold he could win at cards? Do you think they've all found as much gold as Cousin Lewis?"

Maggie steered her mother away from them, took Phillip's hand, and swallowed the lump forming in the back of her throat as the men's leers continued to make her uncomfortable. "I think I saw a stand selling meat pies near the waterfront."

However, as they turned around, their path was blocked when one of the men punched another man in front of them, calling him a cheat. The accused swaggered, knocking Maggie and her mother to the side, then lunged toward the first man to retaliate.

Maggie took the opportunity to tuck young Phillip safely into her side to keep him from harm, but several fists swung back and forth as a few other men joined in, and Maggie, her mother, and Phillip stood trapped right in the middle of them.

As another fist shot forward, Maggie winced, sure she was going to take the brunt of it, when at the last second a broad, dark-haired man, several inches taller than herself, stepped in the way and took the blow instead. The impact knocked him over and dropped him to the ground at her feet.

"Hey, watch out for the ladies," her rescuer growled.

The one who had punched him raised his brows and exclaimed, "Ben, is that you?"

He nodded, rubbed his jaw, and picked himself up off the floor. "It's me."

"Sorry 'bout that," the other man replied, then let out a big-hearted laugh. "I was aimin' for someone else."

"No offense taken," Ben told him. "But if you don't mind, could you clear a path so I can escort these ladies and the young lad out?"

After his friend managed to push the other men away, the man named Ben turned, and Maggie acknowledged that despite the red welt upon the right side of his jaw he'd gallantly acquired for her sake, his facial features were quite handsome. He wore his wavy brown hair parted to the side, and although simply dressed in a beige shirt with brown trousers, the sparkle in his eyes made him appear far more dashing than the other men who flaunted their newfound wealth with their tall top hats, silk cravats, and fob watches.

Ben picked up the straw hat that had been

knocked off his head during the fistfight, and she noticed that his dark brows and hazel-green eyes were startlingly similar to Phillip's.

Once they were safely outside, Maggie asked "Are you by any chance young Master Trescott's uncle?"

"I am," Ben assured her, tousling the hair atop Phillip's head. "He will be living with me now that his mother — my sister — and her husband are no longer with us."

Maggie nodded. "Upon our first meeting at sea, Phillip and I discovered we have much in common. I lost my father too. Almost two years ago now."

Ben frowned. "Are you not my nephew's governess?"

Maggie shook her head. "No. My mother and I met Master Trescott while on board the *Cordova,* sailing out of Boston." She pursed her lips then added, "He was *alone.*"

"*Alone?*" Ben stared at her, then the muscle along his jaw tightened as he looked down at Phillip. "Where is Miss Lang?"

Phillip shrugged. "She decided the trip might make her seasick."

"I paid her a full year's salary in advance to accompany you."

Ben's voice shook with what sounded like fury, as well as fear, which was understandable, considering the situation, and Maggie forgave him now she knew he had not consented to have the boy travel alone. Her thoughts were not so merciful, however, toward Miss Lang, whoever she was. Anyone with any decency at all would never have allowed such a thing!

"If I had known —" Ben continued solemnly, looking his nephew straight in the eye, "I would have come for you myself."

Phillip lifted his chin. "I managed all right."

"He did indeed," Maggie said, her heart going out to them both as they looked warily at one another. "Master Trescott was honorable enough to keep my mother and me company for most of the trip, for which we are exceedingly grateful."

"As am I." Ben shot her a look of gratitude over the boy's head then smiled. "And although you may know one another quite well by now, my nephew and I need some time to get reacquainted." He glanced at Phillip, then turned back to Maggie, tipped the brim of his straw hat toward her, and added, "As do we. I'm Benjamin Freethy."

"Miss Maggie McDermott," she said, dipping into a slight curtsy. "And my mother, Mrs. McDermott."

"We appreciate your help in the eatery,"

Maggie's mother said with a shudder. "This is no place for a lady."

"No, it isn't," Ben agreed with a rueful grin. "Pardon my asking, but what are you doing here?"

"We've come to live with my cousin," Maggie informed him. "However, when we stepped off the steamer, he was not there to greet us. He lives in Gold Bar."

"He may have gotten delayed," Ben assured her. "I'm also from Gold Bar. What is his name?"

"Lewis Parnell."

Ben's jovial expression dropped as soon as the name left her lips. Alarmed, Maggie glanced at her mother then asked, "Is there something wrong, Mr. Freethy?"

Ben clenched his jaw, as if hesitant to respond, then said, "I'm afraid he's gone, Miss McDermott."

Anxiety coursed up Maggie's spine. "What do you mean, gone?"

Had Cousin Lewis picked up and left? Had he changed his mind about marrying her?

Ben heaved a sigh. "Lewis Parnell . . . is dead."

After more than eight months of living in a land devoid of most females, especially *de-*

20

cent single young ladies, Ben never imagined that when he finally found one, he'd have to be the bearer of bad news.

The women didn't take it well. For several moments, Miss McDermott, the sweet young woman with the lilting, soft Irish accent and reddish-blond curls poking out from the sides of her floral bonnet, just stared at him. Then as his words sank in, her delicate pink lips parted, and she let out a small gasp. She looked as if she were about to reach for him but pivoted a half second later to catch her mother, who had started to faint.

"Is she going to be all right?" Phillip rushed forward to help the older woman stand.

"Perhaps if we can get her something to drink," Miss McDermott said with worry lines creasing her forehead. "Our throats are parched, and we haven't had anything to eat in quite some time. I fear this news, after we've traveled so very far, is just too much for her."

Ben nodded. He imagined the news was too much for Miss McDermott to bear as well, but she seemed to be putting up a brave front, despite the helpless look lurking in her beautiful blue eyes. Disconcerted, he quickly moved toward the corner street vendor.

"Four beef pastries and a jug of water, please?" Ben drew a few coins from his pocket and put them on the vendor's counter.

Hastily settling beside him, Maggie dug through her carpetbag. "Thank you for your kindness, Mr. Freethy, but you do not have to pay for ours."

"Please, Miss McDermott," Ben said, brushing his hand briefly against hers. "I insist."

What was he doing? He had no time for intimacies of any kind. Not when he had the boy to raise, and certainly not until he'd panned enough gold to build the kind of life a woman deserved.

Perhaps empathy for the young woman and her mother made him reach out to her. Or, more truthfully, his own selfish desire. He hadn't touched a woman's hand, even gloved, in a very long time. But whatever the reason, he couldn't deny the pleasant jolt of awareness that jumped between them when he did.

Maggie blushed and averted her gaze, as any proper young lady would. Then as the vendor handed her one of the minced-meat pies, her appetite must have gotten the better of her reserve, because she greedily gobbled the food, as if ravished, as did his young nephew. The elder woman, Mrs. McDermott, hardly took more than two bites. She sat prim and proper on a bench amid her many layers of gray skirts, took a sip from the water jug, and looked about to cry.

"What will become of us?" she whispered.

"Seems to me, ma'am, the most practical solution would be to take another ship back home," Ben offered.

"We can't go back." Maggie's eyes widened, and her expression turned more than a little desperate. "After Father died, our finances dwindled, and we had to sell most everything we owned. Cousin Lewis sent money to book our passage, but we haven't enough for a return trip."

"You can't stay here," Ben warned. "This town isn't fit for a decent woman."

"Is there no other option?" Maggie asked, her voice grave.

He swallowed hard as his gaze locked with hers. "I suppose, if you wanted, I could take you to Gold Bar to collect your cousin's things. He left some personal items for you with the postmaster, although I fear it isn't much."

"We must see what it is," her mother insisted. "And pay our respects."

Maggie nodded and looked at him with such hope his heart skipped a beat. "We'd gladly accept your assistance to journey onward to Gold Bar — if it isn't too much trouble."

"It isn't too much trouble," Ben said, his throat raspy as he forced out the words. Somewhere in the back of his mind, a little voice called him a fool. Although, for the life of him he couldn't bring himself to take back the offer — or tear his gaze away from Miss McDermott's beautiful fair-skinned face.

Besides, he was indebted to these women for looking after his nephew these last six and a half months. Taking them to Gold Bar was the least he could do.

"We would be happy to escort you, Maggie," Phillip chimed in.

Ben raised his brows. "Shouldn't you address her as Miss McDermott?"

"I've given him liberty to call me Maggie," she said, the lilt in her voice entrancing Ben as she spoke. "Since you've been so kind, Mr. Freethy, you may do the same."

He nodded and grinned. "If you'll call me Ben."

Maggie's mother didn't share her enthusiasm. Instead, she gave him a deep look of concern. "Will we have to ride a mule?"

"No," he assured her. "I have a wagon."

"Well, thank the good Lord for that," the woman declared.

Maggie gave him a grateful smile that sent his emotions into a tailspin until second thoughts berated him. *What are you doing? It's best not to let yourself get involved.*

But he couldn't very well leave the ladies on their own in this town. Not with more than three-quarters of these brazen, uncouth men starved for the mere sight of a woman, let alone the opportunity to gain one's attention. He didn't trust the fellows to keep their hands to themselves any more than he could trust them not to steal his gold — if he found any.

Even now, scores of men were staring at them, ogling the beautiful reddish-blond locks framing Maggie's face and her dainty floral bonnet tied with those incredibly feminine pink satin ribbons.

Ben escorted the women and his young nephew to the wagon and mule team he'd left hitched to a nearby tree and prepared to swing by the riverfront to collect their trunks.

"Gold Bar isn't much but a mining camp about an hour and a half away," he told them. "Once we get there, I'll take you to the postmaster to inquire after Parnell's personal belongings and see that you get a room at the hotel where you'll at least have a safe place to spend the night."

After that he couldn't make the women any more promises. For better or for worse, they'd be on their own.

CHAPTER 2

Ben glanced back over his shoulder at the two women seated behind him in the wagon to make sure they were all right. They'd been quiet for almost two-thirds of the trip, most likely mourning the loss of Maggie's cousin and contemplating what they would do when they reached Gold Bar. He didn't know what he'd do in their situation.

His chest tightened as he recalled the day he and his sister lost their parents. Ben had been eight years old, six years behind his sister, Lucinda, when an aunt came to take them back to her ranch in Vermont. Ma had become weakened with the influenza first, then shortly after, Pa got sick too. The doctors did what they could, but ultimately Ben's parents passed away within hours of each other.

He glanced over at his nephew sitting on the front seat of the wagon beside him, who had just lost his parents, killed in an overturned wagon accident. One of them, Ben's own dear sister, Lucinda. A deep pang of regret hit him hard. Now with the rest of their family gone, he would look after her son, like she had helped look after him while growing up.

The back of his throat grew tight just thinking about it. Would he be a good father figure to the boy? At the very least, a good uncle?

It seemed to him there was too much sorrow sitting in the wagon with them this day. Maggie and her mother had started sniffling, and Ben decided that if they were going to make it to Gold Bar without their tears flooding the floorboards, he had to do something to lighten the mood. Perhaps a little conversation would cheer everyone up?

He cleared his throat and turned to take another glance at Maggie. Having not seen many marriageable young women this past year under the age of thirty, his blood quickened at the sight of her and it took him a moment to find his voice. "Are — are you originally from Boston, Maggie?"

She shook her head. "No, as I'm sure you can tell from my accent, my family is from Ireland. We came to the States twelve years ago when I was naught but a wee girl and settled in New York."

"I trust your journey to California aboard the *Cordova* was satisfactory?"

"As well as can be expected."

From her good-natured tone, Ben would have believed her experience upon the sailing vessel to have been almost pleasant, except for the subtle twitch of her lips that suggested otherwise.

Beside him, Phillip scowled. "Thunderstorms. High winds. Rough seas. Especially around Cape Horn."

"At least we did not lack for food," Maggie countered.

His young nephew wrinkled his nose. "Yeah, if you like mold and maggots."

"And we slept well," Maggie added.

The boy let out a small laugh. "When the rats weren't nibbling on our toes."

Ben couldn't be sure if he was hearing tall tales or the truth. "Rats?"

"Yes." Phillip's eyes widened with excitement. "Great big ones with tails as long as —"

"Our accommodations could have been slightly better," Maggie hurriedly admitted, cutting him off.

Phillip leaned toward Ben, his expression earnest, and confided, "You've never seen such sorry conditions."

"Now mind your manners, Phillip," Mag-

29

gie admonished. "Remember what I told you about complaining?"

"Yes, ma'am," Phillip conceded. " 'Always look for the positive in every situation, and thank the good Lord that things are not worse.' "

Maggie nodded her approval and slipped the boy a smile, one that lit her eyes with a radiant sparkle and stole every ounce of breath from Ben's lungs. Although he had not seen many women this past year when living in the gold mining camp, he was certain of one thing — he had never seen a woman as beautiful as Maggie when she smiled.

She turned her gaze back to him. "How did you come to California, Ben?"

He grinned, the sound of his name on her lips more alluring than he ever could have imagined. "Signed on with a wagon train west from Missouri last year. Took us four months along the California Trail. When we arrived in August, we learned the rumors claiming James W. Marshall had found gold at Sutter's Mill were true. Most of my party came out to homestead, myself included, but once we heard the tales of twenty-dollar nuggets just lying around in the streambeds waiting to be picked up, we all headed straight for the mining camps along the rivers."

"Have you found much gold?" Maggie asked, her eyes rapt with attention.

"Not enough," he admitted. "At least not yet."

"And who will watch over Phillip while you pan for gold?" she asked, curiosity in her voice. "Your wife?"

Ben met her gaze. "I'm not married."

"Oh. Well." Her cheeks grew nearly as pink as her ribbons. "Surely you will place him in school?"

He hesitated, not wanting to earn her disapproval, then slowly shook his head. "There's no school at the mining camp."

Maggie gasped. "But who will look after the boy's education?"

"I am now nine and a half," Phillip said, lifting his chin. "I don't need to go to school. I can pan for gold like Uncle Ben and get rich."

Maggie raised her brows. "And what would you do with such riches?"

Ben watched his nephew's gaze dart briefly toward him, and then he turned away and shrugged. "I don't know."

"A proper education might help you find out," Maggie said, her voice firm.

Ben knew she was right. "After I find

31

enough gold, I'll see to it the boy has a proper education," he promised.

"Then I wish God's blessing upon you in your gold-panning endeavors," Maggie said, her lilting voice once again filled with pleasant optimism. Then she craned her neck, looked past him, and frowned. "Ben," she said, pointing and drawing his attention back to the road ahead. "Is that Gold Bar?"

"Can't be," her mother said, her voice low. "It's too small."

"It is," Ben said, dismayed to have to be the bearer of bad news once again. "Gold Bar isn't large enough to officially be called a town, at least not yet."

"But Mr. Freethy," Mrs. McDermott protested. "All I see are tents."

"There are a few wooden buildings," he assured her. "But tents are easier to pack up and transport to a new location — if there's no gold."

"What about that wood shack over there in the trees?" Phillip asked, gesturing with a wave of his hand.

Ben couldn't lie. And the women would find out soon enough. "*That* belonged to Lewis Parnell."

Mrs. McDermott groaned. "Surely he didn't live there."

"Of course not, Mother," Maggie whispered. " 'Tis merely a shed."

Phillip pointed. "The sign over the door says 'Home Sweet Home.' "

"The windows are broken," Maggie protested. "There is a gaping hole in the roof, and —"

"Rats!" Phillip exclaimed. "Did you just see that big brown one scurry through a slot in the side wall?"

"This cannot be his only house, not the one he described to us in his letters," Maggie said, her voice strained. "Because he found gold, enough to build another much bigger, better house, with a wraparound porch, and —" She broke off and gave Ben a questioning look. "Is *this* where our cousin lived?"

Knowing how hard this must be for her, Ben couldn't bring himself to answer, only nod.

"What are we going to do?" Maggie asked, her voice weak.

" 'Always look for the positive in every situation,' " Phillip said brightly. " 'And thank the good Lord that things are not worse.' "

Ben brought the mule team to a stop in front of the camp entrance, spotted the crowd of rowdy, women-deprived men coming back from a long day at the river, and knew full well that — unfortunately — things *were* about to get worse.

Gold Bar was nothing like Cousin Lewis had described. With only about two dozen filthy canvas tents lined up in two rows with a single earthen aisle between, and a few ramshackle buildings erected in the background, Maggie couldn't help but wonder what he had been thinking when he'd invited them here. Had he been trying to paint a positive picture for her like she had tried to do for Phillip? As far as she could tell, the stone fire pit near the flagpole in the corner of the camp was the only means they had for cooking, and not only was there no school, but there didn't appear to be a church for Sunday service either.

They did have a small post office, an infirmary, and a bakery, which doubled as a hotel and boasted on its sign of having six rooms.

With her stomach fluttering, Maggie hoped one of the rooms might be available for her and her mother that night. But what if they were all taken?

Minding her skirts, she gave Ben her hand and allowed him to help her down from the wagon. Didn't he promise he'd see to it they would have a safe place to sleep?

She heard a chorus of boisterous male whoops and turned her head to see a half-dozen men carrying an assortment of shovels, pickaxes, and pans coming toward them, most likely returning to camp from a long day of panning for gold at the river. Upon seeing her, several of them stopped up short. Their mouths fell open. And they stared . . . just like the men she and her mother had encountered in both San Francisco and Sacramento.

"Hey, Ben, what you got there?" a jovial, dark-bearded man called out. "Is that why you took the wagon today? To go pick yourself up a wife?"

Ben grinned then shook his head. "She's not mine."

The incoming men were already ogling her with their jaws hanging. Now upon hearing she might well indeed be single, they instantly straightened, some puffing out their chests, broad grins spreading across their dirt-splattered faces.

As if Ben realized her vulnerable position, he quickly added, "Miss McDermott and her mother are cousins of Lewis Parnell."

The bearded man who had first spoken frowned. "Parnell?"

One of the larger-bodied men in the back stepped forward, and Maggie could see the sandy-haired fellow was better dressed than his peers, wearing a clean white shirt rolled up at the elbows, as opposed to the others whose clothing was in dire need of washing and mending.

The man's gaze boldly slid over her, and then he let out a long, drawn-out appreciative whistle. "Too bad Parnell's not here. My condolences, ladies." Bowing, and sweeping his wide-brimmed straw hat off his head, he continued, "Hubert Elias Kendrick at your service. Perhaps I can be of assistance?"

"No need, Hugh," Ben said, stepping around to help Phillip and then Maggie's mother also descend from the wagon.

"Thank ye kindly, Mr. Freethy," Maggie said softly. "I don't know what we'd have done if ye hadn't come along when ye did."

"Well, I'll be," another man exclaimed. "She's Irish!"

Maggie had been careful to keep her speech nearly impeccable until this point, but unfortunately, whenever she was nervous, her native accent invariably slipped out a wee bit more than usual. Ben looked at her with amused surprise, as did the other men, which made her feel even more conspicuous.

The big, bold fellow named Kendrick

36

laughed. "Looks like we struck gold, boys!"

"Not gold. I'd say she's got curls of sun-lit copper," a round-bellied man drawled, then stepped closer. "Or would you say strawberry honey?"

"Red gold," said the lanky fellow to his left.

Mr. Kendrick pulled the man back and stepped in front of him. "My, but have you ever seen such a pretty sight? I'll give you five dollars for a lock of your hair, lass."

Her hair? Maggie gasped and reached up to tuck a loose curl safely back into the confines of her bonnet.

"Ten dollars!" shouted another man.

"Fifteen!" yelled a third, and the entire crowd broke into a clamor of highly inappropriate offers.

Beside her, Maggie's mother let out a soft cry, and Maggie pushed her and Phillip safely behind her. Had no one taught these wild, unruly men any manners? Was it the gold that had corrupted their senses? Like King Midas?

Thank the Lord she had met Ben first. Once again acting as her protector, he stepped forward to place himself between her and the other men. "Sorry, boys, but the young lady and her fine golden tresses are not for sale."

"Says who?" Mr. Kendrick demanded. He raised a brow as if to challenge Ben. "Have *you* staked a claim on her?"

As the two men stood nose to nose, Maggie could sense the rivalry between them and held her breath as Ben replied, "Let's just say the lady doesn't require your attention. Go back to your digging and try your luck there."

"Already did." The glint in Mr. Kendrick's eyes mocked him.

"He found gold!" the round-bellied man shouted, grinning. "Got a fifty-dollar nugget by the look of it!"

"Yeah, tomorrow it will be my turn," boasted another.

Mr. Kendrick held out his hand to show off his newly found treasure, and Maggie couldn't help but peer around Ben to take a closer look.

"That caught her attention," Mr. Kendrick said, giving her a wink. "There's nothing that money can't buy . . . eventually."

The muscle along the side of Ben's jaw jumped, confirming that these two men were most definitely *not* friends.

"Congratulations on your find, Mr. Kendrick," Maggie said, nodding toward the walnut-sized, coppery-golden rock in his hand.

"Please," he insisted. "Call me Hugh."

Maggie nodded. "Thank you. Now that I know your name, I will be able to tell the sheriff, so I may issue a complaint detailing your exceptionally rude behavior."

The other men laughed, and Hugh broke into a smile as if he thought her funny. "You won't be finding a sheriff here in Gold Bar."

"He's right," Ben told her.

"No sheriff?" Maggie frowned. "How do you keep law and order?"

Hugh snickered. "We *don't.*"

"That's not exactly true," Ben assured her. "The majority rules when there's a call to be made on certain matters."

Hugh laughed. "Of course, money has a great deal of influence."

"Not over me," Maggie declared.

The smug, egotistical man leveled his gaze on her. "We'll see about that."

The muscle along Ben's jaw jumped again, and from the look in his eye, Maggie was certain Ben would like to punch him. Maggie balled her own fist and would have been sorely tempted to punch Hugh herself, but then she heard another man claim, "I'll take her mother."

And when her mother swooned, at least ten men swooped in to catch her like a flock of vicious vultures.

"Leave her alone!" Maggie cried.

"I've got you, Mrs. McDermott," Ben soothed, taking her mother's arm and pulling her out of the hammock of hands that had kept her from falling to the ground.

"Just trying to help, miss," said one of the other men, and a clamor of echoing agreements erupted around them, until one voice rose above the others.

A voice that was blessedly female.

"Stand back, or you'll get no bread from my bakery tonight," said a large, bustling woman waving a large wooden spoon. "I'll take it from here."

The men parted, but not before some received a few swats.

A second woman, older and slightly stooped, with gray streaks in her hair, also rushed forward and growled under her breath, "Best we get her inside, away from those mongrels."

The larger woman with the spoon agreed. "Ben, can you help my Samuel carry her into the bakery?"

Ben gave the woman and the dark-bearded man from the crowd a nod, then glanced around and tensed. "Where's Phillip?"

Maggie pulled the boy out from behind her. "Right here."

The taut, worried expression on Ben's

face relaxed as he spotted his nephew. Then he looked back at Maggie and gave her a half grin. "Seems like we keep needing to look out for one another this fine day."

"Yes," she said, her cheeks warm as he held her gaze. "It certainly does."

Ben and Samuel helped guide the weakened Mrs. McDermott up the three wooden steps of the bakery. Samuel's wife, Esther, opened the door then pointed her spoon toward a bench seat in the front of the shop by the window.

"Sit her down, right there," Esther directed.

After Mrs. McDermott expressed her gratitude, Maggie, Phillip, Esther, and the stooped washerwoman, Agnes Henshaw, gathered around her to commiserate. At a loss of what else to do, Ben allowed Samuel to pull him off to the side.

"I thought you went and missed all the excitement today down at the river, but I guess you found some excitement of your own, eh?" Samuel joked.

Ben glanced past him toward the women, and his gaze lingered on Maggie, who had her back to him. "If you call having to fend off every besotted male within fifty feet of Maggie McDermott exciting, then yeah, I

41

guess it's been an exciting day."

Samuel grinned. "How did they end up with you?"

"Parnell sent for them months ago," Ben told him. "They arrived on the same ship as my nephew. Of course with the mail service as slow as it is, they were unaware that Parnell had passed on. I told them I could bring them to Gold Bar to collect his things, but I'm not sure what they're going to do after that."

Samuel poked him in the ribs. "You should marry her quick before she leaves. Who knows when another available woman will pass this way?"

Ben took another glance at Maggie and his pulse quickened. "You know I can't afford to support a wife. I live in a tent. And it will be hard enough to support my nephew if I don't find more larger nuggets of gold soon."

"Did you see the chunk of gold Kendrick had in his hand?"

Ben nodded, his stomach tight. If he hadn't had to go to Sacramento to pick up his nephew today, it might have been *he* who discovered the gold. Of course, if he'd stayed in Gold Bar, he never would have met Maggie.

Ben scoffed, irritated at Kendrick's

haughty higher-than-thou attitude as well as his own lack of financial resources. "Most likely it was one of Kendrick's men who found the gold. Kendrick rarely does any panning himself anymore."

Samuel ran his hand over his dark beard and confided, "He said he found it in one of them river caves. Has me thinking maybe *we* should try panning in some of them caves too."

Ben shook his head. "No. It's too dangerous. The caves can collapse. Remember what happened to Nash? Now he's crippled and has to earn his living as a tailor."

"Kendrick isn't crippled," Samuel reminded him. "And with each new nugget he finds, he's even richer than before. He thinks he can buy anything he wants — including your new lady friend. You might have to fight him for her."

"I'd fight for her dignity, but I can't propose to Miss McDermott or any other woman until I can afford to provide for her like a decent husband should."

Samuel wiggled his brows. "Rumor has it there's quite a bit of gold to be found in them river caves."

Ben frowned. "Sam."

Samuel shrugged, breaking into a broad grin. "Just telling you what I heard."

■ ■ ■ ■

Maggie left her mother and Phillip at the bakery where Esther Watkins had set out a plate of sweet rolls, and followed Ben to the tiny wooden building next door to visit the postmaster. Ben had said she could wait until morning to inquire after her cousin's belongings, but Maggie knew she wouldn't sleep a wink until she found out if Cousin Lewis had left them any money, so they might pay for their lodging.

The post office wasn't so much a building that one might enter, but rather resembled a vendor stand with two large double wooden shutters that opened like the upper portion of a barn door when Ben knocked.

A man with thin, wiry brown hair poked his head through the opening.

"Tom Green, this is Miss McDermott, cousin of Lewis Parnell," Ben introduced. "And she'd very much like to collect what's his."

Mr. Green adjusted his round, black-rimmed spectacles and appeared to give her a closer look. "You got any proof?"

Maggie frowned. "Proof of what?"

"Proof that you're his cousin," Mr. Green said, quirking his brow. "I can't be giving

44

his things to just anyone."

"I — I don't believe I have anything that shows we're related," Maggie said hesitantly. "I didn't expect that he wouldn't be here."

"C'mon, Tom," Ben said, giving the man a hard look. "She's had a rough enough time as it is."

Mr. Green rubbed his chin. "Well then, can you describe what Lewis Parnell looked like?"

Maggie hesitated. "He had brown hair, like yours. Medium build. Medium height?"

"Why, you just described half the men here, miss." The postmaster pressed his lips together, as if considering what to do, then asked, "Can you describe his laugh?"

She took a moment to think about the request. "It's been several years, but as I recall, he had a deep, big-bellied laugh."

The postmaster nodded. "My, but he had a laugh that could echo off the walls of the canyon. Didn't he, Ben?"

Ben chuckled. "Indeed he did."

Maggie hurried to explain. "He was my father's second cousin, earning wages as a crew member on the cargo ships out of Boston until he came here, heard there was gold, and decided to stay." She dug through the contents of her large carpetbag. "After my father died, Lewis corresponded with

45

my mother and me and —"

"You have letters?" Mr. Green asked.

She pulled out the last letter Cousin Lewis wrote to her, the one he'd sent along with the money to pay for their passage aboard the *Cordova*. When she handed it to the postmaster, he took another letter from the shelf behind him and compared the two side by side.

"Parnell left you a letter," Mr. Green said. "He passed away from pneumonia, you know, after he helped rescue those people in Sacramento last winter trapped by the flood. Now, if it's the same handwriting . . . yep, sure is."

He handed the letters over to her, and Maggie put them in her carpetbag to read over later in private. Hoping there was more, she asked, "Did he leave me anything else?"

Mr. Green nodded. "Ah, yes. Well, there is his house, if you want it. He gave specific instructions it was part of your inheritance."

Maggie glanced apprehensively at Ben. "The shack we passed on the way in? The one with half the roof torn off and the —"

She couldn't bring herself to say *rats* but was certain Ben knew what she meant, for he grimaced as he gave her a sympathetic look.

Maggie drew in a deep shuddering breath, wishing she could loosen the confining stays of her corset, and turned her attention back to the postmaster. "Did my cousin leave . . . money?"

Mr. Green reached back for another item on a shelf and handed over a small brown leather pouch.

Maggie opened it and was dismayed to find only three silver coins, two from a US mint and one that was Mexican. "You must be mistaken, sir. This can't be everything. What — what happened to all his gold?"

The postmaster exchanged a solemn look with Ben then said, "Lately, there hasn't been much gold to be found, only gold dust with a larger nugget here and there. Thousands of men have come in from all parts of the world to scour the rivers and stake their claims."

"My cousin said he had found a lot of gold," Maggie insisted. "I doubt he would lie."

"No, he didn't lie," the postmaster assured her.

When Mr. Green didn't elaborate, Ben explained, "Your cousin also had a gambling problem."

Cousin Lewis had gambled away his fortune? Maggie clenched her teeth then met Ben's gaze. "I see."

She saw clearly all right. She saw that after enticing her and her mother to travel halfway around the world, Cousin Lewis had left them with nothing but an apologetic letter, a few silver coins, and a run-down, rat-infested shack.

"So that's it, then," she said, tears stinging her eyes. "I have nothing."

Mr. Green smiled down at her. "Not if you marry *me.*"

CHAPTER 3

Maggie returned to the bakery with Ben, her temper nearly getting the better of her. How dare the postmaster propose to her at a time like this! She didn't even know him. Then again, she hadn't really known her cousin Lewis either, had she? Perhaps that was what made Mr. Green believe she might say yes. The man had been quite disappointed when she turned him down.

Ben, however, had smiled. Which tempted her to think maybe he was glad she'd refused the postmaster. Or perhaps he just thought the whole exchange funny.

She did not think anything about her situation was funny at all. The back of her throat ached, and her eyes stung, but she wouldn't cry. She didn't have time to cry. What she needed was a plan, a way to support herself and her mother, and for that she'd need to remain strong. Besides, she knew her mother would cry enough for them both.

But why would God bring her and her mother out here? For what purpose? She'd been so certain it was His will that she come to California to marry Cousin Lewis. Now what would they do? How would they survive? Didn't God promise to care for those who trusted in Him? That all things would work together for their good? Any good to come from this seemed as far away as Cousin Lewis's promise that they'd be living in a grand house on fields of green with more gold than a leprechaun. How silly she'd been to have believed such a thing!

Oh dear. She had broken her own rule. One that had always helped her to keep going when everything looked bleak. *Always look for the positive in every situation, and thank the good Lord that things are not worse.*

Well, she and her mother were alive, weren't they? Which meant they were much better off than Cousin Lewis. She could thank God for that, couldn't she?

And they had met two other women in this place who seemed to genuinely care for their well-being. Oh, and how could she forget Ben and his nephew, Phillip? Her spirits rose as she thought of their smiling faces. Yes, new friends could be counted a blessing.

She also had her strength, no doubt something else she should be grateful for. At twenty-one years of age, she'd already worked as a seamstress, a maid, and a cook to put food in their bellies and a pillow beneath their heads at night. There had to be someone, somewhere, who would hire her.

She thanked Ben once again for his kindness as he delivered both her and her mother's trunks to one of the hotel rooms in the back portion of the bakery, which — thank the Lord again — had indeed been available. Then after Ben and Phillip left, she joined her mother, Esther, and Agnes at a small table beside the bakery counter for a plate of hot, buttery biscuits and a cup of tea.

Maggie told them what she'd learned from the postmaster and handed the two silver fifty-cent coins from Cousin Lewis's leather pouch to Esther Watkins, who ran the bakery and hotel with her husband, Samuel.

"Will this be enough to cover our lodging for one night?" Maggie asked, even though she suspected it wasn't.

Esther took the coins, gave her a warm, welcoming smile, and said, "Of course it's enough."

"I'll find a way to make more money," Maggie vowed.

"You always do," her mother said, wiping a tear. "But it wasn't supposed to be this way. You were supposed to marry Cousin Lewis and live a life of ease."

Esther set down her teacup, leaned forward, and looked at Maggie. "You were engaged to Lewis Parnell?"

She shook her head. "Not officially."

"But it was presumed he'd propose the moment we arrived," her mother added. "I've just come out of mourning for my dear husband, and now I suppose I'll have to dye my gown black again. Maggie too."

"Oh no! You can't do that!" Esther exclaimed, her face full of alarm.

Maggie's mother frowned. "You do not think we should mourn the ones we've lost?"

"If you wear black, you can't get married," Agnes declared, matter-of-factly.

"That's right," Esther said, and gave Maggie a wink. "A young girl as pretty as you will have no trouble finding a husband at all, and in view of your dire financial situation, the sooner the better, don't you think?"

Maggie's mother gasped. "Doesn't proper etiquette require a woman to wear black for a period of one year after the death of a fiancé?"

"Not if she wasn't officially engaged," Agnes drawled, tossing her napkin aside. "And no one has to know about what didn't happen."

Maggie's mother took a sip of tea then shook her head. "He *was* a cousin, and there is still a three-month waiting period for cousins."

Esther looked at Maggie expectantly, as if measuring her up. "Was he a *first* cousin?"

Maggie looked around at each of their faces, not sure what to think. *Marriage?* Was that her only option? Perhaps she should have taken the postmaster's proposal more seriously.

"Cousin Lewis was my father's second cousin, which would make him my third cousin," she said, hesitantly. "Would that make a difference?"

"Well, let's see," Esther said, bustling to the back of the bakery counter where she retrieved a thick book and flipped open the worn, yellowed pages. "In Godey's Lady's Book, it says a woman must wear solid black for one year for a husband, then another six months of black with some color, and finally lighten her gowns to gray for the last six months of half mourning. For a brother or sister, the proper attire is black for six months, and for an aunt, uncle, or cousin three months, but for a friend or second cousin it is only a matter of weeks."

"Out here rules are different," Agnes said in a gravelly voice. "We live off the land and don't have the money for fancy dye or changes in wardrobe. I should think for a third cousin, Maggie and her mother could pay their respects and not have to change their gowns at all."

Esther nodded. "As the only women in Gold Bar, the only ones who would even notice you aren't following the dictated social norms are sitting at this table. Men don't care much for following the rules of proper society."

Agnes chuckled. "Men don't care for following rules, period. I'm sure they'd be as pleased as a fruit fly on a plum tree if you decided to forgo the formalities."

"I don't know," Maggie's mother fretted.

Maggie considered a moment, then made up her mind. "Esther and Agnes are right. The sooner I find a husband, the sooner we'll have financial support. Seems to me, there's no time to waste."

"You could have a husband tomorrow if you desired," Esther gushed. "Pretty young women in these parts are rare, and the men are lonely, which will have them all vying for your attention."

"The problem won't be finding a husband," Agnes agreed. "It will be trying to decide which man would be *best.*"

Maggie's heart raced. "You think I'll be able to choose my own husband? But how will I make money until I decide upon one? My mother and I still need to eat."

"Can you sew?" Agnes asked.

Maggie nodded. "My mother and I are both quite good with a needle."

"Perfect!" Agnes exclaimed, with a clap of her hands. "You can both help me wash and mend the men's clothes. Charge them whatever you want and keep your own earnings. Eben Nash, who thinks he's the camp's only tailor, won't like it, but Lord knows, there's more than enough work for all of us."

Overcome by an unexpected flood of relief, Maggie smiled. Perhaps God *was* watching over them after all.

Ben tried his best to talk with his young nephew, but soon after they'd left the women at the bakery, Phillip became quiet and withdrawn, barely looking at him. Two years had passed since they'd last seen each other. While Lucinda's family stayed in Boston, Ben traveled west where land was less expensive, hoping to build a horse ranch. A dream he still hoped to achieve, once he found enough gold to purchase the right property and needed supplies.

He glanced over at Phillip's untouched bowl of chicken stew they'd fetched from the camp cook, and asked, "Aren't you hungry?"

Phillip didn't answer but shrugged, his face pale and looking forlorn.

Ben wasn't sure what to say. He wondered if Phillip missed his parents or if he was simply weary from his long journey. Whichever case, a good night's sleep would do them both good.

However, the next morning when Ben asked Phillip if he'd slept well, the scowl upon his nephew's face became more pronounced. "There were no rats. However, I did not think we would be living in a tent."

Ben thought the boy's stiff proper speech out of place here in the wild, where most of the men used a variety of slang, but no doubt the ladies would find it refreshing.

"The tent is temporary," Ben promised. "I've got some money stashed away, and as soon as I find a little more gold, I'll build us our own house."

"There is no school here."

Ben lifted a brow. "You told Maggie you didn't need to go to school."

Phillip shrugged. "There is no one else my age."

"One of the miners has a seven-year-old girl."

"I am nine and a half," Phillip reminded him. "And I do not talk to girls."

Ben grinned. "One day you will."

"Can we go see Maggie?" Phillip asked, a flicker of hope lighting his young face.

For a moment, the thought of seeing her sparkling blue eyes and fiery red-gold curls escaping her frivolously feminine pink-ribbon bonnet didn't seem like a bad idea. Then he remembered he had work to do.

"I think we might let her settle into camp first," Ben replied. When Phillip's face fell back into a scowl, he added, "How would you like to go down to the river and learn to pan for gold?"

His nephew startled him by giving him a direct look. "Can I keep any gold I find?"

Ben assured him he could, and for a while, as they sifted through the stones from the riverbed, all seemed fine. Until the boy tired.

"I wish I'd never come here!" he shouted, wiping tears from his eyes with his fist. "I should've run away from Miss Lang and found my own place to live. At least then I'd still be in Boston, where I belong."

Ben's stomach clenched and the back of

his throat grew tight as his nephew sat down on a large rock a few yards away and tossed stones aimlessly into the water. He couldn't help but wonder — Had he been wrong in sending for the child? If he'd had the money, he could have paid for Phillip to attend private school in Boston. But the nine-and-a-half-year-old was all the family he had left. They needed to stick together. Certainly, that is what his sister, Lucinda, would have wanted.

But what did he know about raising a child?

One thing was clear. Phillip's fine speech wasn't always polished after all. When provoked, his language slipped into something more natural, just like Maggie when she'd suddenly spoken with her heavy Irish accent in front of the other men.

His gaze drifted toward the ragged sleeves and gaping hole in his nephew's shirt, which was in dire need of mending, and realized that providing for another person was going to cost him. Set back his dream of purchasing land and building that house for a while. And most definitely set back his desire to marry a pretty woman and start a family of his own.

Which meant he had no business thinking about Miss McDermott's pretty eyes, hair, and bonnet, or the endearing little quirks in her speech. No business thinking about them at all.

And yet, how could he not?

Especially when she kept placing herself in his line of sight. Ben's gaze drifted toward beautiful, sweet Maggie as she walked along the water's edge with her long, full pink skirt bunched in one hand to keep the hem from getting wet. His heart lurched in his chest, aching to help her. To protect her. Provide for her. Even though his head knew he couldn't.

"Have you come to pan for gold?" he teased.

Maggie laughed, the joyous sound mixing with the tinkling of the river. "I doubt I would be able to tell the difference between gold and these other rocks, even if I did come upon some. But I am not to start work with the washerwoman until tomorrow. However will I spend the rest of my day?"

Ben froze in place, unable to tear his gaze from hers. Was she hinting that she wanted to spend the rest of the day — with him?

Her gaze shifted and she pointed, redirecting his attention to Phillip, who was smiling as he made his way toward them, and Ben realized, with an unbidden pang of regret, that he'd been mistaken. Her target had

59

been his nephew.

"Would you mind if I borrowed Phillip's company for the rest of the afternoon?" she asked, with a lift of her fair delicate brows.

"Yes, can I?" Phillip asked, his voice pleading.

The boy looked at Maggie with stars in his eyes. He probably saw her as a mother figure. Perhaps, more than anything, that was what he needed right now. He certainly wasn't interested in panning for gold. And it sure was good to see him smiling again.

Ben decided small progress was better than none and gave his assent.

Even though that meant he'd later have to retrieve the boy. And see Maggie again. When what he knew he should do . . . is stay away.

Maggie took Phillip back to the bakery, leading him along the path she'd used earlier. They passed Lewis's grave, a rock mound marked by a wooden cross bearing his name. She and her mother had taken Esther and Agnes's advice and visited the site that morning, wearing their undyed, light-colored gowns. While her mother cried, Maggie had stood there biting her lip. She knew that one day she'd have to forgive him, and God too. But right now, she couldn't. Not yet. Her anger over the predicament she now found herself in was still too raw.

Especially after she and her mother visited the shack Cousin Lewis had left them. The moment Maggie opened the door, it fell off the hinges, and a rat ran out through a crack in the wall. Besides being infested with rodents, which Maggie couldn't abide, the wide hole in the roof and half-broken beams made the place uninhabitable.

Esther said most of the damage came that past winter when the camp had been assaulted by wind and heavy rain. A tree had come down on the shack, knocking it off-kilter, forcing Cousin Lewis back into a tent. This was also the same winter storm that made the floodwaters rise in Sacramento. Cousin Lewis had gone into the waters to help others to safety but consequently came down with the pneumonia that later cost him his life. One could say he died a hero, something else she should be thankful for, if she wasn't feeling so sorry for herself.

But now that Phillip was here Maggie was certain his presence would put an end to her mourning.

"Why do you have mud on your nose?" he asked, frowning as he looked up at her.

"To protect my skin from the sun." She laughed and wiped her nose clean with her handkerchief. "Now I see why the men wear wide-brimmed straw hats. Bonnets may look pretty, but do not appear to be very practical to keep one's nose from turning red."

Phillip grinned. "My nose burned too."

"I don't suppose you know how to spot gold?" she asked, taking a small shiny river rock from the pocket of her apron.

Phillip shook his head.

"Nor do I," she said, and sighed. "But it would be exciting if we found some, wouldn't it? I'd buy supplies to fix up Cousin Lewis's shack and turn it into a real home."

"I would buy a horse," Phillip said, his tone wistful.

"A horse?" Maggie lifted a brow. " 'Tis a fine goal. I have a book about a young boy and his horse. Would you care to read it together?"

Phillip nodded, his face radiant. "I would indeed." He hesitated a moment, looked just a wee bit uncomfortable, then confided, "My mother used to read to me."

His tone had turned wistful again and Maggie's chest tightened, for of course the boy must miss his mother. And he was still so young to be without one.

Could this be the reason God had brought her here? What if His intention hadn't been for her to marry Cousin Lewis, as she supposed, but to help this young boy who had no mother? At the very least, she could offer to tutor him. She wasn't heavily skilled in arithmetic, but she could help the boy read and write so he wouldn't fall behind in his schooling.

She could also mend the hole in his shirt, which Phillip insisted had been chewed by rats.

Maggie smiled with affection for this boy, and once she and Phillip were seated at the table inside the bakery, she opened the book and read aloud, whisking them away to a land of awe and adventure, where beauty reigned and dreams could come true.

Ben leapt up the stairs leading to the bakery, then paused to take a breath and told himself to slow down. *You just need to pick up the boy. That's all. Don't go entertaining thoughts of conversing with Miss McDermott. You don't have the money to properly support Phillip and a wife.*

The problem was he couldn't stop thinking about her after she'd left the river that day. Neither could the other men. The afternoon had been filled with boasts to win her hand and accompanying laughter. She'd have over a dozen suitors by the end of the week, if not by nightfall. And while that didn't exactly sit well with him, Ben knew it was inevitable that Maggie would most likely marry someone else.

Someone with money. Someone who struck gold.

He'd redouble his efforts at the river tomorrow, but for now, he had to keep himself from becoming overly attached. For if he failed, it would pain him too much in the end, a lesson he'd learned before and wasn't too keen to repeat.

Just get the boy.

Ben opened the door of the bakery and walked in, determined to do just that, when the sight before him stopped him in his tracks.

Maggie and Phillip sat at the table side by side, so engrossed in the book she was reading that they didn't see him. He watched their rapt expressions change from wide-eyed intrigue to subtle grins, then dart into a look of surprise. But what drew his attention most was the way they leaned toward one another, their heads so close they were nearly touching, and how Phillip's hand gently clutched Maggie's forearm. As if he needed reassurance she was still there, even as their minds wandered within the scenes from the story.

If ever he had a family of his own, this is how he'd picture it to be.

A picture of love.

Phillip's eyelids fluttered closed and his head sank against Maggie's shoulder. Smiling down at him, she laid the book aside, then looked up when Ben walked toward her.

"You're very good with children," he said, his throat tight.

Maggie smiled again, this time at him. "I was an only child, like Phillip, which can be lonely. Especially in a new land. When I was about his age, I used to read stories to the other neighborhood children in the hope of making new friends."

"You've certainly bonded with Phillip." Ben's gaze drifted toward his sleeping nephew. "I wish I could say the same, but he doesn't seem to be as pleased with me as he is with you."

"Just give him time," she said, her face full of sympathy. "You forget we've shared over six months of travel together while sailing west. Relationships grow with patience, persistence, and time."

"I doubt I'll earn his favor by waking him,

but I must get him back to our own tent."

"Wait. There is one more matter I would like to discuss," she said softly. "I was wondering if you would let me tutor Phillip on a regular basis. When I'm not working, that is."

Ben hesitated. He knew it would be in his nephew's best interest to keep up with his studies, but the arrangement would also continue to draw the three of them together and play havoc with his own growing attraction to her.

No. He couldn't do it. Shouldn't do it. But seeing the determined look in her eyes, he sighed with amused resignation. "You're not going to stop harassing me about his schooling until I give in, are you?"

Maggie lifted her chin and smiled. "No, I doubt I will."

"All right. You may tutor him," he agreed, and inwardly groaned.

Yes, it was going to hurt to have to watch her marry someone else.

CHAPTER 4

The following day Maggie and her mother rose early, before dawn, and made their way over to Agnes Henshaw's wash shed, down near the river. The roofed timber-post structure hadn't any side walls and was no bigger than the square wooden stand beside the bakery that posed as the post office.

Agnes introduced them to her husband, Charles, a rugged, soft-spoken man with a lopsided grin, who took a bucket of steaming water off the steel grate over the fire and dumped it into one of the large, half-barrel washtubs. This washtub, Agnes explained, was for the washing, while the other one on the bench beside it was for the rinsing. Maggie's mother assured the woman that she'd washed plenty of clothes before, as their family did not have the money to hire servants, and Agnes handed her a washboard, a plunger, and a cake of soap.

Maggie, who had better eyesight for

threading needles and sewing fine stitches than her mother, took out her leather sewing kit holding her thimble, needle holder, scissors, steel ribbon bodkin, and a small wooden spool of pale cotton thread. Agnes directed her to a chair beside the clothesline and pointed to the straw basket piled with clothing in need of repair.

"Just do what you can with them," the elderly lady told her. "The men don't expect much."

Maggie picked up a white cotton shirt and had not even finished mending the hole in the sleeve when four men came down the path to pay them a visit, followed by two more.

"You'll have to form a line," Agnes commanded, her voice stern.

The men obliged, smiling, and the first one stepped up to Maggie, a pair of trousers in his hands. "I was hoping you might be able to wash these for me, Miss McDermott?"

Tom Green, the postmaster.

Maggie pointed toward her mother, who was busy scrubbing laundry beside Agnes. "Clothing that needs to be washed can be set over by the tubs. I only take the clothes that need repair."

The owl-faced man with round, black-

68

rimmed spectacles pulled at the waistline of the trousers, causing the material to rip. "Looks like these will need mending."

"I've got clothes that need mending too," called out a short, round-bellied man behind him.

Willis Cogsgrove, the camp cook.

"So do I," said a third, his hooknose resembling a bird's beak as he broke into a broad grin.

Obadiah Brewster, the gold digger who also served as the camp preacher.

She'd met most everyone in the Gold Bar camp at dinner the night before, and because of the repeated attention the men continued to pay her, it had not taken long to learn their names.

Maggie set the piece she'd been working on in her lap and stared at all the garments they held up for her. Then she glanced at Agnes, who told the men, "If you want them fixed, you need to pay her twenty cents for each item."

Each man handed over the required amount, which Maggie deposited into her apron pocket. She was thrilled that she'd be able to pay Esther for another night's lodging but thought of Phillip and wondered how she would be able to tutor him when she had so much work to do. The mounting pile would surely keep her busy until night-fall.

She quickly found that mending wasn't the only thing the men were after. By midmorning she'd also received over a dozen marriage proposals.

"If you can mend my clothes, I can mend your heart," one of them promised.

The man behind him swatted the fellow with his hat. "Don't mind him, Miss McDermott. He has no manners, but if you marry me, I promise that I will treat you with respect."

Quincy and Rufus Vaughn, the squat, dark-haired brothers who work for Hugh Kendrick.

"Step aside, boys," the devil himself said, giving his minions a look of warning as he made his way toward her. "And leave the lovely lady to me."

Maggie pursed her lips. "Does your clothing require mending, Mr. Kendrick?"

"No," he replied. "I'd like to mend things between you and me."

"Oh?" she asked, feigning innocence. "Why would you want to do that?"

He took off his hat and leaned forward. "By now you must have noticed there are only four buildings in Gold Bar. Besides the post office, baker's hotel, and the infirmary owned by Dr. Harrington, there is a large house behind the fire pit. Did you know that I am the owner of that magnificent house, Miss McDermott?"

Maggie shook her head. "No, I did not. But I think you are forgetting one other building in Gold Bar, for I counted five."

Mr. Kendrick frowned. "Are you referring to Parnell's shack?"

"*My* house," Maggie told him. "Or else at least it will be, once I can afford to fix it up."

"That old shack should be torn down," Mr. Kendrick said with a scowl, then met her gaze. "Marry me, and I can give you a better house. Everything you've always wanted. I have money. Lots of money. Why, with your beauty and my resources, we could be the finest couple in all of California. Don't you see?"

Maggie picked up her sewing again and averted her gaze. "No, I do *not* see."

"Aw, you reject me now," he taunted, sticking out his chest. "But there will come a day when you will change your mind."

She knew she would have to choose a husband before too long, and perhaps she should be thankful for the offers she'd already received, but if there was one man she would *not* marry, it was Hugh Kendrick.

He wasn't kind, compassionate, or honorable.

Not like Ben.

She glanced toward the other men coming down the path toward the river. Where *was* Benjamin Freethy this morning? Why wasn't he here? Didn't he have clothes that needed to be washed or mended?

One man she had not yet met headed straight for her, a thin, well-dressed fellow with a limp who hobbled down the path with the help of a carved wood cane.

Unlike the other men, his expression did not contain a hint of eagerness, joy, or amusement. In fact, as he glanced at the line of men before her then at the basket piled high with the clothes she was to mend, his countenance darkened.

"You think you can ride into town and steal my business?" he demanded.

"I'm sorry, sir, but I'm afraid I — I don't know what you are talking about."

"Well let me explain it to you, *lassie,*" the man said, in a tone meant to mock her accent. "I am the town tailor. When the men need a new garment made or their clothing repaired, they come to *me.* Understand? Now, if you need a job, I'd be willing to give you ten cents for each article of clothing you mend."

"She's making twice that here," Agnes said, leaving her wash bucket to come around and wave her fist at him. "Now scurry off, you flea-infested rodent!"

The tailor gave Agnes a menacing glare then returned his gaze to Maggie. "Your success won't last long," he promised. "I assure you, I will see that it doesn't."

As the crippled man turned and hobbled back up the path, Hugh Kendrick touched her sleeve, and when she looked at him, he smiled.

"Remember," he said, his voice low. "I can give you anything you want, even save you from the wrath of the tailor."

At the end of the day, Maggie forced herself to recite everything she had to be thankful for as she accompanied her mother back to their room behind the bakery. They had missed the evening meal prepared by the camp cook, so Esther brought in a tray with biscuits, leftover chicken vegetable soup, and a pot of tea and set it on the dresser.

"Looks like you had a very productive first day," Esther said gaily, when Maggie emptied the coins from her bulging apron pocket.

"I suppose I did," Maggie agreed. "I also received fifteen marriage proposals, al-

73

though not from anyone of interest."

Maggie's mother chuckled. "I received three proposals of my own, two from men half my age. I also received a fair compliment from Dr. John Harrington. He said my cheeks were looking as rosy as an apple, much better than my first day in town when after I fainted he helped to catch me."

"Our good Dr. Harrington is certainly of your own age and would make a suitable match," Esther teased.

Maggie looked at her mother, who shook her head. "I already had one husband. I certainly don't need another. Marriage is for the young, for those still strong enough to stomach it, not for someone in their mid-fifties like me."

"I wish I didn't have to marry either," Maggie said, handing Esther several of the coins to pay for their room that night. "But this money is not enough for us to live on forever, and I cannot afford to fix up the house that Cousin Lewis left us."

Esther smiled. "Well then, you will have to raise your prices, won't you?"

Maggie hesitated. "If I raise the prices, I may get fewer customers."

"Not when every man in Gold Bar wants to win your hand," Esther said, giving her a conspiratorial wink. "Besides, the men are used to paying higher prices. Every other business owner in California is doing the same thing, raising the cost of goods and services sky-high to lay claim to some of the miners' gold. The cost of supplies to fix up the place Parnell left you will be far more expensive than you are accustomed to back east."

"That doesn't seem fair," Maggie's mother protested.

"It's not," Esther said, patting her hand. "That's just the way it is."

Maggie's mother sat down on the bed and frowned. "I still do not think it is proper etiquette to overcharge one's customers."

"It isn't overcharging if I charge the same high rate as others, like Eben Nash," Maggie insisted. "Why should women be underpaid for performing the same work as men? Besides, we need food so that we will not starve."

"Surely we would never starve," her mother exclaimed. "I'm certain that you will find a decent man to marry who will provide for us so we do not have to dwell on such things. For now, we're thankful that Agnes and Charles have allowed us to earn an adequate wage through them. For everyone knows a single woman cannot be a business owner."

"Oh, but in California, a woman can," Esther said, her face beaming. "There are not many women who wish to live in such uncivilized conditions as we have out here, yet there are thousands of men who would like to take a wife. To try to solve this problem, and draw more women in, the governing officials in California have decreed that women can own and operate a business the same as any man. And if she marries, any land or property she may have inherited does not fully transfer to her husband, but half remains her own."

Maggie gasped, thinking of the possibilities. "I can run my own business? Free of a man's input or control?"

Esther nodded. "This bakery is not my husband Samuel's, but all mine. I make the decisions and name the prices, the same as Agnes, down by the river."

"Then why doesn't Agnes charge more for her services?" Maggie asked.

Esther laughed. "Because Agnes doesn't have your pretty face and she knows full well that if she raised the cost of laundry, the men would prefer to wash their clothes themselves."

My own business.

If she raised her prices for mending, she could afford to purchase new material.

Design and sew new clothes. Fix up Cousin Lewis's shack and turn the front part into a shop like Esther had done by putting the bakery in the front part of the hotel. She and her mother could live in the back until they could afford to build a separate house.

They'd never have to depend on a man or worry about money again.

Then maybe one day she'd meet a man whom she truly respected, who shared her dreams for the future and loved her for *more* than just her pretty face.

Ben had spent the day at the river with Samuel Watkins. At first he'd wondered where all the other men were, but as they trickled in with their pickaxes and panning supplies, he quickly learned they visited Maggie at the wash shed to drop off their mending.

And ask for her hand in marriage.

Ben clenched his jaw, and Samuel grinned.

"Do you want to try your luck at a new location I found?" his friend asked, arching his brow.

Ben blew out a ragged breath. "Why not? It can't be any worse than here."

But it was.

"It's a river cave." Ben stared into the opening and shook his head. "I told you, it's too dangerous."

"Kendrick's men have been finding several small pieces in the mouth of caves like this."

"Yeah, and this one is too close to the one he's been digging in." Ben pointed to the mouth of another cave fifty feet away. "He may think we're encroaching on his territory."

"Hugh already thinks you're encroaching on his territory by befriending Miss McDermott," Samuel pointed out. "And since when have you ever cared what he thinks?"

"I don't." Ben scowled. "Still, we all remember when Eben Nash got hurt, and now look at him — he has to tailor clothes instead of panning."

Samuel shrugged. "There are always risks."

"But some places are safer to dig than others."

As if to prove his point, a small landslide from the hill above spilled over the cave entrance. Ben pulled Samuel back just in time to avoid getting hit on the head with a rock.

"See?" Ben demanded. "What did I tell you? It's not worth risking our lives."

Except, as the days passed, and the other men found more gold and boasted they were getting closer to winning Maggie's hand, Ben found himself eyeing that cave entrance more and more.

One evening the following week when he stepped into the bakery, Maggie took him by surprise when she demanded, "Why don't you bring me your mending?"

He slid his gaze over the case of fresh-baked muffins to avoid looking at her. "I'm trying to save money."

"Is that the only reason?"

"Well, you did raise your prices," he teased. "Not sure I can afford what you're charging these days."

"I would gladly mend your clothes for free," she said softly.

Ben gave her a quick glance and grinned. "But that wouldn't be good business, would it?"

"It would be if it built good relations."

He moved over to take a better look at a plate of puffed pastries filled with a white pudding that smelled of vanilla cream. "I wash and mend my own clothes when needed."

She stepped up beside him and leaned her head around to catch his eye. "You aren't trying to avoid me?"

He straightened, smiled, and dared to meet her gaze. "Why would I do that?"

"Don't know," she said, her Irish creeping

into each word, a sign she was as nervous talking about this subject as he was. "I just haven't been seein' ye as much of late. I thought — well, I thought — it might be nice if ye helped with Phillip's arithmetic, you see. I've been able to help him with his reading and writing while I mend clothes, but I'm afraid I'm not as advanced with numbers, which is a wee bit discouraging. Especially when I'm trying to calculate how much to charge for my sewing services."

Samuel had said he'd learned from his wife, Esther, that Maggie would hold off on accepting the men's marriage proposals if she could afford to open her own sewing shop. Ben's pulse leapt in his chest. Perhaps if she learned how to run a business it would buy him time.

Time for what? You can't afford to marry her.

Time for him to find more gold.

He cleared his throat. "I can help with Phillip's lesson tonight. Does he have a pencil and paper?"

"Right here," Phillip called over from his seat at the table. "But why should I have to learn my numbers?"

Ben had yet to establish a real bond with the boy and tried his best to keep his tone light. "If you find gold in the river, you will know how much it's worth."

"So no one cheats me?" Phillip asked.

"Yes," Maggie said with a smile. "And so you will know how much it will cost you to buy and keep a horse."

The boy's eyes widened with interest, and when Maggie gave Ben a pointed look, he realized she'd just given him the opening he needed to finally connect with his nephew.

"Let's say a packhorse costs twenty-five dollars, and you find a nugget of gold in the river worth fifty dollars. How many horses could you buy?" Ben picked up the pencil and jotted down some figures.

Phillip thought for a moment. "Two?"

Ben nodded. "Yes, you could buy two, but not if you need to feed that horse. Enough hay to feed a horse for a week can cost roughly two dollars. If you bought just one horse, how many weeks could you afford to feed it?"

Phillip leaned toward him and raised his brows. "Twelve?"

Ben shrugged. "What if the horse needs a saddle blanket? Or new shoes?"

"I'm going to need a lot more gold!" Phillip exclaimed. "Do you think I could go back to the river to pan for gold with you tomorrow?"

"Of course," Ben assured him.

Maggie had walked away, in what Ben

suspected was an attempt to give him and his nephew time alone, but she appeared to still be listening to their conversation as she hovered in the hall between the bakery and the hotel rooms in the back, for she was smiling.

"Let me give you another example," Ben said, glancing back toward Phillip. "If Maggie charges twenty cents for each piece of clothing she mends at the wash shed and can finish ten items in one day, how much would she make?"

Phillip smiled. "Two dollars."

"But what if she doubled her prices?" Ben asked.

"Four dollars."

"And in six days' time?"

"Twenty dollars?" Phillip asked, rapt with attention.

"Twenty-four," Ben corrected. "And in two weeks' time she'd have forty-eight dollars, almost enough to —"

"Buy two horses!" Phillip exclaimed. "Or one horse with eight weeks of hay, a blanket, and new shoes!"

Ben watched Maggie raise a hand to her mouth to try to smother a laugh, and he grinned. "Yes, but she might want to first buy herself some more thread, sewing needles, and material to sew new clothes, so she'd have to calculate those costs on a weekly basis. Then if she sews ten new clothing items and sells each one at ten dollars each, she could cover the cost of the wood beams to repair the shack near the camp entrance and turn it into her very own shop."

Phillip smiled. "Then she could make even more money!"

"Yes, but Maggie would have to subtract her costs from her profits each week to restock her sewing supplies. She and her mother also need to pay rent for their room and pay for their food. So she might keep track of her income and expenses by lining them up in columns."

As Ben drew lines down the page to illustrate his point for Phillip, Maggie walked back over to them, her face filled with wonder. "Where did you learn to budget expenses like this, Ben?"

He shrugged. "I used to work at a bank."

"A bank!" Maggie stared at him in surprise. "I would never have guessed it. You do not seem the type to sit indoors behind a desk."

"I'm not. That's why I came out here."

Maggie nodded. "To find gold. And what will you do with it?"

"For starters, I might invest in your sewing business and ask you to sew me a new set of clothes."

Maggie blushed. "With your skill at calculating numbers, why don't you have your own business?"

"I hope to have a horse-breeding business — one day. I already have a place picked out in the valley, just a short ride north."

Phillip gasped. "Really?"

He nodded. "I just need more gold first."

"How much do you have?" Phillip asked, and Maggie eagerly leaned in also, awaiting his answer.

With a pang of regret, Ben shook his head. "Not enough."

CHAPTER 5

Maggie eagerly returned to her room to make a list of the supplies she would need before opening her own seamstress shop. She tapped the pencil against her paper as she ran the calculations through her head. If Esther was right, and the men still paid the new rates, and Maggie followed Ben's instructions on how to budget her income, she could save enough to start buying supplies in three weeks or less.

And she did. Handing Agnes and her husband, Charles, some of her earnings, she requested they purchase set amounts of new fabric and thread for her during their next trip into Sacramento in mid-May.

Of course, Maggie had mended Phillip's shirt for free. She couldn't have him going around camp looking like a common street urchin. Nor could she accept money from Ben after all he had done to help her business succeed. Whether or not he'd intended for her to overhear how to budget expenses while tutoring Phillip, she paid close attention, and learn she did, to both her and her mother's delight.

One problem remained before her. Although she'd saved more than enough to purchase the windows and wood needed to fix Cousin Lewis's shack, no one would help her make the repairs. Esther said that Samuel told her Hugh Kendrick wouldn't let any of the men volunteer.

"Hugh thinks if you have your own home, you will be less inclined to marry," Esther had told her.

"Why does anyone listen to Hugh?" Maggie demanded.

"Because he pays." Esther shrugged. "Most of the men follow Ben because he's a good friend and helps everyone, and Hugh hates that. So, he pays out large quantities of money, thinking he can buy loyalty and respect."

"And a wife," Maggie added in disgust.

"I'm sure our sweet, kindhearted Ben would help fix up your cousin's place if you asked him," Esther teased.

Maggie's cheeks warmed. Could she ask him such a favor? After all, Ben needed to pan for gold as much as the other men if he was ever to afford his horse ranch. Time away from the river to help her could cost him dearly. Unless she paid him. But would he take her money?

She smiled as the beginning of a plan leapt into her mind. Perhaps there was something she could do for him first, before she asked, to sweeten the deal.

One evening later that week, instead of tutoring, Maggie asked Ben and Phillip to meet her in the grassy field behind the post office.

"What's this?" Ben asked, eyeing Maggie, Tom Green, and the horse the self-appointed postmaster used to retrieve the miners' mail from San Francisco — for a price, of course.

Tom pointed at Maggie. "Her idea, not mine, but I'll go along with it since she gave me a cherry pie."

Maggie nodded. "Which I bartered from Esther at the bakery in exchange for mending some of the hotel room linens."

The postmaster handed the reins to Ben. "You can use Scout each week for an hour, as long as I continue to get my pies."

Maggie met Ben's questioning gaze. "I thought you could give Phillip some horseback-riding lessons."

Phillip's squeal of delight made everyone smile. "How fast can he go? How many miles do you think he can travel in a day?"

"One step at a time," Ben told him. "First let's get you up into the saddle."

Maggie could hardly hold in her own delight as she watched Ben's expert precision in handling the animal, one of the few horses in camp, as most of the men used sturdier mules to pull their wagons up the steep terrain. And Phillip's eagerness to learn how to properly hold the reins so he might turn the horse and direct its steps had been worth the extra work required for the arrangement.

Yet the look of appreciation Ben gave her is what really captured her heart, and she hoped before long he would not only grow closer to his nephew, but also agree to accept her money and help with the repairs she needed to open her own shop.

Ben thought Maggie was very clever in the way she'd bartered services throughout the camp to procure a horse for Phillip to practice on. Yet, he was now faced with a dilemma that kept him on edge.

During their riding session the following week, Phillip fell off the horse and tore his trousers right up the midsection. There was no question the garment was beyond repair, and the tailor's price to sew a new pair of trousers for the boy was much too high.

But if he went to Maggie, would she think he was trying to court her like the rest of the men? He didn't want to do anything to mislead her. Neither did he want to risk losing his heart to a woman before he could afford to do so, a real danger each moment spent in her presence.

With an inward groan he decided there was no helping it. The boy had to have new trousers and that was that. He'd have to go to the wash shed and ask for Maggie's help first thing in the morning. And pray for the strength to keep his heart intact.

Ben shifted his weight from one foot to the other as he waited his turn in line. He'd risen early, but ten men stood in front of him, eagerly waiting for the opportunity to speak to the ever-popular Miss Maggie Mc-Dermott. He'd hoped to speak to her privately about sewing Phillip's trousers and get to the river the same time as usual, but it looked as if that was not going to happen. He'd have to be patient and accept the delay.

What was the adage Maggie quoted? *Always look for the positive in every situation, and thank the good Lord that things are not worse.*

He could be thankful for his tent that sheltered him at night and for the money he had already saved toward his horse ranch. He also had to be grateful he was not still at odds with his young nephew, thanks to Maggie.

Although he did not appreciate Hugh Kendrick or the fact he was now smiling at her and making a show of presenting her with a spool of gold-colored thread.

Ben stiffened. Wondering what the rich rogue was saying to her, he inched forward to listen in. All he heard was Maggie telling the guy, "Mr. Kendrick, all the gold in the world could not convince me to dance with you."

Ben grinned. He could be thankful for that. Very thankful.

Twenty minutes later, after watching others converse with her and ask for her hand in marriage, Ben had his chance to speak.

"It is a pleasure to finally have you step forward," Maggie said, her eyes shining as her pink lips parted into a wide smile.

Heat crept up his neck as she continued looking at him that way, as if she'd been waiting for him, only him, and hoped that he, like the others, would propose.

"I'm not here for myself," Ben said, his voice strained. "Phillip tore his trousers, and

I was hoping you might be able to sew him a new pair?"

Her smile faltered, but only for an instant.

"I have a proposal for you," she said, giving him a direct look.

A proposal for *him*? His heart thumped hard in his chest as he cleared his throat. "What — what kind of a proposal are you suggesting?"

"Simply this," she said, her smile widening again. "I will sew Phillip new trousers, a shirt, an entirely new outfit, and you too if you like, if you will only agree to help repair my cousin's shack so my mother and I might move in and I can open my shop."

Ben felt his face flush. "Your shop?"

"Yes," Maggie said in a hushed voice so the other men wouldn't hear. "My very own seamstress shop. I have money for building supplies but no one to help me. The men have all refused, saying they can't take time away from the river."

Ben nodded. "Everyone is vying to find the most gold."

"Besides the clothing, I can also pay you for your time." Maggie bit her lip and gave him a hopeful look. "I've always dreamed of owning my own sewing business, but back east I never thought it possible. No one there knows of the opportunities available to women out here in California. For me, opening this shop will be a dream come true."

He knew all about having dreams. He'd almost given up, but since he'd met her and had begun teaching his nephew, his desire for a horse ranch had been rekindled, along with his desire for a family and a wife.

Ben was nodding even before his words of agreement left his lips. She had already inspired him and helped him in ways she couldn't even imagine. And he knew in his heart that despite his resolve to remain uninvolved, there wasn't anything he wouldn't do for her.

Three weeks later, Maggie scanned the interior of her new shop, her heart swelling with thanksgiving for the repairs Ben had made. The broken windows had been replaced, the roof and side walls repaired, the interior refurbished, and best of all — there were no rats.

She'd kept her end of the bargain also. Both Phillip and Ben sported new shirts and trousers she designed and stitched. Maggie had even ordered them new straw hats when Esther's husband, Samuel, took a trip to San Francisco. When the other men saw her skill at stitching, they too wanted her, and not Eben Nash, to fashion them lighter summer clothes. Which, of course, soured his attitude toward her even more.

Picking up her most treasured possession, the decorative silver-plated thimble with the intricate scrollwork and tiny heart engraved on either side, she thought of her grandmother in Ireland who had given it to her on her twelfth birthday. Grandmother had said learning to sew could someday lead her to prosperity and freedom — and it had. In fact, Maggie was certain that she was now earning more money than a large portion of the men who were panning for gold.

And she no longer needed to marry out of necessity due to hardship, but could marry for love, if she so chose. *Thank You, Lord, for all Your blessings. My heart is indeed grateful.*

She was pinning a pattern of her own design onto a piece of fine muslin when the door to her shop opened and Eben Nash presented himself, hat in hand.

"Seems I may have overreacted when I saw you deliver new garments to Tom Green at the post office yesterday and said you wouldn't succeed," he stated, his expression contrite as he leaned on his cane. "But having slept on the matter, I think, considering we both have common interests at stake, that a partnership would be beneficial to us both."

Maggie raised her brows. "You want to be my business partner?"

"Of course not," the tailor said, shaking his head. "I am talking about marriage."

"Marriage?" She supposed as his wife, any money she made he could confiscate as his own. "I am sorry to disappoint you, Mr. Nash, but I must decline."

Mr. Nash scowled. "Is it because you fear my limp will prevent me from assuming my husbandly duties? For I assure you, that is not the case."

"No," Maggie said, forcing herself to remain calm, despite the indignation building inside her. "I am flattered by your offer, but I do not believe our temperaments are well suited."

He narrowed his gaze. "Perhaps if I give you a weekly stipend?"

Give her a stipend? Maggie clenched her grandmother's thimble tight in her hand. "My answer remains — no. Now I must kindly ask you to excuse me, Mr. Nash, for I have work to do. Good day."

She pointed toward the open door, and with Mr. Nash's scowl back in place upon his narrow, beady-eyed face, he hobbled through it, purposely knocking his cane against the new doorframe as he made his way out.

For one moment, his expression had reminded her of an old beau, the one who'd broken her heart when he'd said she was too ambitious then married someone else. Yet, she would not give up her dreams. And if she did marry, her husband would need to be supportive, not manipulative or controlling.

He'd have to be someone like . . . Benjamin Freethy, who had still not given her any indication he was interested in moving their acquaintance beyond friendship, much to her great disappointment.

Why was it that nearly every man in Gold Bar had asked for her hand in marriage except him? Didn't he think they were well suited? Or that she'd make a good wife?

Did Ben see her new shop's success and think she was too ambitious?

The June sun shone bright across the water, sending shimmering sparkles through each ripple in the streambed. Many a time Phillip had brought Ben a rock to examine, hoping he'd found gold, only to have it turn out to be fool's gold. "Fool" was exactly how Ben was beginning to feel. He hadn't found more than a few small pieces of genuine gold in the last few months, and his finances were dwindling.

Samuel, who sifted through a shovel full of rocky soil beside him, was also getting desperate. Esther's birthday was in two weeks, and he wanted more than anything to buy her a new cookstove for her bakery.

Except more men were pouring into Gold Bar each day. Ever since President Polk had announced back in December 1848 that gold had indeed been found in the rivers of California, thousands of people had decided to head west to make their fortune. Ben heard rumors the population in San Francisco had practically doubled overnight. New buildings and businesses were expanding across the hillside, some using the hulls from the abandoned ships stacking up in the harbor. And the more people who came looking for gold, the less chance Ben would have of finding enough. Before long, he feared all the easy-picking gold would be gone.

He figured Hugh Kendrick must have the same fear, for he'd hired six new men to work for a share of the profits. Of course, Hugh always got the biggest share.

Frustrated, Ben plunged his shovel into the streambed where he, Phillip, and Samuel were working, a spot in front of the river cave Samuel had shown him. Ben's muscles ached, sweat beaded on his brow, and as he hauled yet another pile of rocky soil up out of the water, he wondered how long he could keep doing this before he had to consider leaving to find other work.

He dumped the contents of his shovel onto the screen he used to sift the dirt away from the rocks and thought he saw something. Not wanting to get his hopes up, he poured some river water over the rocks on the screen to clean them so he could get a better look.

"Uncle Ben, is that —"

Phillip pointed, and Ben froze as he stared at one rock in particular.

Samuel too stopped what he was doing and looked over. "You find something?"

Ben picked up the spoon-sized rock to examine it further, his heart beating faster with each passing second. Could it be? A jolt of energy shot through his body, leaving him light-headed and excited and relieved all at the same time. He looked at Phillip, who stood wide-eyed, and nodded. "*This* is what a piece of real gold looks like."

Samuel let out a loud resounding whoop and swept his hand down into the river to splash them with water. Ben splashed him back and chuckled. Phillip squealed and splashed the water around him with both hands.

"Does this give us enough money to buy the horse ranch?" Phillip asked, his high-pitched voice nearly breathless.

"Yes," Ben said, and laughed. "I believe it does."

He could buy the land in the valley he had his eye on for the horse ranch . . . and more.

Samuel gave him a broad grin. "Anyone else you want to tell before the news spreads through town?"

Maggie. There was no one he wanted to share this news with more than her.

"C'mon, Phillip," he said, unable to stop himself from grinning. "Let's go show Maggie."

Maggie had just finished sewing a new white silk neckcloth for one of her customers when Phillip burst through the doorway of her shop shouting, "Maggie! Maggie! Guess what we found?"

She set her work aside and lifted her gaze to the handsome dark-haired man behind him whose hazel eyes were shining just as bright as his nephew's, and her mouth fell open. "Did you find *gold*?"

Ben nodded then came forward and showed it to her.

"You should have seen it just sitting there in the middle of the screen," Phillip gushed. "It's twice the size of the rock Mr. Kendrick found last week. And worth enough money to help us finally buy a horse ranch. I can't wait to ride my own horse! How long before you think we can get one?"

Ben laughed, and Maggie didn't think she'd ever seen either of them so happy.

"First things first," she said, and handed Phillip a few coins from the pocket of her apron. "Why don't you run over to the bakery and get a cake so we can celebrate?"

After the boy ran back out the door, Ben surprised her by taking her hand. "It's easy to see why Phillip is enamored with you, and he's not the only one."

Maggie smiled. "Yes, there are the men who still line up for my mending."

Ben lifted her hand to his lips, and the kiss he placed upon it tingled her skin.

"I wasn't referring to the other men," he said, holding her gaze.

Maggie stared at him, breathless, her heart thumping wildly in her chest. Had Benjamin Freethy just admitted that *he* was enamored with her as well?

"I think you and Phillip are pretty special too," she said softly. "And it has nothing to do with the gold you just found."

"That's very kind of you," he said, and laughed. "Although we *do* need to keep the gold in a safer place than my tent until I can take it to Sacramento and exchange it for cash. Do you think we could hide it here, in your shop?"

"Yes, of course, but where?" She looked around. "I could sew it into the hem of the window curtain. No one would ever know, except you and me."

"Perfect," Ben told her, then gave her another heartwarming grin. "I'd like to ask one more favor of you. Would you do me the honor of sitting beside me during the church service Pastor Obadiah Brewster is going to hold in the glen on Sunday?"

Maggie nodded, and her heart sang with glee.

Benjamin Freethy's feelings toward her did extend beyond friendship after all.

CHAPTER 6

Ben left Phillip in Maggie's care for a tutoring session, took the wagon and mule team to Sacramento, and arranged to meet with Lionel Riggs. The wealthy landowner had spoken to him twice before regarding the lower section of the valley outside Gold Bar. Eager to turn his dream of building a horse ranch into a reality, he hoped this time they would come to a firm agreement. Until then, Ben decided to keep his savings in the bank and the gold hidden at Maggie's shop.

Riggs reminded him of Kendrick, always looking to make more money and flaunting it in everyone's face. Ben had to remind himself to stay calm if he wanted this deal.

"I've had another offer from someone who can pay more," Riggs told him as they sat across from each other at the eatery.

Ben looked him in the eye. "How much more?"

"Two hundred dollars above the original

ten thousand."

"That's more than I have."

Riggs sat back, his hands clasped around his giant belly, and twiddled his thumbs. "That's too bad."

"You said you wanted to sell to me," Ben pressed.

"I do," Riggs insisted. He expelled a long, drawn-out breath and leaned forward. "I tell you what. I'll give you two weeks to come up with the extra money. After that I'm afraid I'm going to have to sell to the highest bidder. Deal?"

Riggs didn't have to sell the land at all, but the old land tycoon was greedy. Always wanting more money. Never satisfied with what he had. However, Ben was not about to lose this land. If he couldn't find more gold before the allotted deadline to make up the difference in cost, perhaps he could ask Samuel Watkins for a loan or barter services like Maggie had done to get Phillip horse-riding lessons.

Ben gave Riggs's extended hand a solid shake. "I'll see you within two weeks."

By the time Ben returned to Gold Bar it was late afternoon. He'd hoped there would still be enough time to go down to the river to pan for gold. However, he had no sooner unhitched the mules from the wagon and put them back in the camp corral when Tom Green ran toward him with an anxious look on his face.

"Samuel's hurt. Broke his arm. They took him to the infirmary just minutes ago." The postmaster motioned for Ben to follow him toward Dr. Harrington's building less than fifty yards away. "He also has a pretty good size gash on his scalp."

Ben sucked in his breath. "What happened?"

"Samuel went into a river cave and part of the mouth fell down on him. I was standing nearby and saw it happen."

"Oh no." Ben's stomach curled into a tight ball as the dangers of a cave collapse raced through his mind. "I told him not to go in there."

Seconds later, they were through the infirmary door and greeted by Dr. Harrington, Esther, Maggie, her mother, and Phillip, who clustered around Samuel's bedside.

"Ben!" Samuel exclaimed. Wrapped in bandages, his head bobbled as he struggled to sit up. "I saw gold! Real gold!"

Esther pushed gently but firmly against her husband's chest, making him lie back down on the bed. "You were seeing things,

103

all right. Most likely due to that bump on your head. Now, rest up so the doctor can finish your bandaging."

Dr. Harrington asked Mrs. McDermott to hand him a strip of cloth to bind Samuel's arm, and Maggie met Ben's intent gaze and explained, "My mother used to be a nurse."

"I told her good nurses are hard to come by out here," Dr. Harrington added with a smile. "I'm grateful to have her assistance."

Samuel winced, then looked at Ben again, his eyes wide. "There's something else I got to tell you."

"Whatever it is, you can tell him later," Esther insisted, trying to keep her husband from sitting up again.

Samuel took her hand and moved it aside. "I need to tell him now. Ben, you have to be careful. I heard Hugh talking. Him and the tailor. Those two are up to something. I heard them say your name then something about Maggie's shop."

Maggie gasped. "*My* shop?"

Ben looked at her and froze. *The gold.*

He didn't have to say a word for Maggie to know what he was thinking. She simply excused herself and followed him outside.

"No one could possibly know where we hid it," Maggie whispered.

Ben nodded. "I just need to make sure."

Together, they hurried past the bakery and post office toward the small structure Maggie now lived in with her mother.

"I've been in the shop most of the day," Maggie told him. "And I lock the door whenever I leave."

He glanced at the doorway and hesitated midstep. "It's open."

Ben entered, half expecting to see Hugh Kendrick or Eben Nash rummaging through the material laid out on the center table, but there was no one there. No one except —

"*Rats!*" Maggie exclaimed, then shrieked. "They're eating my clothes!"

Ben stared at the dozen or so rodents, the shreds of material littering the floor, and the overturned shelves he'd built for Maggie to store her sewing supplies. Lastly, his gaze focused in on the curtains that had been slashed from the window.

Maggie ran past him, past two of the rats that did not scurry away upon seeing them, and bent down to pick up one of the curtains off the floor.

Ben held his breath. "Is the gold —"

Maggie looked up and met his gaze, her eyes wide. "Gone."

Dear God, why did this happen? Maggie

105

cleaned up the rest of the shredded, half-chewed garments from her sewing table, realizing it would cost her dearly to replace them. Yet she hadn't lost as much as Ben.

He hadn't said much as he helped chase those nasty, destructive, hairy rodents out the door of her shop with a broom. After all, what was there to say?

Someone had broken in, sprinkled sweet-smelling crumbs from what looked to be one of Esther's vanilla spice cakes all over the various bolts of cloth, and set about a dozen rats on top to chew and tear and rip and ultimately take the blame. And in addition to stealing Ben's gold, someone had also taken her grandmother's silver-plated thimble. Yet how could they accuse Hugh or the tailor of these nefarious deeds without any proof? Nevertheless, Ben had decided to call for a camp council the following night to discuss the matter.

Until then, Maggie had nothing else to do but try to pick up the pieces and attend Pastor Brewster's Sunday service with Phillip and Ben.

Except the following morning when she arrived in the shadowed glen where the service was to be held wearing her best green silk day dress and matching bonnet, Ben was nowhere to be found.

"He is at the river," Phillip informed her.

"Panning on a Sunday?" Maggie asked, raising her brows.

Phillip shrugged. "He needs to find more gold, and quick, or we will not be able to buy the land for the horse ranch."

"We were supposed to all sit together," she said softly. *Like a family.*

Hugh Kendrick stepped toward her and grinned. "I'd be happy to sit with you, Miss McDermott."

"No need to trouble yourself, Mr. Kendrick," she assured the big fellow. "Phillip and I will be sitting with my mother."

To her surprise, Dr. John Harrington also joined them.

"I've decided to go walking with Dr. Harrington after the service," Maggie's mother whispered into her ear.

"Without a chaperone?" Maggie teased, pushing her own sorrows aside. "According to Godey's Lady's Book, it is not proper etiquette for any unmarried woman to walk with a man unaccompanied."

Her mother blushed then raised her chin. "I have God to watch over me."

Maggie nodded, wondering where God was when someone broke into her shop. Of course, she had to be thankful she still had a shop. And glad she and her mother no longer needed to pay for a room in Esther's hotel behind the bakery, no matter how pleasant it had been to smell fresh-baked bread each morning.

However, Obadiah Brewster's sermon, no doubt inspired by the past few days' events, filled her with remorse when he quoted from the Bible, "Lay not up for yourselves treasures upon earth, where moth and rust doth corrupt, and where thieves break through and steal. . . ."

Was it her fault that Ben's gold was stolen? The thief could not have known she hid the gold at the bottom of her window curtain. She supposed whoever it was had only intended to sabotage her business, and finding the gold had been a happy accident. And who would want to hurt her business more than that cranky old tailor, Eben Nash?

After the service, Esther invited Phillip to the bakery for a hot buttered biscuit. When asked if she would join them, Maggie declined. She found herself standing outside the tailor's tent instead.

Did she dare go in?

"I'd bet anything he has Freethy's gold stashed in there," Mr. Kendrick said, coming up to stand beside her. "You know he had to be the one who sabotaged your shop."

Maggie scowled. "I don't have proof."

"I don't like that he hurt you, Miss Mc-Dermott. I don't like that at all." Mr. Kendrick clenched his fists. "I'll search his tent and find the proof you need."

As he stepped forward and lifted the front flap of the tent, Maggie grabbed his arm and tried to pull him back. "Hugh, no! You can't!"

He paused to look back at her over his shoulder and grinned. "I like it when you call me Hugh."

"Mr. Kendrick," she said, careful to keep her voice low. "If Mr. Nash sees, he'll think I put you up to it."

"He broke into *your* place," he countered.

"We do not repay vengeance with vengeance," Maggie told him, and glanced around to make sure no one was watching. "It isn't right."

Unable to stop him, she watched Mr. Kendrick crawl halfway through the cream-colored canvas opening. He rustled around for a few moments, then came back out and gave her a pointed look. "Isn't this yours?"

He held up the silver-plated thimble with the engraved hearts that her grandmother had given her, and she gasped. "I thought I'd never see this again!"

"Every man in camp has seen you use this

while sewing," Mr. Kendrick reminded her. "Every man in camp knows it's yours. Yet here it is, in Nash's tent. What do you think he will say to that when you hold it up at the camp council tonight?"

Maggie took the thimble from his outstretched hand. "Thank you, Mr. Kendrick. I am indebted to you for your assistance in this matter."

Mr. Kendrick gave her a warm smile. "My pleasure, ma'am."

Had she misjudged him? Beneath that egotistical exterior, could it be that Hugh Kendrick was a nice person after all?

After he turned to leave, Maggie closed her fingers around the beloved thimble, and hugging it to her chest, she hurried off in the opposite direction before anyone could see them.

Ben heaved shovelful after shovelful of wet rock and riverbed sand onto the wood-framed wire-mesh sieve, his frustrations over the stolen gold and his inability to support a woman like Maggie driving him onward until midafternoon.

"Hold up!" Samuel scolded. "You're not a steam engine."

Ben gave him a quick glance, noticed his head was no longer bandaged and the gash above his brow had scabbed since the day before. His left forearm was supported by a white linen sling that hung down from his neck. "If I just work harder —"

"Then what?" Samuel asked. "You'll have more money? What if I told you there was a better way?"

"Does it involve going into that river cave you found?" Ben demanded. "The one that fell in on you?"

"I saw gold, Ben. And if we don't go in and get it, you can bet that someone else will. As soon as I'm well, I'm going back in with a select group of men. You can be one of them."

Ben dug his shovel into the riverbed once again. "I thought Esther had you on bed rest. You know you shouldn't be out here."

"Neither should you." Samuel frowned. "Thought you were meeting Maggie."

"Miss McDermott?" Ben kept his eyes focused on the river. "I only invited her to sit with me at the church service because I thought we might have a future together. That future slipped away the moment I lost my gold."

"Did you ever stop working long enough to pray about it?" Samuel challenged.

No. I didn't.

"I can talk to God right here, if I want

to," Ben replied. "Although I doubt He's listening."

"Why do you say that?"

Ben looked up. "Because life shouldn't be this hard."

"Says who?" Samuel asked, lifting a brow. "The Bible has a quote from Jesus Himself that says, 'In the world ye shall have tribulation.' It's the afterlife that's promised to be trouble free. Not these days we live in."

An explosion split the air behind them, and Ben froze. "Dynamite?"

Samuel scowled and stomped his foot. "I think that's why part of the cave fell down on my head. Kendrick's blasting is getting too close."

Ben threw down his shovel and walked over to where he could see the man and shouted, "Kendrick! Enough is enough! Stop before anyone else is hurt."

Kendrick and the eight men with him stared at Ben a moment, and then Kendrick grinned. "If you're upset because you haven't found any gold today, you're welcome to join us."

"No thank you," Ben muttered. Turning back around, he retrieved his shovel, took another quick glance at Samuel, and walked away.

■ ■ ■ ■

Ben showed up early for the camp council by the fire pit in the center of Gold Bar that night. Maggie did as well, looking as lovely as ever, with a sparkle reflected in her beautiful blue eyes that he had not seen in several days. Not since before her shop was broken into. Did she hope tonight's council would restore justice?

He too hoped to initiate action to discover who had broken into her shop and stolen his gold; however, past councils had taught him that votes could be bought, which left him fidgeting with the thin metal horse bit he'd taken from his tent to show Phillip. The mouthpiece was all he had left from the harness of the horse he used to ride at his aunt's ranch in his youth. Now each time he looked at the tarnished souvenir, he saw visions of his future horse ranch. With Phillip, and . . . Maggie.

If only he could find enough gold.

"I'm sorry I couldn't join you for the church service this morning," he said, keeping himself a good three feet away from her.

"I am sure you had better things to do," Maggie said, lifting her chin. "Phillip was kind enough to keep me company, and afterward I had the pleasure of conversing with Mr. Kendrick."

"Kendrick? What did he want?"

Maggie smiled. "To help me."

Ben wanted to ask, "Help you how?" However, there was no time. The other residents of the Gold Bar camp had arrived, and the council meeting was called to order by Pastor Brewster.

"As everyone is now aware," the pastor said, scanning the circle of faces, "Benjamin Freethy had a good-sized piece of gold stolen out of Miss McDermott's shop last night. The steel latch on the door was broken off, her sewing materials and linens were destroyed, and the place was littered with cake crumbs and rats. Anyone here know anything about that?"

"My clothes were in that shop," Willis Cogsgrove grumbled. "I had a sleeve that needed mending. Now I'm going to need a whole new shirt!"

"You shouldn't have trusted her," Eben Nash declared. "You should have come to me."

Ben narrowed his gaze. "I believe Miss McDermott has promised to replace all items that were destroyed free of charge."

"That's right," Maggie agreed. "And this next month, anyone who places a new order

114

with me will receive a 10 percent discount on one of Mrs. Watkins's meat pies."

The tailor glanced at Esther, who was nodding. "This is mutiny!" he exclaimed. "Before long, Gold Bar will be overrun by women and their foolish enterprises. We men have to stick together, or next thing you know, they'll all want to have the right to speak in public and — God forbid — maybe even vote!"

"Miss McDermott has every right to speak at tonight's council, since she is involved in this incident," Ben told him.

"And because I think I can prove who is responsible for both breaking into my shop and stealing Mr. Freethy's gold," Maggie said, and held her silver-plated thimble high in the air. "Everyone knows this is my thimble, characterized by the scrollwork and engraved hearts. I keep it on a shelf in my shop with my sewing supplies. Yet this afternoon, it was recovered from Eben Nash's tent."

"What were you doing in my tent?" Nash growled.

"It wasn't her," Hugh Kendrick countered. "It was me."

Ben stiffened, and his gaze darted toward Maggie. Leaning toward her, he whispered, "Since when have you and Kendrick been working together?"

"Since you've become too busy," Maggie whispered back.

Ouch. Ben knew he probably deserved that for standing her up at the church service that morning, but her retort still stung.

Hugh stepped forward, commanding everyone's attention. "Eben Nash has been jealous of Miss McDermott's business ever since she arrived. He must be losing money. That's probably why he broke in and stole the gold."

"It wasn't me," Nash said, scowling at the others around the campfire. "I haven't done anything wrong."

"Explain where you got the thimble," Ben challenged.

"I never touched it," Nash exclaimed. "It must have been Hugh. He planted it in my tent and only pretended to find it."

"Careful with your accusations," Pastor Brewster scolded.

Nash waved the warning aside with a sweep of his hand and continued, "Hugh is the one who's jealous. He set me up so he could act as Miss McDermott's defender and steal her away from Ben!"

Ben tended to believe the tailor was telling the truth. The question was what did

Maggie believe. He heard her gasp, and her fair cheeks turned a rosy pink even though the sun had dipped below the tree line. However, she didn't look at him.

"Are you certain the damage wasn't done by the rats?" Pastor Brewster asked, lifting his brows.

Ben shook his head. "I have yet to see one steal gold. I think we should vote to search every tent and dwelling in Gold Bar to see who is the real thief."

Pastor Brewster looked at the crowd and asked, "Shall we have a vote?"

The men glanced around at each other nervously, and only Samuel, Tom Green, and a few others agreed by putting up their hands. Certainly not the majority Ben needed.

"Searching the camp is not practical," Hugh told him. "After all, we've all found gold in various amounts. How can you prove which hunk of gold is yours?"

Ben hated that Hugh was right.

He also hated to see the look of hope dashed from Maggie's fair face. He should have warned her that there was a slim chance for justice in this place.

Turning from her sympathetic gaze, he vowed to send a letter to the authorities in

CHAPTER 7

Maggie sat at her sewing table and angrily stabbed her needle into the thick velvet. Ben's heart had not been in his apology. Not showing up at the church service on Sunday was rude, and since the council later that night, he had remained distant. She understood how disappointed he must be over the loss of his gold. Maybe he felt it was her fault, thought she should have chosen a safer place than the hem of a curtain to stash his newly found fortune.

A whole week had passed, and instead of the amused gleam she often saw in the looks he gave her, all she saw now was regret. Perhaps he found that he wasn't "enamored" with her after all. Maybe she was foolish to hope there might be a relationship of a more romantic nature between them.

One thing was certain. She shouldn't be wasting time pining after Ben when her finances were under assault. Since the camp council, orders for mending and new clothes had dropped off significantly. Perhaps whoever had sabotaged her shop had also threatened the men trying to win her hand and told them to back off.

Maggie sighed. What would happen if business continued to decline? Should she lower her prices?

And if business did recover, would she have to keep sewing forever? What of marriage? Would she ever have children of her own? A family?

As her mother entered her seamstress shop, Maggie's hand slipped while stitching the velvet waistcoat and she pricked her finger with the needle. "Ow!"

"Are you all right?" her mother asked, laying her shawl aside and sitting at the table beside her.

Maggie nodded and sucked on the tip of her finger. The sharp stainless-steel needle had drawn blood. And it hurt. Almost as much as her heart. Lifting her eyes to keep tears from spilling over her cheeks, she whispered, "Always look for the positive in every situation, and thank the good Lord that things are not worse."

Her mother patted her arm. "Although I am sad that Cousin Lewis is gone, I *am* thankful we came to Gold Bar."

Surprised, Maggie frowned. "You are?"

Her mother nodded as she removed a pair of spectacles from a small leather case and put them on. "I am also thankful that I will now be able to see to help you with all the sewing."

"Where did you get those?" Maggie asked, staring at the delicate gold and glass spectacles perched on her mother's nose.

"They were a gift from Ben." Her mother smiled. "They belonged to his late sister. When I told him how bad I felt that I could not see well enough to help you sew and recoup some of our loss from the break-in, he and our young Phillip both agreed I should now have them. Phillip said, 'Especially if it helps Maggie.' I think that boy would do anything for you."

Maggie smiled in return. "I will have to thank him."

Her mother gave her a coy look, as if withholding a secret, then burst into a smile and announced, "There is one more thing I can thank our good Lord for. Dr. Harrington has proposed! He got down on one knee as we were walking together just this morning. He had the sweetest smile upon his face as he asked me to be his wife."

Maggie dropped her sewing and gasped. "What did you say?"

"I said yes."

"Are you certain this is what you want?" Maggie leaned forward. "You aren't accepting because of the decrease in our finances, are you? I thought you said that you would never marry again, that marriage was for the young."

Her mother laughed, and the new spectacles magnified the shine in her glistening eyes. "I've changed my mind. And no, my acceptance has nothing to do with finances, although I suppose I *am* thankful I will no longer be a burden."

Maggie wrapped her in a hug. "You were never a burden."

"Oh Maggie," her mother crooned, nearly breathless. "He is such a kind, considerate man. He tells me jokes to make me laugh, and I haven't had much to laugh about in a long time. We'll marry next month as soon as you can sew me a proper wedding dress. Dr. Harrington said he would pay for all the materials and, of course, your service."

"We'll have to put in an order for silk, satin, and lace from San Francisco right away!" Maggie gushed, catching some of her excitement. "Oh Mother, it *is* good to see you so happy."

"I wish the same for you, Maggie. Do not give up hope. I was wrong to think you should marry Lewis Parnell or any man you do not truly love."

"What's this about love?" Esther asked, bustling into the shop behind Agnes.

"Mother's getting married!" Maggie said. "To Dr. Harrington."

"Congratulations, Clara!" Esther exclaimed, her round face beaming.

"Haven't been to a wedding in quite some time," Agnes said, and dropped the clothing in her arms on the table next to the hotel-room sheets Esther carried in. "We brought you some mending. Figured you might need the work."

Maggie nodded. "I do. Although I daresay you two have already done more than enough to help my mother and me."

"Much to Eben Nash's disapproval, we ladies need to stick together," Esther teased, then pointed to the new item Maggie had started working on. "What is that you're sewing?"

Maggie held up the thick, double-paneled rectangular piece. "It's a saddle blanket. For Phillip. Until he gets a horse of his own, I thought he could use it on Tom Green's horse during his riding lessons."

Agnes leaned closer. "Why are you tying knots in the cording?"

"It helps strengthen the threading. Especially on the edges," Maggie explained.

Her mother nodded. "In Ireland we call them 'love knots.' "

"They look like hearts," Esther mused. "Hearts sewn with love. You have certainly 'sown' love into the heart of that young boy, as well as into the hearts of most of the other men in this camp."

Maggie lowered her gaze. "I wish I could sow some love into Benjamin Freethy's heart." She placed the saddle blanket back down on the table and searched the other women's sympathetic faces. "Why won't he propose?"

Esther and Agnes sat down in the two chairs opposite Maggie and her mother, and Esther leaned forward and gave her a conspiratorial look. "Well, all I know is what my dear husband Samuel has told me, but it seems Ben has a code of honor that he just won't break. He's said time and time again that he won't marry until he has enough money to properly support a family."

Maggie shook her head. "So this is all about money?"

"Also, about pride," Agnes confided.

"Apparently, long ago," Esther continued, "Ben was set to marry a woman with high standards. Her father encouraged him to work for his bank. After three months, Ben decided working inside was not for him and told his intended bride about his dream to build his own horse ranch. Well, the young lady would have none of that and broke off the engagement saying she didn't think he could provide her with the kind of life she deserved."

"How awful!" Maggie exclaimed. "But I don't need his money. Even though my earnings have been less, I'm still making enough to support my needs."

"The man doesn't think a wife should have to work," Agnes stated, her voice dry.

"So, he does not want me to make money," Maggie said slowly, "but neither will he propose until he thinks that *he* has enough to support me? That is ridiculous."

"It's proper etiquette," her mother chimed in. "Although I think by now, we all agree that in these times, in this place, it is sometimes best to lay those rules aside."

"Absolutely," Maggie agreed. "And the very next time I see Mr. Freethy, I will be sure to tell him so."

Ben pounded on the door of Maggie's shop, the midmorning summer heat already gathering sweat upon his brow. After his second set of knocks she finally let him in, and his heart sank as his gaze swept the vacant interior.

"Have you seen him?" he demanded.

Maggie frowned. "Seen who?"

"Phillip! He's gone."

Her eyes widened. "What do you mean, gone?"

Ben shook his head. "I woke up this morning and he wasn't there. I've already searched the entire camp and run down to the river twice. I can't find him anywhere."

"That does not sound like Phillip. Have you given him any reason to run off?"

"We did quarrel last night," Ben admitted. "I told him I didn't think I will have the money to buy the horse ranch by the deadline on Saturday, and he said the only reason he wanted a horse was so that he could ride back to Boston."

"Have you checked the corral?" Maggie asked, hurrying toward the door. "Is the postmaster's horse missing?"

Ben followed her. "I didn't see it in the corral, but I thought today is Tom Green's day to ride into Sacramento on the mail route."

She bit her lip, her face filled with worry. "We better check and see."

The postmaster was furious when they arrived. Shaking his fist at them, Tom Green shouted, "Today is not lesson day! I have a mail route to run and no ride!"

Ben winced. "When did you discover the horse missing?"

"About fifteen minutes ago," Tom replied. "At first I thought he got loose from the corral. Sometimes coyotes scare up the animals and get them all panicky. But then I heard from Samuel that your boy was missing. That's when I thought to check the tack and discovered the bridle and saddle are gone too."

"Which way would he have gone?" Maggie pleaded.

Desperation edged her voice, and Ben was comforted in the fact that she cared about his nephew as much as he did. If anything were to happen to Phillip —

Ben swallowed hard. "He could have taken any number of paths through the woods."

"He didn't." Samuel ran toward them, one arm still in a sling and his other holding a straw hat with the initials *P.T.* embroidered along the side in black thread. Maggie's work, of course.

"Where did you find his hat?" Ben asked. His heart was thumping so loudly in his chest he feared he might miss the answer and strained his ears to listen.

"On the main road."

Ben nodded. "I'll get the mules and hitch up the wagon."

He had just unlatched the corral gate when Maggie rushed forward and grabbed his arm. "Ben, look!"

He heard the fast-paced clip-clopping of feet and spun around to see the postmaster's chestnut gelding return to camp — unaccompanied.

The reins were dangling loosely over the animal's left side, and the saddle upon its back sat slightly askew. Had Phillip fallen? Or been bucked off?

Tom grabbed hold of the reins and brought his horse to a stop. The animal was sweaty and breathing hard, letting them know he'd been running. He also delivered a few snorts and tossed his head as if to warn them he would not have anyone ride him again any time soon.

"Dear God," Maggie prayed, sinking to her knees. "Please let Phillip be all right."

Ben prayed silently along with her, his guilt gnawing at him. None of this would have happened if he'd been a better uncle to the boy. He finally turned and placed a hand on her shoulder. "I'll find him. I won't return until I do."

Samuel nodded. "I'm going with you."

Ben had the mules hitched to the wagon in less than ten minutes, and Maggie followed them as far as the camp entrance. Tom said he'd give his horse a short rest, then he too would set out to look for the boy.

However, it didn't take that long. Ben had only driven about fifty feet when another wagon came into view. A large man with black hair, a mustache, and beard sat on the bench seat in front, driving his team of mules, with a fair-haired woman beside him. And crouched in the back, looking over their shoulders, were two boys. One who resembled the man in front of him, and the other — Ben's own nephew, Phillip!

A surge of relief flooded Ben as he tossed Samuel the reins to his mules and jumped down from his wagon to greet them.

"I think I found someone you might be looking for," the dark-haired man said with a grin. "My name's George Galloway. This here is my wife, Sarah, and my son, Arthur. We were on our way to Gold Bar when we found the lad walking down the road."

"A snake spooked the horse and I got thrown into the bushes," Phillip said, climbing off the other family's wagon.

Ben put his arm around his nephew's shoulders and went to hug him, but Phillip pulled away. Apparently, still angry with him.

"Thank you for bringing him home," Ben said, thankful the boy was safe, and shook George Galloway's hand. "I'm Benjamin Freethy. Are you just passing through?"

"No, we're here to stay," Galloway told him. "Thought we'd make this place our new home."

Ben gave him a nod. "Welcome to Gold Bar."

Galloway grinned, then looked past him, and Ben turned to see Maggie racing up the road, lifting her skirts high as she ran.

"Phillip!"

His nephew took off toward her, meeting her halfway. They flung their arms around each other, and Ben wasn't sure who started crying first, Phillip or Maggie.

"I was so scared!" Maggie exclaimed.

"I'm sorry," Phillip sobbed, hugging her around her middle. "I'm so sorry."

"Why did ye do it?" she cried, her accent heavy with emotion. "Why did ye run away like ye did?"

"Uncle Ben said he couldn't buy the horse ranch and that we were moving away to San Francisco and I didn't want to go! I thought I could hide in the woods until he was gone and then come back and live with you."

Ben's stomach knotted, then just about dropped down to his boots when Maggie turned toward him.

She gave him a startled look. "You're *leaving?*"

Chapter 8

Maggie could barely contain her fury as Ben walked toward her, bridging the distance between them. "Phillip." She dropped her arms away from the boy. "Let me have a word alone with your uncle."

Phillip nodded, his eyes filled with hope. Likely he thought she could fix the situation, convince Ben to stay in Gold Bar. Since Ben had not informed her of his plan to leave, she did not know if anything she said would make a difference, yet she had to try. Not only for Phillip's sake, but because her own heart demanded it.

As Ben drew closer, she saw the hard set of his jaw, clearly indicating his reluctance to speak to her. She gestured for him to follow her back to the camp entrance where they might have a little more privacy, and then she turned and repeated, "You're leaving?"

"I thought it might be best."

"Best for whom?"

He shook his head. "I can't raise a kid in this environment."

"Why not?" she challenged. "You can see for yourself — Phillip doesn't want to leave."

"He's my responsibility," Ben said, his voice unusually gruff. "He needs a roof over his head, a home. I can't have him living in a tent. And without any hope of building a horse ranch or seeing justice in this town —" He gave her a direct look. "I decided that Phillip and I should move to San Francisco where I can get a job with reliable wages and Phillip can go to school."

Maggie pursed her lips, trying her best to hold back a new wave of tears. "So that's it, then? You've already made up your mind to go — just the two of ye?"

"Yes."

"I — I don't understand," Maggie said, her voice waffling. "I thought ye might — *care* for me, and —"

She shook her head, unable to finish, unable to say what was really in her heart.

A swift look of pain entered Ben's gaze, and the Adam's apple in his throat dipped, then he looked away to stare down at his boots. "It's been a pleasure to meet you, Miss McDermott. However, it has never been my intention to give you false hope. A man should be able to properly provide for his family, and at this point in my life, I am not in a position to seek a wife."

Now she was Miss McDermott? Maggie's heart ached. "What of love?" she asked. "What if a woman does not need your financial support but has money of her own to help with the finances?"

"A man should be able to provide for his family," Ben repeated, then gave her an apologetic glance. "If you're looking for a proposal, I'd suggest you accept the offer of another."

"Marry someone else?" she choked out.

She wanted him to look at her, to see how much she cared, how much she only wanted *him,* and for him to change his mind and beg her to come with him. Instead, the infuriating man clenched his jaw and kept his gaze averted.

"You must do whatever you think is best for yourself," he said softly.

Holding back tears, she asked, "When will you be going?"

"First thing in the morning."

Her stomach constricted and the back of her throat ached, but she wouldn't let him see how much he'd hurt her. Wouldn't let him see her cry.

"I'll want to say goodbye to Phillip," she

said, her chest tight. "Give him the saddle blanket I made for the horse he might buy one day. And encourage him to write me from time to time. With your permission, of course."

Ben nodded, not saying a word, and his Adam's apple dipped a second time. Would she ever see them again? Would she *ever* find the kind of happiness that lasts?

"Goodbye, Mr. Freethy."

She didn't wait for a reply. Unable to stand there another second, she turned, her eyes burning, and as fast as her feet would carry her, she walked away.

While Maggie and Phillip spent the afternoon together and finished saying their goodbyes, Ben went down to the river with the other men to try his luck panning for gold one last time. As if by some miracle he might find enough gold to change his fate.

He dug with his shovel, sifted, and searched through the river rock time and time again, and . . . *nothing.*

Beside him, Samuel scratched his beard and let out a grunt. "Gold Bar won't be the same without you."

"Don't worry. You'll still have Hugh."

Samuel grimaced. "You know he's probably the one who stole your gold, just like the tailor said. If you stood up to him, instead of walking away —"

Ben frowned. "You think me a coward?"

"You might put Hugh in his place for once."

"What would you have me do?" Ben demanded. "Shake the gold out of him? Then what?"

Samuel gave him a hard look. "I know how much money you have saved in the bank. You might not have enough to buy the land for your horse ranch, but it *is* enough for you to take a wife."

"I'm not having that conversation again," Ben warned.

"You keep insisting you need more money, but when will it ever be enough?"

Ben narrowed his gaze. "Did Esther put you up to this?"

Samuel shook his head. "No. I just hate to see you throwing away something you shouldn't because you think you need more than you've already got."

"I appreciate the concern, but I won't propose without more gold," Ben insisted.

"Good to hear," Kendrick said, coming up beside them. "Because I plan to have a ring on Miss McDermott's finger by night-fall."

Ben's pulse raced and heat surged into

the base of his neck as he thought of Maggie accepting Kendrick's proposal. The very idea sickened his stomach.

"Bet you wish you found a nugget like this today," Kendrick said, holding out the shiny coppery rock in his hand. "Except you don't have what it takes to go where the real gold lies."

Ben's jaw clenched as he thought of the nugget that had been stolen from him and the extra two hundred dollars he still needed to purchase the land for his horse ranch — and propose to Maggie.

Willis Cogsgrove and another miner, a Spaniard whom Ben knew as Domingo, came down the trail to the water's edge and gestured toward Samuel.

"You ready?" Cogsgrove asked, expectantly.

Ben frowned. "Ready for what?"

Samuel nodded toward the river cave where he'd injured his arm nine days before. "There's gold in that cave, Ben. And we're going in. Join us, and we'll divide the profits."

Ben hesitated, met Kendrick's mocking gaze, then with thoughts of claiming Maggie as his own pushing him forward, he grabbed his pickax and followed the others into the river cave's darkened mouth.

He doesn't want me. Hot tears streamed down Maggie's cheeks, and her stomach ached from the overbearing weight of her sorrow as she thought of her confrontation with Ben a few hours earlier. She couldn't imagine living in Gold Bar without him, yet despite her protests, the fact remained that he was leaving, and taking his nephew along with him.

She sat on the window seat of the bakery beside Phillip and hugged him tight. How fond she had grown of this boy! She'd enjoyed tutoring him in the afternoons while she stitched. It was going to be hard to see him go. Releasing him, she gulped back a sob. Why was this happening? Wasn't it God's plan for her to care for this boy who so desperately needed a mother?

She'd been wrong before.

Like when she thought she was coming to Gold Bar to marry Lewis Parnell. And the time she thought her beau in New York would propose, only to have him leave and marry another, saying she was too ambitious. He'd wanted a more docile woman for a wife. Someone who would never dream of running her own business.

Did Ben think she was too ambitious? Twice, he'd said "a good man always provides for his family." Was he afraid he wouldn't be considered a good man if he allowed her to help with the finances? Wasn't there anything she could do to change his mind?

Once her mother married Dr. Harrington, Maggie would be living in the back quarters of her shop . . . alone. Sure, she'd be able to support herself, but she doubted she'd find joy in her success if she had no one to share it with.

The door to the bakery opened with a jingle, and as a slender, blond woman and equally fair-haired young boy stepped over the threshold, Esther bustled out from around the counter. "Maggie, have you met Sarah Galloway and her son, Arthur?"

"From a distance," Maggie said, and stood up to properly greet them. "I'm Maggie Mc-Dermott, and of course, you've already made Phillip's acquaintance when you brought him back to camp in your wagon this morning."

Sarah nodded and smiled. "He looks like you. You have similar smiles."

Did they? Maggie glanced at Phillip, and he looked up at her and grinned. Although not related, perhaps their smiles appeared

139

similar because they were always so happy to see each other.

"I've given the Galloways your old room in the back of the hotel," Esther informed her. "Until they can build their own house here in Gold Bar."

Sarah nodded. "I wish my husband would have taken more time to help us get settled in, but he was anxious to go down to the river to meet the other men and pan for gold."

"They've all got gold fever," Esther declared. "Finding gold quickly turns into an obsession as they hope to strike it rich and live a life of ease."

"My uncle and I found gold once," Phillip chimed in, and walked over to the other boy, who was almost his same height. "Can I take Arthur down to the river to watch?"

When Sarah gave her consent and the excited boys raced out of the bakery, Maggie's heart broke all over again. If Phillip didn't have to leave Gold Bar, he and this boy might have become good friends.

"I love the pattern of your dress." Sarah looked admiringly at Maggie's purple three-tiered skirt and fan-front bodice. "The stitching is beautiful."

Warmed by the compliment, she confided, "I made it myself."

"Maggie's a seamstress," Esther boasted with pride. "She has her own shop."

"My sister and her husband have a clothing store in San Francisco," Sarah told her. "I'm certain they would be very interested in seeing some of your designs. I can give you their name and address if you'd like."

"Thank you," Maggie said, and once again questioned God's plan for her life.

She appreciated the seemingly providential help with her business, but how would she ever be happy without Phillip and Ben?

Ben held up one of the tin candle lanterns Willis Cogsgrove and Domingo had brought with them to light the interior of the cave and scanned the rocks littering the free-flowing stream at their feet.

"I knew you'd come with us eventually," Samuel said, his voice smug.

Ben splashed farther into the river cave behind him. "Couldn't let you get yourself hurt again, could I? Especially since you still have your arm in a sling from the last time you got the foolish notion to come in here."

Samuel chuckled. "So now you're my protector?"

"Esther would never give me another one of her puff pastries if I didn't at least try to

141

keep you safe."

Willis smirked. "I may not bake like his wife, but I can cook you up a meat pie for the right price."

Domingo shot the round-bellied camp cook a hopeful look. "Tonight?"

Willis nodded. "As soon as we retrieve the gold."

"Admit it, Ben," Samuel said, using a shovel with his good arm to unearth a slew of rocks. "You came because you believed me when I said there was gold in here."

"I'll believe it when I see it," Ben said, digging his own shovel into the loose rock on the cave's bottom.

Domingo swung his pickax into the upper side wall and then spun around, his dark eyes wide with excitement, and pointed. "See and believe."

Ben's heart lurched in his chest as he raised the lantern higher into the air and stepped up close. Samuel and Willis also gathered around.

"What did I tell you?" Samuel exclaimed, and let out a whoop. "Gold!"

Willis laughed. "Looks like Ben is at a loss for words."

He was. Ben reached up to touch the shimmering vein running through the rock wall, and a half-dozen images played out across his mind. An image of the bank manager in Sacramento falling over backward in his chair when they cashed in. The surprised look on Lionel Riggs's face when presented with the amount he requested for the land in the valley on time. A vision of a large wooden ranch house with a wide front porch, and beyond, in the fields, over a dozen horses. One for Phillip to call his very own. And standing by his side, with a blue-eyed baby in her arms, his dear sweet Maggie . . . his beloved wife.

All of a sudden he felt as light as a feather as euphoria flooded over him, indeed through every limb of his entire body, and Ben found he was laughing along with the others.

"We're going to need a few more pickaxes to get all of this gold out," he said, shaking his head in disbelief.

Samuel chuckled. "And a few more sacks to put it in."

"I may have to put those meat pies on hold until tomorrow," Willis teased, with a broad grin. "This might take awhile."

Domingo nodded excitely. "Dinner can wait."

"First let's get a few more lamps over here to this side," Samuel directed. "And clear some of these sharper rocks by our feet so that —"

A loud explosion rocked the earth, knocking Ben off balance. The small Spaniard to his left fell to the cave floor with a splash, and Willis and Samuel also appeared to be fighting to stay on their feet. Then another rumble, even louder than the first, deafened Ben's ears. A glance toward the cave mouth showed a cascade of debris filling the opening, and with what sounded like a crack of thunder the top of the cave began breaking apart and crumbling in around them.

"Samuel?" Ben raised his arms to shield himself and tried to dodge the onslaught, but something hard hit his head.

And everything went dark.

CHAPTER 9

Instead of allowing herself to dwell on Ben and Phillip's imminent departure, Maggie chose to do what she did best and finished mending every last piece of clothing stacked in her client basket. Next, she showed her mother the address of the clothing shop Sarah had given her that might be interested in her designs. Then she took a pencil and piece of Phillip's tutoring paper and sketched ideas for the wedding dress she was to create for her mother.

Maggie tapped her pencil as she pondered what kind of sleeves the dress should have. "What do you think for summer? Bell or cap sleeves?"

Her mother glanced at the sketches and smiled. "I'll be happy no matter what I wear."

"I want you to look exquisite," Maggie insisted. "I've already ordered material with —"

From somewhere outside came a shout. "Maggie!"

She jumped to her feet. Phillip! He sounded afraid, so she rushed to open the door.

"What is it?" she asked, breathless, as he stood on the threshold.

Phillip's face was flushed, his chest heaving as he struggled to catch a breath. "Rockslide. Down at the river. Uncle Ben and three others were in a cave. And — and are trapped inside!"

Ben?

Maggie's stomach turned and she grasped the doorframe. "Show me where?"

Phillip nodded, and behind them, Maggie's mother called out, "I'll go get Dr. Harrington."

Maggie arrived at the river to see several dozen men searching the massive rockslide for an opening into the cave. The mouth had been blocked off with so much debris it would take weeks to dig out. Their best option seemed to be to remove rock from the upper left side and tunnel in that way.

Esther ran down from the bakery. "My Samuel's in there?"

Agnes moved to embrace her friend, while Maggie nodded. "And Ben."

"Willis and Domingo too," Agnes informed them.

Why, Ben? Why did ye do it?

Maggie recalled Ben's words when they'd argued, and her heart raced as she stumbled over the rocks toward the rescue party. Did he go in there for himself? Or Phillip? Or . . . *her?*

She never should have pressed him for a proposal. She'd rather have him leave than have him put his life in danger.

"Look out!"

Maggie jumped back in time to heed Charles Henshaw's warning, and gasped as another slew of rocks slid down the steep hillside above and splashed into the river.

Then as soon as the embankment appeared stable, Charles motioned for Tom Green, newcomer George Galloway, and a couple of other men to help him lift away several large boulders. Pastor Brewster joined them, and as he worked, he uttered a constant stream of prayer for the lives of everyone involved. Maggie, her mother, Phillip, Esther, Agnes, and even Sarah Galloway and her son also removed debris.

"If only we could find an opening," Maggie murmured. "And find out if they are all right."

She hated to think of the alternative. She

couldn't think about the alternative. She had to stay positive. After all, God did not bring her out here to lose one man, fall in love with another, and then lose him too.

Maggie drew a sudden breath at the realization. She was in love with Benjamin Freethy. Not just a wee bit, but with all her heart and soul and everything within her. Just as she'd heard so many times during Sunday service that she should also love God.

But did she *trust* God? And His will for her life?

She had thought it was His will that she agree to an arranged marriage. She'd thought it His will that she open shop and provide for herself. But none of it had brought her the joy, peace, comfort, and security she truly craved. None of that could bring back Ben. Only God, the Creator of the universe and Master of seemingly impossible miracles could now provide what her heart needed most.

Squeezing her eyes shut, Maggie knelt amid the debris and grabbed hold of the rock in front of her. *Dear God, it is You and only You that I can now trust. Have mercy on us all and help us get these men out.*

She finished the short prayer, but then as she continued digging without any sign of a chink in the rock's armor, she wondered if she should have prayed longer, or used fancier words, for a better chance of drawing God's attention.

Her hands removed another rock, and suddenly, a small opening was revealed between two slabs of rock slanting down into darkness. She dropped a few pebbles through the fist-sized hole and couldn't hear them land, indicating a void, perhaps the interior of the cave and access to the men?

"I may have found an opening!" she cried out, then drew her mouth closer to the ground. "Hello?"

Nothing.

George Galloway rushed over to see for himself then shook his head. "We'll never be able to move these boulders, not with fifty men. We'll have to keep tunneling through the side. Keep talking and let us know if anyone responds."

Maggie called down again. "Ben? Are you there? Hello?"

Please, God. Please let him be all right.

If only she could see. She glanced up toward the heavens, and the last rays of the day's sun rested upon a pinnacle of rock on the hillside above — like a candle. If she went back to her shop and got a candle lantern, and some rope . . . No, a rope would be too thick, but if she used the thin leather cording she'd used to bind the edges of Phillip's saddle blanket, and attached the candle to one of her heart-shaped knots — "hearts sewn with love," Esther had called them — she might be able to lower the light into the depths below . . . and discover the men's fate.

Ben moved his head and winced as a sharp rock poked into his scalp. His cheek burned, raw to his touch where the flesh had been gouged. The sharp metallic smell of blood filled his nostrils and lay on his tongue. He blinked twice but couldn't see through the encompassing dark. The candle lanterns must have been snuffed out by the —
He drew a deep breath into his lungs and coughed. There had been an explosion. A second thunderous rumble. Rocks. Several rocks fell off his chest as he struggled to sit up, and a needlelike twinge of pain shot through the side of his foot as he moved his leg. He must have twisted his ankle. However, he didn't think it was broken. How had the others fared?
"Samuel?"
His call was answered by a low groan a few feet away. "I'm here. A bit banged up but in one piece, I think."

Thank the Lord!

Bolstered by the fact he was not alone, Ben called out again. "Willis? Domingo?"

The two other men had been to his left before he lost consciousness. Careful of his ankle, Ben pulled himself over the rough loose rock and located a large body. Had to be Willis, as the Spaniard was only half the size of the camp cook. Ben found the man's arm and patted his way up the torso to his throat to feel for a pulse. Willis was alive.

Patting the big man's fat cheeks, he shouted, "Willis! Wake up!"

The body beside him stirred and emitted a loud, tumultuous groan. "What happened?"

"The roof of the cave collapsed," Samuel spat, his tone harsh. "Probably because Hugh used dynamite."

"Hugh!" Ben recalled hearing the first explosion before the rumble of rock that had sealed the mouth of the cave and fallen in from the ceiling above. "He did this?"

"I'd bet money on it," Samuel growled.

Fueled by his rising anger against Hugh, Ben crawled on his hands and knees and found Domingo. The small man was alive as well, although the words tumbling out of the Spaniard's mouth were incoherent. "He's only half-conscious," Ben announced.

"He needs a doctor."

"Don't we all." Willis let out another groan. "I — I think my leg's busted up. My right arm too."

The alarming urgency of the situation drove Ben forward as he felt his way around in the total darkness. "Use your hands to search for our tools. There must be something in the rubble we can use to help us get out."

He had no idea how long they'd been in the cave since the collapse, but from his thirst, he guessed it had been awhile.

"I'm sorry," Samuel said, his voice half-choked. "You warned me it was too dangerous. I never should have encouraged you to come."

"You're not to blame, Sam. I'm the one who decided to follow you in. The only one I can blame is myself."

He'd been a fool for gold. Also, a fool for hurting Maggie. The look on her face when she'd confronted him about leaving and asked, *What of love?*" had twisted his heart into a fearsome knot that threatened to be his undoing, if this cave didn't finish him off first.

What had he been thinking? When had he become so prideful, so obstinate about who could or could not be the money earner in a marriage? Especially when it was he who had arranged for her to learn the business skills she needed to help her succeed.

He let out a sigh. He should have proposed to her the moment he first saw her, before anyone else could. Because he *did* love her. He loved her coppery-blond hair, her blue eyes, her Irish accent, the way she mothered Phillip, the way she'd boosted her business and learned to barter. And most of all he loved the way she understood him, the way she looked at him, the way she —

"Ben, do you think there's any hope?" Samuel asked, his voice cracking.

"As long as we're alive, there's always hope," he replied. Then, recalling Maggie's words, he repeated, "Always look for the positive in every situation, and thank the good Lord that things are not worse."

"I suppose I can be thankful I'm not trapped in here with someone cranky like Eben Nash," Samuel admitted.

"I'm thankful for you too," Ben said, then sighed. "And Maggie, and Phillip."

Would he ever see them again?

"Hey, Ben," Samuel barked suddenly. "Do you see that?"

A flicker of light caught Ben's eye and he glanced upward, searching for the source. Unbelievably, a tiny candle descended toward them, from about twenty feet above, its brilliance bouncing off the cave walls and lighting the interior.

And a soft, sweet, angelic voice asked, "Ben, are you all right?"

"Maggie!"

She nearly fainted with relief when she heard Ben's voice respond out of the depths below. He was alive!

"Everyone is working to get you out," she told him.

"The sooner the better," he replied. "Samuel and I are okay, Willis is hurt, and Domingo's head is bleeding. It looks bad."

Maggie relayed the information to the other rescuers, then wrapped cloth bandages from Dr. Harrington around her leather cord in a tight spiral and lowered them through the hole along with more pencil-thin candles secured by her "love knots."

Hours passed, wearing the rescue party down, as well as those trapped in the cave below.

"Maggie?" Ben called. "Will you look after Phillip?"

The way he said it made her realize he wasn't just asking for this moment. It was for in case he didn't make it out.

Her heart wrenched. "You know I will."

She also planned to look after Ben too, once he was out, if he let her. "Phillip's right here beside me. Esther too, and she's anxious to speak to Samuel."

Giving the baker and her husband some privacy, Maggie went back to the rock brigade to touch base with the others and lend a hand. More hours passed as men, women, and children all helped by lantern light to remove rubble from what they believed to be the side wall to the river cave. It began to rain, and, wet and shivering, they continued on through the night, working to save the ones they respected and loved.

To Maggie's surprise, Eben Nash had hobbled down to the river to take charge, unearthing rocks with the rest of them by lantern light until the following dawn.

"Watch your heart," Dr. Harrington warned him.

Maggie frowned. *Eben Nash had a heart problem?*

"Instead of worrying about me, you should concern yourself with those men trapped down there," the tailor said with a scowl and tapped his crippled leg with his cane. "Believe me, I know what it's like to have a cave collapse in on you. And despite that little hole they are conversing through,

155

if those men don't get proper ventilation into that chamber soon, they'll all suffocate."

Ben's next words to her confirmed Eben could be right. "Maggie," he said, his voice strained. "The air is getting thin. It's hard to breathe."

"We're almost there," Maggie said . . . which wasn't exactly true, no matter how much she wished it were.

Many of the tribal natives, who had mostly kept their distance while panning for gold on the river, also offered their assistance and set out diligently to help the recovery effort, but it still wasn't enough. They needed more men.

More specifically, they needed Hugh Kendrick and his team, who hadn't helped at all and were now seen heading upriver with their panning equipment.

Furious over their lack of compassion, Maggie marched toward them.

"Hubert Elias Kendrick," she stormed, stamping her foot, "how can ye even think of panning for gold when there are men's lives at stake?"

The tall, broad-shouldered man grinned. "You remembered my full name."

"As if ye would ever let anyone forget," she retorted.

"What would you have me do?" he asked.

"Help us," she pleaded. "We desperately need the strength of more men."

"Desperately." Hugh glanced around at his men and laughed. "Hear that, boys? She said 'desperately.' "

Maggie narrowed her gaze. "This isn't a game."

"All right, my men and I will lend a hand." The look in his eyes grew hard. "*If* you'll marry me."

"What? No. I will not!" She could never marry him or any other, for that matter. Never again would she consider a loveless marriage. Benjamin Freethy was the only man for her, and if she couldn't have him, she'd die a spinster.

"Well then, it's going to cost you," Hugh said haughtily. "Five hundred dollars."

Maggie sucked in her breath, outraged by his ridiculously steep request, and scanned the faces of the eight other men listening in. "Do ye all agree with this?"

Hugh's men looked nervous but wouldn't budge. He paid them too well.

"I'll get the money," she vowed.

Except when she ran back and told the other miners who were trying to rescue the trapped men, no one wanted to part with any of their precious gold. No one but Esther. The baker offered to give all she'd saved to help rescue her husband. However, Esther's generous donation only provided half the amount, which still left Maggie short two hundred and fifty dollars.

"Time is running out!" she told the others. "Hugh and his men may be our last hope."

She wouldn't let Ben die. She *wouldn't.* But where would she get the rest of Hugh's required fee? If only she had something of value to —

"I'll sell my shop with the back-side living quarters for the second half of what is needed," she offered.

George Galloway stopped pulling away rocks to look at her. "My family and I would be interested. But are you sure that's what you want to do?"

She'd spent everything she'd earned over the last two months to fix up the shack her cousin had left her and turn it into a real home, but Maggie swallowed hard and nodded, her gaze upon the collapsed cave. "Ben's in there, and I can't lose him!"

She'd been surprised that George Galloway had so much cash in his possession. But not as surprised as Hugh Kendrick when she returned with a sack full of money.

Hands on hips, she demanded, "Now will you help?"

CHAPTER 10

Ben dipped one of the cloth bandages into the water on the floor of the cave and placed it over Domingo's forehead. The Spaniard had developed a fever, even though the rest of his body was shivering. Ben shivered too. He'd managed to pull himself and the others up onto the dryer half of the cave, filled with a layer of fresh rubble from the slide. But the air was still damp and the temperature chilly.

A few hours into the new day, Maggie had called down to him, "Don't you dare give up! The good Lord is going to get ye through this. I know He will."

Ben had to smile. Her positive attitude was something else he loved about her. Maggie was always believing, trusting, persevering, even when things didn't turn out as she'd hoped. She always said one should count their blessings, but instead of appreciating the fact that God had given him everything he needed, Ben had kept thinking it wasn't enough. He'd wanted more. Because he didn't trust God to provide. He'd trusted in gold. Yet love and his relationships with others were so much more important than gold. If he ever got out of here, he'd be sure to try to set things right.

Ben chuckled to himself. Maybe because he was losing air, and with it — his mind. Or perhaps because being trapped in a cave and faced with an uncertain future could put everything into perspective, make him realize what really mattered. *Who* really mattered.

If only he'd had the wisdom to see it all before.

"Lord," he murmured, striving to pull in a breath. "I need You. I know I've been trying to make my own way, do things myself, but I need You."

Maggie thought Hugh looked disappointed she had chosen to pay him instead of accepting his offer of marriage. However, he kept his word, and when he and his team joined the rescue efforts, the extra help appeared to make a difference. They were now making significant headway.

She lowered a set of Esther's fresh, stick-thin breadsticks through the rock opening into the cave, realizing she hadn't herself eaten anything since noon the day before. The others had rested and eaten in shifts, but she had declined. She was exhausted, and her stomach growled, but being there for Ben and the other men was more important.

A tug on the cord let her know when they'd taken the food off the line and she could pull it back up.

"Maggie, I'm thankful for you," Ben said, his voice sounding a little sluggish.

"I'm thankful for you too, Ben. How are you doing down there?"

"Oh. You know. Just sitting here staring up at a vein of gold and thinking of you."

He sounded delirious. If she didn't know better, she'd think he was drunk. Better to keep him talking. "You said you see a vein of gold?"

"I do." He chuckled softly. "The biggest vein of gold you ever did see. Hugh would be jealous."

Was he now seeing things?

"Even with the nugget that was stolen, I only needed about two hundred dollars more to buy the land for the horse ranch," he said, his voice oddly bemused. "Now here it is right in front of me."

She thought he must be imagining things and was certain all four men were going to need medical care. Dr. Harrington would be kept busy. Her mother too as she assisted.

"Phillip is here," she told him. "He wants to speak to you."

The young boy drew close to the hole. "Uncle Ben?"

"Yeah, Phillip?"

"I'm not going to run away again. I promise. I'm sorry I took the postmaster's horse without asking. I'll go with you wherever you want to go."

"We aren't leaving. You're going to stay here . . . with Maggie."

"Great!" Phillip lifted his head, looked at her, and grinned. "I can't wait to tell Arthur! Maybe I can teach him to ride a horse."

As Phillip ran off toward his new friend, Maggie bit her lip, conscious of the fact that Ben had told the boy "you're going to stay," not "we."

"Maggie, are you still there?" His voice sounded almost panicked.

"Yes, Ben, I'm here."

"Maggie, will you marry me?"

She'd received numerous proposals over the last two months, but none had ever sounded so sweet. "Yes, Ben," she replied, tears filling her eyes. "I'll marry you."

She thought she heard him sigh. "We would have been happy."

"Ben?"

He didn't respond. George Galloway came over to give her instructions, and she leaned back over the hole.

"Ben, do you hear me? I need you to get the other men away from the left side wall. Can you do that? They're going to break through."

Again, there was no answer, and as she scrambled down the embankment, over the rocks, her heart hammered in her chest as she prayed.

Hopefully, they were not too late.

The tinkling sound of pickaxes and murmurs of outside voices drew closer as Ben helped Samuel drag Willis and Domingo to the opposite side of the cave.

"Looks like we'll be getting out of here after all!" Ben exclaimed. "You first, Domingo."

The Spaniard hadn't roused but was still breathing.

A few rocks fell from the ceiling close to the wall where the rescue party was working. Then the tip of a pickax poked through and more of the wall crumbled. The sudden breeze of fresh air that streamed in when the pickax was removed reinvigorated all of Ben's senses.

He could smell the sweet, earthy scent of the trees, hear the soft rippling of the river, and taste the remnants of Esther's bread on his lips now that there was hope for more. His head cleared so that he no longer felt dizzy. And the sight of Phillip and Maggie hovering behind the rescuers hauling Domingo out through the new, man-sized opening made his chest ache in a way he never before thought possible.

When the rescuers reached their arms inside the cave again, Ben and Samuel helped transport Willis through the opening. Willis moaned and groaned the whole time, but Ben thought it was in a good way, as all their spirits had been lifted.

Samuel went next, the sling on his arm torn and battered and sprinkled with stones and debris, although thankfully he hadn't suffered any new injuries, just a few bumps and bruises.

When they'd gotten every other man out, Ben limped toward the opening last, and at least a dozen hands grabbed hold of his upper arms as he crawled through and stood up on the other side. Cheers rose into the air, along with laughter, and a flurry of excited chatter as everyone began talking at once.

Then he spotted her. His dear, sweet Maggie. Ignoring the pain in his ankle, he took several quick strides toward her, drew her into his arms, and captured her mouth in a kiss. A hungry, lingering kiss that was warm and sweet, yet filled with the intensity of renewed hope and second chances.

Afterward, as they drew apart, Phillip ran toward him and flung his arms around his middle. "Uncle Ben, I was so scared."

"I was scared too," he admitted. "Scared I'd never see you again. Or Maggie."

Ben lifted his gaze to hers, and she whispered, "God is good."

"He is indeed," Ben said with a nod. He had a lot to be thankful for.

"Glad my men and I could come to your rescue," Hugh Kendrick said with a smirk. "If we hadn't come along when we did, I fear you wouldn't have made it."

Upon hearing Kendrick's voice, Ben turned around, clenched his fist, looked the large, arrogant beast of a man in the eye, and punched him in the face.

"If it weren't for *you*," Ben spat, narrowing his gaze. "We never would have been trapped."

"That's right," Obadiah Brewster agreed. "I saw Hugh bring the dynamite toward the mouth of the cave with my own eyes. He knew those men were in there, and he lit off the explosives on purpose."

"I saw it too," Charles Henshaw declared.

"So did I," George Galloway said, slapping a handcuff onto one of Hugh's wrists. "Hubert Kendrick, I'm placing you under arrest for attempted murder."

Hugh's eyes widened. "What gives you the right —"

"County Deputy." George held up a shiny gold badge for everyone to see. Then he pointed at Quincy and Rufus Vaughn, two of Hugh's men. "Think you can give me a hand hauling this guy over to my new office?"

Ben frowned and looked back at Maggie. "He has a new office?"

She nodded and bit her lip. "My shop. I had to trade it to get the money to pay Hugh so he and his men would help get you out."

Ben's disgust with the man increased tenfold now that he knew the full extent of what Hugh had done. "That money won't do him much good if he's sitting in jail."

"I know." Maggie took Ben's arm and

smiled. "Yet for me, it was worth every cent to see you safe."

Maggie and Ben followed along behind as the other men carried Willis and Domingo back to the camp infirmary on makeshift stretchers. Dr. Harrington examined Domingo first, and after he waved a packet of pungent smelling salts beneath his nose, the Spaniard awoke, although he was still groggy. Willis had broken some bones but would heal in time.

Her mother took fresh bandages and helped bind the men's wounds while Maggie placed a supportive wrap around Ben's ankle. The gash on his cheekbone also required some of Dr. Harrington's medicated salve.

"He will heal fast," her mother assured her. "And will look no less handsome."

Maggie blushed, thinking of Ben's kiss and wondering if they were truly engaged, or if the proposal in the cave had been uttered out of delusion.

Before she had time to dwell on the matter further, Eben Nash stepped into the infirmary clutching his chest. Maggie rushed to him. "Eben, what's wrong? Your heart?"

The tailor nodded as she helped him into

a chair. "Racing just a little fast. Thought I might have the doc take a listen as soon as he's finished with the others."

"Thank you for your help with the rescue," she said softly. "Especially with the risk to your own health."

He dismissed her concern with a wave of his hand. "I'd never want to see harm come to another. I'm not like Hugh, nor was I ever in cahoots with him and his malicious schemes. When he came to me and asked if I'd help break into your shop, I refused, which is why I think he tried to set me up. You have to believe me."

Maggie nodded. "I believe you. Perhaps we can work out a way for our two sewing businesses to work together?"

Eben winced and patted the left side of his chest. "I'm thinking I might head back east to see some family. Enjoy life while I still can."

"Let me know if you change your mind," Maggie offered before stepping aside so Dr. Harrington could attend to him.

She glanced back toward Ben and saw Phillip had drawn closer to him and laid his head on Ben's shoulder. Her breath caught as she took in the sight, and for a moment she couldn't move, reluctant to interrupt.

Then Phillip lifted his head and said,

"Maggie, where will you live? Uncle Ben said you sold your shop."

Having already made peace with it, Maggie laughed. "Once again, it appears I am homeless. Now that the Galloways will be leaving the hotel, I suppose I could ask Esther if I could have my old room back. I can still sew and perhaps sell some of my designs, so I will not be as poor as when I first arrived here in Gold Bar. As for the rest, I'll just trust God to work it out."

"You also have us," Ben reminded her. Standing, and then grinning as he had to hobble on his good foot toward her, he took her hand. "I may not have wealth, but if you keep your promise to marry me, I will do my best to give you a life rich with love."

Maggie's heart soared as she held his gaze, and she was so overcome with emotion that she could hardly speak. " 'Tis all I've ever wanted."

Ben's grin broadened as he leaned down to kiss her. "I love you, Maggie."

"I love you too," she whispered, then glanced over at Phillip, who looked up at her earnestly. "And you."

Phillip had just returned her smile when Samuel shouted, "Ben! There's something I need to show you!" He held out his sling as he made his way toward them. "Gold!

There's a whole heap of tiny gold pieces here trapped in my sling!"

Ben gave him a nod. "Congratulations."

"It means you found gold too, partner. Your share of just this little bit is at least a couple hundred dollars. There's a lot more in that vein we found." Samuel held up a small nugget. "Before we went into that cave, we agreed to split all the profits."

"Is it real?" Phillip asked Ben.

"We'll have to test it to make sure, but, yeah, it looks real." Ben handed the rock to Maggie and gave her an encouraging look. "Now you can build a new sewing shop."

"No," she said, and smiled. "Now *we* can build a horse ranch . . . and a happy life together."

Ben grinned. "As long as we're together, I'll be happy."

"Me too," she agreed.

Phillip wrapped an arm around each of them, his eyes shining. "Me three."

Maggie laughed again, giddy with joy as she thought how blessed she was at this moment and how much she would have missed if she had not come to California. God *did* have a plan for her all along. A plan for a life rich with the fullness of family, friendship, and love.

With her heart overflowing with gratitude,

she sent up a prayer of thanks. Then she walked outside with Ben and Phillip and, joining hands, they took the first step together toward a beautiful future.

ABOUT THE AUTHOR

Darlene Panzera is a multipublished author, speaker, and writing coach of both sweet contemporary and Christian inspirational romance. Her career launched with "The Bet," a novella included in bestselling author Debbie Macomber's *Family Affair,* which led her to publish twelve more titles including *The Cupcake Diaries, Montana Hearts,* and novellas in Barbour's *Underground Railroad Brides, Runaway Brides,* and *Sew in Love* collections. Darlene is also a member of RWA, the Oregon Christian Writers, and the Northwest Christian Writers Association. When not writing, she loves spending time with her husband and three kids, teaching at conferences, and feeding her horse carrots. Learn more about Darlene at her website www.darlenepanzera .com.

■ ■ ■ ■

WOVEN HEARTS

BY JACQUOLYN MCMURRAY

■ ■ ■ ■

To my thoughtful husband
who understands my need for
quiet writing days.

ACKNOWLEDGMENTS

A warm *mahalo* to:
Debby Lee, who invited me to write a novella for this collection.
Darlene Panzera for holding my hand from proposal to novella completion.
Jeri Stockdale for critiquing every chapter.
Frank Eaton for editing my final draft.
Kristin Wolfgang, who has been my writing partner for more years than I can count.
Joanne Jaytanie, who serves as my personal cheerleader.
My gems — Marilyn, Marla, and Libby for their encouragement and helping me celebrate each milestone no matter how small.

Now the God of hope fill you with all joy and peace in believing, that ye may abound in hope, through the power of the Holy Ghost.

Romans 15:13

CHAPTER 1

New York City, 1911

"Fire!" A firm hand dragged Millie Pulnik across the eighth floor of the Triangle Shirtwaist Factory as she shrieked her mother's name and fought to free herself from the grasp of the steward. He shoved her into the overloaded elevator with several other young women, edged in beside her, and turned the key to close the door.

Millie lunged for the opening. The steward grabbed her around the waist and held her as she clawed at the door and pleaded with him to wait for her mother.

The elevator lurched and moved. The smell of smoke and terror filled her nostrils, and the sound of desperate screams from the trapped workers echoed in her ears. Mother. Where was Mother? And Father? Had he escaped from the ninth floor?

Please, God. Let them be safe.

At ground level, she covered her ears and

fled across Greene Street with the others before turning to look back. Flames shot out of windows on the eighth and ninth floors.

And then something else. Millie pushed her palms over her eyes.

Workers leapt from the windows to their deaths.

Millie gathered her siblings by their beloved mother's simple pine coffin and cursed a God that let this happen. How would she keep her family together without Mother's wise counsel? With eyes squeezed shut, she whispered her goodbyes. Barely five years old, twins Paul and Celia clung to her skirt while fourteen-year-old Rose held on to Babi, their maternal grandmother. Millie wished her arms were long enough to encircle all her family members at the same time, but all she could offer were words of comfort.

Her forced smile conflicted with the tumbling of her stomach. Why had God spared her from the same fire that claimed her mother's life and damaged her father's legs? Was her new purpose to assume guardianship of her family?

A nervous glance over her shoulder confirmed her betrothed was nearby. With

Nathan's support, her family wouldn't be destitute.

After they lowered the coffin into the earth, Millie turned her attention to those who had come to honor Mother. She thanked their pastor, who walked not twenty yards to perform the next graveside service for another fire victim. Parishioners offered their condolences and a few pressed coins into her palms. Millie pushed the money deep into her pockets, the weight of it a reminder of her loss.

"Such a tragedy." Nathan's father kissed her cheek.

Nathan patted her arm. "She was a lovely woman, Millie."

"Yes. She was."

"Did you confirm your father will be discharged next Saturday?" Nathan asked.

"Yes."

"Then I will be there to drive him home." He pursed his lips and dropped his arms to his sides. "I have something I want to discuss with him."

Nathan walked away and slid into the driver's seat of his family's new Stanley touring car, the vehicle her father had deemed an unnecessary extravagance. Would Father agree to ride in it? What choice did he have? No one could expect her to push a wheelchair more than two miles over the uneven stones of the sidewalks.

The twins tugged at her skirt. Paul whimpered. "Is Father in the ground with Mother?"

Millie smoothed his unruly hair away from his face. "No, Father is in the hospital, remember? He hurt his legs, but he will come home soon."

"Today?" Paul asked.

"No, not today. In one week. His legs need to feel better before he can come home."

Celia whined she was hungry. Millie gathered the twins in her arms and kissed the tops of their tow-haired heads.

"Rose, please take Paul and Celia home." She reached into her pocket where the coins rattled against one another and retrieved two. "Take the bus. The twins are too tired to walk."

With her siblings on their way home, Millie turned her attention to Babi. She had said little since the day of the fire except that a mother should never have to bury her child. Millie scanned the graveyard. Only a dozen funeral guests still lingered, most of them visiting the other freshly mounded gravesites. Babi knelt at the foot of her daughter's grave, the loose earth heaped on top and dust swirling up with each breath of wind.

Millie knelt by her grandmother and wrapped her in her arms. "Let me take you home, Babi."

"She was such a good daughter." Babi covered her face with her shawl and wept. "Such a good daughter."

"And a good mother," Millie acknowledged. She rose and took Babi's elbow to help her stand.

"I keep asking God why He didn't take me instead."

Millie's muscles tensed. "I could ask the same thing. Somehow, I survived, while Mother —" Her voice betrayed her. "While Mother was not so fortunate."

"I cannot imagine life without her." Babi bit at the edge of her thumb.

Millie wrapped her arms around her grandmother again. "Babi, I need you to stay strong for the children. Can you do that for me? Be strong around them? Especially with Father injured, we need to show them that you and I can take care of them, at least until I marry and we have Nathan's family to assist us."

"I'm an old woman, Millie, and the emptiness I feel is vast, but I will do my best to help you with the children." She ground her teeth together. "You are all I have left."

Millie's heart wrenched in her chest. "That's all I ask."

Abe Skala stood at a distance from the grieving family. The acrid taste of bile collected in the back of his throat every time the fire victims came to mind. Would they still be alive if the Triangle Shirtwaist Factory had been a union shop and adhered to basic safety regulations? But what good was wondering? He couldn't undo the past.

Two years before, he'd failed to convince the Triangle Factory workers to stay on strike until the factory bosses met their demands. After five months on the picket line, they agreed to return to work in exchange for better hours and slightly increased wages with no union representation and no changes in safety regulations.

Failure was tiresome. With these survivors, he vowed he'd be of use to someone. This was his fifth funeral today, all victims from the church both he and the Pulnik family attended. And the Catholic and Jewish deaths far outnumbered those from their congregation. Funerals would go on for several days until all 146 victims were buried.

He cleared his throat, and Miss Pulnik

turned toward him. He froze in place with just one glance from this tawny-haired beauty. He'd been this close to her only one other time and that was in the company of the whole congregation. But he knew her features, had studied them from afar — her serious, golden-brown eyes, her heart-shaped face, and splendidly high cheekbones. He'd kept his distance and would continue to keep his distance because she was betrothed to that fellow named Nathan — a conceited dandy as far as Abe was concerned, if he had any right to be concerned.

"My sincere condolences for your loss. Your family is in my prayers."

"Thank you, Mr. Skala."

"I understand your father is confined in Bellevue Hospital. How does he fare?"

"He broke both legs when the fire escape collapsed, but he managed to survive. He'll be released soon."

Abe nodded. "As you know, I represent the International Ladies Garment Workers Union, and I've been working closely with the families of the fire victims." He thrust his hands in his pockets. Why was he talking so fast?

Miss Pulnik's grandmother shook her head. "Mr. Skala, I hardly think this is the time to talk politics. My daughter has been in the cold ground for less than an hour."

"I meant no disrespect, ma'am." He fumbled with his pocket watch. "I just wanted to inform you that assistance is available for families of the fire victims — rent relief, food baskets, assistance finding jobs. Things of that nature."

Miss Pulnik straightened her shoulders. "We appreciate your offer, but I doubt my family will require assistance."

"Then you're one of the fortunate families. Most don't know where their next meal will come from." He offered her a nickel for a pay phone and a business card with his name and union office telephone number printed on it. "If you need anything, please call."

She smiled. "How very kind of you, but as I explained, my family and I will be fine."

Miss Pulnik's grandmother stretched out her palm. "As optimistic as my granddaughter is, I prefer to have an alternate plan in case the need arises."

Abe gave her the coin and the business card. "Well then, I'll take my leave. Will I see you both in church on Sunday?"

The older woman nodded, while Miss Pulnik avoided eye contact with him and drew in a slow, steady breath.

He walked toward his car. How could Miss Pulnik think her family did not need assistance? He knew they lived in a run-down tenement in Greenwich Village and she and her parents had worked at the Triangle Shirtwaist Factory. If it was necessary for a young woman to work in the factory before the fire, and her father was severely injured and her mother dead, how was it that things could be easier now? Was it pride that kept her from accepting his help? Abe would continue to offer his assistance, in case the need arose, as her grandmother had suggested.

The following morning Millie served bowls of porridge to the twins while Babi and Rose spread lard on toasted bread.

"We have no more flour," Rose announced.

"There's money from our church friends as well as what Mother left in the tea tin," Millie reminded her.

Babi looked up, her expression wary. "That money was meant for you and Rose to buy materials to start your millinery business."

"Yes." Millie removed her apron. "But we can use it now, and once Nathan and I are married, we can replace it quickly enough."

Babi let out a doubtful harrumph.

Millie ignored her grandmother and counted out enough coins to buy food supplies. She gave the money to Rose. "After school, please go to the grocer and buy flour, sugar, and tea. I would go, but I have an appointment with Father's doctor this morning."

Celia jumped up from the table and hugged Millie's knees. "I want to go too."

Bending to lift her youngest sister to her chest, Millie swayed and whispered that everything would be okay. She'd be away for a few hours, and Babi would stay with her and tell her a story.

Babi sat in a chair and opened her arms to Celia. Paul finished his last spoonful and joined his sister on their grandmother's lap. Sadness swam in Babi's gray eyes as she told a story about their mother and how she loved to fashion hats and hoped to one day open a millinery shop with her daughters.

"Me?" Celia asked.

"Yes, darling. You and Rose and Millie. Your mother taught your sisters how to make hats when they were just a bit older than you are now. She was fond of saying, 'One day we will make the finest hats in all of New York.'"

The finest hats, indeed. Millie strode into

the bedroom she shared with Babi, Rose, and Celia and stood before the cheval mirror. What would they do without Mother? The fire had been a senseless event caused by senseless bosses who ignored safety guidelines that would have protected their workers. No family should have to endure this kind of pain ever again.

She slammed her hairbrush against the vanity just as her sister entered the room. Rose took their mother's blue satin hat off the dresser, placed it atop Millie's head, and wrapped her arms around Millie's waist. Millie leaned on Rose for a few brief seconds.

"Mother loved this hat," Rose said. "It becomes you."

"I feel closer to her when I wear it." Millie closed her eyes and inhaled. "It still carries her scent."

"Lavender," Rose whispered, her voice catching.

Millie wiped her tears, squared her shoulders, and pasted on a much-practiced smile. Considering all her new responsibilities, there simply was not time to mourn.

There were no available seats in the enclosed seating on the double-decker bus from Greenwich Village to Bellevue Hospital. Millie forced herself up the metal stairs to the upper level and withstood forty minutes of sputtering rain that gathered on her best linen dress and Mother's satin hat. She steeled herself for the visit with Father. It was no secret he was angry over his injury.

At the hospital, the receptionist directed Millie down a long corridor to Dr. Herman's office. Her barrel-chested father sat in a wheelchair near the doctor's immaculate desk.

"Good morning, Father." Millie leaned to kiss his balding head, then greeted his physician.

"Thank you for coming," Dr. Herman said. "I will make this brief. As you know, your father's legs sustained multiple breaks in the fall."

Millie nodded.

"We have done what we can for now. Over time, we will see how well his bones mend."

Father's eyes narrowed and a flicker of fear darted across his face. "Will I walk again?"

Dr. Herman shifted in his seat. "It is too soon to know."

"When might you know?" Millie pressed.

"Five to six months. In the meantime, your father can convalesce at home. As planned, I will release him on Saturday. He will need a wheelchair. The hospital does not provide them." Dr. Herman scribbled a number on a piece of paper and slid it across the desk to her. "The Red Cross may be of some help."

She took the paper and thanked the doctor.

"Push me back to my room, Mildred. And for heaven's sake, take off that ridiculous piece of satin finery atop your head. This is no time to be puttin' on airs."

"I'm sorry, Father. I wanted to look nice for our meeting."

He scoffed. "I don't see why."

Millie blinked back tears as she pushed his wheelchair. She grasped the hat between her thumb and forefinger, all the while wondering why she'd never been able to please him.

She made her excuses to leave as soon as the nurse delivered her father's lunch tray. The spring air soothed her as she walked to the phone booth just outside the lobby. She dropped a nickel into the slot and dialed the number for the Red Cross. The representative apologized but said they didn't have any available wheelchairs as the need was so great after the fire.

Her father had to have a wheelchair. He wouldn't be able to move about the tenement without it. Perhaps Nathan would help her secure one. She called the import business Nathan's father owned and asked the secretary whether Nathan was available. Confident he'd help her, Millie leaned against the side of the booth and relaxed her weary muscles.

"Hello, Millie."

"Hello, Nathan. Thank you for taking my call."

"What is it? Is this an emergency?"

The last time Millie interrupted him at work, she'd told him about her mother's death and her father's injuries. "No, it's not an emergency. I have a request. Father will need a wheelchair to come home, and the hospital and the Red Cross have none to lend. Do you have any suggestions?"

"Why would you assume I'd know where to acquire a wheelchair? I have more important things to do with my time."

Words scrambled together in her mouth. Why indeed? "I wasn't thinking," she murmured.

"I have work to do. I'll meet you at the hospital on Saturday and bring the car around to drive your father home as we agreed."

"Thank you, Nathan." The click on the other end of the line reverberated through her bones. What had she been thinking to interrupt Nathan at his place of business?

Nonetheless, she still needed to locate a wheelchair.

She could call Mr. Skala. Millie cringed and shook herself. She shouldn't have been so quick to decline his help when they talked at Mother's funeral. He did seem like a nice man. She had liked the sound of his voice when he offered his condolences — a smooth baritone she'd heard above all other voices when the church choir led the congregation in song. And his expression of sincere concern had warmed her.

She'd give Mr. Skala a call and resist being so arrogant with him this time. Millie hoped she was not too late. If he couldn't locate a wheelchair, she didn't know how she'd get her father home.

CHAPTER 2

Abe barely stepped inside the office of the International Ladies Garment Workers Union before Sam Jensen, his best friend and colleague, raised the telephone handset in the air and announced, "It's a woman. A Miss Pulnik."

Sam waggled his eyebrows and passed the phone to him.

Abe swallowed hard before he found his voice. "Hello."

At the sound of Miss Pulnik's voice, the edges of his lips curled into a grin. Despite turning his back to Sam, he could feel his friend's questioning gape throughout the short phone call.

As he hung up he wished the conversation had been longer, but her purpose for the call was to ask for assistance in locating and delivering a wheelchair to Bellevue Hospital. She needed it by Saturday. He had no idea where to find such a thing, but he intended to make good on the promise he'd just given her.

Sam slapped him on the back. "Who's the lady? You look like a miner who just struck gold."

"Miss Pulnik needs a wheelchair for her father, who was injured in the fire."

"How about the Red Cross?"

"She tried. None available."

Sam checked his pocket watch. "C'mon. I know a place that might have one. It's on the way to the opera house. We're due to meet with the Committee on Safety in about an hour." Sam produced a comb from his pants pocket and raked his long brown bangs off his brow, then clicked his tongue. "I'll drive. I'm not sure you can see straight."

Abe's mouth went dry. "She's engaged."

Sam nodded. "Well then. That's another story, isn't it?"

On Saturday, Millie entered the formidable Bellevue Hospital. Holding a handkerchief to her nose to ward off the pungent smell of disinfectant, she signed her name on the visitors' log at the front desk before she chose a seat on a faded couch beneath a smudged bay window. She'd just sat down

197

to wait for Mr. Skala when he entered the lobby.

"Good morning, Miss Pulnik. I hope this will do." He removed his hat and tilted his head toward the steel-spoked conveyance he was pushing.

She nodded. "I'm grateful. Thank you."

"You are most welcome. Have you arranged transport to drive your father home?"

"Yes. My fiancé is coming with a car."

"Good. Well, let me know if your family needs anything else."

She stood and looked into his eyes. "We'll be fine once I get Father back home."

"I hope so." Concern creased his brow.

Millie dipped her chin and chastised herself for admiring his gleaming turquoise eyes. She would soon be married.

"All my best to you and your family."

Her gaze followed Mr. Skala while he signed in at the visitors' desk then walked toward the burn unit. No doubt he aimed to visit survivors of the fire.

Millie gripped the wheelchair and pushed it across the lobby. The poorly lit corridor leading to the postoperative ward was a cacophony of misery — gurneys in need of oiling screeched in protest and men cried out in pain. Even the priests' mumbling of prayers took on the sound of hopelessness, but nothing could dampen her spirits today. Nathan was meeting her here to drive her father home. And he had something to discuss with Father. Millie could imagine only one topic of discussion. Nathan intended to marry her right away. With the support of Nathan's family, the financial burden for her own family wouldn't rest solely on her shoulders. Then perhaps she'd be able to sleep at night instead of worrying until the wee hours of morning.

Millie heard Father's gruff voice from behind the privacy curtain at the far end of the long room. "Go away," he shouted. "My daughter will bathe me."

Millie's body tensed and her feet refused to move. Bathe Father?

The nurse's aide attempted to soothe him. "Let me finish your feet and back, Mr. Pulnik. Your daughter will have plenty of work ahead of her after she takes you home."

What other nursing duties are in store for me? Millie shuddered, then remembered Rose's advice to treat their father with compassion.

She slipped behind the curtain. "Good morning, Father."

"Give the cloth to Mildred." He swatted

at the determined aide. "She has to learn, doesn't she?"

The aide clicked her tongue then passed Millie the cloth. "You just need to scrub his feet and back, miss. He can handle the rest."

Millie closed her eyes and sent up a silent prayer. She trembled as she rolled up the sleeves of her shirtwaist, dipped the cloth into the basin of tepid water, and added a few drops of liquid soap from the dispenser. Gaze averted, she leaned over her father and scrubbed one of his feet.

Suddenly her father let out a loud grunt. "You and that hat." He slapped it off her head. "I don't know why you insist on wearing that thing."

Startled, she wiped her hands on her skirt and knelt to retrieve her beloved mother's hat from the floor.

"Leave it," her father commanded. "Finish my bath before the water cools."

Head down and battling tears, she scrubbed his other foot. Through the threadbare fabric of the washcloth, Millie felt the edges of the gypsum plaster cast — a physical reminder of the broken bones Father sustained after the dilapidated fire escape at the Triangle Shirtwaist Factory collapsed.

Millie remembered her vow for compassion and softened her tone. "Shall I wash your back now?"

"When we get home. Take me out of here."

Father's voice twisted up her nerves. Where was Nathan?

"Now, Mildred." He slammed his fists on the bedcovers. "I said take me home. I want to see my son."

She flinched. Poor Celia. For reasons Millie didn't understand, Father favored Paul and paid little attention to Celia except to scold her. "Nathan is coming with the car momentarily."

"Nathan? A good man, your fiancé. Better than you deserve."

Perhaps. Nathan was a good Christian man and maybe she didn't deserve him, but he'd agreed to the marriage pact their mothers made eleven years ago on the voyage to New York. And even if Millie did not love him, she hoped love would come with time.

"Good morning, Mr. Pulnik," Nathan called from the edge of the privacy drape. "Millie."

Thank the Lord, Nathan was here to help her.

He shook Father's hand. "How are you, Mr. Pulnik?"

"Better now that I'm going home."

Nathan frowned. "Millie, why is your hat

on the floor?"

"It fell off. I was just retrieving it when you arrived." Her face flushed as she picked it up and settled it back on her head.

The nurse's aide appeared. "Did you bring clothes?"

Millie reached into her satchel and produced a folded bundle of clothes, a pair of black leather boots, and a shabby leather belt.

"He won't be needin' the shoes," the nurse's aide barked. "You two, come closer so I can show you the easiest way to dress him."

Nathan waved his arms in the air. "I don't need a lesson, miss. I won't be the one dressing him."

"I don't blame you, son," Father said. "Go on to the hallway. This is a job for the women." With a whisk of his fingers, he sent Nathan away.

Dressing her father was akin to wrangling a wee child into a too-small suit of clothes. Maybe after she and Nathan married, he'd offer the resources to hire a caregiver. After all, his family had been one of the few Czech families who had made their fortune in the new country.

"Okay, you old fool," the nurse's aide declared, "the doctor will come shortly to sign your release papers." She gestured for Millie to follow her.

In the hallway, the aide motioned for Nathan to join them. "He's full of the devil, and I don't envy you. Until his bones heal, he will need assistance with bathing, dressing, and toileting." She jammed her finger into Nathan's chest. "Are you the son-in-law?"

Nathan grimaced. "No."

Millie's cheeks burned.

"Well, this young woman will need assistance to lift him," the nurse's aide continued. "Is there someone else at home who can assist?"

Nathan answered, "Her grandmother and sister."

Millie clutched her stomach. Would the woman stop with her incessant questions?

Finally, the aide skittered down the hallway and left Millie alone with Nathan.

Millie glanced up at his face. "Thank you for coming."

"I said I would come to drive your father, and here I am." He smiled weakly but looked away.

"Here you are," Millie repeated. "You mentioned you wanted to speak to Father today."

She reached for his elbow, but he backed

away from her, just out of reach.

"Nathan? What is happening? Why won't you look at me?"

"We should talk. You and I."

There. He's simply nervous. Certain Nathan had reached the same conclusion that marrying sooner was the best solution for her situation, she offered, "Don't worry, Nathan. Father will agree we should marry long before we planned."

The muscles in his neck tightened, and he turned his head away. "You misunderstand."

She touched her throat. "Why else would you want to speak to Father?"

"To explain why I cannot marry you," he said.

She braced herself against the wall. Millie had seen Nathan's mouth move, but surely, she'd heard the words wrong. "But what of our mothers' agreement?"

"My father considers that agreement buried with our mothers."

Millie turned away and struggled for composure. "How could you desert me, given my circumstances?"

Nathan scoffed. "Because my feelings for you do not extend past friendship, and I wish to marry another."

"Please help us, Nathan," she begged. "I can't do this alone. I thought you'd appreciate the position I find myself in. What will we tell Father?"

"Under the circumstances, you can tell your father whatever you like. Goodbye, Millie."

Without a flicker of either compassion or regret, he turned his back on her, strode down the corridor, and left her alone.

Bile rose in the back of her throat as tears inundated her cheeks.

Coward. And he calls himself a Christian? How stupid of me to count on his allegiance. What do I do now? I can't go to work in another factory. Does God have no mercy for me?

She'd foolishly counted on Nathan supporting her family once they married and even imagined him financing the start-up costs for her millinery business. Her family wouldn't manage for long without the proper resources, and she refused to see them split apart like so many of the Triangle Shirtwaist Factory families. She vowed to keep the twins from the orphanage and Rose from the hazardous factories.

Unsure whether she could steady herself enough to thread a needle, Millie knew she had to earn money by working in the only profession for which she had experience.

First thing Monday morning, she needed to secure another garment factory job.

Holding his brown felt bowler hat against the misty gusts of wind, Abe made his way to the bread truck he'd borrowed to transport the wheelchair to the hospital. If he hurried, he could return the truck and still make it back to the union hall in time for the noon meeting.

He drove up a steep incline toward Greenwich Village. Just ahead on the cobblestone sidewalk, a woman strained to push a large man in a wheelchair. Was that the Pulniks? Hadn't Millie told him her fiancé was bringing a car to drive them home?

Abe stopped the truck adjacent to her and jumped out. "Miss Pulnik?"

She stopped pushing and strained against the weight of the wheelchair that appeared destined to roll back down the hill.

"Good afternoon, Mr. Pulnik." Abe offered a handshake. "May I offer you transport home?"

Mr. Pulnik scowled at him. "Aren't you the rabble-rouser from the union?"

"Well, I suppose you could call me that. I do work for the union." He offered his hand again. "I'm Abraham Skala."

Mr. Pulnik eyed him suspiciously and

made no effort to accept his greeting. "How do you know my daughter?"

"We met at church, sir."

Abe held the conveyance and addressed Miss Pulnik. "I thought you had transport arranged?"

"She had," Mr. Pulnik barked, "but it seems Mildred has managed to chase away her fiancé."

Abe set the brakes on the wheelchair. "Let me drive you."

She nodded, her eyes filled with so much sorrow, surely his heart would break.

Her father turned his head and stared at them. "Stop standin' around and get me home."

All through the ordeal of lifting and settling her father in the truck, Miss Pulnik remained silent. Would she ever speak again? He'd talked her through every move — how to stand on one side and make a cradle under her father's backside to lift him and how to bend at the knees to protect her own back. When Abe opened the rear door of the bread truck and offered to help her step up, his concern for her deepened. She seemed disoriented, and when she finally sat on an upturned wooden crate, she wrapped her arms around her middle and hung her head.

Abe lifted the cumbersome chair into the truck then settled into the driver's seat. "Where do you live?"

"Blanch Tenements on 56th Street. Fourth floor," Mr. Pulnik growled. "I hope you have a strong back."

"Strong enough," Abe answered.

"Mildred's fiancé, or should I say her *former* fiancé, is a strong young man. Shoulders like an ox."

Abe clenched his jaw. *But he's not here to help, is he?*

Mr. Pulnik turned his head toward the cargo area and roared, "What did you do to make Nathan break off your engagement?"

Silence.

He continued his tirade. "Do you think you can find someone better? Your mother chose him for you. A fine young man — showy, but from good, solid stock."

What would Mr. Pulnik think of *him* if he found out his father was a con man? But that was unlikely, since he had taken his mother's maiden name years ago.

"Well?" Mr. Pulnik bellowed at her. When she offered no response, he turned his attention to Abe. "Did you have something to do with this? Have you compromised my daughter's engagement?"

"No, sir. I've assisted only when your

daughter asked it of me."

Mr. Pulnik stared out the front window, jaw and fists clenched.

Abe held his tongue. He wanted to lash out at the old man, tell him he should be grateful he lived through the fire and had his children to go home to. That the union was not the enemy. But he didn't. He couldn't. Instead, he prayed God's grace would shine on the old man and Miss Pulnik would find peace.

Outside the tenement building, Abe unloaded the wheelchair and helped Miss Pulnik step down. He tried to catch her eye, but she looked away and maintained her silence.

Again, in the gentlest voice possible, he instructed her what to do. He'd take the wheelchair to the fourth floor, and then they'd carry her father up the stairs together.

Her whole body trembled as she poked the key into the lock. In contrast to the stale onion odor of the stairwell, the tenement smelled of vanilla cake. Miss Pulnik's grandmother acknowledged him and her granddaughter then welcomed her injured son-in-law home. Abe recognized the young woman sewing at the kitchen table. Rose, wasn't it? She set her sewing down and greeted her father while casting a questioning glance toward her sister. Relieved no one asked questions about why he was there, Abe stood off to one side.

The two small children gawked at their father's legs.

"Come here, Son." Mr. Pulnik lifted the boy to his lap and pushed one rubber wheel. The chair spun in a circle.

"My turn, my turn," called the little girl.

"Celia, hush," her grandmother scolded.

"Millie's engagement is off," Mr. Pulnik announced. "Maybe she'll tell *you* why."

"Oh Millie." Rose crossed the small room to take her sister in her arms. "I'm so sorry."

Miss Pulnik bit her fingernail, and Abe sent up another prayer.

"Come." Rose wrapped her arm around her sister's waist and led her toward a door. "You should freshen yourself."

Miss Pulnik's grandmother glanced at him. "We have nothing to give you for your trouble."

"I'm glad to assist your family." Abe dug in his pockets and produced four peppermint candies. "For the little ones."

As soon as Miss Pulnik returned to the room, Abe asked to speak to her in the hallway. "I have a proposition for you."

She folded her arms across her chest and lowered her chin.

Abe realized his blunder. "I've said it wrong. Allow me to begin again."

She nodded.

"You need a job. I know of a seamstress position in a men's sack suit factory that pays union scale. It's across town, but on the bus route."

"A garment factory?" She'd found her voice but seemed to have precious little control over it.

"If you like, I could drive you there today, and you can apply for the position. The truth is Mr. Berg claims to run a union shop, but we suspect otherwise. So far, we've been unsuccessful in identifying anyone who will bear witness to the unsafe conditions. If you're on the inside, you could gather information for us, perhaps persuade others to testify against Mr. Berg if conditions are as bad as we think."

She lifted her chin and tilted her head. "Act as a snitch?"

"I'd rather think of it as working to improve conditions for factory workers to ensure people never again lose their lives because safety is ignored. We can keep your involvement quiet, especially since your father is so opposed to the union."

After several moments, she took a deep breath. "I *do* need a job. Thank you, Mr. Skala."

"Abe," he said, hoping to ease the tension.

She finally met his gaze. "Abe."

CHAPTER 3

Millie boarded the bus that would take her within blocks of her new job at Berg's Garment Emporium and passed the driver the ten-cent fare. Relieved to be out of the rain, she settled on a wooden bench close to the front and confirmed that one more coin rested deep in her skirt pocket for the fare home.

She closed her eyes and pinched the bridge of her nose. *I should've listened to Babi's advice to save some coins from Mother's tin, but I counted on Nathan's support and I trusted he'd honor our agreement to marry.*

The bus screeched to a halt and spewed noxious fumes into the air, then lurched forward three more times before Millie reached her destination. Each start and stop jolted her insides and strengthened her opinion that if God genuinely cared about her, He would have made sure Nathan kept his promise.

Millie jerked her head in disgust, then pinned a few loose strands of hair back into her chignon. Despite the quiver in her stomach every time she imagined entering a garment factory, she needed this job for the money it would provide. More importantly, on behalf of Mother and all the other fire victims, she wanted to do her part to ensure safe working conditions.

She patted the piece of paper and nub of a pencil in her pocket. She wouldn't draw attention to herself but would keep her eyes and ears attuned to the safety irregularities and record them on her way home.

Rain pelted Millie's face as she stepped off the bus and scurried the four blocks to the garment factory. She tugged her rain-soaked shawl around her middle and glanced up at the ten-story wooden building.

Millie gaped at the metal fire escape hanging on the front of the building. Was it secure, or would it break in an emergency like the one that injured her father?

Her body quaked as she followed a group of women through the massive metal door. On Saturday, her new boss, Mr. Berg, had instructed her to report directly to him upon her arrival at the factory. Millie smoothed the front of her skirt then knocked on his office door.

A gruff voice beckoned her to enter.

"I'm reporting to work, sir."

He looked up from the mass of papers scattered across his desk, his bushy eyebrows furrowed as he exhaled foul-smelling smoke from his cigar. "Which girl are you?"

"Mildred Pulnik, sir."

Mr. Berg grunted as he pushed his chair away from his desk, the buttons of his dark satin vest straining across his stout belly, then swaggered through the doorway. "Come."

Millie followed the pompous little man, who led her to an elevator where a group of women fell silent in his presence. Millie chewed her bottom lip. The elevator dial went all the way to floor ten. How could she work on an upper level where escape from fire was slim?

She took a step backward and covered her mouth. One of the women nudged her into the elevator and offered a thin smile. Millie's chest heaved. The last time someone pushed her into an elevator was the day of the fire. She couldn't breathe then, and she couldn't breathe now.

On the third floor, the elevator shuddered to a stop.

"Get to work, straightaway," Mr. Berg barked.

The women bumped into her as they fled the elevator and spread across the crowded sewing room.

Mr. Berg caught Millie's eye then tipped his head toward the middle of the room. Was she assigned to this department? Her gaze darted wildly about until she located the door to the fire escape. Later, she'd check to see if the door was locked as it had been at the shirtwaist factory.

Millie followed her boss past rows and rows of tables where immigrant women like herself sat in front of electric sewing machines, bare lightbulbs strung above them, and great piles of black and gray linen by their sides.

He pointed to an empty stool — nothing more than a metal disk on rollers. "Sit here."

Millie sat on the cold, unyielding seat.

"You," he commanded the girl at the next sewing machine, "show her."

"Yes, sir," the girl answered.

He walked away, but the lingering smell of cigar smoke settled in Millie's throat as if it were a cautionary tale.

The girl's greasy hair fell in her face, and her shapeless muslin dress revealed the developing figure of a girl around Rose's

216

age. Without a word, the girl demonstrated how to sew the trouser pieces together and where to stack the completed product.

Millie thanked the girl and introduced herself.

"Yuri," the girl whispered before turning her attention back to her work.

Millie laced gray thread through the industrial sewing machine and followed Yuri's directions to produce men's dress trousers. She kept her head down and focused on the task. She couldn't afford to make mistakes; mistakes meant less take-home pay for her family and a greater chance of dismissal. If she was to collect information for Abe, she needed to keep this job.

She had already noted Mr. Berg seemed oblivious to the fire hazard of flicking his cigar ashes wherever he pleased, despite the mounds of flammable fabric on the sewing tables and copious scraps on the floor.

At midday, the blare of a horn announced the one sanctioned break. Millie followed the other workers to the benches that lined the exterior wall and sat next to Yuri. Reaching into her pocket, she pulled out the handkerchief wrapped around her meager meal — one piece of bread with a minuscule layer of lard — and laid it on her lap.

Before she took her first bite, Millie noticed many of the girls had nothing. She turned to Yuri. "Do you have food?"

Yuri shook her head. Without another word, Millie tore her bread in half and offered the girl a piece. Yuri took the bread and shoved it into her mouth, then stared at her ragged boots while she chewed.

Millie listened to the grumbling of the workers closest to her. Several whispered complaints about the lack of breaks, the locked doors that made them feel like prisoners, the expected daily quotas, and the lack of ventilation that made the stale air difficult to breathe.

One of the women reminded the others they were fortunate to have jobs at all.

A man who worked at the cutting tables leaned toward Millie. "This boss may not be the best, but he's a far cry better than my last boss." When others nodded their agreement, the man continued, "I'll never vote to strike again."

That was exactly why workers needed to have people like Abe making sure bosses followed their contracts. Did they not understand that their united voices against unsafe conditions provided the only protection they had? If people at this factory wouldn't stand up for their rights, then

Millie resolved to do it on their behalf.

A woman across from her declared her cousin worked as a snitch for the union and was sent to a garment factory to check on safety issues. Within days, he mysteriously disappeared. No one, not even his own mother, had seen or heard from him in several weeks.

Gooseflesh rose the length of Millie's arms. What did the woman mean, *disappeared*? Had the snitch been murdered?

Mr. Berg stepped off the elevator and shouted, "Back to your stations."

The workers scrambled. Millie inserted herself into the throng and headed toward the fire escape door. She had to know if it was locked.

A few workers still provided concealment. She grasped the handle.

It did not turn.

Millie stared at the door, stomach churning, feet anchored to the floor, then glanced over her shoulder. Mr. Berg stood not three feet away. Where had the others gone? His scrutiny rattled her nerves. As he approached, she fabricated an excuse.

"Sorry, sir," Millie said. She lowered her chin. "I know the break is over, but I felt a tad faint and wanted a bit of fresh air."

"If you're not fit for work —"

"I'm recovered now, thank you, and will return to my station."

Her anger mounted with each hurried step back to her sewing machine. Mr. Berg was no better than the Triangle Factory bosses. How dare he lock the fire escape door! Surely he was aware that the district attorney's office sought indictments against the Triangle Factory bosses because they had kept the doors locked. Was he so arrogant he thought himself above the law?

Millie pursed her lips and resumed sewing, but after sewing crooked seams and removing the thread to start again, she questioned whether she'd complete any trousers that afternoon.

Yuri had her own difficulties. She wept when the thread broke on her machine for the third time. Millie reached out and patted her shoulder. Like so many others in the factory, Yuri was too young to be working.

Halfway through the afternoon, the nauseating smell of cigar smoke caught Millie's attention. Mr. Berg stood over the meager pile of completed trousers, rapped his burly knuckles against the tabletop, then took his gold watch from his vest pocket.

"You and you." He pointed at her and Yuri then tipped his head toward the completion pile. "If you can't keep up, I'll replace the both of you."

Millie's nostrils flared. How dare he threaten them! She couldn't wait until his employees testified against him for violating safety regulations.

Yuri's whimpering intensified. This was precisely the reason Millie did not want Rose in the factories. Bosses like Berg thought they were above the law and treated everyone beneath them with contempt. Millie winced. She wouldn't subject Rose to this kind of verbal degradation.

She patted Yuri's forearm. The girl lifted her chin long enough to nod.

Millie fumbled with the coarse linen, too upset to concentrate on her work. She had done exactly the opposite of what she set out to do. She didn't intend to bring attention to herself, yet she'd already had two disagreeable interactions with Mr. Berg on her first day at work. Millie had no doubt that if Mr. Berg suspected her of snitching, he'd do more than fire her.

He'd make sure she was never seen again.

Abe parked his car near the factory entrance as workers poured from the building. He strained his neck to identify Millie in the mass of people but didn't see her.

Had she changed her mind and not reported to work? He pulled his jacket lapel tighter around his neck. Should he go to her tenement? He didn't want to appear forward, but he hoped to spend some time with her and confess his feelings.

The *wumpth* of the factory door drew him from his reverie. His pulse quickened. Millie stood on the sidewalk arm in arm with a young girl. Millie removed her shawl and wrapped it around the girl's shoulders, then crossed her arms in front of her chest and bounded up the cobblestone sidewalk.

She has little and yet she gives away her shawl.

"Millie, I came to drive you home," he called from the car.

She glanced around. "I can take the bus. Thank you."

"You can, but I'm on my way to your building to deliver food. I'd like to hear about your day."

She jerked her head one way, then the other, and jumped into the car. She covered her face and lowered her body in the seat. "Drive, please."

Her voice was riddled with trepidation.

Abe pulled from the curb and drove in the direction of Millie's tenement. "Difficult day?"

"Yes."

"Do you want to tell me?"

"I want to ask you a question, and I need you to tell me the truth."

Does she think I don't tell her the truth?

"I heard a tale during break about someone's cousin at another factory who worked for the union. When they identified him as a union snitch, he disappeared. No one has seen him. Do you have knowledge of that?"

"Yes, but there's more to the tale. The snitch, as you call him, is safe. The union relocated him and his wife."

She inhaled and exhaled slowly. "I'm worried about my own family if I'm discovered."

Oh Lord, am I no better than my father? Have I conned Millie into collecting information for the union as my own avenue for recognition?

"I don't believe you're in danger, Millie, but there are risks. I would never forgive myself if something happened to you. Allow me to find you a position somewhere else."

"No. I want to stay. If you say I'm not in danger, then I believe you."

"Are you certain?"

"I am, but I've already received a scolding from Mr. Berg, and he saw me near the fire escape door, which is locked, just like at the shirtwaist factory."

"Locked? We expected as much."

"He caught me checking the latch."

"What did you do?"

"I made an excuse about feeling faint and needing fresh air. Later, he admonished me because I didn't sew enough trousers." She lamented, "I've sewn on a machine since I was twelve years old, yet today, it was as if I had no knowledge of how to do it."

Abe cleared his throat. "You don't have to work there."

She hesitated for a few seconds. "Yes, I do. What if there's no one else willing to report unsafe conditions? If I can help stop Mr. Berg from causing harm, then I'll stay at his factory and give him reason to form a higher opinion of me." A slight grin formed. "He won't suspect a model worker to snitch on him."

"I admire your resolve, Millie."

"I believe in our cause."

He liked the sound of "*our* cause" rolling off Millie's lips. "Nevertheless, it was wrong of me to meet you near the factory. From now on, we'll meet away from the peering eyes of your boss."

"Agreed."

He gripped the steering wheel. They were mere blocks from her home. If he intended to tell Millie about his affection for her, he needed to say it soon.

"Millie?"

"Yes?"

"I have a confession." He couldn't look at her. "I used the food delivery as an excuse to spend time with you."

There was so much more he wanted to say, like how he admired her determination to care for her family, her commitment to the labor union's goals, and her display of Christian kindness when she gave her shawl to the young woman, but words failed him.

As pink rose on Millie's cheeks, an unfamiliar warmth spread through Abe's body.

In the last few minutes of the drive, silence lingered between them. When Abe admitted he wanted to spend time with her, the day's strife melted away and left only pleasant thoughts running through her head.

Abe was such a good man. Why didn't Father recognize, as she did, how kind Abe was, how dedicated he was to improving conditions for factory workers? If he'd give Abe a chance, she was certain Father would look at him in a different light.

She grasped the coin in her pocket. "Abe?"

"Yes?"

"Would you kindly stop at the tobacconist's? I'd like to buy Father some pipe tobacco."

"Of course."

Even though the union provided food for her family, Millie worried that if Abe delivered the food, her father would treat him as disrespectfully as he had on Saturday. Father had not enjoyed his pipe since before the fire, and it was something that relaxed him. If Father relaxed, he might realize he had misjudged Abe.

Abe parked the car in front of the tobacconist's. When Millie reached for the door handle, Abe called out, "Wait."

He sprang from the car, hurried to the passenger side, opened the door, and offered his hand.

Millie glowed. Never had a man showered her with such attention. She savored the strength of Abe's grasp and held on longer than decorum permitted.

His grin made her cheeks burn anew.

When they got to her building, Millie followed Abe up the stairs to her family's tenement, the familiar odor of onions and baking-powder biscuits blending with the fragrant tobacco she had tucked in her skirt pocket. She imagined Father's delight at her gift and pictured him smiling at her as the sweet aroma of tobacco filled the room.

How long had it been since he'd smiled at her?

She unlocked the entrance door, and Abe motioned her over the threshold ahead of him. Even in the hazy light from one kerosene lantern, Babi's face showed her gratitude as she accepted the box of food.

Millie kissed Babi's cheek and opened her arms to Celia. Her little sister jumped into her arms and buried her face in Millie's hair.

"I want Mother," Celia whined. "I want her home."

Millie rocked the child in her arms and explained for the hundredth time that Mother was in heaven and watched over them.

Father looked up from the history book he was reading to Paul. "Stop your sniveling, child," he demanded. "Go to your bed."

Millie shushed her. "But she hasn't eaten, Father. Perhaps when —"

"Don't argue with me, Mildred."

Celia clutched Millie's neck and Millie rubbed her back. "I'll help her into her nightclothes."

"Stay here. You shouldn't fuss over her all the time." Suddenly, Father pointed at Abe. "What are you doing here?"

"Look, Henryk, Mr. Skala brought us a box of food." Babi tipped the box to show him the contents.

Father ignored Babi and kept a sharp eye on Abe. "Why are you consorting with my daughter? She doesn't need your outrageous union ideas. Remember the strike of 1909? Lot of good that did us." He slapped his legs. "Weeks without pay. Used up all our savings. We never recovered. And for what?"

Abe clutched his hat between his fingers. "I'm here to assist your family, sir, the same as the other Triangle Factory families."

"If you're intent on helping our family, then find a factory job for this one." Father pointed at Rose.

"No!" Millie shrieked. "Mother promised Rose she'd finish school. I'll not allow her to work in a filthy factory."

"*You* won't allow?" Father erupted. "Since when do you make the decisions in this family?"

Millie bit her lower lip. *Since I became the breadwinner, that's when.*

"Henryk, please. We have a guest," Babi urged.

"Just because Millie drags a young man in here does not make him a guest in my home."

Tears gathered in the corners of Millie's eyes as Abe retreated into the hallway with Babi at his heels, calling out an apology.

Millie wouldn't blame Abe if he never spoke to her again. Given all he'd done for their family, how dare Father treat him so rudely!

"Well, Mildred?" Father yelled. "I asked when you became so high and mighty that you assumed the position of head of this household?"

Her chin trembled as she struggled to make her voice audible. "I'm trying to honor Mother's plan for Rose."

"Your mother's plan? Things have changed, haven't they? I'll not tolerate your insolence."

"Father is right," Rose countered. "I should help earn money."

Millie spun around to face her sister. "What about school? Your education?"

"You were in the factory when you were younger than I am now. Do you think I'm not capable?" Rose challenged. "I know how to sew a seam, same as you."

"I know you can, Rose. If you realized the horrid conditions, you'd understand I'm trying to protect you."

"She thinks she's better than you, Rosie," Father bellowed. "Thinks she's better than all of us put together."

Millie fled to the bedroom and curled up next to Celia. She held the crying child while tears seared her own face.

She fingered the pouch of tobacco in her pocket. Father's stubborn attitude toward Abe had not been quelled.

If Father was in the ground instead of Mother, we'd all be happier.

Millie clamped her fist over her mouth. When had she become so wicked even to think such a thing? Evil thoughts were just as sinful as evil deeds.

She was no better than her father.

CHAPTER 4

The next morning Abe stared out his window in Mrs. Dunn's boardinghouse and decided he'd had no other choice last evening than to leave the Pulnik household before he bid Millie good night. Was her father always so ill-tempered?

He must see Millie again soon, for both personal and business reasons. Last night, when her grandmother followed him into the hallway and agreed their church would be the best place to meet with Millie, she reminded him that Millie had not stepped into the church since the funeral. Nevertheless, she promised to do her best to convince Millie to meet him.

A soft knock announced Mrs. Dunn's daily delivery of a kettle of hot water for washing. Abe pulled on the same gray dress pants he had worn the day before and opened the door.

He bid his landlady good morning. Bless

Mrs. Dunn. If she had not offered Mother a housekeeping job and a place to stay after she lost her job at Stark's Bakery, he wouldn't have completed high school.

Abe poured hot water into his china shaving mug, a gift from his mother, and wondered whether she would've liked Millie as much as he did. If she had only lived long enough to meet her.

He lathered his face, scraped the safety razor upward, and the scent of sandalwood shaving soap filled his nostrils. He wiped the remaining lather from his face and neck with a towel then dressed in a white cotton shirt. He retrieved the removable collar from the makeshift clothesline and buttoned it in place.

The salty, oily aroma of bacon frying pleased his senses. Like most men his age, he'd never learned his way around the kitchen and was grateful for the food Mrs. Dunn prepared for him and the other boarders. He could afford a larger place, but he was content here, and the difference in housing fees allowed him to tuck away money for emergencies. Ever since he and Mother had been penniless, he vowed always to have reserve cash stashed away.

Abe pulled out his pocket watch. He was due at the union hall in less than an hour.

Today he'd meet the last family on his list of those affected by the fire. To date, he and Sam had been able to contact and offer support to over fifty families. It gave him such joy to help people in need. He sighed. If only he could find a way to demonstrate to Millie's father how supportive he could be.

Before he left his room, he studied the sepia wedding photo of his mother and considered the missing portion he'd torn away. His jaw tightened. How could he love one and resent the other?

Mother would still be alive if his father hadn't deserted them and sent her spiraling into a chasm of despair.

Thirty minutes later, Abe went to visit Mr. and Mrs. Addario, a couple who had lost two daughters to the inferno at the Triangle Factory. He straightened his collar, buttoned the jacket of his sack suit, and prepared to assess the needs of the family. He'd offer his assistance and assure the Addarios that he and the union were committed to helping them.

Abe balanced a box of food in one arm while he rapped on the door. The boney man who answered towered over him. "Mr. Addario?"

The man nodded.

"I'm Abraham Skala. On behalf of the International Ladies Garment Workers Union, I'm here to offer aid after the untimely deaths of your daughters."

Mr. Addario opened the door wider. Abe stepped into the one-room living quarters and assessed the surroundings. The crowded quarters held one table, four chairs, and two cots covered in threadbare sheets with neatly folded, faded quilts atop them. Two sleeves of crackers and a tin of sardines rested on the otherwise bare shelves.

"Who'd you say you represent?" Mr. Addario tugged at his scraggly gray beard then rubbed his bloodshot eyes. "Any identification?"

The birdlike woman perched on the edge of one of the chairs coughed a dry, shallow cough then took a ragged breath. "It's fine, Ezra. He's from the union."

Mrs. Addario stood, and Abe offered her the provisions, which she set on the table. Tears welled in her eyes. "God bless you."

"I wonder whether I might ask a few questions to better understand your needs?" Abe removed his hat. A lone photo of two young women adorned the bureau. Abe touched the broken glass of the picture frame.

"They were late born," Mrs. Addario said. "We just kept praying for children, and when God answered our prayers, we got two beautiful girls at the same birthing." She coughed again, deeper than before. "And when He took them, He took them at the same time."

She swayed a bit, and her husband rushed to hold her waist and help her to sit. He sat at her side and kept his arm wrapped around her middle.

"We never should've let them go to the factory," Mr. Addario lamented. "We're hard workers, Mr. Skala. Come from a long line of working folks, but the missus and I both got sick after we lost our life's savings in a confidence game."

Bile rose in the back of Abe's throat.

Mr. Addario wiped his eyes with the backs of his pockmarked hands. "Our girls insisted. Barely thirteen. Said they wanted to do it for us."

"You raised good daughters."

"The factory work was meant to be temporary until the missus and I got back on our feet. We wanted to give our girls a better education than we'd had. The con claimed we'd double our money." Mr. Addario rubbed his temples. "We lost everything, all because I trusted him. I'll never forgive myself."

Mrs. Addario patted her husband's shoulder.

Abe's gut roiled. Was it his father who had conned this family out of their money? He stared at the bureau.

"They told us the girls jumped together from the eighth-floor window." Mrs. Addario's voice cracked. "The exit door was locked."

Abe nodded. "That's true, but even after the foreman unlocked the door, the fire escape didn't reach ground level and collapsed under the weight of the workers trying to flee." He surveyed the room. "How can the union best support your needs? We can send food and provide a small fund to pay your rent until you're well again."

"Bless you, Mr. . . . What did you say your name is?" Mrs. Addario asked.

"Abraham Skala."

"Skala. I've heard the name before. Where do I know that name from?" She tapped her fingers on her forehead, then a look of recognition came over her face. "I knew a woman named Lidia Skala. She worked with me at Stark's Bakery. A nervous type. Do you know her?"

Is she asking because she can connect Mother to my father, or is she simply making conversation? Shall I admit to my parentage?

I'm proud to be Lidia's son.

"Lidia was my mother."

Mr. Addario looked him in the eye, contempt sweeping across his brow. "Word round the neighborhood is your mother was married to the con. That she changed her name after he went to prison."

Prison? Mother told me he was dead.

Mr. Addario stood over Abe, his words measured and threatening. "That makes the man who robbed us your father." His voice grew louder. "Why did you really come here? I saw you lookin' round. We have nothin' left to rob."

"I assure you, I'm not here to rob you."

"He sent you, didn't he?"

"No, sir. The union sent me."

"I bet he's out of prison and you're his front man. Tell him for me we got nothin' left." He stepped away and opened the door.

When Abe stood firm, Mr. Addario grabbed him by the collar and hauled him outside. "Don't come back."

Abe straightened his spine and turned to face Mr. Addario. "I'm not like my father. I'll prove it to you."

Mr. Addario grunted and slammed the door in his face.

Teeth clenched, Abe drove to the first pay phone he saw. He crammed coins into the slot and asked the operator to connect him to the Clinton Correctional Facility. He had to know whether Mother had lied to him.

"Clinton Correctional Facility," the operator said. "How may I direct your call?"

"Uh, who can . . . who can tell me whether my father is an inmate?" he stuttered.

"I'll transfer your call to the warden's office."

Should he hang up? What would he do if his father was alive?

"This is the warden."

The gruff voice made Abe want to hang up, but he had to know, didn't he?

"I'm trying to locate my father." His mouth went dry. "Are you able to confirm a Tymon Kowalski as an inmate?"

Abe heard papers rustling then the warden's voice, "Yeah. He's been here seven years."

Abe dropped the handset. He pushed the folding door open and gasped for air. His father *was* alive.

Why hadn't Mother trusted him with the truth?

Three days had passed since Father accused Abe of consorting with her, and no matter how much Millie contemplated what went wrong, she couldn't make sense of it. Father hadn't spoken to her since then, and she didn't know how to end the silence between them. Her only solace came when she had a needle and thread in her hands.

Happy for the excuse to retreat to the bedroom after dinner, she helped Celia prepare for bed. After she sang a lullaby and tucked the sleepy child under her blanket, Millie gathered her sewing basket, scraps of ribbon, and Mother's blue satin hat.

She fashioned ribbon into rosettes and sewed them onto the hat to cover up the imperfections caused by wear and tear. Bone weary, she pushed the dull needle through the satin and longed for the days when Mother was alive and there was money saved in a tin for their millinery shop. But Mother was gone and with her the dream.

Her mind calmed as she transformed the stained hat into a fashionable headpiece. Feeling more settled now, she puzzled through her guilt over the way Father treated Abe. She wouldn't blame Abe if he never spoke to her again, but he had asked Babi to have her meet him at church on Sunday next. She supposed it was the most logical place, and as much as she questioned where God was when she needed Him, she'd enter the church to see Abe.

She wouldn't break her word to him. Furthermore, as an apology for Father's harsh words, she would not only report the safety irregularities, but she'd surprise him with a list of workers who would testify against Mr. Berg.

Yuri was already sewing when Millie arrived on the third floor of the factory the next day. The young girl greeted her then resumed stitching.

Millie hoped this day would be different from the last three. Since Monday, Mr. Berg had stood over them and barked out orders like he owned them, all the while spewing his vile cigar smoke into the stuffy air.

Midmorning, Mr. Berg examined the completed garments and scribbled something in the little notebook he kept in his shirt. Well, he wasn't the only one keeping notes. Millie tapped her pocket and grinned when she anticipated Abe's reaction. After she added names of workers willing to testify, she'd have the best apology gift she could give him.

Mr. Berg strode to the row of tables forward of Millie's work area and stopped in front of a pregnant woman. He stood over her, sucked air through his cigar, and allowed the red ashes to fall to the floor

240

while he waggled his finger and reprimanded her for taking too many trips to the privy. The woman bowed her head and muttered an apology.

A familiar odor assaulted Millie's nose.

"Fire!" shouted the woman next to Yuri.

Millie jumped to her feet but stood frozen in place.

A man shoved her aside and drenched the flames with a bucketful of water. Two more men followed with a second and third dousing.

She sank to her stool, her heart pounding against her chest.

Mr. Berg roared, "Get back to work or you'll all be without jobs."

Like marionettes, workers resumed their duties, except the pregnant woman, who stood agape at the mess beneath her station.

"You, girl." Mr. Berg pointed at Yuri. "Help her clean the floor."

Millie gathered her wits about her. Her boots and hemline were sodden from the splash of water, yet her head was dry. The overhead sprinklers had not sprayed even one drop of water.

The lingering smell of charred fabric spurred Millie's confidence. During the lunch break, she followed the pregnant woman to the washbasin. "I'm sorry Mr. Berg reprimanded you."

"Thank you for your concern."

Millie continued, "There's a movement to report bosses who don't follow health and safety regulations. Surely a woman heavy with child should be allowed an extra privy break. Would you consider joining the movement and testifying against Mr. Berg?"

The woman held her palm in the air and stepped back. "Stay away from me. I don't want any more trouble."

She trudged to a bench where her husband joined her, then cupped her hand over her mouth and leaned into his ear. Even from across the room, Millie could see the scowl on his ruddy face. The woman pointed at her, and before Millie could move, the man sprang to his feet, bounded across the room, and towered over her.

"You've scared m'wife." He lowered his voice, "We don't want no trouble."

"I meant no harm."

He spoke through clenched teeth. "Leave us be or I swear I'll rat you out."

"Understood."

Millie clamped her mouth shut and walked to the benches to join Yuri. She couldn't be the only factory worker who wished to triumph over the factory bosses.

There had to be someone else willing to testify.

After lunch, the hum of sewing machines lulled her into a sort of stupor until Yuri gasped.

Millie jerked her head toward the girl. Yuri had pierced her fingernail with the sewing machine needle and looked as though she'd faint when a red spot blossomed on the gray fabric. Millie scanned the room for Mr. Berg. Seeing no sign of him, she deftly released the broken needle from the machine, pulled the severed portion from Yuri's finger, and wrapped a scrap of fabric around the girl's wound.

Yuri shuddered, her words running together and spilling to the floor. "That's my second warning. If I get three, Mr. Berg will fire me, then how will I support my grandfather and me?"

Millie knew little of Yuri's circumstances. "Do you live with your grandfather?"

"Yes. He was blinded in a workplace accident."

"Your father?"

"Dead for three years now."

"Mother?"

She choked on the words. "Disappeared when I was five."

"I'll help you." Millie pulled the soiled

243

garment from the machine and stuffed it under the table, then replaced the needle with the spare she always carried in her pocket. She did not know how she'd remove the blood, but she had to try. In the meantime, she thrust the trousers from her own machine at Yuri and told her to sew.

Millie stashed the soiled garment under her arm and hurried to the washbasin located at the back of the room near the privy. She was losing time at her machine, but she had to try to save the trousers. She held the bloodstained fabric under the tap while her gaze darted from one corner of the room to the next. Was Mr. Berg on the third floor? She didn't see him anywhere.

She looked down to appraise the situation. The stain refused to surrender to her scrubbing.

Off her guard, she concentrated solely on the blemish until the odor of cigar smoke seeped into her awareness. She wanted to flee, but Mr. Berg stood not five paces away, feet planted and arms crossed.

"What have we here?"

Millie recoiled and swallowed a lump in her throat. She responded in a voice she didn't recognize as her own. "I've soiled a garment, sir. I'm rinsing it out."

"Back to your station, girl. Leave the trousers."

She returned to her machine to sew. Within seconds, Mr. Berg loomed over her. "These are ruined." He shook the dripping wet fabric in her face. "First warning, and the cost of the garment will be deducted from your pay." He waggled his finger at her. "At this rate, you'll owe *me* money at the end of the day."

He stomped off, muttering to himself. Millie pursed her lips. Clearly, profit was the only thing Mr. Berg cared about.

Yuri touched her elbow. "Thank you for shouldering the blame. Bless you."

"We need to stop him, Yuri. He caused a fire today that could've ended as badly as the Triangle Factory fire. Do you know he locks the fire escape door? Think of your grandfather. We must promote safety in our workplaces. Will you join me in testifying against Mr. Berg?" She squeezed the girl's childlike fingers. "It's our only defense."

Yuri pulled away. "I'm sorry, Millie." Her chin quivered. "I'm grateful to you. I just can't testify."

CHAPTER 5

Abe returned to the union hall determined to gather whatever resources he could for the Addario family and to prove to them he was trustworthy. Distracted by Mother's lie and the notion there might be scores of families who had suffered because of his father, he struggled to focus.

Why had his mother betrayed him? He needed to talk to someone. Sam? Too personal even for his best friend. Mrs. Dunn? He didn't want her to worry about him. His aunt? Perhaps.

Aunt Iris had informed Mother about his father's death. At least that's what Mother had told him. His aunt could be the one person to help him make sense of his mother's lie. He had to find out the truth, but for now, he needed to compile a list of the Addarios' needs before his weekly meeting.

Sam entered the office with his usual

swagger. "Ask me what I accomplished this morning."

Abe assumed a poker face. "I hope more than I did."

"I persuaded the landlord over at the Blanch Tenement Building to move a family into a bigger ground-floor unit at one of his other buildings, *for no extra charge.*"

"That's Millie's building." Abe scraped his fingers through his hair.

"Millie?"

"Miss Pulnik."

"Ah. The engaged woman."

"Not anymore."

Sam clicked his tongue.

"How can I contact the building owner?" Abe asked. "I'd like to arrange a deal of my own while he's in the mood."

Within two hours, an arrangement was in place to move Millie's family to the ground level at the Blanch Tenements. Her landlord agreed after Abe explained Mr. Pulnik was in a wheelchair and Abe would hire a crew to refurbish the fourth-floor unit. He prayed the move would put Mr. Pulnik in a better humor and soften his manner toward Millie.

By the time Mr. Crane called him into the weekly meeting, Abe was confident he'd be able to coax the boss into maximum support for the Addarios until their health improved and they could go back to work. His mission took on more importance now that he could put faces to his father's crimes.

Not one for small talk, Mr. Crane announced he'd been in contact with the district attorney's office and they were ripe to bring indictments against garment factory bosses if there were witnesses to testify. "How many we got?"

Sam said he identified three workers from the cloak maker's factory, and he knew of at least one infraction of fire code in the building.

"My informant at the Berg Emporium discovered the fire escape door is locked on the third floor," Abe said, embarrassed he had nothing else to offer.

"Anyone ready to testify?" Mr. Crane asked.

"Our informant, but I haven't spoken to her since Monday. She might have convinced others."

Mr. Crane nodded. "Keep gathering evidence and witnesses. We'll hold off on calling the fire marshal for an inspection. I want a solid case against these guys before we take any action." He flipped through some papers on his desk. "Have we contacted all the families on our list?"

"Yes, sir," Sam said.

"The last couple I visited needs food, rent relief, and support for their medical needs," Abe said. "Neither husband or wife is fit to work."

"The emergency coffer is nearly gone." Mr. Crane screwed up his mouth. "We'll need to divide it between our last two families."

"I'll need one more week of food for my family," Sam said. "The parents and two of the daughters found employment."

Abe scratched his head. "The Addarios could use everything we can offer and more."

"The remaining funds will cover a few boxes of provisions. Keep in mind, the union's main goal is to protect the health and safety of people in their workplace." Mr. Crane looked him in the eye. "Identifying people to testify is paramount."

Mr. Crane dismissed Sam and Abe to the outer office. Sam tipped his chair and deposited his heels on the desk. Hands clasped behind his head, he leaned back and closed his eyes.

Abe twisted his shoulders this way and that. Why wasn't he able to relax the way Sam did? He admired his friend's ability to get his job done and not carry the burden around. Abe rubbed his temples.

He needed to figure out how to help Mr. and Mrs. Addario. They'd suffered because of his own flesh and blood. He had to make it up to them and prove he wasn't like his father. How could he tell them there was no more funding available? Considering all they'd lost, if the union couldn't provide the needed assistance, he had to find the resources to support this couple, even if he had to use his own savings.

Millie wished she hadn't waited until the last day of the workweek to look for safety irregularities on the second floor. After her father's unseemly behavior toward Abe, she hoped to impress him by supplying plentiful information when she met him at church tomorrow. Abe already knew about the locked fire escape door, and she could tell him about the sprinklers not activating during the fire, but that didn't seem like enough.

During the break, the others mentioned Mr. Berg spent every Saturday afternoon holed up in his office counting out money for their pay envelopes. If she intended to examine another floor, she had to do it now.

Millie slipped into the elevator and went to the second floor, where she walked the perimeter of the room, shoulders back and chin up, as if she'd been assigned the task of examining the premises. She checked the fire escape door. Locked, just like the one on the third floor. Her attention settled on the overhead sprinklers. She followed the length of them to the far wall where they were capped off, no water pipes in sight. No wonder the sprinklers had not activated.

Body shaking and sick to her stomach, Millie made her way to the privy where she retched until her stomach emptied of everything but fear.

Mr. Berg must be brought to justice.

At the end of the day, Millie stood in line to collect her pay. She followed Yuri to the exterior of the building before they opened their envelopes. Yuri removed the cash from the packet. A slip of pink paper fluttered to the ground. Millie bent to pick it up, knowing full well what it meant.

Yuri had been fired.

The young girl trembled. "I know what a pink slip means, but what does it say?"

How could Millie soften the outrageous accusation listed as the reason for firing her friend? She hesitated. "It says you are a thief."

"But I'm not. Even when grandfather and I are hungry, I don't steal." She buried her face in her shawl and wept. "I have to talk to Mr. Berg. Plead my case."

"I can go with you."

"No. I should go alone." Yuri stumbled back into the building.

Millie waited. Within minutes, Yuri exited the building flanked by two men at least a head taller than her. Millie wrapped her arms around the sobbing girl.

"Mr. Berg told me to leave or he'd report me to the police. Says I'm lucky he didn't have me arrested."

"Don't worry, Yuri. The union will help you," Millie reassured her. "You'll have another job."

"How can you be so sure?" Yuri scrunched her brow. "Who do you know?"

"I have a friend at the union. I'll see him tomorrow and ask him to help you. What is your address?" She took the pencil and paper from her pocket.

"Village Tenements, Number 18, 232nd Street." Yuri bit her lip. "How can I repay you?"

"Don't trouble yourself about that. I want to help you."

Yuri drew in a breath. "I'll testify against Mr. Berg. Just tell me what I need to do."

Millie gathered the girl back into her arms

and thanked her. "I will be by your side."

"And I will keep you in my prayers."

Abe sat on the risers with the other choir members. From his vantage point he could see everyone who entered the sanctuary, and so far, he hadn't seen anyone from Millie's family.

Pastor greeted the congregation and led them in song. Normally, Abe enjoyed adding his strong baritone to the other voices, but distraction over the absence of Millie's family weakened his voice. What if yet another misfortune had befallen them? This was to be a day of celebration when he surprised Millie's family with the news they could move to the ground-level tenement.

During the pastor's opening prayer, Abe sent up his own request that Millie would appear. As if in answer, when he opened his eyes, she and her family stood in the aisle.

After the service, Abe lingered near the doorway of the church hall. He gripped his hat between his fingers and grew weary when one of the parishioners engaged him in a conversation about the possibility of another strike. Any other time he'd pay close attention to a worker's concerns, but this time he wanted only to be near Millie.

"Is it true?" the older man wanted to know.

Millie's family crossed the room and melted into the crowd.

The old man snapped his fingers in Abe's face. "I say, Mr. Skala, is it true about the indictment?"

Abe nodded. "It's true."

"I heard the Triangle Factory bosses are paying folks to testify on their behalf. Lie about the conditions."

"I've heard the same thing." Abe stretched his neck to keep Millie in his sight. "Excuse me."

By the time he made his way across the room, Millie, Rose, and their grandmother sipped at cups of fragrant hot tea and little Celia sported cookie crumbs in the corners of her mouth. Abe stood opposite Millie, close enough to see her eyes sparkle and distant enough to keep tongues from wagging. Was she as happy to see him as he was her?

"I ate two ginger cookies," Celia announced as she tugged on his jacket.

"Shall we see whether there's one more on the platter?" Millie's grandmother led Celia away.

Abe pushed his hands in his pockets. Not able to contain his excitement, he blurted,

"I have news."

"Oh?" Millie asked.

"I arranged to move your family to a street-level tenement in your building, that is if you want to. My friends from the union will assist."

Rose's eyes widened. "When?"

"Today."

"Oh my goodness!" Rose squealed. "Father will be able to go outside whenever he chooses. Thank you, Mr. Skala. I must go tell Babi."

He looked at Millie for confirmation his gesture had pleased her. Her russet eyes sparkled, and the smile on her face broadened. "Thank you. Father will be pleased. I have a surprise for you as well." Millie glanced about the room, then lowered her voice. "Yuri will testify."

"Yuri?"

"My friend from the factory. After Mr. Berg accused her of stealing and fired her, she changed her mind. I hope I didn't overstep my boundaries, but I told her you could help her find a new job." Millie passed him the slip of paper with Yuri's address.

"I'll contact her tomorrow and see what can be done." Abe looked at Millie. "You are to be commended. My boss will be pleased. I am pleased." Why was he speaking so formally?

Millie's eyes glistened. "There's more. The sprinklers are not connected to the water lines."

Abe raised his eyebrows. "That information just might be the undoing of Mr. Berg."

Abe insisted on driving Millie's family to their tenement building. Babi, Rose, and even little Celia kept up a lively conversation about the move. They decided Millie would ask Father's *opinion* of moving to the ground floor, even though everyone predicted he'd wholeheartedly agree. And once he agreed, she'd ask his permission for Abe and his friends to help them pack their belongings and move the furniture. By treating Father as head of their household, Millie hoped he'd be in better spirits.

Upon arrival at the tenement, she suggested Abe wait in the hallway while she spoke to Father. She swung the door open then knelt at her father's feet. He turned his face away and reached for the wheel of his chair. She laid her hand atop his to stop him from moving. "Father, I have the best news."

"Your news is no concern of mine."

She bit the inside of her cheek and tried again. "Our family has been offered the street-level tenement. We need you to make a decision about whether we should move."

He looked down at her. Was that hope in his eyes?

"Street level?"

"Yes. We can move today if you find the tenement agreeable."

He swiped at the corners of his eyes.

"And, Father, I want you to know Abe made the arrangement, and his friends at the union hall have offered to help us move. They can come today if you'd like."

Then something happened that she had not seen since before Mother died. Father smiled at her.

When Mr. Crane and Sam arrived, the men carried the wheelchair and Father down the stairs. He sat upright in his chair, head held high while he inspected each of the four rooms, including an inside privy. He signed his name to the rental contract and exchanged pleasantries with the landlord. The rest of the afternoon, he rolled his wheelchair up and down the cobblestone sidewalk greeting the neighbors, with Paul *and* Celia on his lap.

Abe and his associates carried furniture to the tenement while Babi directed the placement of each piece. After Mr. Crane and

Sam took their leave, Abe helped Babi pack dishes into wooden crates while Millie and Rose gathered their personal belongings from the bedroom.

Millie hummed one of the hymns they'd sung in church that morning. She asked Rose, "Do you believe the Lord is with us always?"

"I do."

"Even after Mother died?"

"Yes. The Bible tells us to be courageous and not afraid. Are you afraid?"

Millie contemplated the question. "I am, but not as much as the day of the fire or the day Nathan broke our engagement."

"Good riddance to Nathan. Abe is a much better match."

Warmth flooded Millie's cheeks. "I have no idea what you're talking about."

Rose giggled. "I think you do. There's no mistaking the look in Abe's eyes when he sees you."

Millie fanned herself. *Is Abe part of Your plan for me, Lord?*

Father invited Abe to join the family for their first meal in the new tenement. He even delivered the prayer and thanked Abe. The mood in the room was most joyous as Babi served the simple fare of cornmeal muffins and stew made from the tin of beef Abe had delivered last week. After dinner, Rose read to the twins and helped them prepare for bed. Millie fetched the pouch of tobacco she still had stashed away and gave it to Father.

"You're a good daughter, Mildred." He smiled at her once again. "Thank you."

Millie blinked back tears.

Father asked Abe to hold the doors open for him so he could smoke his pipe out on the sidewalk. Babi swooshed Millie out the door behind them. "Go thank Abe before he leaves."

Millie stood near Abe's car and took in the sweet fragrance of her father's pipe tobacco. Father finally gave Abe a handshake, then turned his wheelchair to roll down the sidewalk.

Abe joined her, and Millie smiled at him. "You have made Father very happy indeed."

"He seems more at ease." Abe intertwined his fingers with hers and held her hands to his heart. "I asked him whether I may call on you."

She gazed into his turquoise eyes. "I hope he consented."

"He did." Abe placed the gentlest of kisses on each palm. "My heart is in your hands."

CHAPTER 6

The next morning Abe lingered on the porch swing at the boardinghouse and waited for the mail delivery. He hoped Aunt Iris had responded to his request to visit her come Sunday next. He had not seen her since his mother's funeral six years prior, but their monthly correspondence had afforded him a connection with his sole surviving relative. He scoffed. *Second* surviving relative if he counted his convict father.

He wanted to call her the same day he confirmed his father was alive, but she and Uncle Clarence claimed they had no desire for such a contraption as a telephone in their home. And even if they did have a telephone, wasn't it best to discuss his mother's lie in person?

Abe's head swam with thoughts of Millie. He yearned to see her today, but he'd tamp down his impatience and wait until tomorrow when he'd join her family for her eighteenth birthday dinner.

Had it been a mere twelve hours since Millie's father gave Abe permission to court her? He closed his eyes and inhaled the fragrance of freshly turned soil in Mrs. Dunn's flower beds — the scent of new beginnings.

The mailman arrived and delivered a stack of mail. Abe flipped through the letters and opened an envelope addressed to him in an unfamiliar script. He slit the seal and read the few sentences from his uncle Clarence.

Iris suffered a stroke. Recovery questionable. Come soon.

Abe fetched his hat and coat from his room then drove to the nearest phone booth. He called Mr. Crane to explain why he wouldn't be at work that day. On the four-hour drive to Albany, he prayed his aunt would recover.

When he arrived, he checked the return address on the envelope against the house number of the brownstone. This had to be the right place. He banged the brass knocker, hugged the bouquet of purple irises he'd purchased at a roadside stand, and waited until Uncle Clarence opened the door.

"Abraham." His uncle gave him a hearty

hug. "So good of you to make the drive. Come in."

Abe stepped over the threshold. "How is she?"

"She hasn't spoken since the stroke, but she can nod if asked a question," Uncle Clarence said. "The doctor reports she's not in pain, but her brain is muddled. She will be pleased to see you."

Abe slipped into the darkened room and held his aunt's frail fingers in his. She opened her eyes and blinked back tears.

He smiled and stroked her forehead. Abe wouldn't burden her with his questions, even if she could nod her head to respond. Instead, he told her all about Millie and how her father had consented to a courtship.

Within fifteen minutes, Aunt Iris fell asleep. Abe kissed her cheek and whispered goodbye. For the life of him, he couldn't understand how she and his father could have such opposite personalities.

Abe joined his uncle in the parlor where a tray of hot tea and a tin of shortbread cookies sat on the maple coffee table.

Uncle Clarence served the aromatic black tea — a skill he admitted having learned since Iris's stroke. He asked Abe about his work, and when the conversation waned, Abe broached the subject of his father.

"Did you know Tymon is alive and confined to prison?"

His uncle furrowed his brow. "Where did you hear that?"

"I met a man who claimed my father was in prison. I called Clinton Correctional, and the warden confirmed he'd been there for seven years."

"Did you tell Iris?"

"No."

"Good, because she put him to rest when we received notice he died. I won't allow the good-for-nothing to impose on her again, especially in her current condition."

"Why did you think him dead?"

"All I know is a man who claimed to be your father's friend came to our door." Uncle Clarence shook his head. "He said Tymon was already buried and asked whether Iris would contact anyone else who needed to know. That's when she sent the letter to your mother."

"Why would he lie about such a thing?"

"I don't know, but it was a relief to have your father out of our lives. I think you're aware he swindled his own sister in one of his con games."

"Yes. Aunt Iris told me as much." How many more people had suffered because of his father? "I wonder how long he'll be in prison."

Had he said that aloud?

His uncle muttered, "For the rest of his worthless life, I hope."

Abe bid his uncle farewell. Should he go to the prison and confront his father about the lie they'd been told? No. There was no reason compelling enough to visit a man who had caused so much heartache for so many.

On Wednesday evening Abe arrived at the Pulniks' residence with a bunch of yellow daisies and a gift-wrapped box. Mrs. Dunn had accompanied him to the dry goods store to select one yard each of yellow, green, and blue satin fabric and matching spools of thread.

Millie's face lit up as soon as she opened the door. Abe gave her his presents.

Celia and Paul scrambled to her side as she arranged the flowers in a mason jar then sat on a kitchen chair and laid the present on her lap. "Oh my. It's so lovely."

Abe shifted his weight from one foot to the other. "My landlady wrapped it for me."

"Tell her I can't remember ever seeing such a lovely package."

He grinned and kept his gaze on her.

"Open it," Celia squealed, jumping up and down.

Millie removed the wrapping paper and folded it neatly before she opened the box. Her brown eyes shimmered, and her fingers caressed the fabric and spools of thread. "Oh Abe. How thoughtful. The colors are perfect for hats. Rose, look."

"Hats?" Mr. Pulnik grumbled. "Why would you need more hats? Haven't you two already?"

"The fabric is meant to give Millie and Rose a little inventory to start their millinery shop," Abe answered.

"Millinery shop?" Mr. Pulnik huffed. "Women can't run a business. They don't have the wherewithal for such things."

Millie sank into a chair, arms crossed and teeth clenched.

"Still," her grandmother said, "it's a lovely gift, Abe. Lovely indeed."

"You best forget about a hat shop or any other kind of shop, for that matter. Your mother shouldn't have promoted such a ridiculous notion." Father wheeled himself to the door, and as if on cue, Paul held the door open and followed him out of the building, while Celia scampered right behind.

"Excuse me," Millie muttered as she left

265

the room.

Rose followed her.

"Shall I leave?" Abe asked Millie's grandmother.

"No. Stay. Your presence might be Millie's only beacon of light. I'm sure she'll return once she's composed."

After several minutes, Rose and Millie returned from their bedroom. Millie apologized for her father's behavior. "Tell me how Yuri is doing while Father is out of earshot."

Abe softened the news as best he could. "I have not seen her yet —"

"But it's been three days," Millie interrupted.

"Yes, and on two occasions I've driven to the address you gave me, and no one answered the door."

"I don't understand. I told her you'd contact her and help her get another job."

"Her landlord claims she and her grandfather haven't taken their belongings from the tenement. Says they neglected to pay rent for the week."

Millie opened her mouth to say something, but Abe reassured her. "Don't worry. Their rent has been paid."

"Thank you, but where could she have gone?"

"No one in her neighborhood will talk to

me, but I promise you, I will continue to search for her." Abe scratched his head. "It's a good sign their belongings are there. I've gone only in the daytime. Tomorrow, I'll go in the evening."

"And then contact me."

"Yes." He turned to Rose. "Do you agree your sister could use some uplifting news?"

Rose's eyes widened. "At my urging, Abe arranged for me to work at the newly unionized garment factory over on 114th Street. You no longer need to carry the full burden of our expenses."

Millie shook her head. "Is this news meant to be a prank?"

"I assure you, it's not," Rose retorted. "I intend to help our family. I have the same obligation as you to earn money. I discussed it with Father and Babi, and both support my decision."

Millie twisted toward Abe, fire in her eyes. "How could you do this? You know I don't want Rose in the factories."

"I thought you'd be pleased to have someone share the burden. Can't you see Rose is simply trying to help?"

"You have no business interfering with our family decisions. And Rose will certainly not quit school to work in a filthy factory." Millie pointed to the door. "Leave. You are

267

no longer welcome around my family."

The nerve of Abe to interfere in her family affairs. How could she have made the same mistake again? Trusting that God cared enough about her to send a man who could make her happy.

And to think Babi and Father had championed Rose's decision. Millie simply couldn't abide Rose working in a factory. She'd get a second job if it would keep her sister in school.

One of the women at work had mentioned St. Paul's was hiring part-time laundresses. Millie would apply tomorrow and show her family she could take care of all of them, without anyone's help.

It had been three days since Millie secured an evening laundress job and that many days since she'd seen the twins, or her father, awake. And while fatigue claimed her, sleep eluded her.

Something was amiss in their household. Rose, Babi, and Millie normally had a pleasant conversation over morning tea, but Rose refused to acknowledge Millie, and Babi kept her distance.

Millie mumbled her goodbyes and shuffled out the door for work. Halfway to the bus stop, she realized she'd forgotten bus fare. If she hurried, she could go back home, grab the money, and still catch the bus.

As she rounded the corner to the tenement, Rose dashed across the street and disappeared into a bus headed the opposite direction from her school. Millie ran into the tenement. "Babi, where is Rose going?"

Babi bit her lip. "To work."

"Work? Didn't I make it clear my second job will provide us with ample funds?"

"She wants to help."

Millie rubbed her arms. "She can't."

"You're exhausted, Millie." Babi touched her shoulder. "You have no time to spend with the twins. Celia asks for you every day. Let Rose help."

Millie ground her teeth and insisted Babi tell her the location of Rose's workplace. She clutched a fistful of coins, stormed out the door, and tramped to the bus stop. She'd miss a day of work at Berg's Emporium, but she had to stop her sister today.

By the time she entered Rose's workplace, her head ached, and the bright lights burned her eyes. A man in a stylish suit coat greeted her and asked if she sought employment.

"No, sir. I'd like to speak to my sister, if I may." She gave the name and followed the man to the front of the room where Rose stitched a lapel onto a jacket and chatted with the girl next to her.

"Rose, you have a visitor," the man said.

Rose turned her head. She jumped up, eyes wide. "Is someone hurt?"

"No," Millie told her. "I've come to take you back to school."

Rose put her hands on her hips, elbows out. "I don't need your permission to quit school, nor do I need your permission to work. Father supports my decision." She lowered her voice, her jawline firm. "Please leave."

"I won't leave without you," Millie snapped. "Mother intended for you to complete high school, and that's what you'll do."

Rose stood eye to eye with her. "Leave," she spat. "Haven't you humiliated me enough?"

Millie glared at her sister. When had she become so impertinent? If Rose wanted to act the stubborn child, she'd treat her like a stubborn child.

Millie grabbed her elbow.

"Don't make a scene." Rose wriggled free.

Millie reached for her sister's arm again, but the man who'd met her at the door stepped between them. "Leave the premises or I'll call the authorities."

"Not without my sister. Rose?"

Rose plopped down and resumed sewing.

"We are not done with this conversation," Millie told her.

The meddlesome man asked, "Do I need to escort you out?"

Millie tipped her chin up and marched out of the building. She'd find another way to convince Rose she did not belong in a factory.

Abe trudged through each day. What had he done wrong? After a week of prayer, he drew the same conclusion — his greatest desire was to help Millie and her family. It was never his intention to upset her. When Rose requested his assistance in securing a job, she assured him Millie would approve of her working provided the factory was safe and clean.

And as much as he ached to see Millie, he'd give her more time as her grandmother had suggested at church last Sunday.

If he could locate her friend, perhaps Millie would give him an audience. But for now, if he couldn't remedy his own blunders, he'd remedy what he could of his father's, beginning with the Addarios.

Last week, after Mr. Crane announced the union's emergency funds were depleted,

Abe had used his own funds to fill a box with supplies for the Addarios. He'd asked Sam to make the delivery, with the hope they'd accept the help they needed.

This week, he'd deliver the provisions himself. Nothing he could do would bring back their loved ones, but he could ensure the couple had the financial support they needed until they could rally.

At the end of his workday, Abe drove to the Addario tenement. He wiped his brow, straightened his spine, looked heavenward, and prayed the couple would accept his offering.

A subdued Mr. Addario answered the door and invited him to enter.

Encouraged, Abe passed him the box.

Mr. Addario cleared his throat. "We thank you."

Abe nodded to Mrs. Addario then gave her the rent receipt and a voucher to help defray the cost of medication.

"Bless you." Mrs. Addario blinked back tears. "How can we ever repay you?"

"Repayment is not necessary. After my father's unforgivable behavior, what little I offer is of no consequence."

"That fellow, Sam, vouched for you." Mr. Addario looked Abe square in the eyes. "Me and the missus prayed on it. I owe you an apology."

Abe tried to spare the man some dignity. "You needn't say more." He turned and surveyed the tiny room. "What else can I do to help?"

"We are already stronger," Mrs. Addario said. "Your support has been a godsend, but now that we're able, we want to do for ourselves. Save the assistance for those in worse circumstances."

"Got myself a union job." Mr. Addario stood tall and held his head high. "Thanks to Sam's recommendation, I start work on Monday as a longshoreman. I'll earn enough so's the missus can take her time recovering."

Abe nodded. "Congratulations."

"When I'm able to return to work," Mrs. Addario asked, her expression hopeful, "will you help me find a position?"

"By all means." Abe offered his business card.

"You must resemble your mother's side of the family," she said, "because you're not at all like your father."

With those words, a heavy burden lifted from his shoulders. Now if he could only find a way to lighten Millie's load.

First thing the next morning, Mr. Crane

rushed through the door to Sam and Abe's office. "Gentlemen," he said, "the district attorney's office set the eleventh of May for witnesses to testify against Berg and Grant. That's just a week away. Will you be ready?"

"I have twelve confirmed informants from Grant's Garment Makers," Sam said.

"Abe?" Mr. Crane asked.

Will Millie still testify? If I can't find Yuri, I may be without any witnesses.

"Yes, sir. I'm still trying to locate one of the witnesses, but we'll be ready." He hoped that was true. His reputation depended on it.

"I assured the district attorney we'd make it worth his time," Mr. Crane said. "How many?"

"One, maybe two." Abe frowned.

"I gave my word we'd produce a minimum of five witnesses for each boss." Mr. Crane lifted his brow.

"I won't disappoint you, sir." Abe said the words but doubted every syllable.

CHAPTER 7

Millie arrived home from her laundress job long after the rest of the household had retired for the night. Moonbeams streamed through the kitchen window and provided enough light to brew a cup of peppermint tea. A high-pitched whistling sound, apparently carried from the street through the open window, niggled at her. Too exhausted to walk to the bedroom, she cradled her head in her arms on the kitchen table and fell asleep.

She was at the Triangle Shirtwaist Factory. Rose sat beside her, sewing lace onto a white shirtwaist. A burly man stood over them smoking a cigar. Crimson ash fell at Rose's feet. Flames shot up the length of her body. She screamed. Millie grabbed for her. Rose fell to the floor in a fiery mass while Abe beckoned from the elevator.

Startled, she sat upright. Her body quaked, and tears stung her cheeks. When would she be able to sleep soundly again? The recurring dream accentuated her fear that harm would come to Rose in the factory and increased her dread that Yuri had already been harmed. Add to that her torment over Abe's blatant disregard of her wishes, and it was a wonder she slept at all. Jumbled thoughts competed for her attention, and she wrestled with the notion that the more she tried to protect her family, the more she alienated them.

Fully awake now, she recognized the whistling sound as wheezing, and it came not from the outside but from Father's bedroom. Alarmed, she knocked on the door. "Father?"

"Mildred, bring a lantern. Paul's ill."

She entered the room. Panic creased Father's brow. "He can't breathe. He's aflame yet shakes as if freezing. He needs a doctor."

"I'll take him to the infirmary, straightaway."

Millie directed Babi and Rose as soon as they entered the room. "Rose, go to the phone booth and call a taxicab. Babi, fetch another lantern. We need to check his color."

The extra illumination from the second lantern confirmed Paul's lips and the beds of his nails were blue. Gut wrenching, Millie bundled him in a blanket and lifted him to her chest.

Father pulled himself to a sitting position, terror in his eyes. He motioned to Babi. "Florence, help me dress. I need to go with them."

Rose reported the taxi would arrive in ten minutes. She helped Babi dress Father and lift him into his wheelchair.

The taxi met them at the curb. The driver jumped from his seat. "Can't take the invalid. No place for the wheelchair, but you others can get in."

Father's shoulders drooped. "Go, Mildred. Take Paul."

Millie's chin trembled.

"Go," Babi said. "I'll find a way to bring your father."

Millie held her limp brother in her arms as the taxi sped them to Bellevue Hospital.

Please, God, don't let him die.

On their arrival at the hospital, a nurse asked Paul's name and symptoms, snatched him from Millie's arms, and promised someone would report to her shortly.

The waiting room offered no solace. There were a few other people about who spoke in hushed tones, tapped their fingers on the tables, or paced the floor. With nothing to occupy her time, Millie could only wait and think and worry.

She stared at the lightbulbs dangling from the ceiling, half of which were illuminated, and her mind drifted to her father. How difficult it must have been for him to be called an invalid and be turned away by the taxi driver.

Millie wished Babi or Rose were here with her. She couldn't bear this burden by herself, could she?

What had happened to the close relationship she once had with Rose? She had to mend the rift between them even if it meant embracing Rose's decision to work in a factory. Truth be known, Millie was relieved to share monetary responsibility for the family.

A doctor strode across the vast room. "Miss Pulnik?"

"Yes."

"Your brother has pneumonia and his fever persists. We are giving him oxygen, but he is very weak."

She stood. "May I see him?"

"Not until visiting hours at two o'clock in the afternoon, then for ten minutes."

Could she ask the question sitting in the back of her throat? "Will he recover?"

The doctor opened his mouth, paused, and then said, "It is too soon to tell, but if there are other family members, you should encourage them to come."

Millie slumped to the couch, her gut tight for the unthinkable.

"We should know more in the next twenty-four hours. If his condition worsens, someone will come get you to say your goodbyes."

She stopped breathing. Goodbyes?

"I will apprise you of his condition when I do evening rounds." He turned on his heel and disappeared down the long corridor.

Millie gulped for air. She had no way to contact her family short of going back home, and she could not leave Paul.

It was after ten o'clock in the morning when Millie's family arrived.

Father looked like he had aged ten years. "Where's my son?"

"Resting," Millie assured him. "No one can see him until two o'clock and then for only ten minutes."

He checked his pocket watch. "Where's the doctor?"

"He will be here this evening to examine Paul and tell us his findings. He spoke with me earlier."

"Well?"

I need to tell him all of it. "He has pneumonia. They're giving him oxygen. The doctor recommended the family gather here . . ." Her voice wavered. ". . . in the event —"

Father slammed his fists against his legs then rolled himself to the far side of the room, where he faced the wall. Great heaving sobs overtook him.

Babi sat beside Millie and wrapped her in her arms, tears flowing freely down her wrinkled cheeks. Celia buried her head in Millie's lap and joined the sorrow.

Misery consumed Millie's family. Did she have the reserves to be strong for them? She did it after Mother died, and she'd do it again.

She redirected Babi's attention. "Why isn't Rose with you?"

Babi dabbed at her eyes and blew her nose on her cotton handkerchief. "She chose to go to work. Said your place was with Paul, and since you couldn't earn your wages today, she'd go earn hers."

"Her behavior is quite mature for a girl her age, don't you think?"

"I do. I'm pleased you recognize that."

Celia sat up. "We rode in Mr. Skala's bread truck."

Millie cocked her head. "What?"

Babi held her chin in the air. "I didn't know what else to do. I called Abe to see if he could transport your father here. He was able to borrow the truck after his friend finished morning deliveries."

Millie bit her lip, then allowed tears to flow.

Dear, sweet Abe. Always at the ready to assist them.

Father wheeled himself back and forth across the hospital waiting room, stopping only to check the time on his pocket watch. The longer the wait to see Paul, the more his sorrow turned to anger.

"He's not had enough to eat, I tell you. He's a growing boy and needs more than broth and biscuits. He needs meat."

Millie hung her head and chose not to respond.

At two o'clock, a receptionist came to the waiting area and announced visiting hours. Babi offered to stay with Celia while Father and Millie went to see Paul.

"Let me push you, Father," Millie said, grasping hold of the wheelchair from behind. "You must be weary."

He nodded. "Go quickly, then."

Paul's eyes were closed, his breathing labored, and his body shuddered as if he were packed in ice. Father grasped Paul's arm and begged him to fight.

Millie folded her arms across her chest to quell the shaking. Was she to blame for Paul's condition? Had she been too preoccupied with her own troubles to care for him properly?

As the sun set, Rose arrived with a basket of food on her arm. "How is he?"

Millie rubbed the back of her neck. "We're waiting for the doctor's evening report."

"May I see him?"

"Visiting hours are at seven. They allow two visitors. Babi has not seen him since she arrived."

"I see. And Father. Of course." Rose managed a little smile and held up the basket. "I bought food with part of my wages."

"Thank you. Celia asked for something to eat hours ago."

Rose gave Celia a piece of cheese and a thick slice of bread. She encouraged everyone to eat a little something. "We need to stay strong for Paul's sake."

Millie stood back as Rose took care of the family, and marveled at how grown-up her younger sister acted.

When the doctor reported no change, a tear slipped down Father's face. The doctor shifted his weight from one foot to the other. "I will talk with you after I do rounds

282

in the morning."

He exited, leaving uncertainty in his place.

"Rose?" Millie asked. "I wonder if you'd accompany me to the chapel?"

The sisters set out along the gas-lit walkway. Millie glanced at Rose. "I must apologize for treating you like a child. It was mature of you to want to alleviate the financial burden we face."

Her sister dipped her chin. "I wanted to make it easier on you."

"I appreciate that."

Rose faced her, brows creased. "It was also Abe's intention to ease your burden. He wants the best for you."

"Yes. I see that now."

"And I don't want you to worry about my education, Millie," Rose continued. "I trust that between you and Father, I will learn what I must."

Upon entering the chapel, a stillness settled in Millie's chest. The rose-colored walls and pale blue ceiling calmed her as she knelt beside Rose at the chancel rail and looked above the marble altar to the stained-glass window depicting Christ healing the sick. She prayed God would spare Paul and that Abe would forgive her.

Abe entered Bellevue Hospital at a quarter

to seven. Millie's grandmother, Celia, and Mr. Pulnik were in the same area where Millie had waited for him to deliver the wheelchair, but Millie was nowhere in sight. Disappointment and relief washed over him at the same time. He wanted to see her, but he didn't know whether she'd even speak to him.

Celia waved, ran across the room, and hugged his leg.

"Millie and Rose went to the chapel," Millie's grandmother informed him. "They should return shortly."

He glanced from her to Millie's father. "May I wait with you?"

Mr. Pulnik nodded.

"How is your son?" Abe asked.

"Struggling," Mr. Pulnik answered.

"Henryk and I will see him at seven and should know more then," Millie's grandmother added.

Celia tugged at him. "Are we going to ride in the bread truck again? It smells like cimanim."

"Cinnamon," her grandmother corrected.

The child ignored her elder and begged, "Can I please have another ride?"

"I returned the truck this morning, but you can ride in it again when your father is ready to go home."

She jumped up and down and waved her arms.

Millie and Rose came through the door, arms linked and faces serene. Millie offered Abe a shy smile.

His heart thudded against his chest. Had she forgiven him? Did he dare think reconciliation was possible?

When Millie's father and grandmother went to see Paul, Rose took Celia to count the windows on the other side of the waiting room. Abe and Millie were alone.

Millie looked at the floor. "Thank you for transporting Father."

"Always happy to oblige." Abe's fingers rubbed the edges of his hat. "It was never my intention to upset you."

"I know that now. Rose explained."

"Forgive me?"

She raised her face to his. "If you forgive me as well."

"Of course I do." He stepped closer. "I didn't know what I would do if you refused to speak to me. I really care for you, Millie."

"I care for you too, Abe."

Millie touched his cheek and all his worries dissipated. His future looked promising once more.

After a nerve-racking weekend, Paul's doctor met Millie and her father on Monday morning before Babi and Celia arrived. "Your boy's fever broke," the doctor told Father. "He opened his eyes and asked for you. I'll allow a short visit this morning."

While Father went to see Paul, Millie paced the floor near the hospital entrance and awaited the arrival of Babi, Celia, and Abe. As soon as they arrived, she ran outside to share the good news.

"Thank the Lord," Babi said.

"Yes," Abe agreed.

Celia tugged on Millie's arm. "Can I see him?"

"Perhaps later." Millie bent to pick up her little sister. "The doctor says we should be able to take Paul home in a couple of days."

"I have work to do, but I'll return as soon as possible," Abe promised.

Millie wanted to stand closer, to give him reason to touch her, to brush his fingers across her cheek, but she controlled the urge. "Thank you."

Once inside, Babi set a food basket and a fabric-wrapped bundle on the couch and patted the seat next to her.

"Did Rose go to her job?" Millie asked.

"Yes. She'll join us later."

Celia blurted, "We're going to make a hat."

"We need to keep our hands busy." Babi winked. "And it's high time for Celia to learn how to sew."

Millie peeked inside the package. Babi had remembered everything including the three pieces of satin from Abe. "Shall we take our supplies to the table on the far side of the room and get started?"

Millie threaded a needle for Celia and showed her how to make a straight line of small, even stitches on the muslin scraps. She drew a pencil mark across the fabric and instructed Celia to practice. Babi sat close by and offered encouragement.

Mother would be pleased. Her reverie dissolved when Father rolled into the room, concern stamped on his forehead.

"What is it?" Millie asked. "Did you see Paul?"

"I did." His voice cracked. "He begged me not to leave. The nurse pushed me right out of the ward."

Millie cringed. "How awful for you both."

"We're going to make a hat," Celia said.

"Here?" Father glowered at the materials spread before them. "While my son struggles to breathe?"

Millie tipped her head toward Celia. "We need to keep busy, Father."

"I'm going to make a hat for our hat shop,

right, Millie?" Celia asked.

"Again with the hat shop?" Father shook his head. "Stop filling the child's head with nonsense. Sewing hats does not mean any of you can run a business. Waste of time, if you ask me."

He spun his chair around and called over his shoulder, "I'm going outside."

Little Celia scampered to the door to hold it open for him.

Just before the afternoon visiting hours, the lobby filled with people. Father and Babi went to see Paul while the two sisters continued to sew. Celia graduated from sewing scraps to hemming a square of cotton she called a handkerchief. Millie cut the green satin from self-made pattern pieces and pinned them around the milliner's block.

"Excuse me," a woman interrupted.

Millie looked up from her creation. A well-dressed woman stood over them.

"Allow me to introduce myself. I'm Hazel Wellington. May I take a closer look?" She touched the fabric lightly. "This design is stunning. Where did you study millinery?"

"My mother taught me."

"You do lovely work. Would you consider selling me this hat and one just like it?"

Millie gulped. "Sell it?"

"This weekend, my sister Violet and I will host an annual soiree and we always dress exactly alike. The hats my sister chose are dreadful." Miss Wellington gave a sheepish grin. "I'd need both hats in four days, but I will pay top dollar."

Millie's stomach flip-flopped, but she remained calm and professional on the outside as she and Miss Wellington agreed on the terms of the transaction.

Miss Wellington clapped her gloved hands. "I almost forgot. What is your name?"

"Millie Pulnik."

"I'm so pleased to meet you, Millie. Violet and I will eagerly await your delivery."

Millie was bursting to share the good news with her family. She'd made her first sale — and not just one, but two hats.

CHAPTER 8

By evening, Paul's condition showed marked improvement and his doctor recommended the family go home for the night. Abe borrowed the bread truck to transport them. Celia sat on Father's lap in the front seat while Rose, Babi, and Millie sat on upturned crates in the back of the panel truck. Rose bounced her legs as the women discussed how to budget the money needed to complete the hat order.

Millie took Rose's hand and teased, "If we plan well, we may be able to open a small millinery shop before you are of marriageable age."

Rose blushed, and Babi laughed for the first time in months.

"Stop chattering about hats," Father demanded. "Selling hats won't put food on the table. I expect Paul to have meat every day to help him regain his strength."

Silence blanketed the women. Just like

Father to quell their enthusiasm. Millie did have the business skills to sell hats. All they needed were more hat orders and the willingness to sacrifice where they could. It was unreasonable to demand that Paul have meat every day. What about Celia? When did Father ever consider her needs? Millie rubbed her temples. She'd prove to Father she could run a business.

That evening, after Father and Celia were asleep, the women counted the remaining money from Rose's first paycheck and decided she'd go to the yard goods store after work tomorrow and purchase the needed materials to make the second hat. Millie would return to work, and Babi would accompany Father and Celia to the hospital.

While they talked, Rose and Millie stitched until the first green hat was complete, satin rosettes and all.

Early Wednesday morning Millie and Rose helped Babi plan a special meal in celebration of Paul's homecoming. Babi suggested they buy a few potatoes and carrots and use the last tin of beef to make a stew. Millie figured that should be hearty enough to satisfy Father's expectation that Paul would have meat every day while he recovered.

Babi offered to bake a loaf of bread and a small cake with the last of the flour.

That settled, Millie hugged Rose and Babi and set off to work. The sun's rays had already found their way between the buildings and warmed her shoulders as she waited for the double-decker bus. She'd gladly sit on the upper deck today.

Even before the driver stopped the bus, Millie's vantage point afforded her a glimpse of the area outside the factory. As many as a hundred people were milling about. Were they her coworkers? Why were they not inside the building?

She stepped off the bus and hurried toward the factory.

"There she is!" A gruff voice shouted and pointed at her. "There's the snitch."

Millie dropped her chin to her chest and scrambled up the cobblestones. Would they continue badgering her once she was inside?

As soon as she saw the glint of metal, she understood why so many people were outside the factory. Heavy steel chains hung from the closed doors.

The jeers grew louder. "Look what you've done." Men and women alike shook their fists at her. "How do I feed my family now?"

Her head throbbed and her stomach

tightened. Was she to blame for the factory closing?

The pregnant woman Millie had talked to days ago bowed her head as her husband joined those yelling at her. Why had she trusted this woman? After their conversation that day at the factory, the woman had run right to her husband to expose Millie as a snitch. He must have told everyone she was in partnership with the union. And now, because of the union, the factory was closed.

That meant what they said was true. It *was* her fault chains hung from the doors. Had Abe known this would be the outcome? Had that been his plan all along? To find a way to shut down the factory without regard for the workers? Why hadn't he warned her instead of setting her up to be the scapegoat?

She pushed her palms over her ears and ran through the contemptuous crowd, not stopping until her lungs burned in her chest. What was she to do? After she and Rose and Babi made the perfect plan to improve their family's condition and realize their dream of a hat shop, she'd misjudged Abe's intentions and lost her job. She'd trusted him the same way she'd trusted Nathan. What was wrong with her? Why was she incapable of judging a man's character?

Millie straightened her shoulders. She'd

show them all. She'd go directly to St. Paul's and ask for more hours in the laundry.

Millie smoothed her skirt and pinned a few loose strands of hair back into her chignon before she entered her boss's office suite. His secretary opened his door and announced Millie would like to speak to him.

"Isn't that fortuitous? I hoped to speak with *her* today."

Millie entered, curious why he'd want to speak to her. "Good morning, sir. Thank you for seeing me."

He looked different from when she had first met him. She remembered him to be amiable, but now he leaned across his desk and cast a derisive grin her way. "Did you know my brother-in-law works over at Berg's? Maybe you've met him. He's the foreman on the second floor."

She stuffed her fists in her skirt pockets. "I don't believe I have, sir."

"He saw you snooping around the other day. Checked with some others from the third floor and discovered you're conspiring with the union."

Beads of sweat dampened her upper lip. "I believe in the union, yes, sir."

"Well, I straight up do not condone

unions, or anyone else, telling me how to run my business. And I absolutely cannot have a union informant working for me."

"But sir —"

"Collect your time card and take it to my secretary. She'll pay you for the days you worked. I'd prefer not to give you any money, but I don't want it said I cheated you either. Who knows how you'd report *that* to your union friends."

Millie's mouth fell open, but no words formed. She lost two jobs in one day because of her affiliation with Abe and the union. She'd trusted Abe, relied on his guidance and protection, and been played for a fool again. One would think, after she misjudged Nathan, she would've learned a man's word was not to be trusted.

Abe arrived at the office later than expected after he'd transported Paul home. He rummaged through the files for the list of those hired through the union to work at Berg's Emporium. Of those, he identified six terminations. Yuri's name was absent from the list of those terminated. If Berg fired without the union's knowledge, did he also hire without their knowledge? At any rate, for the rest of the day he'd focus his attention on contacting those on the termination list to see whether any of them would be willing to testify.

He knocked on four doors before he found someone at home. "Good afternoon. I'm Abraham Skala. I represent the International Ladies Garment Workers Union."

"The union was s'posed to protect us," a middle-aged woman spat out. "I made one little mistake and Berg fired me."

"I'm sorry to hear that. Would you like the union to assist you in finding a new position?"

"No. You can leave me alone. Empty promises. That's all. I got myself a night-time job rolling tobacco into cigars. Don't need anybody to find me a job."

"The union needs people like you who were fired unfairly. You can help make conditions better for everyone by testifying against Mr. Berg."

"Why would I help the union? Get goin' now and don't come back." With a scowl, she slammed the door in his face.

It was nearing the end of the workday for Berg's employees, and despite Abe's agreement with Millie to stay clear of the place, he had to go there if he had any chance of talking with the employees.

No workers waited at the bus stop. Something was wrong. Abe rounded the corner and recognized the chains on Berg's factory doors as those of the fire marshal. The property had been deemed unsafe. Had Mr. Crane changed his mind and reported the fire safety violations earlier than he'd indicated at their meeting? Those chains meant all the factory workers, including Millie, were without jobs until the building passed inspection. There was no telling how long that might take. Abe may not be able to assist all of them in finding replacement jobs, but he had to help Millie. Even with her second job and Rose bringing home wages, the family still suffered financially with all the added medical bills. Just this morning when he transported Millie's grandmother to the hospital to pick up Paul, she'd mentioned the rising debt from the hospital as late fees and interest compounded the initial debt. Her voice wavered when she confided that her son-in-law suggested she go to the poorhouse.

He had to help Millie find an alternative position. Millie was not Job. She couldn't be expected to suffer one more setback. She'd be on her way to her laundress position by now. Abe had ample time to go home, freshen up, and have his supper at Mrs. Dunn's before he drove to Millie's tenement and waited for her to come home from the laundry.

Evening shadows fell over Mrs. Dunn's front yard flower garden as Abe walked through the gate. The porch swing creaked against the weight of a man, his silhouette familiar and his presence as repugnant as a sewer rat.

"Abraham?"

"I don't believe it." Abe crossed his arms over his chest as a chill settled deep in his gut. "You are not welcome here, Tymon."

His father stood and stepped toward him. "Come now, Son. After all these years, give your old man a bite to eat and a place to stay until I get back on my feet."

"Why should I help you get back on your feet? I owe you nothing." Abe turned to enter the house.

"Your mother would want you to help me —"

Abe whipped around and poked his finger in his father's chest. "Don't speak to me about what Mother would want. Because of you, we were destitute. If not for Mrs. Dunn's kindness, we would've been out in the street."

"Don't make me beg," he whispered. "I'm asking for a few days. Some food and a place to sleep. I'm a little down on my luck."

"Is that what they call it when you're released from prison?" Abe scoffed. "Down on your luck?"

His father hung his head. "So you know about that."

"You let us believe you were dead."

"Ah, I asked a friend to tell that story. Seemed like it'd be easier on your mother and my sister."

"Easier?" Abe lowered his voice and made no effort to disguise his disdain. "Don't tell me you cared about what was easier for anyone but yourself. Mother went to an early grave mourning your death."

"I never meant to hurt her. She was a good woman."

She *was* a good woman. Better than his father deserved.

"Abraham. I'm sick." His father grasped Abe's arm. "Doc told me I don't have long to live. I'd like my last days to be near my son."

What would Mother want me to do? Please, God, I need Your guidance.

Abe answered through clenched teeth. "I'll ask Mrs. Dunn to prepare a pallet in my room for you and arrange for two meals a day. But not a word to the other boarders about your time in prison. At least spare me that."

"Fresh start?" His father offered his hand.

Abe's arms fell to his sides.

Abe suffered through supper while his father regaled the other tenants with stories of his early days in Poland. At the end of the meal, Abe offered to help Mrs. Dunn clear the table.

Once inside the kitchen, Mrs. Dunn questioned him. "Are you sure you want him here?"

"I don't, but I think it's what Mother would want me to do."

"Don't be too sure after the heartache he put her through."

"He says he's dying." Abe raked his fingers through his hair.

"If you're comfortable with your decision, then I'll support you."

"Thank you."

Abe went back to the dining room and escorted his father to his bedroom, then made his excuses to leave. He had to talk to Millie before he could get even one minute of sleep.

Millie sat at the bus stop near St. Paul's, unable to move. She clutched her pay envelope and watched the buses come and go. Once she finally boarded, the chill of the spring evening wrapped around her.

How would she tell her family she was no longer employed? Even with Rose's wages, they wouldn't last two weeks without her paychecks. Her family was one step from the poorhouse all because she'd blindly trusted Abe.

By the time the bus ground to a halt, her head throbbed. A group of children played hopscotch on the sidewalk fronting the building. Even their laughter did nothing to lighten Millie's mood.

Movement in the alleyway caught her eye. She took a step backward.

Celia reached into a trash can and held up an apple core. She took a bite.

"Stop," Millie called as she ran to her sister.

"But I'm hungry." Celia stuffed the rest of the apple into her mouth before Millie reached her.

Millie gagged and gathered the child into her arms. "Didn't you eat leftover stew today?"

"Father said the stew was for Paul. Babi gave me food, but my belly hurts. Are you angry with me?"

"No. I'm not angry with you." Millie

clenched her teeth. She wasn't angry with Celia. She was furious and couldn't decide with whom she was most furious — Nathan for his lies, Abe for his manipulation, or Father for his blatant disregard of Celia in favor of Paul.

With Celia in her arms, Millie marched into the tenement, where Babi and Rose washed the supper dishes and Paul listened to Father reading.

Millie helped Celia wash the stench of garbage from her hands and face. "Is there any beef stew left?"

"Henryk thought it best to save the stew for Paul," Babi answered. "The rest of us ate bread and broth."

Millie pursed her lips and spread lard on a piece of bread for Celia. "I found her in the alley eating from a garbage can."

Babi gasped and clutched the edge of the table as she swayed on her feet. Rose wrapped her arm around Babi's waist and helped her to sit, then lowered herself into a chair and bit at her knuckles.

"Too many mouths to feed." Father glared at Babi.

Babi shook her head. "I should've kept a better watch on her. She asked to go outside to play hopscotch with the other children."

"We can't leave her unsupervised," Millie

said. "Celia, do you understand? You're not to eat from the garbage cans again."

Celia whimpered. "I was hungry."

Father frowned at Millie. "Why aren't you at St. Paul's?"

I might as well tell them. "Berg's factory is chained closed and my boss at the laundry fired me."

"I've never been fired in all my life," Father exclaimed. "What did you do wrong?"

Millie clenched her jaw and turned away from him. *Why does he always assume I'm the guilty party?*

"I could ask my boss for extra duty," Rose offered.

"I'll tell you what we need to do," Father said. "Florence should go to the poorhouse and Celia to the orphanage so we have enough food for Paul."

"No." Millie slammed her fist on the table. "No one will be sent away. Rose and I will find a solution. We'll have money from the hat sales. I'll ask my buyer to recommend me to her friends."

"Get your head out of the clouds. There's nothing more to figure out," Father insisted.

"I don't want to be a burden." Babi's chin shook. "I'll go."

"No, Babi," Millie said firmly. "I won't let

303

you. Father has no say in the matter."

"Who are you to tell me what I can say?" Father bellowed. "You're not the head of this family."

"What am I, then?" Millie scowled at him. "Since your injury, I'm the one who has kept this family housed and fed. Me, Father."

A knock silenced them all. Rose opened the door a crack. "May I wait here for Millie to come home from work?"

Millie ground her teeth. It was Abe.

"I'm here." Millie strode into the hallway, slammed the door behind her, and spun on her heels to face him. "Do you want to know *why* I'm here when I should be working?" She didn't wait for an answer. "I'm here because I lost both jobs in one day. You could've warned me the union planned to shut down the factory."

"I didn't know."

"How could you *not* know? There are just three men in your office."

"I promise you, I didn't know until I went to Berg's this afternoon and the doors were chained."

"The others shouted and shook their fists at me," she yelled. "Called me a snitch. Blamed me for the loss of their jobs."

He reached for her.

She recoiled. "Don't touch me. Because of my involvement with you and the union, I can no longer provide for my family."

"We can remedy this. I'll help you get another job, maybe at the same factory as Rose."

"I've been labeled a snitch, and all the garment factory bosses know one another. Thanks to you, no one will want to hire me." Millie clutched her torso, elbows pressed to her sides.

"I hate to see you like this. Please, allow me to help."

Millie spat out, "The last time I trusted you to help me get a job, you took advantage of my vulnerability and set me up as a union spy, knowing full well the implications."

He took a step backward and shook his head. "Are you saying you don't trust me? Without trust, we've no future together."

Millie swallowed and tried to ignore the ache in her heart. "I don't trust you."

CHAPTER 9

Abe strode out of the building and left Millie alone in the hallway outside her tenement. She leaned against the wall, squeezed her eyes shut, and balled her nervous hands into fists.

Has it been only a few weeks since Nathan walked away? Am I to repeat the same pattern with each suitor? Trust their word is true, then be left alone?

Millie slammed her fists against the wall.

Am I incapable of judging a man's character? Was I so desperate for a job I was blinded to the real reason Abe helped me get a position with Mr. Berg? Fine. I have no more obligation toward him or the union. The union had all the information they needed to close the factory.

Millie covered her eyes and slumped to the floor, determined not to give in to what her heart begged her to believe. *What if Abe did tell me the truth when he said he didn't know the factory would be chained shut?*

He had seemed like such a gentleman, ready at every turn to assist her family, a devout man who had demonstrated his allegiance to her. *How could that man be the same one who set me up as the scapegoat?*

None of that mattered anymore. She told Abe she did not trust him, and he walked away without a backward glance. How could she ever trust a man again when the man she hoped she'd spend the rest of her life with simply walked away from her? Wasn't she worth fighting for?

Her thoughts reeled back to the message in last Sunday's sermon and the scripture the pastor had quoted from Psalms — *"My help cometh from the Lord, which made heaven and earth."*

Although she couldn't rely on men, she could no longer deny her need for God's provision. She prayed God would reveal His plan.

Millie took two measured breaths. She needed to earn money to contribute to the family, but she wouldn't seek employment in another factory. She'd rather work as a scullery maid on her hands and knees than work for another garment factory boss.

Of all nights for Abe to have his father sharing his room, this had to be the worst. Certain his face would give away his heartache, Abe drove with no direction in mind and ended up in Yuri's neighborhood. He parked along the sidewalk in front of her building, slumped down in the seat, and scrutinized the darkness. At this point, he assumed Millie wouldn't testify, and he had no one else. Perhaps if he had been more attentive to his union duties instead of helping Millie's family, he'd have the number of witnesses Mr. Crane expected.

What was more important? He loved his work and the notion he participated in making factories safer for generations of workers to come, but he also loved Millie.

I do love her. Had he known before this moment? If he was sincere in his love for her, why had he ended the argument by telling her they had no future together? Would he allow his wounded pride to keep him from a chance at happiness?

Abe had to show her how much he cared, even if it compromised his job. He'd locate Yuri for Millie's sake and not concern himself with finding people to testify.

The illumination of a kerosene lantern caught his eye.

Someone was in Yuri's tenement.

■ ■ ■ ■

Millie was determined to cut the fabric for the second hat before bedtime. She helped Babi clear the kitchen table while Father read to Paul and Rose helped Celia write the letters of her name. Millie retrieved her sewing basket and lifted the luminous green satin from atop the blue and yellow yardage.

Don't think about Abe. Tears pooled in the corners of her eyes. She positioned herself with her back to the family and surrendered her worries to God. She cleared her mind of Abe and Nathan and Father and inhaled and exhaled to the methodical in and out of the needle through fabric.

Warmth radiated throughout her body as inspiration enveloped her. She'd use the blue and yellow satin to make two more hats to show to her buyer when they met on Saturday morning. Three hats in less than three days, but she'd stay up all night, if needed, to finish them. Lifting her eyes to the heavens, Millie thanked God for giving her the ability to sew and the creativity to design hats.

She hummed her mother's favorite hymn as the scissors sliced through the green

309

fabric, barely aware her family was still in the same room.

"Mildred, I hope you see now what your association with the union has yielded," Father barked at her. "No employment."

She chose neither to respond nor to allow Father to dissuade her from her vision.

"Is there meat for tomorrow?" Father asked.

Millie looked up from her project. "I will buy some after breakfast."

"Won't you be seeking employment?"

"No." She kept her voice steady. "I'll be sewing hats to sell."

"May I remind you that if we don't have meat for Paul every day until he's fully recovered, you'll deliver your Babi to the poorhouse and Celia to the orphanage?"

Millie held his gaze. "I don't recall agreeing to that solution. Rose and I are aware of the need to provide for the family. It's our concern, not yours."

Without a word, Rose picked up a needle and stitched two sections of the green fabric together. Babi removed her apron and followed Rose's lead. Even little Celia threaded her own needle and stitched a straight seam.

Father harrumphed. "Mark my words, nothing good will come of fooling yourselves. You are not businesswomen."

"Perhaps we are not," Rose said as she approached Father and knelt at his knee. "But you and Mother always taught us to persevere."

He opened his mouth, then clamped his jaw shut.

"Shall I make you a cup of tea before you retire?" Rose asked.

"No. I'm ready for my nightclothes."

Relieved Rose had calmed their father, Millie assisted her sister in lifting him into his bed. "Good night, Father."

"Kerosene costs money. Shut down the lanterns and go to bed."

Millie understood Father's need to have the last word, but she chose to ignore his command. Hadn't she and Rose earned the money to buy the fuel? They'd burn the lanterns all night, if necessary, to complete the green hat.

On Saturday morning Millie packaged the completed hats — one sky blue decorated with peacock feathers and ribbon rosettes, one yellow cloche style with embroidered floral details, and the two mushroom-shaped green hats — and set out to meet with her buyers. She'd practiced how she'd ask the sisters for referrals and prayed she wouldn't lose her nerve when the time came.

She steadied herself then knocked on the door of the brown-stone. An elderly maid, dressed in a full-length black cotton dress and crisp white apron, opened the door and invited Millie into the formal sitting room where the two elegantly dressed sisters perched on a rose-colored settee. Millie paused. She'd never seen a room more luxuriously appointed. She adjusted the hat boxes she carried to disguise her own threadbare skirt.

"Come in," Hazel called. Her fingers flitted to the lace collar on her turquoise gown. "Violet, meet Millie. Millie, my sister, Violet."

"Well now." Violet smoothed the skirt of her pink taffeta dress. "Please sit, and let's see what you've brought."

Both women gasped when Millie pulled the green hats from the first box.

Violet held her hand over her chest. "Breathtaking. We will be the talk of the gala, won't we, Sister?"

"Yes, we most certainly will. The hats are gorgeous. Simply gorgeous."

"I'm so happy you like them," Millie said. She swallowed hard then held her head high and her shoulders back. She reached into the second box. "I brought two more styles to show you."

"Oh my." Hazel leaned closer. "They are both divine. Are they for sale?"

"Yes." Millie willed her body to quit trembling. "The price is a dollar more for the embroidered cloche."

"We'll take both, won't we, Sister?" Hazel caressed the peacock feather on the blue hat.

Had Millie heard correctly? She wanted to dance a jig, but she'd wait to celebrate with Rose, Babi, and little Celia.

A surge of confidence coursed through her. "Have you other friends interested in designer hats?"

"Oh yes." Violet clapped. "Our friends in the Women's Club would love to see your creations."

Hazel nodded. "Most certainly."

"May I bring a selection to your next gathering?" Millie asked.

"Oh my, that's a perfect idea." Hazel babbled on, "Do you take custom orders? Do you ever work with chiffon or silk?"

"Yes, I can take custom orders." Millie's palms were moist, but she maintained the voice of a woman conducting business. "My grandmother, sister, and I have worked with a variety of fabrics and embellishments."

Violet scanned a daybook. "Our next meeting is the eighteenth of May. Bring your hats and join us for lunch. We will promote you ahead of time."

"Thank you." Millie's mind tumbled with hat design ideas.

"This is not my business," Hazel said, "but do you have an inventory of supplies?"

Millie's voice wavered. "No. I started selling hats just this week."

The sisters looked at one another and stepped to the side for a whispered conversation. *What are they discussing? Have I presented myself as an amateur?*

Violet took paper and pencil from a desk and scribbled something. "We'd like to sponsor you by setting up an account at our dry goods store. Here is the address and a note to the proprietor to record all the supplies you require. You can pay the debt after you sell the hats. We will guarantee the account."

Millie tipped her head back for a moment and tried to compose herself. Despite her efforts, tears gathered in the corners of her eyes. "I . . . I don't know how to thank you."

"Pish posh." Hazel waved her hand in the air.

Millie dabbed at her tears. "How many

hats shall I bring to the meeting?"

"As many as you can."

Millie left the brownstone with more money in her pocket than she'd ever earned in one week. She went directly to the dry goods store with the letter from the sisters and charged a variety of satin, silk, chiffon, thread, grosgrain ribbon, embroidery thread, and ostrich and peacock feathers — enough for ten hats.

She bought food, including a big slab of beef, tobacco for Father, and kerosene for the lanterns. With her arms full of parcels and money left in her pocket, she rode the bus home, determined to convince Father she knew how to run a business.

Once inside the tenement, she set all her packages on the table before sharing her good news with Babi. "The buyers paid top dollar for all four hats."

"How wonderful," Babi said as she hugged Millie. "I'm so proud of you. Your mother would be proud too."

"There's more." She bounced from one foot to the other. "I asked if they knew other women who would like to see our hats, and they invited me to bring as many as possible to the next gathering of their Women's Club."

"The Women's Club?" Babi hugged her again. "Rose will be thrilled. This calls for a celebration."

"I'll put a roast in the oven with potatoes and carrots. Shall I make apple dumplings?" Millie asked.

Father rolled into the room with Paul and Celia at his side. His gaze darted to the parcels on the table and settled on Millie. "What have we here?"

"I wanna see." Celia climbed on a chair and peeked into one of the parcels.

"Celia, why don't you ask Babi to take you and Paul for ice cream while I speak with Father?" Millie passed some coins to Babi, waited for the trio to leave, then silently unpacked her purchases and laid them on the table.

She rocked back on her heels. "Come look, Father."

"I can see." He made no movement to roll his chair closer.

"Proceeds from four hats paid for all of this." She tossed her head back and swept her arm across the bounty on the table. "I know how to make and sell hats. If I sell three hats each week, I'll earn more money than going to work in a factory. Three hats, Father. With help from Babi, Rose, and Celia, we can produce much more."

He spun his chair around. Were his shoulders slouched? Had she become an obstinate brat with no regard for her father's feelings?

Millie knelt at his side, offered him the tobacco, and softened her tone. "I arranged to sell hats at the Women's Club meeting in two weeks. I can run a business and I can take care of our family. Babi and Celia cannot be sent away."

He turned the plug of tobacco over in his hands while tears welled in his eyes. "I never meant for you to take care of the family. That's my responsibility."

Her cheeks burned. She dropped her chin to her chest. "I appreciate your need to take care of us, Father, but until you're able —"

He balled up his fists and jabbed at the casts on his lifeless legs. "I was supposed to be successful in this country. Promised my father on his deathbed I'd make something of the Pulnik name in America. Why do you think I spend so much time teaching Paul? I've failed, and he's the only one who will carry on the family name. If Paul succeeds, then I've kept my promise to my father."

Millie remembered Grandfather Pulnik as a tyrant — always demanding something and leaving guilt in his wake. "What does the name matter? Your blood courses through the veins of your daughters, and our successes can also be attributed to you."

"Perhaps you're right."

"Father." Millie held his hands in hers. "Celia needs to know you love her as much as you do Paul. She is devastated by Mother's death."

"That's just it. Every time I look at you girls, I see your mother. You all have her eyes. Most days, it is more than I can bear."

How could she have discounted the effect of Mother's death on Father? "Then I pray you will one day be able to look at us and find comfort rather than despair."

She attempted to release his hands, but he clutched her fingers.

"If they'd hired me at the university, I could have provided for all of us, but they wouldn't even read my curriculum vitae. They tore it up right in front of my face and said they had no need for foreigners on the faculty."

Millie fumbled for the right words. "I'm so sorry. I didn't know."

"If I'd been more persistent, I might have been able to teach elsewhere, and you and your mother wouldn't have been working in the factory when it caught fire." He ignored the tears that dampened his cheeks. "I blame myself for your mother's death."

"Oh Father." She laid her head in his lap as she'd done when they lived in Poland. "Please don't blame yourself. The real culprits are the factory owners who place profits above the health and welfare of their workers."

He wiped his eyes with his sleeve.

"That's why I agreed to help the union." A lump formed in Millie's throat. "We need to fight for workers' safety so there are no more fires like the one that claimed Mother."

"I wish there was something I could do." He shook his head. "I'm useless in this chair."

Millie kissed his forehead. "How would you like to help with our millinery business?"

"I'll leave the sewing to women."

"You're good with numbers, Father. Would you assist me in recording sales and expenditures?"

His shoulders straightened. "I'll need a record book."

"I'll purchase one tomorrow. And Father, I propose we discuss, as a family, how to allocate the money we earn from our hat sales." She retrieved the remainder of the cash and held it out. "What do you think we should do with these funds?"

She hadn't seen a spark in her father's eyes since the day the twins were born.

"We should replenish the savings for the millinery shop."

The plunk of coins inside the tea tin sounded like hope restored.

When Babi and the twins returned to the tenement, Babi waved a copy of the weekly newspaper at her. "There's an article about Mr. Berg's factory. The fire marshal chained the doors after receiving an anonymous tip that he should inspect the building. The union denies making that call. Berg is scheduled to appear before a judge on the eleventh of May."

Millie sank into a chair. "Then Abe told me the truth. He wouldn't necessarily have known about the closure."

Had she dissolved any future with Abe by not trusting him? Should she apologize for her mistrust or accept that she seemed incapable of maintaining a relationship with a suitor?

Millie had to do more than apologize to Abe. She'd help him by showing up at the courthouse to testify, and she'd bring as many other workers with her as she could. They'd face Mr. Berg together.

■ ■ ■ ■

Abe arrived at the office early on the eleventh of May and informed Sam and Mr. Crane he'd meet them at the courthouse with his witnesses, even though Yuri was the only confirmation he had. If, by some miracle, Millie *did* decide to testify, he'd still have just two of the five witnesses Mr. Crane expected.

He looked around the office and prayed he'd still have his job tomorrow. He'd spent most of his time the past week looking for Yuri instead of pursuing other witnesses to testify against Mr. Berg, but he'd finally found her the night before and knew she was safe. Hungry and exhausted, but safe. Even at the risk of losing his job, it would be worth it if Millie viewed the act as a token of his affection.

He straightened his tie, grabbed his hat, and left to pick up Yuri.

The young girl stood on the sidewalk outside her tenement building, wrapped in the shawl Millie had given her.

Abe opened the front passenger door and bid her good morning.

She leaned in, her gaze sweeping the vehicle. "Where's Millie?"

"I've not spoken to her in several days. I'm not sure she plans to testify."

Yuri bit at her lower lip and bowed her head. "She promised to be by my side."

"I know Millie meant to be with you. It's just that —"

"I don't know if I can do this without her."

"Would you be willing to go to the courthouse and then decide if you want to testify? I will make sure you see Millie today. You have my word."

The girl hesitated for several seconds before she slid into the car.

Ten minutes later, Abe parked near the back entrance of the courthouse. When he and Yuri rounded the corner to the front of the building, several people stood on the limestone steps.

"Millie!" Yuri shouted as she ran toward her.

Millie opened her arms to the girl and mouthed a thank-you in Abe's direction.

He joined them at the entrance. Millie reached for his hand and squeezed it, but before they exchanged any words, she pointed. "There's Mr. Berg."

Abe looked over his shoulder. Mr. Berg, flanked by men Abe recognized as notorious lawyers for the garment factory bosses, bounded up the steps.

Words were no longer necessary. They linked arms with the others to block the entrance.

Berg's entourage stopped in front of them. "Out of our way or we'll have you arrested," one of the lawyers demanded.

"Not until Mr. Berg admits he compromised the safety of his workers," Millie said.

"You." Mr. Berg pointed his finger in her face. "I should've known. You little snitch."

"She's not the only one," a man near Millie said. "We all saw the violations, and we're all here to say so."

"Say it." Abe glared at Mr. Berg.

"Have you told your lawyers about the fire you started with your cigar ashes?" Millie asked, her voice strong and sure.

"Have you?" Abe repeated.

Mr. Berg lunged at him.

Abe jerked his head and stumbled backward. Millie held firm, preventing his fall.

Berg's lawyers pulled Mr. Berg back and held him, but he managed to thrust out his chest. "You'll see who triumphs in this hearing."

The lawyers kept their grip on Berg and urged him toward a side door.

As soon as Berg's group disappeared around the corner of the building, Yuri and Millie hugged again and wiped tears from their faces.

"Where *were* you?" Millie asked.

"Grandfather fell. I took him to the infirmary and stayed with him until yesterday when he was released into my care."

"Abe?" Millie asked.

"I waited outside her tenement. Three nights ago, I saw a lantern light, so I knocked on the door, but no one answered."

"I was afraid to answer the door in the middle of the night," Yuri said. "I thought Mr. Berg discovered I made the call to the fire marshal and sent someone to harm me."

"You?" Abe and Millie asked in unison.

Yuri nodded. "When I told my grandfather about the locked fire escape doors and how Mr. Berg accused me of stealing, he insisted I call."

Millie glanced at Abe with eyes that begged his forgiveness.

His heart full, Abe continued, "I finally intercepted her last night before she entered her tenement."

"This means so much to me," Millie whispered.

"And it means a lot to me," Abe answered, then addressed the whole group. "Thank you all for coming and not giving up on the union's purpose."

"We had given up," a woman heavy with

child exclaimed. "My husband and I blamed Millie for the factory closing. When we read the announcement in the newspaper that the fire marshal closed the factory, we knew we had to do something for the next generation." She patted her belly. "Millie located us, and we were ready to testify. My sister, who worked for Mr. Berg last year, asked to testify against him too."

Millie and the woman regarded one another. "Fortunately," Millie said, "I remembered their last name from the time cards, and I'd heard they lived within two blocks of me. I went to every building and asked if anyone knew them."

Abe nodded. "Shall we go inside?"

The witnesses entered the hearing en masse — Millie flanked by Yuri on one side and Abe on the other.

Mr. Crane took a seat and looked down the row of witnesses. His lips moved as he counted to five. "Well done, Skala."

Abe beamed. Thanks to Millie, he would not lose his job.

One after another, the witnesses answered questions about the locked fire escape doors, the fire caused by Mr. Berg's cigar ashes, the penalties for extra privy breaks, and the sprinkler system not connected to a water source.

Mr. Berg could no longer deny the allegations.

The judge indicted him on three counts of malicious endangerment and told Mr. Berg he could not conduct any business in the garment industry until after his fate was decided at trial.

Abe jumped to his feet and cheered. Millie cheered right beside him.

CHAPTER 10

Millie sat in her tenement, needle in hand, and shared the events of the morning with Babi and Father. She'd wanted to spend more time with Yuri and Abe, but Yuri wanted to go home to attend to her grandfather and Abe had work obligations. He promised to bring Yuri to see her that evening.

She kept busy by sewing and relied on the familiar push and pull of the needle to calm her. Would Abe forgive her for mistrusting him? Every image of the future she imagined included Abe at her side.

She marveled at her family. Babi was teaching Celia and Paul how to make a hearty stew with chunks of beef and fresh vegetables, and Father was recording expenses for the hat business in his new ledger. Only Rose was absent.

"How many hats would we need to sew in a week to make more money than Rose earns at the factory?" Millie asked.

Father took a minute and tapped the pencil against his head. "Just two of the embroidered cloche."

"What do you think?"

Father straightened his shoulders and held his chin high. "I propose Rose quit her job and sew hats."

"And I agree."

Abe whistled as he approached Mrs. Dunn's boardinghouse. The events of the day had gone better than expected. An indictment against Mr. Berg, a vote of confidence from Mr. Crane, and a pleasant conversation with Millie. After supper he'd see her again. He prayed she'd forgive him and agree to resume their courtship. He could no longer fathom life without her.

He freshened up in the hall bathroom. His father's booming voice carried down the hallway, but Abe could only distinguish a few words — deal, lifetime, double your money. He squeezed his eyes shut. Had he heard correctly? Was his father trying to con the other boarders?

He rushed to the dining room.

Upon his entrance, his father said, "Well, we can discuss this another time."

His father greeted him and changed the

subject to the New York Giants and how he'd met Red Ames and how the World Series pitcher autographed a baseball as a gift for Abe.

The youngest boarder in the bunch, a pasty-faced delivery boy, turned to him. "Can I see it?"

Abe stared at his father. What baseball? He had never even heard the story before. "I don't have it. I guess my father forgot to give it to me."

Mrs. Dunn entered the dining room carrying a shepherd's pie and apologized for the delay in supper.

"That's okay," the pasty-faced kid said. "Abe's father was telling us how he can double our money by investing in a bridge-building company."

Abe's father brushed the kid's comment aside. "Wouldn't that be something to double our money? I'm sorry you misunderstood, young man. I meant to say I have a friend in upstate New York who *claims* he can double our money."

"Oh," the kid replied. "Then tell Mrs. Dunn about the signed baseball from Red Ames. Where is it?"

Abe threw down his napkin and excused himself from the table. He'd heard enough of his father's lies. Had he also lied about being sick? About not having long to live? Abe needed to get him out of Mrs. Dunn's home before he conned anyone here.

He entered his room and fell to his knees. *Lord, help me do the right thing.*

Thirty minutes later, his father entered the room. "You could've covered for your old man. Said you lost the baseball. Make me look good to the others."

Abe gave his head a quick shake then repeated, "Make you look good? Now how would I do that? By following your lead and lying?"

"I'm just saying, before you entered the room, I had the kid's respect. Nice to have someone look up to you."

Anger swirled in Abe's gut. "Respect is earned."

"We're really not so different, you and I." His father lowered himself to sit on the edge of the bed. "You con people into joining the union. Make promises you can't keep. Lies can get us what we want."

"And lies can destroy us." Abe sank into a chair, too exhausted to stand. "Tell me the truth. Are you dying?"

"We're all dying, Son."

With every sound from the hallway, Millie flew to the door. She'd expected Abe and

Yuri to be there by now. She was eager to introduce Yuri to her family and even more eager to speak privately with Abe.

Rose giggled when Millie jumped for the fifth time since they'd washed and dried the supper dishes. "You're as nervous as a young bride."

Millie's cheeks warmed. A bride? *I hope the opportunity presents itself.*

The tap at the door brought her back to her feet. Millie rushed to greet their guests. She embraced Yuri and looked at Abe, her gaze lingering on his face.

Babi insisted they sit at the table and eat sweet baking-powder biscuits topped with fresh strawberries and rich, thick cream — a delicacy Father recommended they serve their guests.

Father rolled his wheelchair up to the table, welcomed Yuri to their home, greeted Abe, and conversed with him as though they were lifelong friends.

Celia waited until Abe finished dessert and then showed him two pieces of fabric she had stitched together. Paul handed him an atlas and pointed to several cities in Poland and named them.

Rose whisked Yuri to the corner of the living area to show her the sketch of her next embroidery pattern for an aqua-blue silk hat trimmed in beige chiffon. Yuri asked Rose to show her how to embroider, and the two sat in the corner, heads together, whispering, smiling, and stitching.

Babi sat down beside Millie.

The tableau pleased her. Her family had not been torn apart.

This is what it means to be part of a family.

Abe had never heard Mr. Pulnik speak so enthusiastically. He told Abe how Millie had sold two hats, then that order doubled, *and* she'd arranged for a hat sale at the prestigious Women's Club. "I'm the accountant. We all have our jobs. Paul threads the needles, Celia bastes the straight seams, their Babi cuts the pattern pieces and sews, and Mildred and Rose design and sew. I project we'll soon be able to move into a larger tenement that affords a work area, perhaps even buy a sewing machine." He raised an eyebrow. "Did Mildred tell you Rose agreed to quit her factory job to help with the millinery business?"

Abe glanced at Millie. "We haven't had much opportunity to speak."

"Mildred may like to take a walk on this grand evening." Father slapped him on the back. "I wonder, would you be so kind as to escort her?"

Abe offered Millie his arm. She looped her arm through his and offered him an encouraging smile.

They walked out of the tenement and onto the cobblestone sidewalk.

"Thank you again for testifying and bringing more witnesses," Abe said. "What you did on the steps of the courthouse was very brave."

"Thank you for your dedication to the cause."

They walked in silence for several minutes. "Millie." Abe cleared his throat. "I hope you can forgive me for walking away from you and saying there was no future for us. It was impulsive of me. I will forever regret it."

"I also have regrets. I hope you don't think it forward of me," Millie said, "but I pray you'll forgive me and offer to court me again. That is, if you're interested."

He stopped walking then turned to face her.

She touched his cheek. He clasped her hand and kissed the tips of her fingers, one by one.

"I'm more than interested."

A sliver of moonlight stretched across Abe's bedroom, enough for him to see his father sleeping in his bed. Not that he cared. He changed into his nightclothes and eased onto the pallet in the corner of his room. Sleep evaded him. His mind, abuzz with the possibility of a future with Millie, kept his eyes wide open.

How had he been so fortunate? He had a job he was proud to do, a woman he loved, and a family that embraced him.

He murmured prayers of gratitude until sleep finally claimed him.

Abe's bedroom door creaked. He raised his head. His father was not in the bed. The earthy aroma of morning coffee had likely drawn him to the kitchen.

Abe stretched and anticipated his day. He and Sam would meet with Mr. Crane this morning to discuss ways to keep up the momentum of identifying garment factory bosses who ignored safety regulations. Later, he'd join Millie's family for supper and take Millie to an ice cream parlor. Last evening he'd learned her favorite dessert was vanilla ice cream, her favorite color sky blue, and most importantly, she'd forgiven him and asked him to court her.

He dressed in brown linen trousers and a freshly pressed beige shirt. He reached for his pocket watch from his dresser. In its place was a note scrawled on a scrap of paper.

Abraham,
    I can't stay where I can't make money, so I've moved on. I borrowed your pocket watch, a few dollars from your wallet, and a blanket. I will repay you when I can.

Your Father

Abe opened his wallet, peered at the empty space where his spending cash had been, and confirmed without question what he now knew to be true.

He wasn't at all like his thieving father.

Summer was a flurry of designing custom-made hats for high society ladies to wear to their parties. Wide-brimmed styles reigned as New York City experienced a heatwave that kept fashionable ladies fanning themselves and drinking cold lemonade. By the end of the season, Mother's tin overflowed.

Father graduated from his wheelchair to a cane and took a walk with the twins every day. Before bedtime, he read to them from Frances Hodgson Burnett's *The Secret Garden* or a tale from *Aesop's Fables,* then tucked them in, kissed their cheeks, and told them both how much he loved them. Babi hummed her way through the day, and Millie and Abe spent most evenings together. Rose and Yuri were best of friends and often sat with their heads together giggling and embroidering. None of the young women worked in factories. The millinery business provided more money than they'd ever made.

The first Sunday in September, Abe borrowed the bread truck and drove Millie's whole family to church. The men were in especially good spirits. During the fellowship hour, Abe and Father talked with hands cupped over their mouths and mischief dancing in their eyes. Millie delighted in the camaraderie between them.

On the drive home, Abe parked the truck in front of a two-story redbrick building with a large plate-glass window next to the entrance door, presumably a former mercantile. Abe and Father quirked their brows and beamed as they assembled the family on the sidewalk.

Abe asked Father, "Ready?"

Father pulled a key from his trouser pocket and presented it to Millie.

Abe opened the back door of the bread truck and unveiled a simple wooden sign, PULNIKS' MILLINERY.

Millie tilted her head and stared first at the key and then the sign.

Abe hustled her to the door and urged her to try the key. Inside the shop, Millie admired the rich maple wood of the display cases along one wall. Rose stood behind the sales counter that ran partway down the middle of the room, and Babi ran her hands over the worktables on the back wall. A cloth-covered object sat on one of the back tables. Father asked Celia to pull off the cloth to expose the surprise.

Eyes wide, the women gathered around an electric sewing machine.

A full minute passed before Millie stammered, "Oh Father . . . Abe . . . how?"

Father stood tall. "Abe and I pooled our resources and rented this building for your business."

"And the rest of the building?" Babi asked.

"Our quarters. Come with me." Father led them through a storage room, and behind that to a tenement with two bedrooms, a large kitchen, an indoor privy with a bathtub, and a parlor.

"We have electricity and running water." Father knocked on a large table in the kitchen area. "Sewing and business in the morning and lessons at this table after lunch. It's time to teach Celia and Paul how

337

to read and do arithmetic. Rose can take her lessons in the evening, and Yuri asked me to teach her to read and write."

"I don't know what to say." Millie placed her palm over her heart. "You've considered every detail."

Abe regarded Millie and added, "Upstairs is a smaller apartment where I will live."

They toured the whole of it together, one big family. Afterward, they stood in a circle in their new shop while Father led a prayer of gratitude. God had answered Millie's prayers and restored her faith.

On the drive home, the women and little Celia talked about how to prepare their new store for a grand opening.

Abe held Millie back while her family entered the Blanch Building. He took her hand and knelt on one knee. "Mildred Pulnik, your father gave permission for us to marry. Will you trust me to love and care for you for as long as I live?"

She knelt beside him, her heart full, while joyous tears fell to the cobblestone. Millie held Abe's hands in hers, locked her gaze on his, and kissed one palm, then the other.

"Abraham Skala, my heart is forever in your hands."

ABOUT THE AUTHOR

Jacquolyn McMurray writes both contemporary and historical romance and has published two novella-length romances. She and her husband live on a macadamia-nut farm on the island of Hawai'i where they feed a clowder of cats and a flock of hodgepodge chickens. Jacquolyn is a member of the Romance Writers of America, the Greater Seattle Romance Writers, and American Christian Fiction Writers. When she's not writing, Jacquolyn enjoys spending time with her family, reading, sewing, and solving crossword puzzles. In her past life, she was an elementary school teacher. Keep connected with Jacquolyn at www.jacquolynmcmurray.com.

■ ■ ■ ■

A Language
of Love

BY KIMBERLEY WOODHOUSE

■ ■ ■ ■

To my precious friend, prayer partner, and encourager — Jeni Koch. I could never adequately tell you how much you mean to me, but this will hopefully give you a little piece of my heart.

Thank you for your friendship and support, your love and prayers, and all the laughter, hugs, and smiles. I'm looking forward to decades more with you.

Give Gary a hug from his favorite bell-ringing ding-a-ling, and tell him how much I love it that he reads my books too.

Love you dearly,
Kimberley

Note to the Reader:

What an exciting time in our history to write about — 1911. For this story, I used some real people, but since this is a work of fiction, their personalities are contrived in my imagination.

It is important to note that Alva Vanderbilt Belmont was a huge supporter of the suffragette movement and extremely wealthy. Adding this historical figure to *A Language of Love* along with Carrie Astor Wilson — great-granddaughter of America's first millionaire, John Jacob Astor — was so much fun and I think an interesting addition to this story.

While the New York Giants were a real team in the National League in 1911, our hero is not real. He's completely fictional. The team played at the Polo Grounds (III) in Coogan's Hollow, which actually did burn down on April 14, 1911, and was rebuilt — Polo Grounds IV — by June 28 of that same year. (Today, the Polo Grounds Towers stand on the location with a plaque on the property marking approximately where home plate was originally located.)

Some of my favorite attire is from this Edwardian era. The "big hat" time period is actually my favorite and so I truly enjoyed having Jeni be a designer and milliner.

What was even more fun was researching linguistics and accents for this story since my heroine is Irish and my hero is from Brooklyn. Because it's a novella, there's not a lot of room to get to show you the uniqueness and fun of these two characters' speech, but prayerfully, you get a snippet and see what a challenge it would be to try to change your "accent."

Let's head back to 1911 in *A Language of Love.*

Enjoy the journey,
Kimberley Woodhouse

CHAPTER 1

Manhattan, New York
Monday, February 27, 1911
"Yer gonna do *what,* lass?" Auntie Bridget's voice screeched into an upper octave only a soprano could manage.

Jeni O'Brien felt the heat in her face grow as her ire built. Placing her hands on her hips, she took a deep breath. "Exactly what I said, Auntie Brig. I'm gonna take linguistics lessons." She turned toward the mirror and patted her hair before putting her latest creation — an incredible design if she did say so herself — in place and securing it with a pin. She wanted to look her best for today. Nothing like a new hat to make a woman feel beautiful.

"Why on earth do ya need linguistics lessons? Ya speak jest fine."

"Because we're not in Ireland anymore. Because I'm tired of NINA. The *No Irish Need Apply* groups are still around. They're condescendin', ridiculin' us just because of how we speak. And frankly, I'm tired of everyone lookin' at me when I speak and peerin' down their noses at me because I'm Irish. I'm not a lesser person just because I speak differently."

"But ya *are* Irish. And ya should be proud of it." Auntie Bridget's Irish brogue thickened. On purpose, no doubt. "Come here to me, you'll be regrettin' this for sure."

"Oh stop, Aunt Brig. No bodge tryin' to convince me otherwise. I'm just as proud of my heritage as you are —"

"No, yer not. I can't believe ya would do this to yerself. And to me. Ye are Irish and yer heritage is everything." Her aunt took a deep breath. "All this will do is lead ya down a rotten path. That'll lead to conversations with non-Irish men. Non-Irish people of all sorts. And all they will want is for you to become like them. That's not why we came to America. We came to be free. To be who we are."

"That's exactly what I'm doin', can't ya see that?" Softening her tone, Jeni knew the only way to convince her aunt was to plead with her Irish practicality rather than get into one of their heated arguments. "By workin' on my speech, I'll have even *more* of a chance to own me own shop one day.

How many times have you told me that ya hate the fact I create the best hats for all the wealthiest of New York City and yet absolutely no one knows my name? Mr. Crawford keeps me in the back all the time. Another point on which yer disdain has been made clear. But why does it happen? Because I'm Irish. I would think you would want me to succeed, rather than be hidden in the back like a slave." So much for keeping her temper at bay. Her voice had risen in volume the more she talked and brought up all of her aunt's points. Which would probably work against her.

"I don't think yer being treated like a slave. For heaven's sake, yer paid more than triple of all the other girls, ain't ya? Isn't that special treatment enough?" Auntie Bridget crossed her arms over her chest and stomped her foot. "The fact of the matter is yer doin' this so people won't *know* that yer Irish. *Not* that ya want them to know yer heritage. Yer ashamed and want to become American. I'll have none of that. I'm ashamed of ya. Yer a good Irish lass, why do you want anythin' more than that?" The look on her face told Jeni all she needed to know.

The scolding from Aunt Bridget just about did her in. If she wasn't careful, words could be said that neither of them could take back. Jeni kept a firm tone as anger bubbled inside her at an alarming rate. All this time, she'd been too timid to move forward. Little did her fiery aunt know that the very words she used to try to change her niece's mind only proved to give Jeni the stubborn bravery she needed to move ahead with her plan. "Auntie Brig, you can't talk me out of this." She lifted her shoulders. "I pay all of our bills. I pay for our housing. I pay for our food. You should respect the decision that I'm making. It's the best thing for us." She put on her gloves and grabbed her purse. "Now, if you'll excuse me."

"We are not finished, lass. Yer parents left ya in my care, and I won't stand for —"

Jeni walked out and closed the door on her aunt's words. "Aye, we are." Whispering to the wood that separated them, she turned and walked down the hall. She'd never done anything quite so callous, even though they'd had plenty of knock-down drag-out arguments over the years. Before they'd come to America, they'd even had a couple of donnybrooks in the street outside their home. Two stubborn Irish women didn't make for congenial conversation when they both had ideas of their own. Especially as Jeni became an adult and started to earn enough money for them to live on. As soon as she felt like she should have an opinion, Auntie Bridget had tried to make sure that she remembered who was the elder and who was in charge.

As Jeni walked to the professor's office, she looked around at the streets and shops of New York City. She loved it here.

Never would she tell her aunt this, but she had no desire to return to Ireland. Too much heartache remained there, and she had no reason to go back to her homeland, even though it was a beautiful country. Auntie Bridget often talked of returning one day. When things were better. But Jeni held no such desire.

For years she'd worked her way up in millinery. In fact, it was true, the owner of the shop where she worked was known as the best milliner in the city — all because of Jeni's designs. He paid her a pretty penny because he knew that if he lost her to another shop, he'd lose the majority of his business. But so far she hadn't had the gumption to do anything more than threaten to leave. So he just raised her pay and she stayed hidden in the back.

Something that needed to change. And soon.

It wasn't that she wasn't grateful. She was.

But what she lacked was confidence. If she could simply get rid of her strong Irish accent, she could be accepted among society as a valuable contributor. Despite her aunt's opinion, Jeni truly was proud of her heritage. Even though attitudes weren't as intense now against the Irish as they'd been at the turn of the century and decades prior, there was still discrimination — especially among some of the elite. The very people who were her clientele. So what was the problem with her improving herself so that she could be a respected business owner? Couldn't God honor that desire?

Her dream was to one day own her very own shop and serve the wealthiest women in New York City. The latter of which she already did — not that any of her clients knew it. Jeni wanted to do it out in full view. Not hidden behind the curtain.

Deep down, she longed to be a part of them one day. Oh, she didn't have to be extraordinarily rich, but she would like to at least be in their social circles. They carried themselves differently. Had money to help the poor, and were well respected.

Some of the ladies she'd seen on the streets had been people she desperately wanted to speak to. After all, they were wearing her hats. But it hadn't been her place. At least not yet. She'd have to earn it.

Why was class such a big deal anyway? Why did it matter the color of someone's skin or the color of their hair, the land of their birth, the accent of their speech, or how much money they had? This was supposed to be the land of the free and the home of the brave. A place where all men were equal.

If only that were true for women.

And women who were Irish.

As she entered the building that housed the professor's office, she took a deep breath. This would be a lot of hard work, but it was time. Maybe it took Auntie Bridget's arguing this morning to get Jeni's ire up enough that she'd have the gumption to follow through with her dream. Whatever it was, she was ready.

God, help me to do my best and to honor You.

Knocking on the door, she put what she hoped was a confident smile on her face. Her dress was of the highest fashion, and of course so was her hat. If she could simply impress the professor and get through this first lesson. Everything would be wonderful. She hoped. One step at a time. That's what Da used to always say.

Even though this first step was a doozy, it was one she needed to take. And then after that, maybe each step would be a little easier. Each step, that was, that didn't include dealing with Aunt Bridget, but that couldn't be helped. She'd just have to deal with her later. Much later.

Several seconds passed and only served to increase the racing of her heart. What on earth could be taking so long? She looked in her purse to make sure she'd read the number on the paper correctly. Sure enough, the door number matched. Checking the watch pinned to her shirtwaist, she noted she was a minute or two early, but wasn't that proper etiquette?

The door swung open, and the tall, blond-haired man coming through the doorway looked a bit stunned. A smile quickly filled his face, which made his blue eyes shine. "You don't have ta knock on the door. Just go on in and sit in the waitin' area." His thick Brooklyn accent came through as he pointed behind him and then tipped his hat at her.

"Um, well, thank you." He allowed her entrance, and she sent him a small smile. All this time, she must have looked so silly, standing outside the door, knocking.

"I made the same mistake my first time."

He tipped his hat again and hesitated for a moment like he was about to say something else and then turned and walked away.

"Thank you," she called after him. Whoever he was, at least he hadn't laughed at her or sneered when he'd heard her accent. Perhaps this was going to be a good day after all.

CHAPTER 2

Thursday, March 2, 1911

Philip March sat in the waiting area of Professor Montgomery's Linguistics School, his right knee bouncing. When the New York Giants' manager told him to take linguistics lessons, Philip had laughed at him. Until he realized the man was serious. What was wrong with the way he talked? Yeah, his accent was thick, but shoot, he'd grown up on the streets in Brooklyn as a newsboy and bootblack. In fact, he'd never even had a last name until his manager gave him one. This was his life. His history.

He'd always been proud of the way he talked. Of his rags to riches story. People loved it. At least . . . he thought they did.

But apparently, since he was one of the world's best baseball players, his adoring fans wanted to hear more from him. As he signed hundreds upon hundreds of trading cards and talked to fans all over the country,

remarks rolled in that they couldn't understand him. And now? The owners and
management had come up with some hare-
brained idea that he needed to do live
speaking to the crowds. Because that was
what the fans wanted. Which meant speech
lessons for him. On a daily basis.

The first two days with the professor had
been brutal. Not that the man was a bad
guy. But Philip was a baseball player. And a
really good one at that. Why on earth did he
need to waste his time on "rounding out his
vowels" or "brightening his tone"?

It didn't make sense. That is, until he met
her.

Inspiration struck.

For more than a week, he'd been mulling
over the conversation he wanted to have
with the professor. And it all had to do with
the dark-haired beauty he'd seen every day
for the past nine days.

The first time they met, he'd opened the
door to find her ready to knock. Her cheeks
had bloomed pink when she realized she'd
been waiting for someone to come answer
the door. Exactly the same thing he'd done
his first time at the professor's. But each
morning after that, he'd looked forward to
seeing her as he left his lesson.

She hadn't let him down.

Every day she gave him a tiny smile as he exited and they greeted one another. She always sat in the same chair, prim and proper, with a massive hat atop her head. How women carried around the weight of such things, he had no clue, but it was the style today. And she wore it well.

Her voice had a beautiful Irish lilt to it. Sounded so musical and bright compared to all the brash and harsh Brooklyn accents he'd heard his entire life. It made him smile just to think about it. Maybe learning how to speak right wasn't such a dumb idea after all.

Since the only thing he'd learned was her name — Jeni O'Brien — and all they could do was smile and nod at each other between their early morning lessons, the past few days he'd concocted an idea that he hoped Professor Montgomery would agree with. While it didn't appear that Miss O'Brien was in need of help financially, he hoped his offer would entice her.

"Philip!" Professor Montgomery called from the doorway of his office — the room they used for the torture he went through each day trying to learn how to add *r*'s to his vocabulary and "move his speech back." Whatever that meant. The older man rubbed his hands together. "Have you been

358

practicing?"

"Not as much as you would prob'ly like, but yeah, I'm tryin'."

"Pro*bab*ly."

"Sir?"

"The word is pro-bab-ly. Three syllables. Not two."

"Oh." Not that it mattered much to him, but his instructions were to listen to the highly esteemed professor so that he could speak to the masses — his adoring fans — before and after the games. Something the manager reminded him of daily. The sooner the better, they said. Which made Philip all the more anxious. So far, there hadn't been any real progress. But they wanted these special events for the fans to start in June. That didn't give him a whole lot of time to relearn how to speak. Or maybe it was unlearning the way he already spoke — which meant almost twenty years' worth of living on the streets before baseball made him famous. He shook his head. None of that mattered. "Sir, I'd like to discuss an idea I had."

"We really must get working on your lesson —"

"I understand, sir. This is about that, if you'll give me a second to explain?"

Professor Montgomery took a long breath

and leaned back in his chair. "All right. Let's hear your idea. But I doubt it will change my mind about my methods."

Philip held up a hand. "Your methods are just fine. I know I haven't made much progress . . . that's why I had this idea. I thought if I had a partner — that is, some-one else tryin' to learn how to speak all proper-like — that I might do better. Ya know, hear how they are tryin' to do it, and then I could try to do it too. I'm not just a dumb baseball player —"

The professor sat up straighter. "No one has called you dumb, Mr. March. You just haven't progressed. There's a difference. Your accent is thick and it might take some time . . ." The man let his words hang while he rubbed his chin. "Your idea has merit though, I must say. I've never taught two people at the same time. It's either one at a time or a group. I have another student who speaks very much as you do, but he only comes once a week." He stood and went to his schedule he kept open on his desk. "Perhaps I could speak —"

"Actually, sir, I had another partner in mind."

"Oh?"

"Yeah. The lady who comes after me. She comes every day, and she also likes early

360

mornin' appointments. If she's willin' to come a bit earlier, I would offer to pay for half of her tuition with you. Then we could work and learn from each other as well as from you."

"But she's Irish."

"So?" Was the man prejudiced? If so, Philip didn't want anything to do with him. He'd seen way too much of that in his life already.

Montgomery tilted his head as he appeared to think it through. "While you both tend to have forward speech patterns, the two accents are *entirely* different. It might pose great difficulty."

"I understand that. That's why I thought it would help. If I'm listenin' to someone who sounds just like me, how am I s'posed to know the difference? Miss O'Brien and I both have to learn how to talk right. And we're both comin' from different backgrounds. Maybe if we could hear each other's mistakes, it would help us to learn ourselves." The reasons he'd rehearsed over and over in his head didn't sound as convincing now.

The professor crossed his arms over his chest and paced. "That is precisely why the class model works so well, so I agree it has merit . . ." He turned on his heel and paced toward the window. "Actually, the more I think about it, the more I like the idea. But I'm not certain Miss O'Brien would have the time. Her job keeps her quite busy."

"Would ya mind askin' her?"

"Of course not. I wouldn't mind at all. In fact, at the end of your lesson today, I'll invite her in and we will discuss the parameters. Does that sound agreeable?"

"Yeah. Thank you, sir."

"Yes." The man lifted an eyebrow as he corrected Philip.

"Yes. I'm sorry. I should know that one."

"Now, about my fees —"

"I will pay for half of Miss O'Brien's regular fees. In addition to that, I'm willing to offer you double for my lessons — for the added work this might make for ya. Just so you know I'm serious about learnin'."

A large smile grew across the man's thin face. "Wonderful." He stuck out a hand. "I believe we have a deal."

Bridget O'Brien twisted her hands as she stood in front of the parlor window.

Cheeky lass, her Jeni. Her niece was getting too high and mighty. And while Bridget admitted that she enjoyed the fine things Jeni's salary could afford, it wouldn't do for her to allow her charge to be sucked into the dregs of non-Irish society.

Life had been entirely too hard back in Ireland, and things hadn't been much better in New York until Jeni started to become a rising star in the millinery business. Why couldn't she just be content to stay in the back?

Bridget shook her head. She should have never said anything to her niece about being acknowledged for her work and that her boss shouldn't hide her in the back. But Bridget had to admit that she'd gotten caught up in the money. She liked the fact that Jeni could earn more than the others because of her talent. Especially after all the years they'd lived in the squalor. All because they were Irish.

It was nice to be out of the slums.

But now she had a bigger problem. Jeni liked this new world in the city. Had a little too much liking for all the high-and-mighty clientele she served. It was one thing for her to demand better circumstances and pay because she deserved it, and another entirely to throw away her Irish heritage in order to do so.

Jeni had worked her magic with those enormous hats she loved to make. But it was all for naught if the lass didn't remember where she came from. Bridget realized she should've done a better job of instilling the pride of the Irish in her niece.

If Bridget could get her niece away from this godforsaken city, then maybe there was a chance to help her find a good Irish boy in a small town out west. Where there were other Irish people. Lots of them. Who wouldn't demand Jeni have linguistics lessons. A few of their neighbors had gone to Wisconsin. Maybe she should write a few letters.

Jeni would probably pitch a fit, but too bad. Bridget was the elder here. And good Irish girls always listened to their elders.

CHAPTER 3

Opening the door to Professor Montgomery's Linguistics School, Jeni took a deep breath. So far she hadn't felt like she'd made much progress. Other than remembering not to drop her *g*'s. Maybe that was something.

She smoothed her long blue skirt that matched her hat perfectly. As she looked up, she saw not only the nice gentleman — Philip — but Professor Montgomery watching her.

"Top o' the mornin' to ya." The normal Irish greeting slipped out before she could yank it back. "I mean, good morning, gentlemen."

"Good morning, Miss O'Brien." The professor turned sideways and motioned toward his office. "Would you join Mr. March and me for a moment to discuss an opportunity?"

Blinking rapidly, she looked from one man

to the other. "I'd be happy to." What was this about? While she enjoyed seeing Mr. March every morning, they hadn't spoken more than a few words to each other.

She entered the room ahead of the men and took her normal seat. Spine straight. Chin lifted.

Mr. March took the chair next to her, while the professor took his seat across from her.

Professor Montgomery clapped his hands together. "Let's not waste any time. Mr. March here is in need of a partner for his classes. I believe you two would be a good fit, and you both come daily for lessons. So here's my idea: If you wouldn't mind coming an hour earlier each day, I would offer you the chance to have your lessons for half the price, but twice the time. I think it would be beneficial to you both to hear and learn from one another."

Half the price? That would help her save even more for her own shop. Calculating the figures in her head, the thought made her smile. But a dozen questions flitted through her mind. "While your offer is very generous, I wouldn't want to be a hindrance to Mr. March's progress. I've struggled quite a bit with the assignments so far."

Mr. March chuckled next to her. "So I'm

not the only one."

Professor Montgomery cleared his throat. "You've only just begun. Please don't take that as any indication of your success or lack thereof."

Taking the moment to glance at Mr. March, she pondered the sacrifice of time it would take. Two hours each day was a lot. But she'd still arrive at the shop on time. So Mr. Crawford wouldn't have any reason to complain. But oh, how she dreaded telling Auntie Brig about it. There was certain to be another squabble over it. Maybe she could just leave before her aunt woke up? How long could she get away with that? A shiver raced up her spine.

Tired of cowing to everyone else's demands on her life, Jeni lifted her chin another smidge and smiled at each of the men. "I think it's a grand idea. The sooner we learn, the better, aye?"

"Then let's get started. I'd like us to do a trial run to make sure it's going to be helpful to you both." The professor stood and clasped his hands behind his back. "While the two of you differ in a great many speech patterns, I want you to examine how the other speaks and then listen to my examples of correct linguistics. So please, if you would, turn and face one another." He cleared his throat. "But first, let's make an agreement."

"Oh?" Philip gave her a look and then turned back to Professor Montgomery.

"Yes. I think it would be beneficial to you both to talk freely to one another in here. Speech is what we are working on, and the best way to do that is through conversation. And so, to put you at ease, let's agree that nothing discussed here is to leave this room."

Philip shrugged. "I can do that. But I don't want Miss O'Brien to be uncomfortable in any way." He turned to her. "I think we should just be honest and be ourselves. What do you think?"

She bit her lip for a moment. "I can agree to that."

"Good. Now turn to face each other."

Jeni set her handbag on the floor and turned to face Mr. March. His blue eyes seemed to dance with merriment as he turned toward her as well. He wouldn't laugh at her . . . would he? Especially after they'd just agreed to be honest and be themselves?

The professor began. "Now, Mr. March —"

"Let's get rid of the formal stuff. I'm Philip." He held out a hand to her.

Taking it, she gave it a gentle shake. "Jeni."

"Now that we've accomplished that, let's continue. Philip, I want you to tell Miss O'Brien — Jeni — about what you do and why you came for linguistics lessons." The professor looked at her. "Your job, Jeni, is to watch his mouth. Listen to the sounds of his words and see how he pronounces them."

Giving their teacher a nod, she looked back to Philip and specifically watched his mouth. She thought that would be easier than looking into his magnetic blue eyes, but for some reason, it wasn't.

"Well . . . I play baseball for the National League New York Giants. Last year I hit the most home runs, which made me famous according to management, so they think I need to start talkin' to the fans at special gatherings. And they want me to learn how to speak better. Some days I wonder why I ever agreed to this crazy idea. I'm from Brooklyn, and I don't think you can ever get rid of a Brooklyn accent." Philip shrugged his shoulders and laughed.

"Very good. Thank you, Philip. All right, Miss O'Brien, what did you hear?" The professor's brow was furrowed.

"That he's a baseball player from Brooklyn."

"Yes, that's true. But what did you hear in his voice? His words?"

Tilting her head, she tried to replay it. "Would you mind repeating it for me?"

"I'll do my best."

As Philip started again, it took a moment for her to focus on the sounds rather than the actual words. The fact that he was a baseball player — and a famous one at that — had given her quite the shock. But as she watched his mouth, she paid attention to *how* he spoke. "The corners of his mouth seem to be really forward as he speaks. Am I describing that correctly?"

"Very good observation."

She looked back at Philip and saw him smile. "Which makes his mouth a bit narrow? Is that a good description?"

"Yes. Very good. Go on."

"He doesn't pronounce *r*'s. At least not like I do. You've told me on several occasions that my *r*'s make an extra sound. Almost an extra syllable. Like *er*. Where his aren't there much at all. For instance, he said 'New Yahk' and 'staht' instead of start. Ever sounded like 'evah.' " Trying to imitate Philip's accent, she made herself laugh.

"Also great observation." Professor Montgomery looked back and forth between the two of them. "I think this is going to work well. Now, let's give Mr. March a chance. Miss O'Brien, why don't you tell Philip what you do and why you want linguistics lessons."

With a deep breath, she wondered what the baseball player would hear. "I am a milliner. That is, I make hats. And I'd like to own me own shop one day. Since there's still a good deal of people who look down on the Irish, I'm trying to get rid of the accent so people will see me for who I am. The best hat designer in all of New York."

"I can see that's the truth." Philip pointed to the creation on her head.

His words made her blush.

"All right, Philip, what did you observe?"

"That's tough, because I love the sound of her accent. It's . . . what would you say . . . brighter than mine? You've mentioned that my tones are dark. So that means hers are brighter. Right?"

"Yes, that would be an accurate assessment. Good job. Now, what else did you hear?"

As Philip's blue gaze studied her face, she couldn't pull her eyes away even though she wanted nothing more than to look down in her lap. But his scrutiny wasn't offensive in any way, and she found she couldn't wait to hear what else he said.

"I don't think I'm as good at observing as Jeni, but I did notice that the words that have a *th* in them sounded more like a *d* or a *t,* and the long *i* vowel — like when she said 'Irish' — sounded more like an 'oy' sound but a bit different."

"Very good. Now, Jeni, I want you to say the word *Irish* again."

"Irish." She lifted her brows.

"Now, Philip, say Irish the way you would pronounce it, and then say it like you heard Jeni say it."

Jeni looked over to her new lesson partner. He furrowed his brow. "I-rish. Oi-rish."

"Jeni, now it's your turn. Pronounce it the way you normally say it, and then try to say it the same way you heard from Philip."

As she did what the professor asked, she felt the difference in her mouth — and the sound to her ears was . . . odd.

"Good, good." The professor gave them a wide smile. "I believe this is going to work splendidly."

A rush of warmth filled her middle, and her stomach did a little flip. As Jeni looked at Philip, she agreed with the professor. Already she felt like she understood a bit more, so perhaps her practicing would make more sense now.

It also didn't hurt that her new learning

partner was a handsome, blond-haired, blue-eyed baseball player. The extra hour for lessons would be well worth it. Especially if she got to spend time with this interesting man every day.

CHAPTER 4

Friday, March 3, 1911

The sounds of bats making contact against baseballs echoed across the field. Philip turned toward the pitcher and set his stance so he could get some hitting practice in too.

The windup. Then the pitch.

Crack! The ball flew over the fence.

A few moments later, another pitch . . . *crack!*

"Hoo-ie, March! Look at 'em fly. Another home run." Coach Joe walked over and slapped him on the shoulder. "Think you can do three in a row?"

"Why not?" Philip smiled as he got back into position.

The ball whooshed toward him and he swung. *Crack!*

"World Series, here we come if you keep this up, kid." Coach Joe whistled at him and then walked over to the next player. "All right, boys, March has set the bar high.

Let's show everyone who the New York Giants really are!" The coach's voice resounded around the batters, and they cheered and hollered back.

After a few more solid hits to the outfield, Philip swung the bat around with one hand and then the other. He stretched out his neck and shoulders and went back to the batter's box. Twelve more pitches.

Twelve more over the fence.

He felt unstoppable.

A smile crept up his face as he thought about why. Yeah, he'd been the home run king this past year, but he'd never had a practice quite like this one. The only thing that had changed in his life was one Miss Jeni O'Brien. And she provided lots of inspiration. The past two days had been better than any he'd ever had. All because of four hours with a stuffy linguist professor as he and Jeni conversed.

Professor Montgomery's idea was for them to talk naturally. Normal conversations, but where each sentence the professor stopped them and corrected their sounds. And then they would repeat what they said, trying to make it sound right. Which made a fascinating way to really learn about Miss O'Brien.

So far, he'd learned that her favorite color

was blue, she was twenty-three years old, and she lived with her aunt Bridget because her parents were both gone. It had only been a few years since she'd come to the States, but she loved it here. She loved the city. Loved the people. And had a hankering for a taste of high society like her clients.

She was obviously a master at designing hats, because she worked for the top milliner in the city. But of course the man kept her in the back of the shop and took credit because she was Irish.

Just the thought of it made Philip's blood boil. If he ever met the man, he'd be tempted to give him a piece of his mind. Not that it would do any good. And she had admitted that he paid her triple the amount of any of the other girls because he knew he'd lose all his business if he didn't have her designing for him. Which was better, but still Philip wanted to see her with her own shop, delighting the wealthy women of New York City with her talent.

After he and Jeni had their first session together, he must have earned her trust, because today's session was even better. She seemed completely at ease and ready to learn. The way she tilted her head when she was thinking about a pronunciation was one of his favorite things he'd noticed about her.

And they'd shared plenty of laughter as they worked on vowel sounds with Montgomery after their first hour of "conversation correcting," as the professor put it.

The coach blew a whistle, which brought him out of his thoughts. He tossed his bat to little Scotty, who kept track of all the wooden bats, and the batters switched places with the guys in the outfield. It was time to work on his fielding. As he grabbed his glove and jogged out to center field, Jeni's smile came to mind. In most situations it wasn't proper to study a woman's lips, but in linguistics, they spent a good deal of time staring at each other's mouths and trying to mimic the professor's sounds. It seemed so intimate to be studying her that way, but he couldn't deny that he liked it.

Balls flew at him from the different batters on the field. This was one of his favorite exercises — fielding for more than one batter. It kept him on his toes and kept him moving. Something that was good for his mind as well. But as much as he chased baseballs around the field, his mind wanted to chase something else entirely.

Jeni O'Brien.

The more he thought about her, the more he actually considered the fact that he wanted to settle down some day.

To have a family.

Something he'd never had growing up. The other newsboys had been his only family. At least the only family he could remember. And they'd stuck together a long time. Played stickball in the street every day. That's how he'd gotten discovered.

Seeing real families at games and at church always made him a bit sentimental. Until just lately, it'd been easy enough to push those thoughts aside and focus on baseball. But then he met Jeni.

A classy lady. Smart, feisty, and determined.

Someone who made him *want* to settle down. Sooner rather than later.

Two years ago, on his twenty-fourth birthday, he'd told God that he would play baseball for as long as He allowed. And he'd be grateful for the chance he had, because it was a miraculous thing. Especially for a kid with no name from Brooklyn.

He jumped for a ball that went over his head. The smack of it in his glove made him smile. Yeah, he wanted to play ball as long as the good Lord let him. This game was in his blood. But every time he saw one of the other guys with a pretty gal hanging off his arm, he wondered if his chance would come.

After today, he'd begun to believe that it had.

"What's got you grinning like that, Wedge?" Tony — another kid rescued from the streets to play ball — had been his closest friend for the past few years.

The reminder of his childhood nickname made Philip laugh. "Oh, just somethin' good."

"If I didn't know any better, I'd say it had to do with a lady friend. But you don't have any of those."

Philip wasn't ready to reveal all his secrets, so he simply shrugged.

"Ah, so it *is* a girl." Tony spit on the ground and put his hands on his hips. "I shoulda known. You gonna tell me about her or not?"

"Or not." Philip caught another ball and sent it rocketing to first base.

Tony's laughter followed him all the way to the dugout.

CHAPTER 5

Peeking through the curtain that separated the storefront from the back area, Jeni watched Mr. Crawford show one of her hats to Mrs. Carrie Astor Wilson — a woman Jeni desperately wanted to meet.

A great-granddaughter of America's first millionaire, John Jacob Astor, she was a daughter of *the* Mrs. Astor who had been the leader of the Four Hundred until her death just a few years ago.

Mrs. Astor Wilson was the woman to impress. Apparently, Jeni had done it. Although Crawford's shop would take the credit.

This was the seventh hat that the wealthy socialite had bought in the last two weeks. And Jeni had designed them all. What she wouldn't give to be introduced to the woman whose tastes she knew so well. Every time the wealthy socialite asked for something, Mr. Crawford said he would need time to think it through and design it. Then he'd give the project to Jeni and she would create it. The woman had been thrilled with each one and raved about them to her friends. Which drove even more customers into the store. Crawford had made more than double Jeni's monthly salary off of only five of the hats he'd sold to Mrs. Astor Wilson. She'd kept track. And he hadn't done a bit of the work. Granted, he supplied Jeni with everything she needed to create them, but she'd also made more than forty other hats that he'd sold this month alone. This was the time to make her move again and demand a raise. With the spring season ahead of them, all the women of the city would be looking for new hats. They'd only grown larger the past year, which meant they were more expensive. And Jeni could supply what they wanted, she'd proven that.

For a moment, she let herself imagine her very own shop. And with Mrs. Astor Wilson as a client, she'd certainly do well for herself.

Not that she wanted to see Mr. Crawford fail — even though he kept her and the other Irish girls sequestered in the back — but she knew what skills the good Lord above had given her. She didn't necessarily want to steal Mr. Crawford's customers

381

either . . . but, then again, they weren't really *his* customers, were they? If she could run her own shop, perhaps she'd even be able to employ some of the other girls as well, and not make them work in the dingy and dark rooms in the basement of the store. At least Jeni was allowed to work in a room with a window and light just behind the storefront.

Crawford finished the sale, and Mrs. Astor Wilson was describing what she wanted next. This would be the perfect opportunity. Jeni slipped back into her workroom and sat on her stool finishing the details on a cream-and-peach hat that was over two feet wide while she waited for her boss to come to her.

The hooks of the curtain scraped on the rod. Then footsteps.

Jeni took a deep breath and then shoved a few pins between her lips. She kept sewing on the beautiful roses she'd made for the hat.

"Miss O'Brien."

"Mm-hmm?" With her lips pursed around the pins, she pretended to be preoccupied.

"I've got another order from Mrs. Astor Wilson." The emphasis he put on *Astor* was a typical ploy. He always dropped the names of the influential clientele he served.

But Jeni wasn't going to let it sway her —
she knew very well that the only reason he
had Mrs. Astor Wilson as a client was
because of her. "Wonderful. What would she
like?" She spoke around the pins.

Mr. Crawford placed a piece of paper in
front of her. "I believe everything you need
is listed here. Let me know if you need any
specific supplies."

Jeni held up her hand. Removing the pins
from her mouth with her other hand, she
shot him a smile. "Mr. Crawford. As you
know, I can provide you with exactly what
Mrs. Astor Wilson wants. She's purchased
seven of my creations in the last two weeks,
and it sounds like she is telling all of her
friends about your shop."

"Yes, and I appreciate all you do."

"If I wasn't able to produce what these
women wanted, you wouldn't have their
business."

"That's taking it a bit far, don't you think,
Miss O'Brien? I do provide the very best
here in my shop."

"Yes, sir. That you do. But if I were, say,
to take one of the other offers that have
come my way, and I were to leave your
shop . . . do you think that would continue?"
Trying to sound as confident and yet as
meek as she could, she raised an eyebrow at

383

him. And hoped that he couldn't hear the pounding of her heart.

He lifted both of his hands as if to surrender. "Miss O'Brien, I give in. I know my competitors would like nothing more than to steal you away. What if I were to offer you a dollar more per week?"

She allowed herself a small smile. "That would be wonderful, Mr. Crawford. Thank you."

"And you'll agree to stay?"

"For at least another three months, yes, sir. As long as you put it in writing." She stuck out her hand.

He always liked to shake on it. "I'll have a new contract drawn up today." He reached up and straightened his tie. "You do drive a hard bargain, Miss O'Brien."

"I know how much you make off of my designs, Mr. Crawford, so I believe it's *you* who deserves that praise." The comment was cheeky, especially for someone in her position.

But thankfully, Crawford laughed. "As long as you keep my shop known as the best in town, I'll allow you to say such things in private. Just remember your place, girl." The bite at the end of his tone told Jeni that she'd better tread carefully.

At least she'd gotten what she wanted.

Another raise. If she put all of it back, plus the money she was saving on her linguistics lessons and with everything else she'd already saved, she might be able to start her own shop perhaps in a year or so? The thought gave her a little thrill. Then maybe . . . just maybe, she'd find a dashing gentleman who would whisk her off her feet. Philip's face flashed before her. It was a bit too soon to really know anything about the man, but lots of girls had crushes on baseball players. So she let her imagination soar. One day she'd have a family. And they'd have a better future than what her poor parents had. Which was exactly the reason why she and Aunt Bridget had come to America in the first place.

The walk home that evening had her smiling the whole way. Just wait until Auntie Brig heard the good news about another raise. Perhaps that would get the sour look off her aunt's face for a little bit and they could celebrate together.

A new future awaited them, and it was closer than she had hoped!

But when she opened the door to their small apartment, Aunt Bridget stood there with her arms crossed over her chest and Jeni's bubble burst. "Why did you leave this mornin' afore I was even up? What are you up to, lass?" She pointed a wooden spoon at Jeni. "And don't give me no lies. I raised ye to be a proper woman, not one to go gallivantin' around in the wee hours."

Jeni huffed but promised herself to practice her language skills. "I was not gallivant-*ing* around, Auntie." She took a moment to breathe and took off her gloves. "My linguistics professor has increased my lesson time."

"Whatever for?" And the spoon waved around. "It best not be anything improper —"

"Oh, for pity's sake, you should know me better than that." Jeni hung up her coat and purse. "It will help me progress faster by working with a partner, on top of the fact that he's offered me the lessons for half, which means I'll be able to put more of me money back for a shop." She smoothed her skirt and walked past her aunt.

But Auntie Bridget's arm was quick to grab the back of Jeni's dress. "What is this about a partner?" The older woman's voice raised in volume and pitch.

"There's another student taking speech lessons from the professor. We've been paired together to help each other improve as the professor teaches us."

Her aunt stomped her foot and mumbled several things under her breath. "Ridiculous notion of you taking these lessons in the first place. There's nothing wrong with the way we talk. Who is this partner? It better not be some woman of the night or some other such personage that'll ruin yer reputation. Who is this professor anyway?"

Jeni tried — she really did — *not* to roll her eyes, but she couldn't help it. "It doesn't matter what any of my answers are to your questions, because you're not listening to me anyway."

"I listen to ya —"

"No. No, ya don't." Defeat rushed through her. Why did she ever think her aunt would be proud of her? All her life she'd tried, but Auntie Brig had just gotten harder and harder on her. "When are ya gonna learn that I'm an adult and can take care of meself?" All her good practice flew out the window as words flew out of her mouth. "Ya don't get to boss me around or scold me anymore, Auntie Brig. I have a good head on my shoulders and have been makin' hats for the wealthiest of New York's society. If I want to make it as a reputable milliner, I need to educate myself in the ways of America. That's why we came here. To be free. To escape the debt and poverty and ache of all our loss. I have the right to own my own business now. I think I know what

I'm doin'."

"Don't you take that tone with me, missy. Your parents left ye in my care."

"And I will be forever thankful for all you did after Da died, Aunt Brig. But that was years ago. Now *I'm* the one takin' care of you. Takin' care of us both. And I've done pretty well, ye'll have to admit."

"Ungrateful girl. Such disrespect to your elder shows you're headed down a dangerous path." Her aunt pointed a finger in her face. "An' I'll not stand for it." She marched off and slammed the door to her bedroom.

Jeni looked to the ceiling and lifted her hands in frustration. "So much for celebratin'." Her words tumbled out in a soft murmur. "I didn't even get to tell her about my raise. . . ."

CHAPTER 6

Bridget paced in her bedroom. The lass had gone daft, that's what, and there was nothing she could do about it at the moment. Other than make plans.

But she'd have to do it all behind Jeni's back. There was no reasoning with her right now. Maybe the only thing she could do was make peace with her niece but give her a bit of the cold shoulder. It always worked with the girl when she was younger. Over time, Jeni would come around. She always wanted the approval of her only living relative. Bridget could use that to her advantage.

A few months of being patient couldn't hurt. By that time, enough money would be saved for them to travel to Wisconsin and start fresh there. Bridget needed to be strategic, but it sounded like Mr. Crawford would keep Jeni busy enough. For now. Then Bridget would demand they move to

Wisconsin.

Her niece would thank her. One day.

Monday, March 20, 1911

Jeni watched Philip's face as he listened to Professor Montgomery. Even after two hours together every day for almost three weeks, she loved watching Philip puzzle over a new assignment or instruction. What if he studied her the same way when she was thinking through the professor's directions?

A rush of warmth hit her face. She shouldn't be having such thoughts. Philip was her friend. And a real friend at that. Something she hadn't realized that she didn't have until recently. He didn't care that she was Irish. She didn't care that his Brooklyn accent was thick. He seemed unfazed that she worked as a milliner, and the fact that he was a famous baseball player didn't mean anything to her anymore. They'd talked about everything imaginable during their sessions. He was just Philip. Her friend. She never wanted to do anything to jeopardize that.

But that didn't mean she wasn't still fascinated by him.

The two men chuckled and it brought Jeni's attention back around. Hopefully, they hadn't asked her anything.

"Philip, no. That's not what I'm saying at all. When I said 'pull your lips back,' I didn't mean to bare your teeth like a grizzly bear. I simply meant that your lips are always very far forward when you speak — like the corners of your mouth are down and forward." The professor mimicked Philip's accent to a T. "So why don't we try something else."

Philip made a silly face at her. "I'm game for anything, Professor, because apparently I'm not gettin' it."

"Getting. *Ing-uh.* Come now, Mr. March, you've been doing so much better than that. Don't drop the *g* — let it make the sound it's supposed to make." Professor Montgomery let out a little huff.

"Sorry, Prof. You're correct. Gett*ing.* I'm not gett*ing* it." The overenunciated *ing* made Jeni giggle.

Professor Montgomery shook his head and smiled. "I know this has been difficult on you both. But you truly are making progress. We've got to keep at it."

"Yes, sir." Jeni tried to swipe the smile from her face and straightened her spine as she sat.

"All right, Philip. Let's try this. I want you to smile. And smile big. Right here at Miss O'Brien. While you keep that smile glued in place, you're going to say the sentence 'My dog ran away to the park; have you seen him?' Now I want you to remember that each syllable needs to be made with your cheeks back and your smile full. We're aiming for bright tones, and don't forget that *park* needs to have an *r* in its pronunciation. Got it?"

Philip nodded and quirked an eyebrow. He looked at Jeni and smiled broadly. With his lips pulled back into a smile, he asked her the question "My dog ran away to the park; have you seen him?"

"Very good, Philip." She clapped, truly proud of how far he'd come, and then leaned forward. "But you don't have a dog." She couldn't help the laughter that bubbled up.

"Maybe he's invisible."

"So why are you asking me if I've seen him?"

Soon Philip was laughing with her, and they couldn't seem to stop the silliness of the moment.

"What is so funny?" The professor wiped a hand down his face. "What am I going to do with the two of you?"

Jeni made a face at him. "I'm sorry. I couldn't help it. We've just been working so hard, and you know quite well that Philip doesn't have a dog. The moment just needed some levity and it tickled my funny bone." She tried to keep a serious face in place, but it didn't work.

"I'm sorry too. I can be serious." Philip smashed his lips together.

In the next moment, the professor was laughing along with them. A ridiculous mention of a dog that didn't exist had put them all over the edge. But as they laughed, she felt tension ease. The Bible did say that laughter was good medicine. Jeni hadn't laughed this hard in a long time. Tears streamed down her cheeks as she tried to catch her breath — which wasn't an easy task for a woman wearing a corset. Totally unfair that the men didn't have to deal with that.

She pulled out her hankie and dabbed at her eyes. "I'm sorry. I know I started it. But we should get back to work."

The laughter died down, and Jeni took a deep breath.

The professor sat up straighter. "Yes. Now, Philip. You ask Jeni a question. Act like you are coming into her shop to purchase a hat for a lady."

Philip nodded. He looked at Jeni and appeared to think about it for a moment. He gave a slight smile and spoke with it in place. "Miss O'Brien, I need to purchase a hat for my boss's sister."

The professor made him correct the word *boss* and try again. Twice.

After their teacher was satisfied, he looked at her. "All right, Jeni, now it's your turn to reply."

"I'd love to help you, Mr. March. What colors would you like?"

"Perfect, exactly what I was hoping for." The professor stood up. "Say that response again."

Jeni repeated herself.

"All right, now let's concentrate on two words. *Love.* And *colors.* Listen to the sound *love* makes and then the first syllable of *co-lors.* Do you hear it?"

"I think so." She made sure she said *think* rather than *tink* like she used to.

"Very good. Now listen to it again. Luhve. Co-lors." He stretched the sounds out. "The way you naturally use this 'o' sound is more like the sound we use for *book,* so it sounds like *loove,* rather than *luhve.* Rather than pushing the vowel through the roof of your mouth, I'd like you to drop your jaw and try the 'uh' sound. Why don't you try it."

"Uhhhh . . ." It sounded wretched. "Is that correct?"

"Yes. It is. Now try the response again."

"I'd luh-uhve to help you, Mr. March. What cuh-lors would you like?"

"Much better, Miss O'Brien. Much better. Now just try to keep *love* to one syllable."

Jeni looked back at Philip and repeated the sentences. The professor made her say them five more times. But every time she said the word *love* she felt a bit more heat creep up into her face. What had come over her? Willing herself to focus back on the task at hand, she couldn't help but wish that she and Philip could just sit and talk. By themselves. Without the professor around to tweak every sound they made.

The more time she spent with the handsome baseball player, the more time she *wanted* to spend with him. But was that a good thing? For the first time in a long time, she felt completely at ease with someone. There was no facade to be held up. No pretense. Just getting to know one another. Albeit it was during linguistics lessons. Could all of this mean something entirely different to Philip? What if it meant . . . nothing?

The thought plagued her as they continued on.

The two hours of their lesson passed in a blur. But at least she felt more and more confident each day with her speech. Since Aunt Bridget was barely speaking to her, Jeni hadn't conversed with her much, but she couldn't help but hope that her aunt would notice and be proud of her. For bettering herself and making her way in this tough world.

Was that too much to ask? Probably. Especially since Aunt Bridget felt like Jeni was giving up her heritage. But perhaps over time she would come around. Because above everything else, Aunt Bridget was loyal and loved her. Jeni knew that.

"Jeni?" Philip stood over her. His coat and hat in his hands, he tilted his head toward her.

Blinking away her train of thought, she shot him a quick smile. "I'm sorry. What did you say?" She stood up.

"I was going to ask you a question, but you looked lost in thought."

"My apologies. You have my full attention." She clasped her hands in front of her.

"Why don't I walk you out?"

"That would be lovely. Thank you." She nodded at him as he held out her coat for her. Even though spring attempted to break through, the chilly temps still lingered.

"I hope this isn't inappropriate . . ." He spun his hat by the brim as they left the professor's office. "But seeing how you and me have become friends, I was hoping I could offer you an invitation to go to church Sunday? With me, that is. Then maybe we could take a drive afterward?"

The invitation stopped her in her tracks. The expectant look on Philip's face made her believe that he was enjoying their time together as well. An invitation to church was a big thing. But a drive afterward as well? Her heart picked up its pace. Dare she hope? She cleared her throat. "I'd love to."

"May I pick you up at 9 a.m.?"

"That would be lovely." She faced forward and they started to slowly walk down the sidewalk.

"But of course, I'll see you tomorrow at lessons as well."

"Of course." The air sizzled in the awkward moment around them.

"I'm looking forward to it."

"Me too."

"Well . . . uh . . . I need to get to the Polo Grounds." He grinned at her.

"All right. I'll see you tomorrow."

"Until tomorrow." He tipped his hat and hurried away.

The racing of her heart drummed in beat with his jogging steps as she watched him. It all seemed like a dream. Just this morning she'd thanked God for Philip's friendship, and now she wanted to shout from the rooftop.

She'd have to find something special to wear because Philip didn't go to just *any* church. It was the church that she knew some of the wealthiest in the city went to. She couldn't embarrass him.

Nervousness built in her stomach as she hurried to Crawford's shop. She couldn't do this. Her boss didn't even let her out to the front of the store. What made her think she could be seen on the arm of a famous baseball player? Could this ruin him?

What would people say about her? What if she said the wrong thing?

Her thoughts swirled around her in confusion and worry.

What had she agreed to?

CHAPTER 7

Tuesday, March 21, 1911

As opening day of baseball season approached, Philip had been putting in longer hours at the field. Now that he held the home run record, expectations were high for him to perform as well or even better this year. And he didn't want to let down his team *or* the fans.

The press loved his rags-to-riches story, and the whole city seemed to love it too. But if he didn't play well, that could easily turn on him.

That's why he'd been willing to give the speech lessons a try. Anything to improve himself, right? But meeting Jeni had changed everything. He found that he actually enjoyed the learning now. Especially when he was able to see *her* every day.

Walking up to Montgomery's building, he couldn't help the spring in his step. She'd said yes! Since he really had no idea what

399

he was doing, it encouraged him that he'd at least gotten that far. What to do now, he really wasn't sure, but hopefully they could continue building their friendship.

As soon as he entered Montgomery's office, he looked for her face. But when their gazes collided, he knew that something wasn't right. Her normal smile and greeting weren't there. Something troubled her.

He walked up to her side. "Is everything all right?"

"I'm fine. Let's just get on with the lesson." She didn't look him in the eye.

Her comment made him raise his brows. All the guys said that women could be temperamental. But he'd never seen it personally. And it seemed more than that. Had someone hurt her?

Since this was new territory to him, he decided it was better to sit back and see how the morning progressed.

It didn't go well.

By the end of their two-hour session, Jeni was in tears, and Professor Montgomery was trying to console her. Philip took his coat and hat and decided to give her some time alone with their teacher. He'd just wait for her outside.

The minutes ticked by slowly, like a slug moving in the early morning dew.

Finally the door opened, and Jeni appeared. She gasped when she saw him. "I'm sorry. I didn't realize you were still here."

"I was waiting for you."

"I'm sorry I was such an awful partner today." She headed down the hallway.

Trailing behind her, he kept his hat in his hands. "You weren't awful. I'm just concerned about you."

She stopped, and he almost ran into the back of her. Turning around, she gulped and took a step back. "I don't think it's a good idea for me to go to church with you, Philip. I'm sorry."

"I don't understa—"

"You're a wonderful gentleman, and I have so enjoyed our lessons together. In fact, I truly think of you as my friend, but don't you see?" Her eyes pleaded with him. "We're two different classes. I don't belong with the set of people that go to your church. You know how much discrimination there still is toward the Irish. What if I say something and it embarrasses you? What if one of the papers writes up some derogatory story about you? All because you were seen with me? I couldn't bear it if my presence did anything to besmirch you. You mean too much to me. I'm sorry."

"But —"

"I'll see you tomorrow morning, Philip. Again, I'm sorry." She turned on her heel and walked away.

As he watched her hurry down the hallway, all of her statements tumbled around in his mind. It came down to two major points.

One — she cared for him. She'd said it herself.

And two? She didn't think she was good enough for him.

As the shock of the moment left him, he headed out of the building and mulled it all over. He'd never met anyone like Jeni O'Brien.

Shaking his head, determination flooded his mind.

He was just going to have to convince her otherwise. Because Philip March wasn't giving up that easily.

The hat in her hand came together faster than she'd imagined. That was one thing about being upset — somehow it worked to her advantage for her to create rather than think about her distress. Attacking the jobs before her this morning, she'd already finished almost an entire day's work, and it wasn't even lunchtime.

Oh well. She could just work more. Mr.

Crawford wouldn't mind her increasing her output.

But her heart ached. As much as she didn't want to think about it, she was furious with herself on the one hand, and then trying to convince herself that she did the right thing on the other.

Philip was such a nice man. And they'd really become quite good friends. With their lessons they'd had the perfect opportunity to get to know one another on an easygoing basis. They both felt comfortable with the other.

So why had she turned him down?

Shaking her head, she tried to make the thoughts go away. But the argument continued in her mind.

She wasn't famous. She didn't have money. How was she supposed to be seen with the most famous baseball player in the country? Not to mention that she was Irish. Exactly the reason why Mr. Crawford kept her in the back of the store.

It infuriated her. God created all of them. Why couldn't they get along and treat one another with love? Why did it matter about class? She'd thought it was bad enough back in Ireland. But the world wasn't that much different in America.

Either you had money. Or you didn't.

That's why she couldn't attend church with Philip. She would be seen as a fraud. She had no place being at his side.

The bell rang over the door at the front of the shop, and Jeni got up from her work stool to go peek through the curtain. If it was another socialite ordering a hat, she often liked to see who it was so she could design the hat to fit their face and frame.

But when she peeked through the slit in the curtain, her heart stuttered and she tried not to gasp.

Philip stood at the counter, a large bouquet of roses in his hand.

What was he doing here?

Her heart raced. Silly girl. He was there for her. She knew it. But Mr. Crawford would never let him see her. She let out a sigh. She wanted to see him. And then she didn't.

As her thoughts warred with each other, the men's conversation floated back to her.

"I'd like to see Miss O'Brien." Philip offered her boss a smile.

Mr. Crawford's back was to her, so she couldn't see his face, but she noticed his shoulders stiffen. "I'm sorry. That's not possible."

"Why not? She works here, doesn't she?" Philip frowned.

"Well, yes, but she is very busy." Her boss's voice sounded awkward and stilted.

"Too busy for you to allow her a moment's break?"

"I'm afraid that's quite impossible, sir."

Jeni watched Philip stare down the man. He stood straighter and lifted his chin. Shifting the roses to his left hand, he stuck out his right hand. "Well, Mr. Crawford, I thank you for your time."

"Yes, thank you for coming in, Mr. . . . ?"

"Philip March. Center fielder for the New York Giants." The men shook hands.

"Mr. March, what an honor it is to meet you. I was there at the game last year when you broke the record for the most home runs. I can't begin to tell you how exciting that was."

"It was exciting for me as well." Philip beamed the man a smile.

"Thank you for coming in."

Philip stepped closer and leaned his right arm on the counter. "Mr. Crawford, you're a businessman."

"Yes, sir." Her boss tilted his head.

"Did Miss O'Brien design and create all of the hats in the front window?"

The man swallowed but didn't answer.

"Let me put it a different way. What if I were to offer to purchase every hat in the

CHAPTER 8

"Uh . . . oh my . . . *every* hat? Well, that would be . . . Why yes, yes . . . of course. I'm sure I could ask her to slip away from her work for a moment."

"Wonderful." Philip pulled out his wallet.

Crawford went to the window with his ledger and scribbled the numbers, then he came back to the counter and spoke to Mr. March. "That will be two hundred thirteen dollars. Would you like them delivered?"

"We can discuss that in a moment. Why don't you get Miss O'Brien, and I can speak with her while you box them up." Philip handed the man a stack of bills.

"Of course. Certainly." Mr. Crawford turned on his heel and headed for the curtain.

Jeni jumped into action and ran back to her workroom. Philip had just purchased more than two hundred dollars' worth of hats! Just to see her. She put a hand to her chest to steady her heart. Footsteps approached.

"Jeni. Quick. I need you out front. Someone has asked to see you." Mr. Crawford grabbed her arm and practically dragged her to the counter.

Face-to-face with Philip, she offered a slight smile. "Good morning, sir."

Crawford went to the front window and started boxing up hats.

Philip leaned a bit closer. "I need to talk to you."

"All right." She kept her hands clasped on the counter in front of her.

"I've been thinking about what you said this morning, and I would like to offer an argument on my behalf."

She felt her eyebrows raise. "Oh?"

"You see, you think that we are different classes. We're not. I believe that all are equal in the sight of God. And it's nobody's business anyway. I think you're the most incredible milliner in all of New York City, and I'm just a lowly baseball player."

"Philip. Please —"

He held up a hand. "I thought we were friends? That we'd always be honest with each other? Wasn't that part of our agreement when we began? To just be ourselves?"

"Yes, but —"

408

"No buts. Don't argue with me. I don't care what anyone thinks. I don't care that you're Irish. In fact, I love it. I love how you speak. I've spent enough time with you to know that I want to know you even better. Yes, there will probably be press there. But they follow me everywhere. I had to sneak through two different alleys just to keep them from following me here. Please, won't you reconsider? I thought we were friends?" He held out the bouquet of roses to her. "These are for you."

After his rush of words and the thrust of flowers in her face, Jeni wasn't sure what to think. He was the most amazing man she'd ever met, and, if she was honest, she'd have to say that she truly wanted to go with him to church. But fear kept creeping its way up the back of her neck. "I don't know . . ."

"I just purchased a bunch of ladies' hats so I could speak to you, Jeni." The expression on his face made her want to giggle. "As ridiculous as that was, you realize I'm serious, don't you? That I won't give up easily?"

With a nod, she gave him a slight smile. "Yes. I think I can see that."

"Please? Will you reconsider?" The eagerness on his face just about did her in. Never in her life had she had a man pay such extravagant attention to her. And she really liked him.

"Yes. I'll accept your invitation."

The smile that spread across his face made her heart flutter. "Thank you, Jeni." He reached out and squeezed her hand. "See ya tomorrow morning?"

She bit her lip and nodded.

"Great." He picked up his hat but kept staring at her with that great big grin on his face.

"You better tell Mr. Crawford where you want to have all your new hats delivered."

"Oh. Right." He dipped his chin to her and then turned toward her boss.

Watching him walk away, Jeni picked up the bouquet and took a long inhale of their scent. No one had ever given her flowers before. And these were roses — weren't they expensive? Her heart did a little flip.

She couldn't wait for Sunday.

Opening the letter with a quick rip to the envelope, Bridget yanked out the sheets of paper and started to read.

According to her friend Betsy, the Irish community in Wisconsin wasn't thriving as well as Bridget had hoped. While a number of them had done well with dairy farming, it was still a tough economy, and if one didn't have the money to start up a brand-new business, the wages offered to the Irish were still lower than others.

After reading all the news from her friend, Bridget sat down with a huff in front of the window. The news wasn't what she wanted to hear. She'd hoped for excitement and enthusiasm and a prosperous economy to be able to tell Jeni that Wisconsin was where they needed to go. So what was she going to do with this?

She squinted her eyes as a new plan unfolded in her mind. Jeni didn't need to know all the details. With the money she was saving up for a new shop, they could manage the move and still probably open a small shop too. Bridget stood up and paced the floor. Perhaps there were other things she could do to help them save money faster. Maybe she could sell some of her baked goods like she used to before Jeni started making all the money. No reason to tell her niece what the plan was. Bridget could just surprise her with the news and the extra money once she had everything in place. It could work. Perhaps she could even write to Betsy and find out if there were any storefronts that could be rented. The more she thought about it, the more her plan made sense.

"Aunt Bridget?" The apartment door shut. "Are you here?"

Shoving the letter into her apron pocket, she squared her shoulders to greet her niece. "In here."

Jeni came to the doorway of her room. "Did you have a good day?"

" 'Twas decent enough." While she hated the distance between them, the cold shoulder treatment worked better than anything else to keep her niece in line.

"That's good." Jeni turned around.

"What's that over ye arm?" It looked like a garment bag.

"Oh nothing. Just a new dress for Sunday."

"What're ye doin' spendin' money on a new dress? I thought ye were savin' up for a new shop."

Jeni's spine stiffened. A sure sign of her stubbornness. "Don't worry, Auntie. My friend Mary made it."

"Why do ya need a new dress anyway?" She'd been giving her niece the silent treatment, but whatever her Jeni seemed to be hiding made her prod.

"Oh Auntie Brig, I'm tired. I don't have the energy to argue with you over a dress." Jeni walked away with a sigh to her bedroom. Which was actually a large storage closet, but Bridget had insisted on having

412

the one bedroom to herself. She was the elder, after all. Now she wondered if she should have rethought it. Her niece had entirely too many secrets.

"It would have been nice if you would have asked about *my* day." Jeni's words were mumbled, but Bridget still caught them.

"What was that, dear?" Her tone was too sharp, which was a sure giveaway, but she had the right to be aggravated.

"Nothing. I'm going to bed early."

"But what about yer dinner?" Bridget placed her hands on her hips. What a rebellious child.

"I'm not hungry. Good night." Jeni cut off the conversation and closed the door to her room.

Well. The city was having a bad influence on her girl. And that wouldn't do. On top of the fact that her cold shoulder treatment — a tactic she'd used for years with Jeni — didn't seem to be having the effect Bridget had hoped for. Maybe she needed to change her game plan.

When her niece left for work tomorrow, she'd just have to see what the girl was hiding. No self-respecting young woman would keep things from her aunt who only wanted the best for her.

CHAPTER 9

Sunday, March 26, 1911

A rapping on the front door brought Philip scurrying out of his room with his tie only halfway tied. He flung the door open to see his manager, Charlie Jones, with a big grin on his face. "You ready to go to church and smile for all the cameras?"

"Um . . ." Philip went back to tying his tie. "I'm picking up a friend today."

"Okay, well let's go get him." He waved his hand like he was waving Philip into home plate. "Come on, come on. I want to get there early."

"Charlie, you go on without me."

His manager's eyes widened. "Oh, I see. This is a lady friend you're picking up?"

"Yep. And I'd like to do it alone."

"Well, this is a first. Who is she?" The smile that spread across Charlie's face made Philip want to grin along with him.

"You wouldn't know her. But I'll introduce you this morning." He finished with his tie and picked up his suit coat and hat. "Now, if you don't leave, I'll never get there on time."

Charlie held up both hands. "All right, all right. I'm leavin'."

Leaving his apartment, Philip jogged down the stairs and headed to the front where his doorman had his Stoddard-Dayton 50 11-K Torpedo ready. He'd only bought it this week when he realized that he wanted something sleeker to impress Jeni when he picked her up.

They'd shared several glances and even a couple of private conversations before and after lessons this week. Their camaraderie was better than ever, but every once in a while it actually felt like they were flirting with one another. He didn't know if it was acceptable — or if that was what it was even called — but he sure enjoyed their banter. So on an impulse, he'd gone out and bought a new car. A very expensive, very fast, new car.

He'd paid almost three grand in cash for it, and Philip wondered if it had been a bit too extravagant. But he'd been blessed, and he wanted to shower Jeni with everything.

The breeze tugged at his bowler hat as he navigated the streets to Jeni's apartment.

Maybe his thoughts were getting ahead of him, but as soon as he'd convinced her to go to church with him and then for a drive, he couldn't help but think of the future. Yeah, baseball would be an amazing part of that for a while, but he wanted to dream about life after baseball. When he could have a family.

Now everywhere he went, he was noticing couples. Families. And he wanted that.

It had been one thing to keep his heart closed to everyone all his life because that was how a kid made it on the streets. But now it was entirely different. It was like his eyes were open for the first time. He didn't want to wake up from it if this was dreaming. Because it was wonderful.

When he found the block for her building, he slowed down and pulled to the curb. He hopped out and looked at the numbers. Finding the right door, he pulled on the handle and opened it to see Jeni standing at the threshold. Her green eyes shimmered in contrast to her almost black hair. His breath escaped him as he took in her beauty.

While she was always dressed like a lady, he guessed what he always saw her in must have been her working clothes. Because the dress she wore today was different. The material matched her eyes and shimmered and sparkled in the light. The hat on her head had to be one of her elaborate designs, because it was exquisite and matched the dress perfectly. It sat at a slight angle and made the line of her jaw beg for his touch.

What had come over him? He shook his head. "Miss O'Brien, you look . . . beautiful."

A shy smile lifted her lips before she ducked her head. "Thank you, Mr. March."

He held the door for her while she exited and then offered his arm to walk her to his car.

"Excuse me, Jeni. Now ya wait just a minute." The door slammed behind them.

Philip turned, and he heard Jeni sigh.

"Aunt Bridget, I didn't think you were awake."

The older woman stomped toward them. She lifted her chin and narrowed her eyes at Philip. "And who might you be?"

He gave a slight bow. "Philip March, ma'am."

"Ye're not Irish." The woman looked affronted.

"No, ma'am. I'm from Brooklyn."

Jeni tightened her grip on his arm. "Mr. March, I'd like to introduce you to my aunt. Bridget O'Brien." The words were a bit stiffer than usual.

"Nice to meet you."

The older woman just stared at him.

"Well, we better get to church." Philip wasn't sure what to do with the fiery and angry-looking woman in front of him. He tried to turn Jeni around.

"I'll be back later this afternoon, Auntie."

"What is it that ya do, Mr. March? To afford such a fancy car? Yer not into gamblin' or any criminal activity, are ya?"

The woman's words made him stop and turn his head back to her. "No, ma'am. I'm a baseball player for the New York Giants."

"He hit the most home runs in 1910, Aunt Bridget. Isn't that amazing?"

"Pshaw. Where did ya meet my niece?"

"At Professor Montgomery's office." He blinked at the woman, waiting to see if she would ask any more probing questions.

"Ah, so you're tryin' to fix Jeni's speech too?" The woman planted her hands on her hips. "She's not good enough for you?"

"No, ma'am. I'm not. And I think she's entirely *too good* for me." Philip turned completely around to face Jeni's aunt. "I love the way she speaks. I love the fact that she's from Ireland. It's my own speech that needs improvement. The boss wants me to talk to crowds, and they think I need to be more understandable."

"Humph."

"We really must be going, Auntie." Jeni grabbed Philip's arm and steered him back toward his car.

He looked back to the older woman and nodded his head.

Opening the passenger-side door to the Torpedo, he held Jeni's hand as she climbed in. Then he raced around, cranked the car, and drove away.

"Is she still watching us?" he dared to ask.

"Of course she is." Jeni sighed. "I'm so sorry about that, Philip. Auntie hasn't been herself for a while now. And I'm not quite sure what to do about it."

"So . . . I take it you haven't told her about me."

"There hasn't been a good opportunity. I'm sorry. I was hoping it would be under better circumstances when you met."

"She's very protective of you. It's endearing."

Jeni let out a long sigh. "It feels more like smothering."

Philip reached over and squeezed her hand. "But it's got to be wonderful to have family." He pulled his hand back and felt her gaze on him.

"I'm sorry, Philip. I know you don't have anyone. You're right. Aunt Bridget is all I've got left. I should be more appreciative."

"You don't need to apologize. I can see that she's quite the handful. But every once in a while, it would be nice to have someone be that protective of me." He wasn't sure why he'd said it out loud, but now that the words were out, he was glad he'd shared them with Jeni.

"What was it like growing up on the streets without anyone to look out for you?" Her voice was soft and tender.

He gave a half shrug. "I guess I didn't think about it much. All us newsboys stuck up for each other and made sure everyone had something to eat and a place to sleep. When we'd get kicked out of a place, we were always on the lookout for something new. Even if it was underneath someone's porch. We were just kids. And we worked a lot. Then played stickball in the streets as much as we could."

"That's how you got to be so good at baseball?"

"Yeah, I guess so." He pulled the car up to the church. He should've known better than to tell his manager what he was up to.

Because out in front of the polished steps were several reporters with Charlie grinning wide.

All watching him.

"Uh, Jeni?"

"I see them."

"Why don't I park around the corner?"

"That sounds like a good idea." She took a deep breath as he moved and parked the car.

"Are you ready for this?"

"I think so. Whatever made you choose this church?"

"It was kinda a requirement when I started playing for the team."

"Really?" The statement puzzled her.

"Well, they gave me three to choose from." He shrugged.

"And who was that man waiting for you?"

"My manager."

"Oh." Her hands twisted in her lap. Then she turned her green eyes on him. They sparked like fire. "This isn't some sort of publicity stunt, is it?"

His heart ached at the look on her face. "No. Oh Jeni. No. Please don't think that I would ever do anything like that to you. Or to anyone."

She looked him in the eye for several seconds. "All right. I believe you. Now what do we do?"

He got out and rounded the car to open her door. "Well, the way I see it, the best way to deal with situations like this is to face them head-on. Just smile and keep on walking. You don't have to talk to anyone or answer anyone's questions. You don't owe them anything. So just hold tight to me and I'll get you into the church as quick as I can."

"Sounds like a plan. I think I can handle that."

"When there's someone I'd like to introduce you to, I'll let you know. Otherwise we'll just smile and nod our way through the crowd."

She nodded. "Good."

"Good." He offered her his arm and headed for the front of the church. "Here we go."

CHAPTER 10

Jeni gripped Philip's arm tighter and tighter the more people they passed through. But it was like the parting of the Red Sea. Everyone moved aside as they walked at a brisk pace up to the entrance of the church.

Doing her part, she smiled and nodded at everyone she made eye contact with. But it was distracting to hear all the chatter.

"Who is that on Philip March's arm?"

"I don't think I've ever seen him bring a woman to church."

"She must be someone famous."

"She's a beauty."

"And so glamorous. Look at the gorgeous hat."

She tried not to blush under the scrutiny and kept smiling.

On and on the comments went. The stairs to the entry were one thing, but then they entered the massive building, and Jeni realized she had a long way to go. People were everywhere. Lots of the wealthy women she recognized from Mr. Crawford's shop. Of course, she'd only seen them as she peeked through the curtain. But she recognized them nonetheless.

As the massive pipe organ began to play at the front of the sanctuary, she breathed a sigh of relief. A signal that the service must surely be about to start. At least she could be thankful for Aunt Bridget's stopping them. The delay had helped keep her from having to converse with strangers. But oh, how she wished that she could sit down and let her heart return to its normal rhythm. Maybe by the end of the service, she'd be able to do it all over again. And not embarrass herself.

Philip directed her into a pew where it was obvious that other baseball players waited for him.

"Wedge. Good to see you." A skinny man with dark hair smiled at her. "Who's this pretty lady?"

Philip held out his hand to his friend. "Tony. May I introduce you to Miss Jeni O'Brien?"

"Lovely to meet you." She moved into the pew.

"And you, Miss O'Brien." Tony waggled his eyebrows. "And where did you meet my friend, here?"

Unsure of how to respond, she gave a smile as they settled themselves. Safely ensconced between the two players, she ignored the question as the organ began to play louder. Thankful for the moment to collect her thoughts, she leaned closer to Philip. "Why does he call you Wedge?"

Philip gave a quiet chuckle. "I'll explain after the service."

At that moment, a loud chord was played on the organ and the congregation stood and burst into a song Reverend Richards called the Doxology. With its marble floors and high ceilings, the cathedral lifted up the sound like an angelic choir. Jeni couldn't help but watch the people around her as the song continued.

Philip opened a hymnal and held it out for her. It seemed an intimate gesture — to share a hymnal with this man — but she found it made her feel special. Taken care of. Chosen.

The song finished, and Jeni found herself reflecting on the thought. For years, she'd worked and worked to provide and take care of herself and Aunt Bridget. She hadn't realized that it would be almost a relief to have someone care for her for a change. Even just the simple act of sharing a hymnal.

As they sat, she relaxed and knew that Philip would guide her through whatever took place today. There was no reason to be on edge or to worry. So she might as well enjoy the service. The reverend prayed.

Then they stood again for another song. Philip pointed to the correct page for her so she could follow again.

When the singing was done, the reverend stepped to the pulpit and in a loud and booming voice told the people to repent.

"This morning's sermon might be a tough one for many of you to hear. You see, my dear congregation, we're going to talk about those less fortunate than ourselves."

Jeni's ears perked up. At a church where the wealthiest of society seemed to be gathered, this would be interesting to watch.

Even though she longed to be among their ranks, she wasn't a fool. She'd seen how the upper classes treated the lower. But how was that going to change? It was the same way in Ireland and England. It must be the same way around the world.

Reverend Richards held his Bible up in the air. "Please turn with me in your Bibles to James chapter one."

The sound of rustling pages echoed throughout the marble room. She had her own Bible but had paid a pretty penny for it. Most people she knew had to borrow one or look on with a friend. The contrast with the people in this sanctuary was startling.

"Please stand and read with me aloud from verse twenty-two to the end of the chapter."

The congregation stood, and voices raised together as they read.

" 'But be ye doers of the word, and not hearers only, deceiving your own selves. For if any be a hearer of the word, and not a doer, he is like unto a man beholding his natural face in a glass: for he beholdeth himself, and goeth his way, and straightway forgetteth what manner of man he was.

" 'But whoso looketh into the perfect law of liberty, and continueth therein, he being not a forgetful hearer, but a doer of the work, this man shall be blessed in his deed. If any man among you seem to be religious, and bridleth not his tongue, but deceiveth his own heart, this man's religion is vain.

" 'Pure religion and undefiled before God and the Father is this, To visit the fatherless and widows in their affliction, and to keep himself unspotted from the world.' "

"Amen." Hundreds of voices around the church spoke at the same time.

Shuffling sounded as everyone took their seats.

Jeni looked down at the words on the page. The reverend paced for a moment and then stood behind the pulpit with his hands braced on either side. "Ladies and gentlemen, please take careful note of verse twenty-two. We are to be doers of the word and not just hearers. What does this mean? Well, let me ask you this. Did you hear the Word read this morning?"

To Jeni's surprise, heads bobbed around the sanctuary.

"And are you willing to be doers of that same Word from this day forth?"

Again, heads nodded.

"Good. I'm glad to see that. Because if you look closely at verse twenty-six, it clearly states that if a man bridleth not his tongue and deceiveth his own heart, his religion is vain. This morning I want you to think about this next question very clearly. Reverently. Have you bridled your tongue this week? And I don't just mean to keep your mouth from speaking profanity or taking the Lord's name in vain, but have you spoken in an unkind way . . . in an unholy way, to anyone at any time?"

Reverend Richards looked around the room while he let his question sink in. Jeni was mesmerized. She'd never been taught this way before. Did that mean that her

428

words to Aunt Bridget had been sinful? Because she hadn't bridled her tongue? How many times had they had heated arguments between the two of them? Jeni thought it was normal because most Irish families seemed to be a bit hot-tempered. At least all the ones she knew.

It was quite convicting. As she mulled over all the conversations she'd had with people lately, Jeni realized that she needed to work on bridling her tongue. Perhaps a lot.

The reverend had continued speaking, but she'd missed it.

Shaking her head, she tuned in to what he was saying. "Let's not ignore verse twenty-seven. Simply put, if you want to have pure and undefiled religion in the sight of God, you need to be taking care of the widows and the orphans. Now I know many of you contribute to organizations that help people less fortunate, but I'd like to ask you . . . When was the last time you visited a charity in person?" He let the question hang. "And then the last part of this verse is crucial. Are you keeping yourself unspotted by the world? It means to not be stained. My brothers and sisters, we are living in an age of defiance toward God. Everyone seeks the best for themselves. This needs to stop. To be unspotted in this world means we need to keep our eyes on what the Word of God says for our lives and not to be conformed to this world. Let us determine how we can help those less fortunate around us this week. Let us pray."

Jeni bowed her head and thought about the words the reverend had spoken. She'd always come to believe that she was one of those less fortunate. And yet, hadn't God blessed her in her work? She and Aunt Bridget no longer lived in the slums. They had plenty of food to eat and clothes to wear. Her heart ached as she thought about kids on the street. Kids that were just like Philip had been. Without parents. Without family. Working all hours of the day and night just to earn enough for a meal.

At that moment, she wanted to cry. She'd walked her own path for so long, but coming here today reminded her of the fire she'd had for God when her parents taught her as a young child. How she longed for that again. *Gracious heavenly Father, I can't even remember the last time I truly prayed, because I've been so focused on myself. But You've changed my heart today. Please help me to see how I can help others. Thank You for all You've given to me. All the blessings. And for Your Word to study.*

During the last song, Jeni followed along

with the words but felt a new sense of joy inside. She didn't know what to do with it, but she ached to find out more.

CHAPTER 11

With Jeni on his arm as they left the church, Philip felt a surge of pride. He'd heard all the comments about the beautiful lady on his arm. She took it all in stride and was gracious to everyone they passed.

When he noticed that Mrs. Astor Wilson was headed in their direction, he wasn't sure what to think. The woman was an intimidating presence.

He gave a quick bow.

"Mr. March." The woman clasped her hands in front of her. "You simply must introduce me to this enchanting friend of yours."

"Of course." He squeezed Jeni's hand that was wrapped around his arm. "Mrs. Carrie Astor Wilson, I'd like you to meet Miss Jeni O'Brien."

"It's a pleasure to meet you, Mrs. Astor Wilson." Jeni spoke confidently and clearly.

"I must say, Miss O'Brien, your hat is

432

simply delicious. Might I inquire about your milliner?" The older woman smiled.

Philip wasn't quite sure how to help. Mrs. Astor Wilson wasn't accustomed to not getting her questions answered. And he didn't want Jeni to be embarrassed in any way.

Jeni squeezed his elbow. "Thank you, Mrs. Astor Wilson. I designed it myself."

"Really? It's exquisite. You are quite talented." The woman's eyebrows raised. "Oh, I simply must hear more about this."

Philip looked down at Jeni and saw the look she gave him. Did she need rescuing? "Mrs. Astor Wilson, I'm so sorry to cut our conversation short, but we really must be going. Perhaps you and Miss O'Brien could talk about this some other time?"

"I would love that." Mrs. Astor Wilson nodded. "I wouldn't want to keep you two young people away from your plans this afternoon." She reached out a hand to Jeni. "Miss O'Brien, I look forward to meeting you again."

"And I you." Jeni gave a gracious nod of her head.

Philip led them out to the car, and they made it with just a few more simple introductions. As he opened the door for her, he lowered his voice. "What did you think?"

She put a hand to her chest. "It was

433

wonderful, Philip. Absolutely wonderful."

Her words put a bounce in his step as he walked around to the front of the car. "That makes me very happy."

After he cranked the car, he settled himself in for a pleasant drive. Once they crossed the Brooklyn Bridge to Long Island, he meandered through the streets he'd known so well as a kid and then let the car gently ramble along a country road.

Their conversation had been light as they'd driven along, and a comfortable silence fell over them as Jeni seemed fascinated with everything around her. "So back there . . . that was the Brooklyn that you grew up in?"

"Pretty much. Have you never seen it before?"

She shook her head and shot him a smile. "No. In fact, I've never even been over the bridge before."

"Why didn't you tell me? I could've given you a tour."

She laughed. "It's fine. Next time, how about you give me that tour. Today, I just want to enjoy the drive and think about Reverend Richards' sermon."

"It was a good one, wasn't it?" His comfort with this woman made him feel content. Was it the beginnings of love? They definitely had a solid foundation of friendship. But how did they get to that next step? Philip realized he had no clue.

Jeni shifted in the seat to face him and put her arm up on the seat behind her. "Tell me about your relationship with God."

The comment made him look over at her. "I'm not sure what you mean."

"Well, I guess I want to understand what I'm feeling. Your preacher inspired me this morning. I felt a fire within me that I haven't felt in a long time. It reminded me of my parents. My da used to always talk about a personal relationship with Jesus. And I really want that. But after they died, Aunt Bridget didn't take me to the same church anymore. Then we moved to New York, and she refuses to go to church because she's certain that unless it's with other Irishmen, we'll be looked down upon."

Philip found a lovely spot to pull off on the side of the road where they could see the water. He turned off the engine and shifted to face her. "Ya know, it wasn't until a few years back that I think I truly understood what a real relationship with God meant. Oh, I'd prayed lots of prayers as a kid, ya know, hopin' that I'd done it right so that God would save me. But I think I

435

was more scared of hell than I was truly wantin' to know about Him. I got into all kinds of trouble as a kid, but most of it was just tryin' to fend for myself. I didn't feel right stealin' like some of the other boys. Sorry, I'm dropping my g's again. Professor Montgomery would scold me."

She laughed with him. "So when did you truly start to follow Jesus?"

"A few years ago. My manager invited me to church, and I went and met the reverend. He asked me if I was saved and I told him I wasn't sure. So without knowing a stitch about me, he took me through the book of Romans and asked me several pointed questions. I knew I was a sinner in need of a Savior. I knew that Jesus had been the sacrifice for my sins and was resurrected. But it wasn't until that moment that I longed to give my life over to Him."

"Thank you for sharing that with me."

"What about you?"

"I haven't felt this alive in a long time." She smiled. "Would you mind if I go to church with you again?"

"I'd love that. Next week?"

"Sounds lovely."

They talked about the songs they sang in the service, which apparently were all new to Jeni. Then she talked about the fact that she had so much more now than she had before. She wanted to start giving back to help widows and the orphans.

Philip looked at the car he'd just purchased. Maybe there was more that he could do as well. A *lot* more.

He pulled out the picnic he'd asked the deli to put together for him, and they enjoyed a leisurely lunch and joked about Professor Montgomery's techniques. They talked about their childhoods and favorite memories.

Jeni was scared of spiders.

Philip always slept with a light on because he grew up in the dark.

As they shared snippets of their lives with each other, Philip didn't want the day to end. But he forced himself to say, "I better get you home before your aunt comes hunting for me."

Jeni laughed and shook her head. "I just need to talk to her more. She's built such a tough wall around herself lately that I'm not quite sure what to do. Maybe I should pray about it."

"That's probably the best idea." He started the car up and headed back to the city. "I really enjoyed our day today. Thank you for spending it with me."

"Thank you for asking. I really had a nice

437

time." The smile she gave him sent heat up his neck.

As they drove, the wind tugged at strands of her hair underneath the giant hat, and her neat coiffure came undone. Her dark hair was so pretty. He wanted to reach out and touch it, but it wasn't his right to do that. At least not yet.

But with everything in him, he longed for that day.

Yep. He had it bad.

The thought made him smile.

"What's caused that grin, Mr. March?" Jeni's voice was playful.

"Oh, just a little secret."

"You won't tell me?"

"Nope. Not yet."

"All right. Well, how about you tell me about your nickname."

The reminder of his nickname made him chuckle. "Well, you see, Tony and I grew up on the streets together."

"Oh, so now I know who to go to for all the secrets about the famous baseball player Mr. March." He loved the way she sounded when she teased him.

"Yep. You do. Tony pretty much knows it all." He shook his head. "Anyway, I was a husky kid. Sometimes, when I had to chase down a ball in the streets, I had to climb through fences, over walls, et cetera."

He looked at her in time to watch her eyebrows raise.

"And I would often get wedged into tight places and Tony would have to come rescue me. So he started calling me Wedge, and the name stuck."

"Do the other players call you that?"

"Yep. Most of the time."

"That's a fun story."

"So now you know."

The moment stretched out, and Philip chanced a glance at her. She just sat there smiling at him.

"What?" He couldn't help but smile back.

"I really like you, Philip March."

His heart thumped in his chest. "I really like *you*, Jeni O'Brien." He took his right hand off the wheel and on an impulse, reached for her hand and lifted it to his lips and kissed it. "More than you know."

CHAPTER 12

Bridget stomped up the stairs to their apartment. It hadn't taken much to find out that Mr. Philip March was indeed a baseball player for the New York Giants and held the home run record. He was basically a celebrity and everyone loved him.

She'd even heard the famous "rags to riches" story about how he'd grown up on the streets of Brooklyn with no family and had made himself into the incredible man that he was today.

It made her sick.

When she'd snooped in her niece's room the other day, she had no idea that the lass was planning on going to church with some rich baseball player. In fact, it didn't seem that the girl had anything to hide, which had relieved her somewhat. But now to know that she'd been hanging out with that March fellow . . .

It didn't bode well. The boy wasn't Irish.

And for goodness' sake, he didn't even have a real job; he played a stupid game with a stick and a ball! What was it with these Americans paying good money to go watch a bunch of men run around in the dirt? It made no sense.

And she wouldn't stand for it.

There had to be a way to separate the two without Jeni knowing that she'd meddled. Bridget had a plan to get them out of this wretched city. But this good-looking man might present a giant obstacle. And she couldn't stand for that.

Sunday, April 2, 1911

The week had passed in pure bliss. The lessons each day were wonderful. It wasn't that she felt all that confident in correcting her speech, it was simply spending the time with Philip that made all the difference in the world. And then today they'd gone to church again and then on another drive. This time, he'd given her a tour of Brooklyn and they got out at the bridge and looked out over the water. They talked about God and prayer, and he shared with her about the new program he and some of the other ball players were starting to help feed the orphans in the city.

It had all been wonderful. Refreshing.

Her fire for God hadn't waned all week, and she found herself waking early to read her Bible before she left for the professor's office.

She prayed for Philip every day.

And realized she'd already given him her heart.

"Penny for your thoughts?" Philip's voice interrupted her musings.

"I was just thinking about you." She felt her face heat instantly. That was an awfully bold and brash thing to say.

He touched her cheek with his hand. "I think about you all the time, Jeni." He pulled back with a sigh. "We better head back."

When they reached her street, he slowed to find a place to park. "We might have to walk the rest of the block."

"That's all right. I'm used to it." She waited as he came around to open her door. When he offered his arm, her heart sped up again.

"Opening day is coming up. I've got a really full schedule this week, so would you pray for me?"

"Of course. I'd be honored."

"Would you like to come to a game one day?"

"I'd love to." The adoration in his eyes

made her heart pump even faster.

Instead of walking, he stood there, and his blue gaze penetrated hers. It had been a perfect day. Her heart pounded at his nearness.

He pulled her hand up to his lips and kissed it. Then he leaned in very slowly and kissed her on the cheek. "Thank you for another perfect day, Jeni."

Her heart flooded with emotion. "I was just thinking the same thing."

He walked her the rest of the way to the door of her building and waved goodbye as she entered. "I'll see you tomorrow."

"See you tomorrow."

If she were capable of floating on air, she probably would. How had she gotten so lucky?

She shook her head as she climbed the stairs. It wasn't luck. God had seen fit to bless her, and she would be forever grateful.

She'd never been this happy in her life. And she couldn't wait for tomorrow.

When Philip made it to his apartment, he was still on cloud nine. He needed to tell Jeni soon that he loved her. He couldn't keep it in any longer. And every day that he saw her, he felt like his heart might explode.

In the back of his mind, there was a little

niggle of doubt.

Aunt Bridget.

She hadn't spoken to him again, but she'd made her presence known when he'd picked up Jeni this morning. And judging by the sour look on her face, she didn't approve.

But maybe she just thought it was too soon. That they hadn't known each other long enough.

Philip thought about it for a moment. He couldn't wait to tell Jeni how he felt. But what if they had a long engagement? They could both deal with that, couldn't they? Besides, baseball season would keep him really busy.

A smile split his face. Yeah, he could do that. Maybe he could talk to her one day after their lessons. He could offer to walk her to work like he did most days.

Loosening the tie at his neck, he went into the kitchen for a glass of water. Tomorrow.

He would tell her tomorrow.

Walking back into the main room, he noticed an envelope by the front door. He must have missed it when he came in.

Probably from one of the guys. Reaching down to pick it up, he realized he hadn't introduced anyone to Jeni other than Tony. And it had been all over the papers. Maybe it was time to introduce her to the team.

He ripped open the envelope and pulled out a single sheet of paper.

As he read the words on the page, his collar became tight and anger boiled up inside of him.

Why are you interested in that tramp? She's only out for your money. The Irish are no-good, lazy, filthy vermin.

If you don't stop seeing her, I'll go to the press with a sordid story that will ruin Miss O'Brien's reputation.

He crumpled the paper and threw it in the wastebasket. How could anyone write such horrible things about Jeni?

Stomping to his bedroom, he ripped the tie from his neck and unbuttoned his shirt.

As his anger stirred hotter and hotter, Philip knew in his heart that it couldn't be true. Someone just hated the Irish and didn't want him and Jeni together. That had to be it. Which only made his anger grow.

But then he felt convicted by his own hate-filled thoughts. Crushed by the emotion surging through him, he got down on his knees and prayed. *Lord, I don't know who wrote that letter. But I need Your help. I'm asking for Your blessing on my relationship with Jeni. But Lord, if this isn't Your will, if I need to end it to protect her reputation, please help me to be willing. I know You can take care of her better than me, anyways. I need Your guidance and direction. You know that I love her, Father, but I don't know what to do.*

Feeling a gentle peace wash over him, Philip stood up and walked over to the open window. A slight breeze fluttered the curtains. Tomorrow, he'd see Jeni and he'd decide what to do.

CHAPTER 13

Monday, April 3, 1911

Sleep had eluded Philip most of the night. But he dressed and went to Professor Montgomery's office. More than anything, he just wanted to see Jeni's face and know that she was okay. As the night had worn on, he'd had horrible thoughts of someone coming after her. All because of him. He couldn't let that happen.

As he drove through the streets of New York City, he tried to think of anyone who might have a grudge against him. Could it be another baseball player? It wasn't that he truly had any rivals. At least he didn't think he did. But many of the guys were competitive. And ever since he'd won the home run record, the public had crowned him the king of all baseball. Could someone be jealous?

But why would they go after Jeni? It didn't make sense.

When he made it to the office, she was

already there. Sitting in her chair with a smile just for him. He tried to act as if everything was all right.

He didn't remember making it through the lesson. It was brutal. And he sensed that Jeni knew something was wrong.

Professor Montgomery must have as well. "Philip, it seems like you are not fully invested today. Maybe we should stop early."

"That sounds like a good idea." Jeni smiled at him.

Philip nodded, and they gathered their things.

As they walked out of the office, Jeni grabbed his hand. "What's wrong?"

He held on to her hand and walked with her down the stairs. Once they were outside, he stopped and released her. "There's something I need to tell you, Jeni."

Her face fell. "All right. I'm listening."

"I care about you a great deal."

Eyebrows lifted, she didn't say a word.

"In fact . . . I . . . I'm in love with you. I was so happy last night and couldn't wait to see you again so I could tell you."

Relief flooded her features, but then her brow furrowed. "But . . . I don't understand. You look miserable, and frankly, you're scaring me, Philip."

"I'm sorry. I don't want to hurt you in

any way."

"Then just tell me. What's wrong?"

Should he tell her the truth? If he did, would that put her in more danger? He looked around. Someone could be watching them. The thought made the hair on the back of his neck stand up. He took a deep breath. Honesty was the only way to go, best to just get it out there. "I received a threatening letter yesterday, and I'm worried about your safety."

She pulled back with a gasp. "Threatening? Threatening how?"

"Someone doesn't like us being seen together."

"What? Why would they . . . ?" She looked down. "Does this happen to you often? What did the letter say?"

"I can't repeat it. It was too ugly. But someone targeted you."

"Oh. But why me?"

He longed to pull her into his arms. The look of hurt and confusion on her face made him ache. "I don't know. Other than the fact that you've been seen publicly with me."

Several moments passed as they stared at each other.

Philip didn't know what to do.

Jeni took a deep breath and stepped

closer. Her eyes brightened. "Philip, I can't undo what some person said in a letter, but did I hear you tell me that you love me?"

He nodded.

"I love you too. Isn't that enough?"

Oh how he wished it were. What if the writer of the letter just wanted to scare him off? What if it was a joke? It was a horrible one, but maybe it was.

"I'm not sure what to do, Jeni. But I definitely don't want you in any danger."

"I understand that. But what exactly are we dealing with? Someone who just doesn't like me?"

"That's what I don't know. They said that if I didn't stop seeing you, they would take some sordid story of you to the press and it would ruin your reputation."

"But I don't have any sordid stories. . . ."

"I think that's the point. They will make up whatever they have to. All to ruin you. Or me. I don't know which."

She chewed on her lip, and even though she straightened her shoulders and looked brave, he could tell she was worried. "What are we going to do?"

"I'm not sure. But I won't let anything happen to you. I promise." He reached for her hand and squeezed it. Looking around him, he didn't want to risk any public displays. "I need to meet with my manager. But I'll see you in the morning."

"Oh, okay." She appeared defeated. Hurt that he would leave in the middle of this crisis. But the fact of the matter was he needed to *not* be seen with Jeni.

Fear niggled at Jeni at every turn. Who would do such a hateful thing? And why would they target her? Just because she'd been to church with Philip?

She'd thought that there were plenty of people who might be upset that one of America's favorite baseball players was seeing a woman of a lower class, but to go so far as to threaten her? Who would do such a thing? And why? Jeni didn't have any enemies. She made hats for goodness' sake! Tossing things around on her worktable, she wanted to vent her frustration but had no opportunity and no time. Several clients would be coming in for their special orders. And her heart wasn't in it. In fact, her heart hurt. How was she supposed to be creative in the midst of all this?

The thrill of Philip's confession of love stayed with her, but now that she'd had a chance to think about it, she was more nervous than she wanted to admit.

It had taken her a lot of time to build a

reputation with Mr. Crawford. Now he trusted her and depended on her for the wealthiest of clients. In fact, she created all the designs for his shop. The other girls made some of the simpler hats, but Jeni was still the one who designed them all. And anything complicated was her job to make. How many handmade flowers had she sewn onto hats over the past couple of years? Probably thousands. Could this person that threatened Philip actually be capable of ruining her reputation? She wouldn't be able to stay in New York City or possibly ever be able to work in a reputable shop again.

Were her dreams of owning her own shop to be destroyed too?

The thought made her sick.

She'd told Philip she loved him. And she did. But was she ready for this? Yes, they were really good friends, but were they ready to throw away not only her reputation but his?

Doubts fought at the edges of sound reasoning. How long she had waited for love, and now that it was within her grasp, it seemed unattainable. All because someone wanted to ruin her.

Which brought her back to the same question. Why?

Something Reverend Richards said yesterday came back to her mind. That God was within reach every moment of every day. So when scripture said to pray without ceasing, it meant that anyone could talk to the Father anytime. Anywhere. The lines were always open. Rather than standing here and worrying about it all, she should be praying.

Without hesitating, she got down on her knees in her workroom and poured out her heart to God. *Heavenly Father, I want to know You more. I feel like I've gotten a taste of a relationship with You recently, and I know that I want more. And God, I need Your help. I praise You for who You are and that You are the Most High. I come to You now, broken and afraid. Thank You for bringing Philip to my life. He has been the best friend I've ever had. And Lord, I feel like this love I feel for him is a beautiful gift from You. But Father . . . what if I have to give him up? Please, God, I don't want to . . .* She choked on the words but lifted her chin and raised her face to the ceiling. *I am seeking Your will, Lord. Not my own. Help me to remember that. Please guide me. Please take away this fear. Help me to follow You.*

With a new peace and a calmer spirit, Jeni rose to her feet. While the threat seemed very real, so was her love for Philip. It was a

CHAPTER 14

Wednesday, April 5, 1911

On his way to the linguistics lesson, Philip knew it probably wouldn't be a pretty scene waiting for him. Yesterday, he'd canceled his lesson. He hadn't said anything to Jeni, had only left a message at Montgomery's office.

Regret filled his thoughts. So many demands had been placed on him with the team, he hadn't slept well for a few days, and now, he hadn't handled this situation with Jeni well at all. But he was tired. Aggravated. Worried. And just a bit overwhelmed by it all.

Stressed. That's what his manager said. He was probably right.

Taking the stairs two at a time, Philip made it to the top and found Jeni standing there with her hands on her hips. "Uh . . . hi." His words sounded strained to his own ears.

"Hi, yourself." A whimsical smile filled

455

her face. What was going on? Wasn't she mad at him? She tugged at his arm and walked him to the professor's door. "I realize that you have a lot going on with the beginning of the season next week, but I have a request."

"Oh?" His eyebrows lifted.

"Yes. You see, the other day I was really struggling with this whole threatening letter situation, and I started to worry. A bit too much. It affected my work and my creative process, and I was a mess. Then I remembered what the reverend said about prayer and about worry. So this is my request . . ." She drew a long breath. "Why don't we meet every morning fifteen minutes before our lessons and pray together? That way we're not seen together out in public, and we bring our burdens to the Lord. What do you think?"

His heart already felt lighter. She wasn't mad at him. "I would be honored to pray with you, Jeni. I really would."

"But you're still concerned. I can see it on your face, so why don't I just save you from having to say what's really on your mind. You want to stop seeing me in public to protect me. I understand. So . . . I don't have to go to church with you for a few weeks — even though I like it very much —

just to see if it all goes away."

"And if it doesn't?"

"Well then, we'll just take it one day at a time." She let go of his arm and clasped her hands in front of her.

All he could manage was a nod.

"I have to be honest with you, Philip. I've given it over to God. And as much as I care for you, I've asked for *His* will to be done in the matter." A sheen of tears appeared in her eyes. "Even if that means that I have to give you up."

Even though he understood what she was saying, it couldn't have hurt worse if she'd stabbed him with a knife. *God, what do we do? It felt like You orchestrated this whole thing, and now I'm worried and afraid. But I don't want to let go of Jeni. Please . . .*

Friday, April 14, 1911

Bridget placed her fists on her hips and examined the letter. Had it been long enough since the first one was sent? Jeni hadn't gone to church with the baseball player again, neither had she mentioned Mr. March for a while. But she left earlier and earlier each day. And she continued the lessons. Bridget had confirmed it herself by following her niece yesterday. At first, she'd hoped that her niece wasn't seeing the man

457

anymore, since no one had seen the couple together. But yesterday, she saw the two on the stairs. They looked quite close.

Which was completely ruining Bridget's plans.

Jeni had seemed supportive when she talked of traveling to Wisconsin. But was it enough?

Now that Bridget knew that the March fellow was still in the picture, she knew she had to take the next step.

She looked back down at the piece of paper. It was pretty harsh, even to her own ears. But it had to do the trick. It had to.

Then it would all be over and they could leave.

A grin split her lips. It was a good plan. And no one was the wiser.

The day was starting out beautifully. Spring was in the air. It made Jeni feel invigorated as she walked to Professor Montgomery's.

The past two weeks had been hard and incredible all at the same time. Jeni loved getting to spend a few minutes praying with Philip each morning but found that she longed for more. They grew even closer during that time. Probably because they were growing spiritually.

Even during their lessons, she found her

mind and her heart pleading with God to allow them to be together. She'd laid her heart on the altar and told her heavenly Father daily that she sought His will. But she found it harder to think about letting Philip go. What would she do if God closed this door?

She'd be heartbroken. That's what.

The thought made her shiver. And yet, she'd promised God that she would do His will. No matter what it cost her.

The past couple of weeks had also seen a change in Aunt Bridget. She wouldn't stop talking about her friends in Wisconsin. How beautiful it was there. So much more open area and clean air. Did her aunt wish to move there?

It made Jeni shrug. Perhaps if her aunt wanted to move away, Jeni could grant her that wish. There was enough money saved up to send her beloved aunt to Wisconsin. Maybe she would finally find a bit of joy there. And Jeni would be free to continue her life here. It would take her a bit longer to save up for her shop, but she was willing to sacrifice for the woman who'd done so much for her after her parents died. Besides, the mail route was getting faster and faster. There were also trains. So they could still stay in touch and see one another.

It was funny . . . a few months ago, she wouldn't have been able to stand the thought of being on her own. Or of her aunt leaving. But now she felt confident and hopeful in the Lord. It was a beautiful thing.

Rounding the corner of the building, Jeni spotted Philip outside the door. He was filthy. Covered in black . . . soot? She ran the last few steps. "What's happened? Are you all right?"

He took a deep breath and shook his head. "The Polo Grounds burned down early this morning."

Covering her mouth with her hand, she shook her head and then lowered her hand. "Oh Philip, I'm so sorry. What will happen?" The opening game had been just yesterday.

"I'm not sure . . . it's pretty much gone. But they're already talking about rebuilding. The owners just need to decide what to do in the meantime for the next part of the season." He opened the door for her and they entered together, and he steered her toward the stairs. Sitting on a lower step, he swiped a hand at his face. When it came away black, he pulled a handkerchief out of his pocket. "We — all the players — went down as soon as we could and tried to help, but I don't think I'm going to be able to come to lessons for a couple days. You continue on without me. At least for now. I'll send a message soon about when I'll be back, but the team needs me."

"I completely understand. Is there anything you need me to do?"

"Prayer is the best answer. This is going to be really stressful on everyone."

She gave him the most sympathetic smile she could muster. But she really just wanted to sit down and cry. It seemed like so much was keeping them apart right now. She really didn't want to be selfish, but she wished she could keep him with her. For just a little longer.

"I better get back. I'll be in touch." He stood and let out a long sigh as he turned for the door.

"I'll be praying for you . . . and, Philip?"

He looked over his shoulder. "Yeah?"

"I love you."

A soft smile spread across his soot-covered face. He took a step back toward her. "I would take you in my arms right now, but I don't want to get anything on your clothes. Thank you, Jeni. For praying. And for everything." He leaned in and kissed her cheek. "I love you too."

CHAPTER 15

Thursday, April 20, 1911

Kicking a rock with his shoe, Philip stuffed his hands into his pockets. Not only had he missed almost a week of seeing Jeni, but he had been working around the clock with some of the other baseball players. Cleaning, salvaging, trying to help in any way they could at the Polo Grounds. On top of that, they'd played four games since the fire.

Then he went home this morning and finally had a chance to look at his mail.

Another letter had been sent. Even more threatening than the last. Saying something terrible would happen if he didn't stop seeing Jeni. Of course, the writer had used some other distasteful terms for her, but he didn't even want to think of them.

So he'd gotten cleaned up and had stewed over the note. But the more he thought about it, the more angry he became. Who dared to think that they could threaten

462

someone like that? It was beyond his imagination.

To make things worse, the manager of the team told him yesterday that morale was low with the fans because of the fire and the fact that they were having to rent Hilltop Park — an American League Park — from the New York Yankees until their own field was rebuilt. This meant that they didn't want to wait until June to have the special events for the fans. The team needed his support.

But Philip was tired. Weary to the bone. The only thing that seemed to be going right was his batting average. What if that went down the drain too?

As he walked the rest of the way to Montgomery's office, the stress, weariness, and aggravation built inside him. And he let it. Because frankly, he was tired of all of it. It seemed like he was being pulled in too many different directions.

His time with God had been limited recently. And his time of prayer with Jeni had been obliterated by all of this. Maybe that was what was wrong with him?

Climbing the stairs to the professor's office, he thought about everything else that he had to do today. With only a few weeks to prepare for the first fan event, he'd prefer just running away and hiding. If only he could just play ball.

But sadly, that wasn't an option.

Jeni's smile greeted him as he entered the office. "Good morning."

"Good morning." He tried to put a smile behind it, but he just wasn't feeling it.

She obviously noticed. "Didn't get enough sleep?"

"Not for a week." He knew his tone was gruff. What was wrong with him? The woman he loved was standing in front of him and being kind. "I'm sorry to be such a grump."

"It's all right. Let's get in for the lesson. The professor has been quite difficult to work with without you." Her light laughter floated over him but didn't stick. Oh, how he wished he could go back to different days. Or just start today over. With plenty of sleep beforehand.

"All right, Mr. March. Your manager sent over the specifics about your speech being moved up to the middle of May, so why don't we start with some work on the actual script you will be reading." The professor turned to Jeni. "I need you to listen and tell him what you hear. Are you able to understand what he's saying? Is he reverting back to his old habits? Be specific about what you hear, because this is just as much a benefit to you as it is to him."

"Of course. I'll do my best." She sat up straighter in her chair and clasped her hands in her lap. A trait that had endeared her to him.

Lord, help me. Please. I'm afraid I feel like a bear today.

Montgomery handed him the script. "Whenever you're ready, Mr. March. Start at the top. Speak slowly and think about your words. Enunciate clearly. The listeners need to understand you."

Philip gave him a nod. He could do this.

Thirty minutes later, he took the sentiment back. He couldn't do this. It was ridiculous to even think that he could. For one thing, he was so tired the words almost blurred on the page in front of him. And for another, with everyone correcting and nitpicking every little thing, he couldn't remember how to say anything correctly. But he kept going.

"To all the fans out there, we want to thank youse for bein' supportive —"

"*Youse* is not a word, Mr. March."

"You dropped another *g.*" Jeni and the professor spoke at the same time.

"That's it." He stood up and threw the paper at their teacher. "I've had enough. I

465

don't need anybody tellin' me what I'm sayin' wrong and when. I'm exhausted, I haven't had any sleep, our ball field is in shambles, now I'm expected to talk to crowds even sooner so that the fans can have their spirits boosted, and oh, while I'm at it, I'm supposed to keep hittin' home runs so I can break my own record."

Jeni reached out to him. "Philip, we were just trying to help, don't —"

"No. Don't say it. Don't tell me one more thing I'm doin' wrong. This was a bad idea. I don't know why I even thought it would work." All his frustrations were coming out of his mouth, whether he wanted them to or not. And his voice kept increasing in volume. Like he was a volcano about to explode. "It's not like you can help me anyway. This was stupid. I can't deal with any more expectations. I'm sorry. I'm not perfect. I can't be the perfect man. I can't protect you. I can't deal with any more threatening letters. All because of us spendin' time together."

Jeni stood, a fire in her eyes that he hadn't seen before. "Well, forgive me for helping you. You'll be good to remember that it was *your* idea that we work together."

"It was a sorry idea. . . . I need to be focused more on my job, anyway."

466

"Far be it from me to keep you from your precious baseball! It's obviously where your true heart is anyway."

"Don't go comparin' baseball to our friendship. That's not fair!"

She crossed her arms over her chest. "I thought we were working together and learning from one another quite well. But I wouldn't want to inconvenience you any further, Mr. March."

"Maybe I should just leave."

"Maybe you should!" Her eyes narrowed, and she grabbed her handbag. "You know what? Maybe it's best that we don't continue. I don't think I want to see you again, Mr. March. Good day." She stormed out of the room, the feathers atop her red hat bouncing along with her.

The slamming of the door knocked a bit of sense back into him. What did he do?

CHAPTER 16

Stomping out her fury on the sidewalks, Jeni marched her way to the shop. Stubborn and foolish man. Why had she ever given her heart to him?

When she entered her workroom, she took off her hat and gloves and slapped them on the table. Well, she would just show him that she didn't need him. She didn't need anybody. And she definitely didn't need love. Forget the linguistics lessons. She could speak just fine. If Philip wanted to continue them, well, by golly, he could very well do them without her.

She was done.

But as soon as she thought it, tears sprang to her eyes. Her stupid temper. Why had she blown up like that?

She wanted to sit down and sob.

No. She wasn't going to let herself get all melancholy over a man.

A man she loved.

A man she missed already. A man she had just pushed away.

But he pushed first.

The argument went round and round in her head.

Stop. The only way to get over the ache in her heart was to pour herself into her work.

She looked down at her hat and gloves and went to move them to the cupboard where she kept her things. But underneath them was a note. In a dark envelope with block script.

As she looked around the room, she noticed that two of the hats she'd been working on yesterday were slashed. Practically in half.

With shaking hands she opened the letter.

This time the threat wasn't against her.

Stay away from Philip March. If you don't, I'll ruin his baseball career and he'll go back to the gutter he came from.

The sender was after Philip too.

Someone was serious about keeping her and Philip apart. But why?

Feeling defeated as fear and worry crept into her limbs again, she could only pray and pour out her heart to God.

Then there was work. Whoever it was

wanted to see them both fail.

Well, Jeni was too stubborn to allow that to happen. She wouldn't let a bully win.

They might think they could take Philip from her, but they couldn't take away her ability and talent.

Four hours later, she'd cleaned up the mess and created the two designs all over again. On top of drawing the designs for three new hats. She found that if she poured herself into her work, she could forget Philip. At least for a few minutes at a time.

Maybe that was for the best. After their altercation earlier, she didn't think that anything could fix how her heart felt. Like it was broken in two.

Footsteps sounded behind her. "Miss O'Brien, I am in need of your assistance."

"Of course, sir. How may I help?"

"I have several extra orders that came in earlier today, and they all need them soon."

"How soon?"

"In the next couple days." Mr. Crawford handed her a paper with the orders and his notes on it.

"Oh. Well of course." She swallowed. "I'll stay late if I need to."

The man beamed a grin at her. "I knew I could count on you, Miss O'Brien."

"Of course, sir."

"You just let me know of anything that you need, and I'll make sure you have it."

She nodded and looked at the paper. Of course the designs wouldn't be easy. Elaborate. Large. Full of ribbons, flowers, feathers . . . One woman even requested white beads that looked like pearls to be woven through hers. Jeni could guess which customer *that* order belonged to.

Oh well. If it would help keep her mind off her heartache, she'd work until midnight every night.

The rest of the day passed in a flurry. It surprised her to discover that as she poured herself into her work, the hats turned out even better than she imagined. Perhaps that might continue. She'd need something to keep her going.

As she walked home, Jeni dreaded telling Aunt Bridget anything about Philip or her work. But her aunt was a perceptive person. She'd know something was wrong. And Jeni didn't have the energy to hide it.

Auntie Bridget opened the door before Jeni could even pull out her key. "Where ya been, lass?" Hands on her hips, the woman looked worried and mad all at the same time.

"I'll be needin' to stay at work a bit late the next few nights. Mr. Crawford has some extra orders that need to be finished fast-like." Her Irish accent grew strong again. Probably because she was tired.

"Oh. All right." Her aunt ushered her in and then closed the door. "Is something botherin' you, dearie?"

Jeni collapsed into a chair at the kitchen table. For a moment, she didn't want to say anything, but then she realized that Auntie Bridget was all she had in the world, and tears sprang to her eyes. "Oh Auntie . . . it's horrible . . ."

After she'd told Aunt Brig everything, her heart felt even heavier and her eyes burned from the tears. A nice headache was brewing too. A lot of good it did her to get it all off her chest.

"I can't believe that someone would threaten you. Why, that's just awful." Her aunt clucked her tongue. "What're ya gonna do about it?"

"Not a thing. Philip and I had a huge fight this morning, and I told him I didn't want to see him again. So that's the end of that. But to think that someone would be so hateful to come into my shop and ruin all my hard work too? Just to be hateful? What have I ever done to them?" Jeni stood up and wiped her nose with her hankie. "I'm afraid I don't feel up to talkin' about it anymore. I just want to go to bed."

"All right. I'll see ya in the mornin'."

As she walked to her room, her feet felt like lead. Her conversation with Philip washed over her again and again, and she realized she'd been quite harsh and unforgiving. He'd been under so much stress and had lashed out, yes, but then she'd told him she didn't want to see him anymore.

But that wasn't what her heart wanted. She wanted to apologize to him and ask for his forgiveness. They could face anything together, right? But how would that ever happen? She'd slammed the door on him. Literally and figuratively.

Tears sprang to her eyes again. She loved Philip. No matter what.

Had she thrown it all away?

Philip paced his apartment. The day had spiraled downward as it went on. How had he allowed himself to speak that way to Jeni? He couldn't believe it himself when he thought back to their altercation at the professor's.

What seemed like an unbelievable nightmare had actually happened.

And now he had to deal with the consequences.

As his heart ached with the weight of losing Jeni, a swell of determination rushed up, and he took a deep breath. No. He didn't have to accept that he'd lost her. Yes, he'd been stupid. Yes, he'd lost his temper. But he could ask for forgiveness. Beg for it, if need be. He'd been in the wrong. The least he could do was admit it.

Scrambling for paper and a pen, Philip looked around the apartment. Words filled his mind. Everything he wanted to say . . . everything within his heart that he wanted to share with Jeni. With another deep breath, he sat down and prayed for the Lord's guidance. Then, setting the pen to paper, he poured out his soul to the woman he loved. If he needed to send her letters every day until she forgave him, he would do that.

Because she was worth it.

CHAPTER 17

Wednesday, May 3, 1911

Mr. Crawford's shop was seeing incredible sales — thanks to the number of hats Jeni was cranking out daily — and he voluntarily gave her another raise. But even with that good news, she couldn't keep her mind from wandering back to Philip. How was he doing? Did he miss her as much as she missed him? She tried to keep track of the baseball games and how he played, but it had been almost two weeks since she'd seen him, and her heart ached for him.

While she'd continued to practice her linguistics on her own, she missed the lessons at the professor's. Missed talking with her best friend. Missed their laughter together. Missed the fact that she could simply be herself.

She longed to see him again, but they were busy rebuilding the field and she was sure the games kept him busy. She'd sent an apology to him but hadn't heard back. Maybe he couldn't forgive her for her words.

What if he didn't love her? It crushed her to even think about it, but their last argument . . . what if he'd realized she wasn't what he wanted after all? The threats, the differences in class . . . maybe it had become too much for him.

Even as the thoughts stirred around her brain, in her heart Jeni knew that wasn't true. Philip was above all that. He was a good and decent man. He'd just been overwhelmed, frustrated, and worried that day. Maybe it was simply going to take him time.

A new plan hatched in her mind. If Mr. Crawford would grant her a day off, it might work. She could go to a baseball game . . . send him a note that she was there . . . and pray that he would see her.

There were just a few things she needed to do first. And she would give him a little more time. A smile spread across her face, and for the first time in two weeks, she felt hopeful.

A customer's voice out front caught Jeni's attention. She stayed silent for a moment. Why did the woman's voice sound so familiar? Setting down the piece she was working on, she stepped quietly over to the curtain and listened.

"This is absolutely lovely, Mr. Crawford. My favorite so far."

Her boss cleared his throat. "Thank you, Mrs. Belmont, I was thinking you would be particular to this one."

"It's perfect."

Jeni dared to open a slit in the curtain and peek through.

Mrs. Alva Vanderbilt Belmont was a proud supporter of the suffragette movement. Jeni had heard her speak on several occasions in rallies in the streets of New York City. While Jeni loved the idea of being able to vote, she hadn't really thought too much about rights for women. It had been hard enough to earn her way as an Irishwoman.

Mrs. Belmont had turned and was pointing to the window. Jeni had been lost in thought and missed what she said.

Mr. Crawford looked a bit perplexed. "Well . . . um, I'm not sure."

"I understand it's a bit last-minute for me to ask you to design something right now, but I need it for tomorrow evening and I want to make sure you are envisioning the same thing that I am."

"Of course, I'm sure I can have something in time for you tomorrow, I'm just having some difficulty creating in front of a customer."

"Isn't this what you do, Mr. Crawford?" The woman was used to getting her way, that was easy to see.

Jeni watched her boss hem and haw. The client was asking him to come up with the idea for the design then and there. So she could approve it. And she wanted it now.

A surge of bravery ran through Jeni's heart. Without giving it another thought, she split the curtain and walked confidently to the counter. "Perhaps I can help?"

Crawford cleared his throat again. "Yes, Mrs. Belmont, I think you would love Miss O'Brien's work."

Jeni pointed to the hat Mrs. Belmont had raved about. "I created that one, ma'am."

"Well . . ." Mrs. Belmont's eyebrows lifted and she turned a questioning gaze to Mr. Crawford. "Why didn't you tell me you had this talented young woman back there?" She didn't give him the opportunity to answer. "Miss O'Brien, I have a fund-raiser tomorrow evening, and I simply must have a new hat to go with my dress. It's an aqua color with a silver sash."

Jeni reached for a plain, cream-colored, satin-covered hat. "What if we were to match the silver sash on the dress with a silver band around the hat here." Demonstrating what she envisioned, Jeni couldn't believe she'd been so bold to jump in like that. But she turned to Mr. Crawford. "There's some aqua feathers on my desk, would you mind fetching them?"

The owner didn't respond but moved in quick strides to the back.

"What if we added some handmade flowers on this side over here. The feathers could be at the crown, and I could dye some tulle to match your dress that could surround the entire design." With deft fingers, she grabbed flowers, tulle, and the feathers from Mr. Crawford and laid them out on the hat to show their customer.

"I can see it." Mrs. Belmont's eyes lit up. "That will be perfect."

"Could you bring your dress by this afternoon so that I can ensure the colors match?"

"Of course. I'll have my maid bring it within the hour."

"That will be perfect. I'll have it ready for you by tomorrow at noon." Jeni gave the woman a confident smile.

Mrs. Alva Vanderbilt Belmont lifted her chin slightly and gave a sideways glance to Mr. Crawford. "Where have you been hiding this genius, and why haven't I seen her before in all the times I've frequented your shop?"

"Well, ma'am, Jeni likes to work in her office. But she does make the very best of the hats here." Mr. Crawford puffed out his chest. "I only hire the best."

"Hmm . . . I see that." Mrs. Belmont eyed them both. "Miss O'Brien, how would you like to help me with my campaign?"

"Campaign?" What had her moment of bravery gotten her into?

"A campaign for women. You shouldn't be hiding in the back of this shop any longer. Especially since you are the designer of such glorious pieces of art. You should be praised for your accomplishments." She turned her attention to Jeni's boss. "And, Mr. Crawford, I guarantee you will gain even more clientele if you back my campaign and keep Miss O'Brien out front here."

"I'm not entirely certain —"

"Oh, but you should be, Mr. Crawford. Don't you realize that the majority of your clients are women? Just imagine the influx of customers you will have when they realize that you are supporting them. Mrs. Astor Wilson, I know, frequents your shop a great deal. I've heard her praise your designs again and again. But what if she found out that your master designer is kept in the back . . . because she's a woman. Now, you wouldn't want to lose her business, would you?"

Mr. Crawford blinked several times. "Of course I'll support you, Mrs. Belmont. It would be my privilege."

"Wonderful." The woman was obviously a master at this. "Miss O'Brien, it was a pleasure to meet you. From now on, I'm sending all my business to you."

"Thank you, ma'am. That's very gracious of you."

The austere woman headed for the door, where her driver waited. "I'll be back tomorrow at noon."

In a flurry of movement, she was gone.

Jeni stood rooted to the spot. Would her boss be mad at her now?

Mr. Crawford moved a few things around and then coughed. Then cleared his throat. Then coughed. Again. "Miss O'Brien, I believe I owe you a debt of gratitude for coming out when you did. Thank you." He moved to the curtain. "Why don't we move your workstation out here? The women might all enjoy watching you work. Especially if you can design exactly what they want while they are here. I think Mrs. Belmont is onto something brilliant." He

481

slipped through the curtain, and all Jeni could do was stare after him. No discussing what had happened. He acted as if this was perfectly normal and they would move on from here.

In the course of twenty minutes, everything had changed. Hadn't she wished to be out in the front of the store?

Excitement filled her as she watched Mr. Crawford move a worktable out from her little area. It put her feet into motion, and she went to grab the rest of her things.

In less than an hour, she'd set up a lovely little area in a corner of the shop where women could come and order a special design or watch her work. It was posh and elegant.

Her heart rejoiced as she praised God for all that He had allowed her to do.

Now if she could just share it with Philip, everything would be perfect.

Her elation sank for a moment. If only she could reach him.

But then she lifted her chin. She had a plan and she would follow through. If God saw fit to keep them together, then He would make a way. She would move forward with confidence and pray for His will.

CHAPTER 18

Bridget lit a match and tossed it into the metal waste bin. Once the paper in the bottom caught fire, she dropped a stack of letters on top. That March fellow was persistent, she'd give him that. Since Jeni worked all day, Bridget had been able to intercept all the mail from the baseball player. She'd hidden them until now, but the fear that Jeni would find them caused her to take a more final approach. Jeni didn't need to see them. There was no reason she needed to read any of them. It was better this way.

Wiping her hands on a towel, she watched the papers get eaten up by the flames. When there was nothing but ash left, she flicked some water into the bin to make sure the flame was gone. Now all she had to do was finish making dinner and she could show Jeni the letter from her friend in Wisconsin. It was time.

Jeni came bounding in the door a few

minutes later. "Auntie!" Her excited voice filled the room as she ran over and hugged Bridget. "You won't believe what happened today!"

"Go on. I can see it must be exciting." She turned and stirred the stew she had bubbling on the stove.

"Mr. Crawford moved my workstation to the front of the store. You wouldn't believe it. Mrs. Alva Vanderbilt Belmont came in and asked for a hat designed right there in front of her . . ."

Bridget tuned out the fast-talk from her niece. Let her have her say, then while she was still happy, they could sit down and discuss the move to Wisconsin.

". . . it's everything I'd been hoping for and more! Well, not owning my own store, but right before I left, Mr. Crawford even talked to me about being a partner with him. Can you believe it?" The exuberance in her niece's voice pricked at Bridget's conscience.

"That's wonderful, dear." She set two bowls of stew on the table. "Now, let's sit down. There's something very important I wish to discuss with you."

Jeni did as she asked, but her face fell.

Bridget said a quick blessing and placed her napkin in her lap. "I've been wanting to talk to you about this for a while, and I think it's finally time. What with your falling out with that baseball player." She shouldn't have brought that up, because Jeni looked even sadder. "Anyway, it doesn't matter. A friend of mine is in Wisconsin, and we've been writing back and forth about the area and the lovely community of Irish that are there. I think it's time we left New York City. We could pack up and leave next week and be all settled in Wisconsin before the beginning of June." She glanced at her niece. "Won't that be nice?"

Jeni sat there with her mouth wide open. "You didn't listen to a thing I said, did you?"

"Of course I did, dearie. Your boss moved your workstation . . ." The rest of it escaped her.

"While that's a great plan for you, Aunt Brig, I have no intention of moving to Wisconsin."

"You'll do what you're told, young lady."

"No."

"What did you just say?" Bridget put her hands flat on the table.

"No. I won't move to Wisconsin."

"Yes, you will." She narrowed her eyes.

"No, Auntie. I won't. After all the work I've put in, after I've supported you for all these years and worked my way up. You just

485

decide that we're going to leave? No. You didn't even listen to one of the greatest blessings I've ever had."

"But —"

Her niece held up a hand and stopped her. "No. No buts. I'll not stand for it. I won't be moving to Wisconsin. I have an opportunity to really excel with Mr. Crawford and Mrs. Belmont. They believe in me. And the baseball player? His name is Philip. I'm not leaving him. I don't want to live without him. I . . . I love him." She stood from the table and slapped her napkin down. "I'm going to bed."

Bridget leaned back in her chair and let the shock wash over her. Why hadn't that gone as planned?

One thing was certain, she'd underestimated Mr. March's charms.

And her niece's stubborn streak.

Well, she knew how to break that.

Thursday, May 18, 1911

For three days in a row, Jeni had purchased a ticket and watched the New York Giants play at Hilltop Park. For three days, she'd learned all she could about this fascinating game that Philip loved. And for three days, she'd hoped and prayed that he would notice her in the stands.

486

Baseball had become her favorite pastime now. She loved it. And not only because she loved and adored a certain center fielder. The game was quite enjoyable. In her imagination she could see herself proudly cheering on Philip for years to come, and she would love doing it.

If only she could get his attention. Each time, she'd worn a hat that he would recognize. But center field was a long way from her seat.

An idea struck, and she didn't waste any time putting it into action. Taking her program, she tore it in half and wrote a note to Philip. Telling him she was in the stands and where to look for her. Then she begged for his forgiveness.

When the Giants ran in from the field to the dugout, she made her way down the stairs and leaned over the railing. Waving frantically, she got the attention of one of the other players. He jogged over to her.

"Would you give this to Philip March, please?"

The player nodded at her and smiled. "Sure will."

"Thank you so much!"

"You're welcome." He ran into the dugout, and all Jeni could do was wait.

She went back to her seat and prayed that

Philip would read her note.

When he came up to bat, he turned and looked toward her section.

Jeni stood.

Their eyes connected and she clutched her hands to her chest. Had he forgiven her?

Still on her feet, she took a deep breath and watched as he swung.

"Strike!" The ump's shout could be heard across the field.

The pitcher wound up for another . . .

Crack!

The ball went flying, and Jeni clapped and jumped up and down. Another home run! Pride filled her chest.

A nudge to her right made her turn. A large man stood there. "This is for you, miss."

Jeni smiled and took the missive. With anxious fingers, she opened the note, so excited to see what Philip would say. But it wasn't from him.

Someone was threatening her. That if she didn't leave the game, something horrible would happen to her aunt.

Jeni scurried out of her row of seats and raced up the stairs so she could get out. On her way, she bumped into the man who'd delivered the note. Grabbing his arm, she tugged. "Who told you to give this to me?"

The man shrugged. "Some lady paid me two dollars to deliver it."

The answer threw her off. Two dollars was a small fortune for someone to pay just to deliver a letter. "A lady? What lady? Is she still here?"

The man looked around. "Nah. I don't see her."

"What did she look like?"

"About this tall" — the man demonstrated with his hands — "blue dress. Big hat."

Jeni didn't need to hear any more. She stuffed the letter into her handbag and headed toward the exit.

Thirty minutes later, she stomped up the stairs to her apartment.

Unlocking the door, she fumed. As she turned the knob she prayed for God to help her to calm down. "Aunt Bridget!"

"Whatever is the matter, dearie?" A look of dramatic innocence was plastered on the older woman's face.

"Don't even attempt to lie to me. I know you paid that man two dollars to deliver your little threatening note."

Her aunt's jaw dropped. "I don't know what you're talking about."

"It's written all over your face. Don't deny it. I'm sure it was you who sent the notes to Philip. And you went to my job and ruined some of my work? What? Just to prove a point? To keep me from seeing a non-Irish boy?"

The facade dropped and Aunt Bridget put her hands on her hips. "How dare you speak to me in such a tone! I did what I had to do. It was for yer own good too. You ungrateful —" She gasped and grabbed at her chest.

Several seconds passed before Jeni realized that her aunt wasn't faking it. She rushed to her side. "What is it? What's wrong?"

Her aunt's eyes glazed over and then her whole frame went limp.

Jeni laid her down and ran out the door. "Help! Someone please, help!"

CHAPTER 19

Friday, May 19, 1911

Jeni paced in the hospital room. The crazy events of the past days had turned everything upside down.

Once she'd gotten help to take her aunt to the hospital, everything seemed to speed up only for it to come back to a screeching halt. The doctors weren't sure if Aunt Bridget could completely recover from her heart episode.

Auntie had woken up and apologized for what she'd done. Said she couldn't face the good Lord without confessing her sins. While Jeni forgave her aunt, it was still hard to believe that her own kin — her own blood — had been so hateful and cruel.

It all seemed like a bad dream.

Aunt Bridget lay pale in her hospital bed. The sun shone through the window.

But what would *she* do now? Would her

aunt recover? Would she need Jeni to care for her?

Then there was the matter of Jeni's own heart. She'd thought for certain that Philip saw her at the game yesterday. The question was . . . would he have come to see her after the game?

She'd never know, because the note from her aunt made her leave the game. And even though Aunt Bridget had been wrong and had done some horrible things, it sounded selfish to Jeni's own ears to even be thinking about her own desires and hopes at a time like this. Wondering whether her last living relative would live or die.

Walking over to the window, Jeni wrapped her arms around her middle. *Lord, what do I do?*

She looked at the clock. It was almost the top of the hour. Maybe she could go grab a paper and find out what happened at the game yesterday after she left. Anything to connect her to Philip.

Swiping her hands at her tears, she decided a cup of coffee would be a good idea. She hadn't slept much last night.

Walking down the hall to where the nurses kept coffee and tea ready for the families of their patients, Jeni stretched the kinks out of her neck and arms. Mr. Crawford had been very gracious about her not coming in. Of course, she'd made so many hats the past little while that he was probably set on inventory for at least a few more days.

The aroma of the coffee perked up her senses. As soon as she poured herself a cup and took a sip, her mind was a little more at ease. God knew what He was doing. She would rest in that.

Walking down the stairs and out of the building, she searched through the crowd at the corner for a newsboy. As she weaved through the people, Jeni spotted a young boy waving a paper over his head.

"Paper, miss?"

"Yes, please." She gave the boy a coin and tucked the paper under her arm.

When she walked back into Aunt Bridget's room, Jeni noticed her aunt was awake. "Good morning, Auntie. How are you feeling?"

"A little tired." Aunt Bridget shifted in her bed. "Is that a paper?"

"Yes. I wanted to see the baseball score from yesterday." Fully expecting a sharp retort from her aunt, Jeni was quite surprised there was none. "Would you like me to read to you?"

"That would be nice. I haven't seen a paper since last week."

"Of course." She flicked open the folded paper and saw the face of the man she loved on the front page. Jeni gasped.

"What is it?"

"It's Philip." Scanning the article, she couldn't believe her eyes.

"What?"

"He's proposed!"

"To who?"

"Me!" Jumping up from her chair, she ran back down to the street and searched for every paper she could find. She had the *Tribune* in her hand then found the *Herald* and the *World.* Standing in the middle of the sidewalk, she checked them.

They all had the same front-page story. HOME RUN KING PROPOSES.

Apparently, Philip couldn't find her and decided to do something drastic. So after the game yesterday, he'd talked to every reporter he knew and asked them to run his proposal in their paper.

Not only had they run it, but it was on the front page. Philip proposing to *her.*

She looked up from the papers and couldn't help but laugh out loud. He loved her! And he wanted to marry her!

Racing to the closest telegraph station, she composed in her mind what she wanted

to say and how Philip could find her.
Thank You, God!

Friday, July 14, 1911
Jeni took a deep breath and looked out at the crowd. The manager of the New York Giants had suggested they get married at the newly rebuilt Polo Grounds and Jeni had agreed, but she hadn't expected to have the seats completely filled. She'd never been in front of this many people before.

The past few weeks had been wonderful. Philip had found her at the hospital after his ball game and proposed again in person.

She accepted.

Aunt Bridget had gotten well and had even invited Philip over for dinner and apologized for burning his letters and sending the threatening notes. They got along surprisingly well, although she still had to throw in the occasional barb that he wasn't Irish. Philip handled it all beautifully and with such grace and forgiveness. Even to the point that now he could banter with Aunt Bridget. It made Jeni love him all the more.

Mrs. Belmont and Mrs. Astor Wilson had become her biggest supporters as she and Mr. Crawford signed the papers to become partners. She'd spoken at a suffragette

495

meeting, the shop saw its profits double in the first week alone, and she'd made time to see *lots* of baseball games.

But the best part had been praying with Philip every morning. About their future, about what God had for them, and thanking Him for bringing them together. It had been a whirlwind, but God made beauty out of their messiness.

A gust of wind blew over her and caused her hat to tilt. Her thoughts came back to the moment at hand as she reached up to straighten it. Looking around her, she smiled. It wasn't a dream. This was all very real. She was about to marry Philip March.

Since she didn't have anyone to give her away, she and Philip had decided to walk out onto the field together. It was a little unorthodox, but so was everything about their relationship.

They'd fallen in love in a linguistics lesson.

She was Irish. He was from Brooklyn.

The papers had a field day with the story. Especially after Philip's gallant, persuasive, and *numerous* proposals in the papers. Philip and Jeni had become the king and queen of New York. At least for a little while.

No one had said anything derogatory about her being Irish. A fact that shocked and surprised her. But times were changing, and she was grateful.

Straightening her dress of gauzy layers of white, Jeni adjusted her gloves at her wrists. Nerves were beginning to get to her, and she just wanted to marry Philip.

Reverend Richards walked up beside her. "Are you ready?"

"Yes. Very."

He laughed. "I'll make it quick and painless, I promise."

Philip jogged over to her. His blond hair moved gently in the breeze, and she gulped. This handsome man — this baseball player and her best friend — would soon be her husband. The thought thrilled her.

"Penny for your thoughts?" He winked at her.

"I'm excited that soon you'll be mine."

"I like how you think, Miss-O'Brien-almost-Mrs.-March."

Reverend Richards cleared his throat. "Well, I think we should get started."

"That's a fabulous idea." Philip laughed.

The minister walked out to home plate. The crowd cheered.

Philip offered her his arm. "Are you ready?"

"I am." She gave him a big smile.

He led her slowly across the field. The

crowd was standing, shouting, and applauding, but she tuned them out. She took a deep breath and started to sing softly:

"Take me out to the ball game,
Take me out with the crowd;
Buy me some peanuts and Cracker Jack,
I don't care if I never get back.
Let me root, root, root for the home team,
If they don't win, it's a shame.
For it's one, two, three strikes, you're out,
At the old ball game."

Philip beamed at her and laughed. "You memorized it for me?"

"Well, you loved it so much when we saw it on vaudeville that I thought it was a good present for you."

"It was perfect. Thank you." They reached home plate, and the reverend told them to turn and face one another.

Reverend Richards kept with his promise. It only took them a few moments to recite their vows to one another, but it was beautiful and something that Jeni would never forget. Even though the crowd couldn't hear them, they'd kept silent — almost reverent.

Until Philip was given permission to kiss her. When he leaned in and took her in his arms, the crowd cheered.

The rumble and roar that coursed through the new Polo Grounds was loud and felt like it could burst her eardrums.

But it was nothing like the joy that exploded in her heart when Philip's lips met hers.

He'd hit a home run.

AUTHOR'S NOTE

The famous song "Take Me Out to the Ball
Game" is the third most sung song in
America, inspired when Jack Norworth saw
a billboard that read "Baseball Today —
Polo Grounds" — an advertisement for the
National League's New York Giants in
1908. It was an instant hit that year and
was performed for vaudeville audiences,
recorded for the Edison Phonograph Company, and actually ended up being the most
popular song of the year. Both Norworth —
who wrote the lyrics — and the man who
wrote the tune, Albert von Tilzer, had never
been to a baseball game.

But in 1934 its fame would be immortal-
ized as it started to be played at baseball
games. This iconic tune — and the story
behind it — were too much to pass up, so I
had to include it in the story. Every time
you hear it, or sing it in the seventh-inning

stretch, I hope you remember Philip and Jeni's story in *A Language of Love.*

God bless you!

Kimberley Woodhouse

ABOUT THE AUTHOR

Kimberley Woodhouse is an award-winning and bestselling author of more than twenty fiction and nonfiction books. A popular speaker and teacher, she's shared her theme of "Joy through Trials" with more than half a million people across the country at more than two thousand events. Kim and her incredible husband of twenty-five-plus years have two adult children. She's passionate about music and Bible study and loves the gift of story.

You can connect with Kimberley at www.kimberleywoodhouse.com and www.facebook.com/KimberleyWoodhouseAuthor

■ ■ ■ ■

TAILORED
SWEETHEARTS

BY DEBBY LEE

■ ■ ■ ■

CHAPTER 1

Dutch Harbor, Alaska
April 1945

In spite of the late spring sunshine, the blustery wind blew through Stella Mc-Govern as she walked home from her job manufacturing parachutes. She wrapped the scarf tighter around her head. Would she ever get used to such bitter temperatures? She tucked her chin against the cold and stepped faster. The answer didn't matter so much. The circumstances were something she would gladly bear to help bring an end to the terrible war, to help bring Papa home.

Work at the small warehouse that day had not gone well. The constant humming of the many industrial-sized sewing machines and the tedious, meticulous work required for each chute proved to be too much for three women. That, combined with the harsh, rugged conditions of the Alaskan Fort Mears Army Base, had motivated the three women to quit and plan to move back to their home as soon as possible.

Their departure would leave Stella working longer hours, but a smile warmed her face. It meant a bigger paycheck and another few months' worth of iron pills for her anemic mother. And she didn't mind working with the Singer sewing machines and rolls and rolls of nylon fabric. Each parachute required sixty-five yards of material. She loved piecing together panels.

Papa, a career army officer, had been stationed at Fort Mears at the onset of the war in early 1942, and the family had moved back to the Alaskan Territories. Then, right after Christmas 1943, he'd been shipped off to England to prepare for D-Day, the retaking of France.

Papa was in charge of getting supplies to troops stationed in Europe. In spite of the war effort back home, supplies often ran short. His convoys of C-Rations and medicines were often under attack from the German Luftwaffe.

Mama hadn't been the same since Papa left. It was one thing for a woman to be apart from her husband because of military duties; it was another when his duties put him in the line of fire and at risk of being killed. Stella could hardly coax food into her heartbroken mother, even when it was plentiful, which wasn't often enough.

If only a letter would find its way from the farmlands in eastern France to the Aleutian Island chain a half a world away, and into her mother's small, bony hands. Mail moved slower than a spring thaw, and Papa's letters were few. Stella bit her lower lip and steered her thoughts toward more hopeful things.

A pale blue, two-story clapboard house came into view as she crested a rolling rocky hill. Her childhood home, at least it had been before the Great Depression had landed on their doorstep. With her father out of work, they could no longer afford the house Stella had played in as a child. That's when Papa had joined the military and they left the Alaskan territories before coming back in 1942.

She paused to stare at it, as she often did when on her way home from work. Shutters covered the large windows, and the balcony was in serious need of repair.

A lump formed in Stella's throat. How many times had Mama walked that balcony as she waited for Papa to come home from work?

Flower boxes underlined the windows beside the front door. At least they were still in good shape. Stella remembered the bright yellow daffodils and orange tulips that sprang to life every spring, in spite of such frigid weather.

What drew her attention the most were the two chimneys at each end of the palace-like structure. They had always looked like bookends to Stella. Mama wouldn't be cold again if they could move back into the house with two fireplaces.

Her heart fluttered like bird wings at the dream of someday living once again in such a home. But the entire world was embroiled in a bitter war, and fancying such notions seemed foolish. She dreamed anyway. Someday the war would be over. Someday Papa would come home. Someday they would live in this grand house again, and she would have a whole room set aside for her sewing.

A B-17 airplane thundered overhead. Stella slapped her hands over her ears. How was Mama to get any rest with the planes roaring over the Alaskan Territories day and night? The thought of her mother made Stella forget the blue house and hurry home.

Twilight crept across the barren tundra by the time she reached the windowless two-room shack, a hovel really, where she and her mother resided. A thick fog spread over the island like a heavy eiderdown quilt. The soupy condensation made seeing difficult, but it did serve a purpose. It helped keep the Japanese from attacking the tiny town of Dutch Harbor. It was harder to bomb what they couldn't see.

Dutch Harbor had been bombed back in 1942. Stella would never forget the terrifying night of June 4, when Japanese fighters had dropped their bombs. Steel oil tanks were destroyed, fire erupted from a barracks ship, and the hospital was demolished. Forty-three people lost their lives.

Stella's heart still ached at the loss of life, but at that moment her temporary home came into view. She walked faster to get there.

"Mama, I'm home." With a hard push, Stella forced the ill-fitting door to close.

"I'm glad you're here. I rested well today. I thought we could work on your quilts again tonight by the fire." Her mother smiled.

Stella's heart thumped a bit faster. She loved to see her mother so happy. A surge of warmth swept through her and it seemed the temperature in the shack warmed by several degrees as well.

"Sounds wonderful, Mama, right after dinner." Piecing together the quilts from the scraps of material Stella scrounged from her work kept her mother occupied. Donating them to the military hospital gave Mama, and also Stella, a purpose. And it was practical, due to the perpetual cold of an Alaskan spring. Many a brave soldier had thanked them for their contribution. She liked to think those hand-sewn blankets brought comfort to the men who made so many sacrifices for their country. She hoped the quilts would keep them warm for years to come.

Stella added several pieces of driftwood to the fire and hung a cast-iron kettle of water over the flames. To it she added fish, vegetables, and a dash of salt. Before long the aroma of the stew hung in the air and Stella sat with her mother at the rickety table. Two square feet of plywood was hardly enough space to hold the bowls and silverware, but that didn't stop Stella from giving thanks to the Lord for all they *did* have — food, shelter, warmth, and each other.

Yet, the longing for news of Papa was a hunger that could never be filled. How many months had it been since they'd heard from him? Three, and the postmark bore the name of a town close to the German border. She said a silent prayer for her father's well-being as she finished eating.

After dinner, she washed the dishes, placed them on the shelf above the sink, and added another few pieces of driftwood to the waning fire. She sat down to sew with her mother. Dare she burden Mama with news that she'd be working longer hours at the factory?

An image of the blue house popped into her mind. If the Nazis weren't trying to conquer the whole of Europe for themselves, Papa would be home to take care of Mama and working a good job to support them all. Then perhaps she could take in sewing jobs and every penny she made could go toward buying back their house.

She chastised herself. Pointing blame and allowing resentment to creep into her heart was no way to live. She silently asked God's forgiveness as she stitched a small square into a quilt block. Nine small squares sewn together made one quilt block. The block in her lap needed one more square to be complete. When she finished her handiwork, she snipped the loose ends. Soon she would need more thread.

Quilt-making supplies weren't easy to come by in their remote location, but several local native women, namely her friend Mary, had come through for her in the past. She hoped they would do so again.

When Stella finished sewing for the evening, she tucked her quilt block into her sewing basket. Then she rubbed her tired eyes and stretched her tired muscles. Not more than two minutes passed when a loud commotion sounded from nearby Fort Mears Army Base.

Shrill sirens pierced the night air.

Heavy diesel engines revved to life.

An airplane overhead whined and sputtered.

Nausea roiled in Stella's stomach. She glanced at her mother, whose face blanched. The cacophony meant only one thing.

A brave but unfortunate pilot was coming in for a crash landing.

Captain Irving Morgenstern gripped the yoke of the shrapnel-riddled B-17 with both hands. No easy feat considering the tremors reverberating throughout the aircraft. He said a quick prayer for his nine-man crew and one to make sure he was right with the Almighty.

"Open that hatch and get the belly gunner back up here," Lieutenant Jack Blankston, Irving's copilot, shouted.

The nose gunner scrambled to the back of the plane.

The radio operator barked their position

over the radio, and the number wounded. Frisco and Tex had both been shot, but Irving didn't know where or how bad. It took every ounce of his skill and concentration to keep the bucking, wavering plane from going into a tailspin.

Steady.

Steady.

In spite of the danger, and the odds against them, Irving vowed to land the plane safely so his crew, his comrades, stood a decent chance of survival. If he could land without the plane exploding, he would count them all lucky. The dense fog coating the runway didn't make his job easy. He was grateful for the large metal drums of burning oil lining each side of the airstrip that gave him an idea of where to land. And he was determined.

The bomber bumped onto the ground with a jolting thump, bounced, and then thumped down again. The screech of the brakes tore through his ears. He held the yoke steady and pulled back on the steering column. A quick glance at the instruments echoed what instinct told him. The plane was slowing down. Hope flickered through him.

One front wheel collapsed and spun the plane sideways.

The left wing skidded onto the ground.

Fire erupted from the engine.

Irving gritted his teeth, fighting the yoke that tried to leap out of his grip. Another jolt, then sudden impact as the rest of the landing gear gave way. The plane's belly walloped the ground. In a matter of seconds that felt more like hours, they lurched to a stop. He released the breath he didn't realize he'd been holding.

"Everybody out!" he bellowed.

Smoke crept into the cockpit. The fire could spread, and fast, or cause an explosion while his crew scrambled for the exits. Even though they had landed safely, they could still perish before they had the chance to escape the wreckage.

He reached for a fire extinguisher to fight the flames so his men could escape.

Blankston jumped from his seat and assisted the waist gunner with Frisco and Tex. Wounded men first. Considering the camaraderie between them all, Irving expected no less. The tail gunner, the last man aboard, leapt from the side door.

Something in front of Irving exploded. He screamed in agony and fear.

Flames licked his hands, singeing his heavy gloves. He peeled the smoking remnants of leather from his hands. Black smoke thickened around him, and his eyes smarted and watered. He scrambled from the cockpit, crawling toward the door on his knees, belly, and elbows. Violent coughing sent his upper torso into spasms.

Air.

He needed air.

Two more feet until he made it to the door. He reached, stretched . . . but sapped of breath and strength, he couldn't quite get to the exit.

A pair of hands emerged from the cloud of thick black smoke. The hands grasped hold of his jacket and pulled.

Irving was yanked into the dark frigid air. Dropping to the ground, he sucked in breath after breath until his lungs ached from the icy temperatures. Another coughing fit tore through his chest. Pain reverberated through his hands, his fingers.

The wail of an ambulance siren pierced the atmosphere.

"My men," he croaked. "Are my men all right?"

"Easy, Captain. Lieutenant Blankston is riding with Frisco and Tex to the infirmary. The medic said they just might be all right."

Irving turned his head to see a squad of men hosing the flames engulfing his plane. He was no mechanic, but he knew the charred wreckage would never fly again. A medic tried to examine Irving's wounded hands.

"Ahhh!" The scream flew from his lips in spite of his determination to be brave in the presence of his crew.

"You're good, Captain. You're gonna make it, you hear me? You're gonna make it," the medic said.

Irving swallowed hard. He clenched his teeth. A glance at his hands revealed black curled fingers, gushing blood, and a stench that frightened him more than the landing.

"Lord," he prayed. "Please don't let me lose my hands."

CHAPTER 2

The smells of alcohol, gangrene, and hopelessness crashed into Stella's senses when she stepped into the hospital ward during visiting hours. She prayed she'd be able to bring some peace and comfort to the wounded soldiers from the previous night's airplane crash.

When she told her boss, Mr. Hapsock, that she wanted the afternoon off to visit the hospital, he'd readily agreed. For the past two weeks he'd been quite irritable, so his willingness to let her go brought a smile to her face.

The charge nurse and Stella's best friend, Colleen Gardner, sat at her desk. "Afternoon, Stella. How is your mother? Any word from your father?"

"Mama is doing all right. Of course, she'd be better if we'd get a letter from Papa."

Colleen reached for Stella's hand. "I'll continue to pray for your folks. How is work

519

going at the factory?"

"Busier than usual now that three more workers quit. How are things going here?"

"We have two new patients today."

"Yes, I heard," she replied. "I'm here to see them."

"Right this way." Colleen stood and motioned toward the beds in the back of the room.

Stella clutched her purse and swallowed hard. Holding a perfumed handkerchief to her nose, she followed her friend down the center aisle. Beds lined the walls and were filled with men suffering with everything from frostbite to dysentery to cholera to amputated limbs.

It was never easy visiting the soldiers, but considering the hardships and sacrifices they endured to keep the Japanese from occupying the Alaskan Territories, she would bear any uneasiness. She'd offer them whatever comfort she could provide as a volunteer.

"How badly were they injured?" she asked. Sometimes the more seriously wounded men didn't care for company for a while. Although she'd heard a few stories from friends, she couldn't imagine the horrors the soldiers suffered. She understood why some of them might need time to adjust to their surroundings before having visitors.

"Corporal Francisco Valenzuela was shot in the leg." Colleen pulled the dark green wool blanket up over the man's shoulders and tucked it in.

Stella's gaze lingered on the man with black wavy hair sleeping on the cot. Did he have family? The men seemed to recuperate better when they had loved ones back home.

Colleen continued, "The surgeon was able to remove the shrapnel without having to amputate. Thank the Lord."

Stella did just that.

"On the other hand . . ." Colleen pulled Stella toward a closet in the narrow hallway. Her hoarse whisper bespoke of her heartache. "Private Eugene Cotton was shot in the chest. The doctor and I worked on him for almost an hour. He wasn't so lucky."

A slow, awkward moment passed.

Colleen said sadly, "If only he'd worn his flak jacket."

A sheen of tears glistened in her friend's eyes. Not being able to save a patient was always hard on Colleen. Stella ached for her almost as much as for the wounded soldiers.

"I'm so sorry," Stella said. Trite words for such a painful situation, she knew, but what else could she say? Some situations were best served by silence.

"The War Department will be sending a telegram to his home in Texas, where he has, um, had, family." Colleen took a few more steps down the aisle and Stella followed her.

Colleen then motioned to a bed in the back corner. "And this is Captain Irving Morgenstern, the pilot. It took a lot of skill to land a shot-up plane with damaged landing gear, but he did it. And then he stayed in the plane, fighting the fire, giving his crew time to get out."

"A true hero." Stella gulped. But weren't they all? Due to the man's tall frame, his feet hung off the end of the bed as he slept. His short blond hair was ruffled, likely from sleeping fitfully. Thick bandages covered his hands. What price would his Purple Heart cost him? To lose one hand would be tragic enough, but to lose both? That would cripple his spirits as much, if not more so, than his body.

Stella's heart thudded in her chest. She would not let this man be crippled, in mind or body, if she could help it. "I think I'll just sit here by his bed for a spell."

"Sure," Colleen said.

Stella pulled up a chair and hardly felt her friend's gentle pat on her shoulder as she prayed for Captain Morgenstern. Did he have a family who cared about him, anyone who wondered if he was alive or wounded?

"I need to get back to work," Colleen said. She gave Stella a small squeeze and then went back to her desk.

If the pilot had family, a wife or a sweetheart, he'd surely want them to know he was all right. But he couldn't very well write the letter with his hands in the condition they were in. No matter, she could pen the letter, or letters, for him. She'd feed him too, if necessary, and if his pride allowed. It was likely that over the next few weeks she would get to know Captain Morgenstern and the other wounded men.

A smile creased her face, and a warm blush crept into her cheeks. She would delight in bringing her next finished quilt to him. If only he could keep his hands, to feel the soft fabric.

Stella caught herself. Colleen hadn't mentioned if Captain Morgenstern was married, but he might very well have a sweetheart. She shouldn't be daydreaming of getting to know him too well.

Focusing on other things kept her mind busy for a while. Why hadn't she thought to bring her Bible? At least then she could read.

An hour later, she moved her chair back a

few feet. She stood, stretched her achy muscles, and went in search of a book. If she read to the captain, even if he was asleep, it might make him feel better. And the rest of the men in the ward too.

In the small hospital cafeteria she found the book *Of Mice and Men* and returned to the pilot's bedside. She sat back down and turned to the first page. Just then the captain stirred and tossed on the bed.

Stella had dealt with a few men coming out of sedation after being wounded. Some thrashed so hard they were a danger to themselves.

"Colleen! We need a doctor," Stella called. She placed a hand on the man's chest and spoke soothing words.

He screamed, bolted up in bed, and knocked her to the floor.

Flames!

The plane was going to explode!

He had to get out of there.

Where was the exit? He couldn't find a way out.

Irving heard himself scream and then a soothing voice.

Felt cool starched sheets enveloping him.

He popped his eyelids open and gazed into a pair of green eyes peering back at him. The owner of those eyes had the prettiest shade of auburn hair he'd ever seen. She held a firm hand on his chest.

"Easy, Captain, you're all right. All your men are out of the plane. Rest easy now." Her voice, soft as his favorite flannel shirt, distracted him for a moment.

A doctor approached with a nurse following close behind. The young physician didn't look old enough to shave, but Irving shoved the thought to the back of his mind.

"My crew," he gasped. "Are they all right?"

The auburn-haired lady and the nurse looked at each other. They glanced back at him and then to the floor. The doctor cleared his throat.

Irving's brain tried to tell him something, something his heart didn't want to believe. Not everyone made it out of the plane alive. He shook his head.

No! Not his men.

He attempted to rise, to see for himself, but pain surged in his fingers, through his hands, and up his forearms. Determined not to scream, he clenched his teeth.

"Easy, Captain," the doctor said. "Lie back down. Everyone made it out of the plane, but your top turret gunner, Private

Eugene Cotton, didn't survive. I'm so very sorry."

Irving demanded, "What happened? I want to know how he died."

The doctor straightened his crisp white lab coat and looked Irving in the eye. "He was shot in the chest and lost a lot of blood by the time he was brought in. We worked on him for over an hour. We tried, but I'm sorry, sir, we lost him."

Irving squeezed his eyes shut and dropped against the pillow. Poor Cotton, he'd just married a year ago and had a baby on the way. Some poor child who would never know his or her father. Riled with indignation, he tried once again to rise, but the doctor eased him back.

"Relax, Captain, the rest of your crew is fine. Frisco is right there. He asked about you for half the night."

Irving turned to see Frisco sleeping. All his men should be sleeping as soundly. He closed his eyes. The nurse had called him a hero before putting him under so they could operate on his hands. Only he didn't feel like a hero. If he was, wouldn't all his men be alive and well?

"Nurse," the doctor continued, "will you please bring a dose of morphine and something for this man to eat?"

The nurse nodded and hurried away, but the auburn-haired lady remained. The doctor held a stethoscope to Irving's chest and instructed him to take deep breaths.

"Let's check those bandages." The man unwound several layers of gauze.

Irving grimaced as the doctor poked and prodded, but the pain of losing one of his men hit harder and ached a dozen times worse. How was he to write a letter of condolence to Tex's widow with his hands all torn up?

After swallowing hard, he managed to squeak out, "Can you leave me alone, Doc, please?"

"Sure thing, Captain." The doctor rebandaged his hands, patted him on the chest, and walked away.

The auburn-haired lady remained. Irving eyed her from head to toe and wondered why she stayed.

As if she'd read his mind, she said, "I can write a letter to Mr. Cotton's family for you. I can write letters to your family too."

As nice as this lady seemed, he didn't want her pity.

"I'm so sorry, where are my manners?" She cleared her throat. "Good afternoon, Captain Morgenstern, my name is Stella McGovern. I'm pleased to make your acquaintance."

Who on earth was this woman, and where had she come from? Irving wanted to be angry at someone, at her, but she was too pretty, and he didn't want to think about pretty ladies. A good soldier thought of his men at all times. He turned his head toward the wall. He should have never gone back for another pass over the target. Risks like that cost lives. But his orders were to bomb a particular target, and he wasn't about to fail and leave the job to someone else.

"Captain?"

The woman drew him from his thoughts to repeat her offer.

"I can write some letters for you, if you'd like."

"Maybe later," he mumbled.

Footsteps echoed down the aisle. It was the nurse carrying a silver tray. On it were two pills, a glass of water, a cup of green gelatin, and a spoon.

"Here you are." The nurse set the tray on the nightstand.

How on earth did she expect him to take his medication and eat? He looked at Miss McGovern, who sat in a chair holding a book. She wouldn't be any help, not that he needed help.

"Here, let me assist you." The nurse took

the spoon and dipped it into the gelatin. Did she really think he'd allow her to feed him like he was a helpless infant? In the presence of a lady? No way. He'd learn to eat with his toes before he'd let that happen.

Summoning every ounce of stubborn pride he could muster, he glared at both of them.

CHAPTER 3

A week had passed since Stella had last visited the men in the hospital ward. May arrived as well as news of the victory over Europe. Hopeful for Papa's return, she put an extra bounce in her step.

Extra shifts at the factory were still a must, which hadn't left her time to revisit wounded soldiers. Still, she wanted to know how they were doing. Colleen had been kind enough to stop by Stella's house and keep her updated on the men's status. Frisco's leg was healing and he was scheduled to be sent home soon. She thanked the Lord and prayed that the war with Japan ended soon and that *all* the men would be shipped home as well.

Captain Morgenstern's hands were doing better. The muscles in his fingers were healing, but he still faced an arduous road to recovery. According to Colleen, the man risked losing his fingers, if not his hands, if gangrene set in.

On the way to work that morning, Stella stopped at her friend Mary's house. In Stella's opinion, Mary could be flighty, but she had a caring heart, and having grown up near Dutch Harbor, she knew the area. Plus, Mary was a shrewd trader and could barter well.

After a brief catching-up with Mary, Stella checked her watch and hustled into her coat. She'd be late to work if she didn't hurry.

"Sorry, Mary, I have to run." Stella gave her friend a hug goodbye. Although Mary lived not too far from the parachute manufacturing plant, it was far enough to cause Stella to worry about making it to work on time.

"I'll see you Sunday, for church, maybe?" Mary asked.

Hope emanating from her friend's dark eyes made Stella smile. "Of course, I'll swing by here beforehand and we can walk together."

"And perhaps get a ride home from a handsome soldier, eh?" Mary chuckled and pressed her fingers to her lips.

At the mention of handsome soldiers, an image of Irving Morgenstern flashed in Stella's mind. Warmth rushed to her cheeks.

"I have to run, literally, or I'll be late."

Stella bolted out the door and sprinted down the pathway, her friend's laughter echoing behind her.

Usually she restricted her time with friends to her days off. Today she'd made an exception because Mary had obtained a treasure and wanted to share it.

Four spools of navy-blue thread.

In spite of the rationing and the remoteness of the base, Mary had really come through for her. Stella carried the spools in her pocket. Mama would like the color and be happy to sew again that night. She wondered what her friend had bartered to obtain the bounty, but there had been no time for idle chitchat.

As she hurried along, she passed the outskirts of the military base and, once again, thought of Irving Morgenstern.

"Lord." Stella voiced her prayer aloud as she walked. "Please bring healing to the captain's hands, and his heart. And please keep Papa safe."

She continued to pray as she hustled to her job, walking briskly past the blue house with the shuttered windows. No time for daydreaming about the future today. She couldn't risk being late, not when they were so far behind their quota.

Mentally chastising herself for visiting too long, Stella rushed to her small locker and shook off her coat.

"Miss McGovern, you're late!" her boss growled. "Get your safety gear on and get out onto the floor."

"Yes, Mr. Hapsock." Stella rushed to her station amid the hum of sewing machines.

Throughout the day she worked hard sewing the long panels of nylon together and fitting the industrial machines with twelve-inch spools of heavy-weight thread. By the end of the day, her hands and fingers ached. In spite of how tired her body was though, her heart smiled as the workers grew closer to meeting the quotas.

Another thing that made her smile were images of the handsome captain that kept popping into her mind. It was a wonder she didn't accidentally sew her shirt sleeve to a parachute.

The next stream of workers flowed in as Stella's shift ended. She bid goodbye to Mr. Hapsock, who barked at her again.

"Don't be late tomorrow."

Stella nodded. "Yes, sir," she said, and hurried out the door. Considering the man's mood, she didn't want to ask for the day's leftover scraps. At least she had new thread to work with.

Think what a grand quilt she could make for the captain with four spools of navy-blue thread. Now all she needed was some sturdy cotton of the same color. There was one place to look. She hurried into the post exchange to see if any new shipments had come in.

One small shipment had arrived, but it didn't contain fabric.

"I'm sorry, miss." The store clerk shook his head. "We received 258 cases of Spam, 104 cases of powdered milk, and three #10 cans of peaches."

Stella groaned. "Anything else?"

The clerk continued. "We also received 200 pairs of winter boots, 200 pairs of army-issue wool socks, an inflatable wading pool, and 200 pairs of baby rubber pants, minus the diapers and pins."

Stella groaned louder and tried not to be too disappointed. Maybe her friends from the factory who'd gone back to Seattle had mailed her the material they'd promised to send. She wasn't holding her breath.

Perhaps there'd be another letter from Papa. Stella allowed hope to dance in her heart as she left the exchange and stepped lively through the warm spring sunshine on her way to the post office.

Grateful for the warmer temperatures, she

almost hated to step inside the small square building. But she wanted new fabric, so she smiled at the postmaster.

"Any packages or letters for Ness or Stella McGovern?" she asked.

"No packages, but I do have this."

Stella stifled a squeal when the postman handed her a letter from her father. No new material, but a letter from Papa! The Lord's grace had sidled up to them after all.

Stella ran all the way home, her lungs burning when she burst through the front door.

"Mama." Stella gasped for air and placed her hand on the wall to steady herself.

"What is it? A telegram?" Mama dropped into a chair and grasped the table's edge.

"No, Mama." Stella rushed to the table then leaned down and rubbed her mother's knees. "It's a letter from Papa, see?"

"Oh, thank the Lord." Tears streamed down her mother's cheeks. She swiped at them with the hem of her apron.

Stella fought her own tears while Mama regained her composure. She silently thanked the Lord it wasn't a dreaded telegram from the War Department.

Stella's heart thudded in her chest as she handed her mother the envelope. Mama used a hairpin to tear it open.

Mama began to read.

" 'My dearest Ness, I miss you and Stella so very much, but I'm happy to say the bombings have stopped and war in Europe is over. I suffered small injuries when my supply truck hit a land mine and turned over, but I am alive, and whole. The folks back home who put together the deuce and a half did a good job. You must be asking yourself where I'm carrying supplies to, and why. Well, I'll tell you. My company has been asked to bring food and medicine to some places in Germany. I saw things at these so-called work camps, things that are very difficult to talk about. Why, just the other day we heard about one called Ravensbruck, and —' "

Mama's hand flew over her mouth.

Panic surged through Stella. "Mama, what is it? Is Papa all right?"

Her mother closed her eyes, swayed, and leaned back in her chair.

"Mama, continue, please," Stella begged.

Without saying another word, Mama rose from her chair and tucked the letter into her apron pocket. "I'm sorry, dear, but you don't need to hear the rest. It would only distress you needlessly. Just know that your father is alive and well."

■ ■ ■ ■

A week had passed and the pretty auburn-haired Miss McGovern hadn't returned to visit the hospital. Irving's heart gave a small tug. He missed her.

"Here you go, Captain," Nurse Colleen placed a tray of food on Irving's lap.

Lunch, he presumed. He nodded at her. "Thank you."

He studied his meal before digging in. A hunk of Spam between two slices of anemic-looking bread, another cup of green gelatin, a glass of watery milk, and one very thin, nearly transparent peach slice. How appetizing.

Spam wasn't all that bad, not when soldiers in the South Pacific and in Europe were half-starved. Yet, when he was served the stuff for three meals a day, seven days a week, for weeks on end, the monotony was enough to make his taste buds cry mutiny.

"I'll be back in a jiffy to see if you need anything."

Irving watched the nurse disappear down the corridor before reaching for his utensils. He managed to grip the spoon between his thumb and fingers, as if he were wearing a pair of mittens. Somehow he managed to get the morsel of gelatin into his mouth without spilling it down the front of his pajamas. Not as gracefully as he liked, but at least he could do something for himself. Gone were the days when his copilot and his best buddy, Jack Blankston, had to feed him when he hoped nobody was looking.

At least now the bandages weren't wrapped quite so thickly around his fingers. This allowed him to eat. The first few days it was all he could do to lift a glass to his mouth and drink from a straw with the glass cupped between both hands.

Pain reverberated through his fingers, but he only had a few minutes before the medications kicked in and left him snoozing for an hour. He'd have to eat fast. He lifted another spoonful to his lips as quickly as possible.

The lime flavor filled his mouth, and he was grateful for the sustenance, but he longed for the day when he could simply cut into a steak with knife and fork and pop a bite into his mouth.

"Lord," he prayed, "help me get strength and dexterity back into my fingers and hands."

Nurse Colleen emerged from the linen closet, a handful of adult-sized bibs in her hand. "Would you like one of these, Captain?"

Irving swallowed the mass of gelatin, which felt more like a rock in his throat, and counted to ten before replying. "No, but thank you."

He used his elbows to help him sit higher in bed and then took another bite, more graceful than the last one, but a long way from where he wanted to be. Much as he missed Stella, he was almost glad she hadn't been back. He didn't want her to feel like she had to feed him or clean up the mess he made from feeding himself.

Grateful, but he missed her too. She'd read Steinbeck with such emotion. He admired her literary knowledge and figured she was well educated, but he wondered where she'd gotten that education. There was no such thing as a university on this giant barren rock the army and navy liked to call a military base.

"Hey, pal, would you like some help with that?"

Irving glanced up to see Jack standing over him. "What are you doing here, and how are things at the barracks?" Irving asked.

"Things are rowdy as usual at the barracks, and I came to say goodbye to Frisco. I hear he's being shipped home tomorrow."

"Hi, Lieutenant." Frisco waved and aimed a salute at Jack.

Frisco pushed his empty tray aside. How had the man finished his lunch already? Oh yeah, he had two hands with fingers that worked properly. Irving bit back bitter jealousy.

He was alive and whole after all, unlike Tex. Irving silently asked God to forgive him then allowed a genuine smile to play across his lips.

"Captain Morgenstern, Lieutenant Blankston," Frisco said.

"What can I do for you, Corporal?" Blankston asked.

"They're shipping me home tomorrow, and I want you to have my address. Promise you'll write to me, okay? And if you give me your addresses, I promise to write to you."

"Sure, Frisco," Irving said. "I'll ask the nurse to give you my address and have her put yours in my file. I'll send you a good long letter as soon as I'm able."

"You'll be all healed up before you know it." Frisco saluted again.

Irving returned the gesture. Jack wandered over to converse with Frisco.

Irving went back to eating. He trusted his life to God, but he didn't want to think about how hard trusting the Almighty would be if he lost both his hands.

Just then he lost his grip and upended his glass of milk.

"Aah," he growled. He wiped at the mess soaking the front of his pajamas and his bandages. It was then he noticed a foul odor, and his heart dropped to his stomach.

CHAPTER 4

Stella added a small piece of driftwood to the waning fire and leaned back in her chair, sewing with her new navy-blue thread. She was grateful it was Friday night and she had the weekend off. She would have plenty of time to sew all the next day.

On Sunday she would attend church with Mary, although it was getting harder and harder to pray for the war to end. She was getting so weary of sending prayers heavenward without seeing the Japanese willing to surrender.

A handsome Irish mechanic had his eye on Mary, but he tugged on his whiskey flask a bit too often. Most soldiers had seen a myriad of grisly sights, which in turn ushered them to the bottle. It worried Stella. She vowed to watch and pray, for the sake of her friend.

Stella gripped the needle and continued to sew tiny stitches in the quilt block. She had three spools of new thread left but only enough scrap material for one more quilt block.

"Are you warm enough, Mama?" Stella shifted to get more comfortable in the rickety chair. She wished for a bigger table, one large enough to hold the quilt top so she could more easily sew the small quilt squares and nine-blocks together.

"Yes, I'm fine for now, but there isn't much more wood to keep the fire going the rest of the night. It makes me wonder, and worry, about your father."

"Well, at least it's not winter where Papa is. Yes, May is still a cold month in Dutch Harbor, but it's different in Europe. I hear that France is lovely in the late spring, nice and warm. That's something to smile about." Stella didn't want her mother fretting about her father freezing to death, like so many had in the Ardennes Forest last winter.

It wasn't lost on Stella, the suffering the brave soldiers had faced the past December and January. Gangrene, frostbite, hunger. And what of the psychological horrors they witnessed while liberating the concentration camps, providing the stories she'd heard at work were true?

Anger boiled in her heart. How could she

not be furious at an enemy who did such horrible things to innocent people?

She wished her father, and the whole United States Army, would squash every Nazi in Europe. Why, if it wasn't for them —

The needle jammed into Stella's thumb.

"Ouch!" she cried, and placed the aching appendage to her lips. It served her right. She rubbed her sore thumb, shook her hand in the air, and silently asked God to forgive her for thinking such unkind thoughts. Then she prayed for the soldiers, even the Germans and the Japanese, that their hearts would be opened to God's love.

"I peeled the paper label off a can of beans and wrote another letter to your father on the back of it. Can you stop by the post office before work on Monday and mail it for me?"

"Of course, Mama, but we only have two more envelopes. I'll ask the postman if he can get us more." Stella finished the quilt block and snipped the loose end of thread. Then she flipped the block over and admired the colors. Her back and shoulders ached from hunching over in the dim light.

She thought of her boss. "Mama," Stella began, "will you pray for my boss, Mr. Hapsock, please?"

Mama dropped her sewing to her lap.

"What happened?"

"Today he barked at me for working too slow. He's never done that before, and he seemed so upset about it. Later, when I mentioned it to one of my coworkers, she told me why Mr. Hapsock has been so upset."

"Go on." Mama resumed her stitching.

Stella continued. "Last month Mr. Hapsock received a telegram. His son, a fighter pilot, was shot down over the island of Okinawa. He's listed as missing in action."

Mama shook her head. Stella saw her lips moving in prayer. She was reminded once again that it wasn't just the men who were paying a psychological toll for this war. Across the country, women were enduring heartaches all their own.

Stella's heart ached. No wonder her boss was so grouchy. The next time she and Mary attended church, she would remember to add his name and family to the prayer list. The list was getting so long, it seemed as though every family in town had somebody on the front lines.

The minute hand on the wind-up clock ticked as the rest of the evening passed in silence.

Her mother's voice brought her back to the present. "I'm ready for bed, dear. I'll see you in the morning."

"Good night, Mother. Sleep well." Stella watched Mama hobble into the small bedroom. If Papa went missing, it would be the death of her mother.

This renewed her resolve to keep up the spirits of the wounded in the nearby hospital, to write letters and mail them so families weren't left to wonder and worry. When would this horrible war be over so all the soldiers could return home?

Victory in Europe Day had come, but what about Japan?

Blankston had bid his farewell to Frisco and left to go back to the officers' quarters. Frisco had been given a sedative so he could get a good night's sleep before being transferred back to the States.

The dinner trays were cleared before Irving found the courage to ask for assistance. "Can somebody help me over here, please?" He cleaned his spilled dinner from his pajama top the best he could.

Nurse Colleen rushed to him. "Yes, Captain, what is it?" The panic on her face echoed the frightened feeling that gnawed on Irving's insides.

"Does this smell odd to you?" Irving held his bandaged hands to her nose.

Colleen sniffed, wrinkled her nose, and bit her lower lip. "It smells like the milk was made with contaminated water."

Irving took another sniff and realized she was right. Embarrassed at his paranoia, he decided to keep his mouth shut about his fear of gangrene and amputation.

"Let me get some fresh bandages and I'll re-dress your wounds."

"Thank you." He offered a half-hearted, crooked smile. "I wouldn't want the germs from the nasty water to cause an infection."

The nurse returned his grin and then proceeded to the supply closet. Moments later, he held his breath and clenched his jaw as she unwrapped the old bandages that tugged at his raw skin. When the last layer came off, it was all he could do to keep from retching.

Thick, black thread laced together the meat on his red swollen fingers. It looked as though Doctor Frankenstein had done the honors instead of the talented army surgeon. He told himself he was healing and improving every day, but they still hurt a lot.

"This should help prevent infection." The nurse sprinkled sulfa powder onto his hands and gently rubbed it into the cuts. "The stitches will come out in a few days."

Irving gritted his teeth so hard his jaw

muscles ached, and he could hardly grind out his words. "Thank you."

Nurse Colleen grimaced. "I'm sorry this hurts. I'll get you something for pain, but be sure and tell me if you feel nauseous. It's one of the side effects of the medicine. I'll keep checking you for fever too."

"Well, I am getting sick of eating Spam for every meal, day in and day out," Irving quipped.

Nurse Colleen chuckled but didn't say anything more. As she wound fresh bandages around his hands, he noticed a wedding ring on her finger. "So, where's your husband, if you don't mind me asking?"

Dimples cut into her cheeks and she blushed. "He's a doctor on one of the hospital ships in the South Pacific, the *USS Mercy.*"

"You must be real proud."

"I am, but not a day goes by I don't worry about him. The Japanese are putting up a good fight, and he's under bombardment almost every day."

Irving noted the sheen of tears in her eyes and decided to steer the topic a different direction. "How did you two meet?" he asked.

"My father was a doctor during World War I. He did so well that after the war he became a specialist at Walter Reed Medical Center. I went to nursing school and became a charge nurse there. Luke Gardner strolled into the cafeteria one day while doing his residency and swept me off my feet. We've been sweethearts ever since."

Irving swallowed hard, shifted his weight, and ignored the beads of sweat gathering on his forehead. "So, um, Nurse Colleen, does Stella have a sweetheart?"

She smiled. "No, she doesn't, but I'm sure she'd be open to the idea of having one. That is, if you have someone in mind."

Irving's cheeks burned hot.

"If you're interested, just ask her out." Nurse Colleen patted his arm and stood. "Thank you for bringing the bad milk situation to my attention. I'll let the cook know right away not to serve any more of it. You just take care of those hands."

Irving watched her walk away, feeling foolish but exceedingly grateful it wasn't gangrene. How much longer before he was in no danger of losing his fingers?

Not wishing to dwell on the possibility or to wake Frisco, Irving rolled from his bed, donned his bathrobe, and headed for the small cafeteria to see if he could find the military newspaper, *Stars and Stripes*. Paper was in short supply, and he wondered how the army kept it going.

Irving's mind wandered. So, Stella Mc-Govern didn't have a sweetheart. Irving's cheeks warmed once again, as well as his stomach. Should he ask her on a date? It wasn't like he could waltz her into a fancy hotel and order her a steak dinner. He reached the cafeteria and stood in the doorway.

What was he looking for?

Something to read, that's right.

Perhaps if he couldn't find the newspaper, he could find a copy of The Maltese Falcon. He'd heard the author, Dashiell Hammett, was the editor of a local paper, the Adakian, but Irving had yet to meet the man.

He hadn't shuffled more than three steps when the wail of ambulances punctuated the cold night air. He shivered.

An army doctor bolted from his office, rubbing sleep from his eyes with one hand and clutching a medical bag in the other. Nurse Colleen grabbed a sweater. They shouted orders at a candy striper and then disappeared out the front door, presumably to meet the ambulances.

Irving plunked down on his bed. Frisco sat up and stared at him with wide eyes. Neither of them uttered a word, but Irving knew his comrade must be thinking what he was.

Had the Japanese decided to retake the Aleutian Island chain? Had one of the many ships dotting the harbor encountered the enemy? Or had some freak accident happened on the base?

He didn't have the answers, but one thing he did know. More wounded were coming in.

CHAPTER 5

Working ten-hour days at piecing parachutes together, the week had passed quickly. It was Saturday once again, and Stella longed to visit the hospital ward.

First, she wanted to work on the latest quilt. Hours later, after spending the morning sewing, Stella noticed Mama looked weary.

She placed a hand on her mother's arm. "You've been working so hard. Why don't you go rest for a spell?"

"A nap does sound good." Mama set her quilt block in her basket.

"Here, let me help you." Stella grasped her mother's hands and pulled her up. She helped her onto the rickety bed in the small room off the dining area. Relief went through her when her mother was all tucked in.

"While you're resting, I'm going for a walk. I'll check the pharmacy to see if more iron pills have come in, maybe stop at the hospital." Stella fluffed the small pillow.

"Thank you." Mama closed her eyes.

Quietly, Stella padded back into the main room. She added more wood to the fire and reached for a book. It was visiting hours at the hospital, and she felt the need to be there. Captain Morgenstern might need her to write a letter for him or help him comb his hair or, well, anything, actually.

Was she making excuses to see him? No, she assured herself, she wanted to be there for all the soldiers. She needed to ask Colleen if she'd acquired any scraps of material from the hospital, bits of old uniforms or worn-out nurses' aprons. On her way back home she could stop by the pharmacy and maybe the beach for more driftwood.

Stella wrapped her scarf around her neck and stepped outside, thinking about the captain and how nice it would be to see him. Now that he was getting his strength back, he was able to take short walks around the hospital, or so she'd heard from Colleen. The brisk wind did nothing to cool the warmth flooding into her cheeks.

Later, Stella ignored the unpleasant smells as she stepped into the hospital ward. Colleen, who was busy taking a soldier's blood pressure, looked up and waved.

"I brought a copy of *A Farewell to Arms,* by Ernest Hemingway." Stella held the book up for all the soldiers to see. Many of them cheered.

At home, she was reading *Gone with the Wind* to her mother. They had gotten to the part where the character Melanie was nursing all the wounded men with kindness and compassion. In the movie Melanie said that she cared for the wounded soldiers the way she hoped another woman would care for her Ashley if he were wounded.

Stella wanted to be like Melanie. One of these wounded men could be her father. This way of thinking made her more determined than ever to be there for the soldiers. These men had family at home. Family that prayed their son, brother, or husband was being well cared for. Stella hoped someone would take good care of her father if he were injured.

Two men, one blond and one redheaded, occupied beds close to where Stella stood. "I haven't seen you men here before. What happened?"

"We had an accident on our ship last night, but never mind about that. Would you like to sit here, please?" the blond man asked.

Stella made it only one step toward the

chair between the two men before Captain Morgenstern called and waved her over. "Miss McGovern, you can sit here and read."

"Aw, Captain," the redhead protested. "We asked her first."

"Hey now," Irving said. "Last time I checked, captain was a higher rank than corporal."

"You pulling rank on us?" the blond asked.

Nurse Colleen laughed, and Stella did her best to keep her composure. "I have an idea," she said. "I can read one chapter while sitting next to each one of you. I'll start at one side of the room and work my way around."

"As long as the chapter you read while sitting next to me is a really long one." Irving flashed a lopsided grin at her.

So, the man was not only handsome, but he had a sense of humor too. Stella's stomach suddenly felt like jelly. She sauntered over to the chair next to the first bed and sat. She opened the book and began on page one.

When she finished the first chapter introducing an Italian ambulance driver and a lovely English nurse, she moved to sit beside the man in the next bed. Time passed as she moved around the room, and before she knew it, she had almost half the book read. One more afternoon and she'd finish it. She'd have to stop at the library for another.

She stood. "Sorry, I have to get home now." Worry about her mother clouded her mind. She'd have to hurry if she was to make it to the pharmacy before it closed.

"Will you be back tomorrow?" Irving asked.

"Yes, but it won't take me long to finish reading this book to you, and I'm afraid I don't have another book, unless you all want to hear *Gone with the Wind.* I'm reading it to my mother, and I'm getting quite adept at the voices."

"I'll put up with a sappy love story if it brings you back here." The red-haired soldier gleamed at her with enough stars in his eyes to illuminate the entire military base on a moonless night. The poor man was outvoted, though, as everyone else in the ward vehemently objected to the tales of Scarlett O'Hara.

"Miss McGovern." Captain Morgenstern rolled his eyes. "Ma made me take my sisters to see that movie when it came to town. They cried enough tears to fill the rain barrel behind the house."

Stella laid a hand over her mouth to stifle a giggle.

Irving continued. "Pearl Harbor happened two days later, and they cried all over again. Of course that was good reason to cry, but all the same, and I mean no offense, I've seen enough of ladies crying to last me a lifetime."

Admiration for his chivalry had Stella swallowing hard and blinking back her own tears, lest she upset the poor man. Then she had an idea. "Maybe I'll bring my sewing to help pass the time so I can visit with you all and get to know you better."

"What do you sew?" Irving asked.

Stella allowed a smile to play across her lips. "My mother and I make quilts from scraps of material, and we donate them to the wounded soldiers here."

"That's very noble of you," Irving said. "Where do you get the material?"

"Bits of worn-out or torn clothing, whatever we can find. We waste nothing," Stella replied. She noticed the gleam in his blue eyes. Could a handsome pilot of a bomber plane really be interested in her sewing?

Stella added, "It gives my mother something to do, something that makes her feel useful. Maybe next time I come, I'll bring her with me. I'm sure you'd all love to meet her."

Irving continued, "Ma and my sisters

sewed. Times were hard growing up. We had to sew if we wanted clothes to wear. I'm not too proud to admit I wore a pair of flour-sack pajamas when I was ten years old. I helped my ma make them too."

"Each one of my sisters wore at least one flour-sack dress growing up," another man said. "We'd be honored to have your mother come visit us while she sews."

The rest of the men agreed. Stella warmed inside and fought the urge to cry. Mama would love this.

Irving motioned her to his bed.

Stella moved and sat on the edge. "Yes, Captain?"

He motioned for her to lean in. "Would you like to go for a walk with me tomorrow? There isn't a whole lot to see around here, but I think some time alone would be nice."

Her heart revved like a jeep in high gear. She put her hand on his arm, shocked at her forwardness. Lord, what would Mama say? When he covered her hand with his and gave it a squeeze, she had to clear her throat before answering his question.

"Yes, I'd like that."

Colleen entered the ward at that moment and announced it was dinnertime. She pushed a cart loaded with trays of fried

Spam and potatoes.

"Yum," she said, rubbing her stomach, and hoping to remain upbeat. "That smells delicious. You guys sure get fed well here."

Stella cast another glance at the captain. His features darkened.

Had she said something that upset him?

Irving watched her go, his heart tugging. He'd asked her to go for a walk with him, but what did he have to offer her? If they weren't in the middle of a war, he'd take her to a nice dinner, one where Spam wasn't being served as an appetizer, main course, and dessert all in the same meal.

Irving didn't really think one could create a dessert from Spam, but best not give the cook any ideas.

He picked at the tray in front of him. At least it was food in the belly. He said a prayer of thanks, for the food and the fact he could hold a fork. He shoveled food into his mouth more gracefully than he had in a long time.

How much longer could this war last? Now that he was recovering, he thought about going back up into the skies and finishing the job he'd begun the night the crash had taken place.

As if on cue, three-star General Valens

marched into the room, followed by an entourage of military aides and underlings. Irving's buddy Jack entered the ward a moment later wearing a somber expression. Jack leaned against the wall and folded his arms across his chest.

Normally, his friend was a party boy and quite the ladies' man. Jack and General Valens often disagreed on things, to say the least. But Jack's mood was more dour than usual. Something didn't seem quite right.

Irving watched the general move from bed to bed, shaking hands and saluting each man he spoke with.

The general stepped in front of Irving's bed. A sick feeling lurched in Irving's stomach when the man saluted, and it had nothing to do with his umpteenth meal of Spam. He returned the salute, not quite sure what to say.

"Your country thanks you for your service, Captain," the general said. "How long before you're ready to fly again?"

"It's only been a few weeks since the crash. My hands are still bandaged, albeit loosely, as a precaution against germs."

"Yes, you must be proud to be wounded for your country. You'll get a Purple Heart for your injuries and be ready to go up again."

"I'd feel better if the doc okayed me to fly." Irving wasn't sure he liked where the conversation was headed.

The general furrowed his brows and emitted a deep sigh before he continued. "The war is winding down, as you must know, and the enemy is throwing everything they have at us. We need you, your country needs you, in the skies, son. So I'll ask you again, how long before you're ready to fly?"

Irving swallowed hard. He sat a bit higher in his bed. "Just give me another week, sir, for my hands and fingers to finish healing, and I'll be ready, with or without the doctor's okay."

"You're a brave pilot, Captain." The general saluted again and made his way to the next wounded soldier.

What was the quickest way to get dexterity back into his hands and fingers? Stella said she'd bring her sewing with her on her next visit. Maybe he could help her with it. Spending more time with her was certainly good medicine, in his opinion anyway.

Another wave of sickness rolled through his stomach that had nothing to do with the side effects of the sulfa powder medicine. Was it fair to pursue her, to allow a relationship to blossom between them, only for him to get shot down and possibly killed?

CHAPTER 6

In the waning daylight, Stella left the hospital with her copy of *The Keys of the Kingdom* and stepped quickly toward the pharmacy on the base.

Every day for the past week, after she'd finished her shift at the parachute factory, she'd gone to read to the men at the hospital. Irving was able to get up and take short walks. They strolled to the cafeteria and back, and on warm days they sat in the lounge area outside the hospital and basked in the sunshine.

This afternoon, he told her about his mother and sisters and what wonderful cooks they all were. She told him about her father and the blue house they'd once lived in.

Stella said, "Someday, when you're well enough, I'll take you to see it."

"I'd like that," he replied, giving her hand a squeeze.

The rest of the afternoon passed as they listened to the birds cawing and the wind blowing over the landscape.

A short time later, Irving's dinner arrived. Stella left the hospital, promising to be back the next day.

On her way home, she intended to stop and pick up her mother's medicine; if she had time, she planned to stop at the post exchange to see if any material or sewing supplies had come in.

She walked past the blue house but didn't take the time to stop and daydream like she usually did. The dreams kept hope alive in her, that Papa would come home soon, that rationing would end soon and Mama would have more food. But those same dreams, if she pondered them for too long, kept her from doing work that needed done.

The door to the pharmacy swung open, and she nearly bumped into Mr. Hapsock as he exited the building. The grim lines carving a frown on his grizzled face stirred pity in her.

Hoping to lighten the burden he carried, she said, "Evening, Mr. Hapsock, I hope you're doing all right."

The man emitted a low grumble and walked on without a word. Stella ached for him and his family. At least she and Mama had proof that Papa was alive. And they knew where he was. That was more than Mr. Hapsock and his family had.

More men were being trained and prepared to invade Japan. It made Stella's heart twist with worry. How many more had to be wounded, or worse, die?

"Lord," she prayed as she stepped into the pharmacy, "please give the family the answers they're looking for and peace of mind in the meantime."

The pharmacist gave Stella the bottle of iron pills. Checking the time, she hurried out the door. If she ran, she could make it to the post exchange before it closed.

Five minutes later, huffing for breath, Stella burst into the store.

The clerk rolled his eyes at her and smiled. "Ten minutes until we close, miss. You made it just in time."

"I heard you received another shipment of goods from Seattle. Has any material come in?"

"Sorry." The clerk shook his head. "We got 241 cases of Spam and 100 cases of powdered eggs."

"How about some thread, or any other sewing supplies?" Stella asked, still hopeful.

"We also got 300 rolls of bandages, 100 rolls of toilet paper, a pair of roller skates, and 5 rolls of Christmas wrapping paper."

"Christmas paper? Memorial Day is next Monday, and then it's June!"

"Hey, lady, I don't order the stuff; the supply officer does that. I just take inventory on what comes in and sell it the best I can."

Stella stifled a groan and silently questioned the wisdom of the supply officer.

"If it's any consolation, the Christmas wrapping has really cute pictures of Donald Duck on it."

With stationery and other products in such short supply, she contemplated using the Christmas paper to write letters to Papa. What would he think of getting mail from home with Donald Duck all over it? Of course he wouldn't care. News from home would be welcomed no matter what it was written on. One couldn't be picky when items were in such short supply.

"I'll take one roll, please," Stella told the clerk.

The young man tallied up her order. She paid for it and exited the store. On the way home she combed the beach for some driftwood to burn that night for warmth. Even in late spring, she was surprised how cold it was. Maybe she could talk her mother into keeping one of the quilts they made. That would help keep her warm at night. And if the war was almost over and all the soldiers went home, maybe there wouldn't be such a demand for them.

Stella stepped through the front door to see Mama standing at the stove stirring a pot of something that smelled good. Vegetables rested on the cutting board, and she was putting some kind of meat in the icebox. Where had Mama gotten that?

Stella dropped an armload of wood into the woodbox and asked, "Is that beef I smell?"

"It sure is. Your friend Mary dropped it off along with a necklace she made for you. The girl does such lovely beadwork."

"But where did Mary get the meat?" Stella shook her head, perplexed.

"Now that the war is over in Europe, the army is preparing the men to invade Japan. That includes feeding them well. Not only is it good for their morale, but they need fattened up to shore them through the hard times ahead."

"So Mary's father butchered their only cow."

"Yes, and he's dropping the meat off at the hospital tomorrow."

"And Mary brought over a little bit for us?" Boy, wouldn't the men all but do cartwheels at a meal containing beef instead of Spam.

Mama nodded and smiled. Actually smiled. She hadn't done that for so long. But the bittersweetness of it wasn't lost on Stella. It made her chest squeeze tight.

Would Irving Morgenstern volunteer to go? Of course he would. If given the opportunity, he'd fly right into the heart of Tokyo and . . . and possibly not come home! Like some of the brave men from the Doolittle Raid. Like maybe her father. It made her heart hurt to imagine it. The realization made her stomach churn, and she dropped into a chair.

No, not her dear papa.

Not her Irving.

The spring sunshine filtered in through the windows on Sunday afternoon, which helped buoy Irving's spirits. That, and Stella had stopped in for another visit. She sat by his bed and finished reading *The Keys of the Kingdom.*

The sound of her voice nearly made him dizzy, or was that the medication he was taking? No matter. Colleen's words about Stella not having a sweetheart propelled him forward.

"The doctor said I could walk around the hospital grounds," he said. "Would you like to go with me?"

Her smile made his stomach flip, and that had nothing to do with his medications.

"Where to? I mean, you probably don't want to go very far," she said.

"Just outside for a spell, breathe in some fresh air, feel the sun on my face while we walk." Irving sounded so sappy he wanted to bite his tongue. She didn't seem to mind though. She rose and put on her coat.

Irving donned his bathrobe, and soon they strolled around the hospital grounds.

"My father is in France, and it's just my mother and me at home," she began. "Tell me a bit about your family, if you don't mind."

Irving warmed from the inside out. Family must mean a lot to her, as it did him. "Well," he began, "my pa and ma run a chicken farm a ways south of Seattle. They've been making it go pretty good with the war on and all. My sisters help the folks out a lot."

"What a small world. I have an aunt. She's married and lives in eastern Washington."

"Well, it is a small world." Irving took her by the hand and they made another lap around the hospital. An hour later, when he heard the call for dinner, he wondered where the time had gone. She gazed up at him, her eyes as green as the fresh grass sprouting up in the countryside.

Irving's mouth went dry. He swallowed so he could speak. "I best be getting back."

"I'm off work a bit early on Wednesday. I can come back with another book. I can't stay too late though. I don't want Mama to worry."

"I'd like that." Though his hands were still bandaged, he reached for hers again.

"Hey, Morgenstern." Jack chuckled as he approached. "I come to visit you, but I see you already have a visitor, one who's a lot prettier than me."

Stella giggled and said, "I'll see you Wednesday."

Then she darted around the corner and was gone. Jack laughed and gave Irving a playful shove. If Irving ever wanted to put his buddy in a headlock, it was right then.

Irving counted the days until Wednesday. To make it an even better day, the young doctor discharged him from the hospital. Signing release papers was a tad painful, but the pain was welcome. Not only did it mean he'd keep all his fingers, but that he'd regain full use of them.

In the past few weeks, the involuntary twitches surging through his hands had given way to greater control. Given enough time, only scars would remind him of that fateful night.

Jack strolled into the ward sporting a cocky grin. "You ready to get sprung from this place?" he asked. "The Officers' Club has missed you."

"More than ready." Irving grinned.

That night he would finally return to his quarters and sleep in his own cot, but not before he enjoyed some more time alone with Stella.

"But I'm not going straight for the Officers' Club. Nurse Colleen said Miss McGovern planned to stop by tonight and read another book. After that, we're going for a walk."

Jack burst into a hearty laugh and slapped his leg. "You're sweet on her, aren't you?"

"So what if I am?" Irving shot his buddy a scowl that he hoped would silence the joking.

The other men had teased him about it. When he'd threatened to write them up for insubordination, they'd laughed harder. Teasing from the enlisted men was bad enough, but he sure didn't want to hear it from Jack.

"Here." Irving tossed Jack a small bag. "Carry my stuff back to my room for me, will you?"

When his stomach gave an audible rumble, he decided to make one last visit to the hospital's cafeteria but was stopped short.

Stella breezed into the hospital ward. Her buoyancy lit up the room like the afternoon sun. "Afternoon, gentlemen. I brought *The Grapes of Wrath* with me. The librarian must really like the works of John Steinbeck. He's put in an order for the author's latest work, *Cannery Row.* It should be here soon."

Under any other circumstances Irving would delight in seeing her, but now that he was being discharged, he wasn't so sure. Ever since the visit with General Valens, he'd waffled on what to tell her regarding his determination to fly again.

The general had scheduled a meeting the next afternoon to check Irving's progress. From there he'd be in training for a few days and then off to fly his next mission. A meeting that, to Irving, was bittersweet. He was happy to be flying again but anxious about invading Japan.

What would he, could he, tell Stella? He prayed she didn't see him cringe.

The other soldiers in the room expressed their pleasure at her presence. They smiled, clapped, and motioned for her to sit by their beds.

Irving was glad to see her too, but he feared moving too far too fast. If Jack hadn't interrupted his last walk with her, he might have kissed her. Why did he feel guilty about the possibility of deepening their relationship? Maybe it was the thought of hurting her that made his heart ache. If he was killed, that would wound her for certain, but indefinitely? There was no way for him to know for sure.

"Hello, Irving, I'm so glad you're healed up enough to be discharged."

The rosy shade of her cheeks and the twinkling in her bright eyes nearly undid him. She flashed a bright smile in his direction.

"Afternoon, Stella," he said.

She placed a hand on the shoulder of a tail gunner who had cut his arm while bailing out the back of a wrecked B-17. She sat down next to the soldier and said, "I'd like to read to the wounded men before we go for our walk. Is that all right?"

Such a pretty girl, and so caring and considerate to all the folks she met. How had he been so lucky to be the one she spent time alone with? "That would be fine. I'm off to the cafeteria to get something to eat.

I'll be back soon."

"It's nice to see you've got a healthy appetite. I hear the cook's making beef stew for dinner. I bet you're glad he's not serving Spam."

"Yes," he replied. She had no idea.

Did he detect the sheen of tears glistening in her eyes? Rumor had it that every available man was being sent to the South Pacific to prepare for the invasion of Japan. If she knew about the beef at the canteen, she likely knew his mission. The knowledge probably frightened her silly, especially realizing that her father could be sent there. Yet here she was, doing her patriotic duty to help in any way she could.

Not only did she have beautiful eyes and beautiful hair, but she had a beautiful soul too.

"I'll be back soon," Irving said again.

"Okay, enjoy your dinner." She opened the book and began reading.

He took a few steps toward the cafeteria but, hearing her voice, turned to watch her. She tucked a stray auburn curl behind her ear, placed a hand on the gunner's arm, and then looked to the other soldiers as she spoke.

Filled with compassion as she tended the wounded, strength as she faced the uncertain days ahead without fear, and kindness in stitching quilts for those around her. Above all, she feared the Lord. Yes, these were the makings of a beautiful soul.

Irving pulled himself away and strode to the cafeteria.

Before he reached it he smelled beef cooking. Pausing for just a moment, he inhaled and allowed the aroma to permeate his nostrils. His mouth watered and his stomach gave an audible grumble. Anticipation filled him, and he hurried to where the meal was being served.

Moments later, seated at a table, he stirred the beef, potatoes, carrots, and onions swimming in the thick broth. The first bite sent shock waves radiating through his taste buds. The second bite nearly made them dance and holler for more.

Torn between gobbling up the meal and slowly savoring each bite, he decided on the latter. His stomach wasn't used to rich foods, and he still battled bouts of nausea from the sulfa powder. He didn't want to get sick, so he ate slowly.

He took his time eating a healthy portion, savoring every season-filled mouthful. As tasty as it was, he passed up the chance for seconds. No sense in making some poor wounded man go without, just so he could be a glutton.

There wouldn't be much gorging on beef in the days and weeks to come. He thought about his meeting the next day with General Valens. The man wanted him back in a plane and ready to fly his next mission by early the next week.

When he finished his meal, he went back to the post-op ward. Stella had finished reading to the men. Nurse Colleen wheeled in a cart loaded with bowls of steaming food for the soldiers. It was time for their dinner.

Cheers erupted from the men and they clapped their hands. Content in heart and belly, a smile played across his lips. Time to take Stella for a walk.

He held her coat so she could slip her arms into it.

"Thank you." Her eyes twinkled as she spoke.

Irving took her hand and they walked outside.

A short time later, they stood in front of a blue clapboard house. To Irving's untrained eye, the structure looked sound but was in serious need of repair. He turned to face her, to say something, but noted her far-off expression.

"It's beautiful, isn't it?" she asked.

"Yes, it is." And it was, because it was

beautiful to her.

"I pray that God sees fit to allow me and my parents to move back into it someday."

"I'll pray for that too." He lifted her hand to his lips and brushed her fingers with a soft kiss. The radiance in her eyes made his heart sputter.

A brisk wind blew over the barren hills as they hiked down to the water's edge. The tide was coming in, and water lapped at the rocky shores like a zealous Labrador, ecstatic to see its owner after a long absence.

"I want you to know," she began, "I support you soldiers in whatever you have to do to win this war."

"I appreciate that." Irving picked up a rock and tossed it into the surf.

She continued. "But I'm afraid you won't come back."

Dare he entertain the notion that he'd become something special to her? He certainly had grown to care a great deal for her. Not much else was said as they strolled along the beach, hand in hand, watching the sun say good night as it slipped beneath the horizon.

The thought of hurting her tore through him like hot sniper lead. Much as he wanted to protect her from the possibility of heartbreak, he respected her enough to allow her to make her own choices. Isn't that the way romantic relationships were supposed to work? Oh, why did love have to be so complicated?

Love?

The word sucker punched him in the gut. He pulled her into a tender embrace, ran his fingers through the soft curls at the nape of her neck. He whispered her name, again and again, but the roaring in his ears refused to dissipate.

Wait.

Roaring?

What roaring?

That wasn't his heart revving into overdrive.

Irving looked up in time to see an enemy aircraft hurtling through the sky.

Instinct kicked him in the backside. He scanned the surroundings for a place to hide. A large boulder, hardly enough to cover one of them, sat a few feet away. He dragged Stella that direction and shoved her to the ground at the base of it, then covered her body with his.

A final glance at the heavens revealed the Zero coming straight at them. Had he survived a fiery plane crash just to die here and now?

The cracking of gunshots made his stom-

CHAPTER 7

"Stella, are you hurt? Are you all right?"

Irving sounded calm but firm. Once she'd taken a few deep breaths and collected her wits, she realized that, yes, she was unhurt.

"I'm fine, Irving, but I need to get home and check on Mama."

"Very well, let's go."

Stella clung to Irving as he walked her home. Still shaken from being shot at, she tried hard not to cry. The bombing of Dutch Harbor had happened years ago, at the onset of America entering the war. Yes, the threat of additional attacks occupied the back burners of her mind, but she'd prayed it would never happen.

Tonight it had.

Irving spoke with gentle words and tone and held her close as they walked briskly toward her house. Fear hummed through her veins in a steady rhythm. She'd never considered herself a shrinking violet, but

Irving's arms gave her strength. Not only did this man have physical brawn, in spite of his wounds, but he possessed a gallant courage that had shielded her from the incoming gunfire.

Then again, she'd received a taste of what the soldiers went through every time they were shot at. No wonder some of the soldiers were such a mess. She vowed to pray harder for the war to end. How much longer could it go on? Hitler was dead, so why couldn't the enemy forces just give up?

Stella fought the anger that brewed in her stomach as she and Irving approached her home.

Mama burst through the front door. "Stella? What happened? I heard Japanese aircraft and gunfire."

Her mother's pale face, her wide eyes, sent shivers down Stella's spine. No sense in upsetting her further. As if Irving read her mind, he set about calming Mama's fears.

"Not to worry, ma'am, likely just some rogue Japanese pilot trying to make a name for himself. Your daughter is safe. The enemy plane is gone. Everything is fine now."

Mama ushered everyone inside. Stella, upon finding her manners, made the introductions. "Mama, this is Captain Irving

Morgenstern, the Army Air Corps pilot I told you about. Irving, this is my mother, Ness McGovern."

"Wonderful to meet you, ma'am." Irving shook her hand.

"I'll make some tea." Stella placed another piece of driftwood on the fire. She added water to the kettle and placed it on the burner to heat.

Mama motioned toward Irving. "Don't sit in that corner. There's a hole in the roof, and it leaks something fierce."

Dear, sweet Mama, looking out for her company. But Stella cringed inwardly. She was embarrassed for Irving to see their poverty. Her cheeks flushed, and she looked to the floor. Granted, many people were poor, and with rations the way they were, not many folks lived in luxury, especially in the Alaskan Territories.

"You know, I can get some materials and patch that hole in no time, if you'd like," Irving offered.

Stella noted the tears pooling in her mother's eyes and knew what she was thinking.

If my husband were here . . .

Stella mentally finished the sentence . . . *he'd have this place fixed up.*

Mama must have drawn courage from

somewhere in her underweight body, because she squared her shoulders, smiled, and said, "That would be kind of you, Captain, thank you."

They made small talk while Stella poured water into the mugs and placed the well-worn leaves into the steaming water to steep.

"Don't you worry about a thing, Mrs. McGovern. The officials in Washington are working hard at peace talks and discussing solutions to end this war." Irving nodded at Mama as Stella handed him his cup.

"My copilot, Jack Blankston, heard this directly from General Valens."

Stella wondered if he was telling the truth or if he was simply placating a delicate old woman. She admired his chivalry and prayed he was being truthful. She pulled the current quilt from the basket and sat next to her mother.

"May I help you with that?" Irving set his cup on the rickety table and reached for her needle and thread.

To Stella's amazement, he unraveled the last of the navy-blue thread and poked one end through the eye of the needle with seeming ease. He knotted the end and handed it back to her. *Well,* Stella thought, *he's certainly regained the use of his hands.*

"Here's a pair of scissors, Captain, if

you'd like to cut the rest of this nurse's apron into squares."

"Thank you." Irving took the scissors and cut the material, making use of every inch possible. When the squares were ready to be sewn together, he set them aside. Then he managed to unravel threads from the scraps and wind them around the empty spool.

"You're doing quite well with that." Stella warmed at having him near.

"I guess it helps with dexterity." He smiled at her and winked.

His eyes were blue, but she hadn't realized until now just how blue they were. Her heartbeat, which had hopped along at a steady pace, did a sudden flip and took off like a jackrabbit. Whew, the effect this man had on her. Where had it come from? She cared a great deal for him, as she did all the soldiers, but there had been something about this man from the beginning.

Dare she allow her heart to fall in love with him, when he was all but guaranteed to head south for preparations for the invasion of Japan? As handsome and gallant as Irving was, she wondered how he'd fit into her dream of the big blue house with white shutters. Would Irving want to live in the house with her parents if Papa came home? What if Irving came through the war unscathed but wanted to live in, say, Detroit? These were questions she didn't have answers to, but she couldn't imagine developing a relationship with him and then watching him fade into the horizon like the last rays of warm sunshine.

Stella stole glances at him while she stitched the squares together. Then she added the nine-block to the quilt top. Her heart and mind were all a tizzy.

To her surprise, he fished through the pile of squares and picked one out. Then he took another square that had been cut from an old blue work shirt and began sewing the two together.

"There are nine squares to a block, if I remember correctly."

"That's right, Captain." Mama smiled.

"Remember, Stella, I told you my mother and sisters all sewed." He aimed another of his winks at her.

Stella blushed but managed to keep her tiny stitches in line.

For the next thirty minutes they sewed in a silence that wasn't the least bit awkward. Then there was a sharp knock on the door. Mama, who'd been resting in her rocker and sipping the last of her tea, said, "You two stay put. I'll get it."

Stella peeked around her mother's thin

frame to see a young enlisted man with papers in his hand.

"Sorry to bother you, ma'am, but I'm looking for Captain Morgenstern. Nurse Colleen Gardner said he might be here."

"Yes, he is." Mama stepped aside and motioned toward Irving.

Why would an enlisted man come looking for Irving? Stella's breath hitched in her throat. This didn't look good.

"I have orders here for him." The soldier handed Irving the papers. Irving tore them open, and for a few seconds Stella thought her heart stopped beating. Was he being called to the South Pacific right then?

"Thank you for the fine evening, ma'am, Stella. I'm sorry, but I need to go." Irving nodded at both of them. "I need to get to my quarters."

He grabbed his coat and hurried out the door. Stella followed him.

"What's going on? Why do you need to rush off?" she asked, fearing the answers. "It's nothing serious or dangerous, is it?" It was difficult enough having her father at risk, but to have the captain in danger as well? It was too much.

Irving grasped her shoulders. "Look, I'm only telling you this so you know why I won't be around for a few days. I could be

585

court-martialed for telling you this."

He paused, looked around. Stella's stomach barrel-rolled like a B-17.

"First thing tomorrow morning I'm meeting with General Valens. He's briefing me on my next mission and giving me an opportunity to get acquainted with two new crew members before we go up. We've been ordered to fly a mission day after next."

"Gracious." The word flew from Stella's lips before she could harness her tongue. It frightened her to realize just how much she cared for this gentle but courageous man.

A sob rose from her middle and stuck in her throat as she spoke. "You will let me come see you off, see you before you go up, won't you?"

His grip on her shoulders tightened. "Stella, no. You can't. I need to focus on my mission, and nothing else. Do you understand?"

She nodded. He gave her a tender squeeze and walked away. Would it be the last time she ever saw him?

An empty ache took root in her heart and bloomed into a gnawing fear as she watched him go. She imagined the Japanese were a real threat now, if the army was sending planeloads of men on missions.

That night she prayed and cried like she

hadn't before. Papa had somehow survived D-Day and those long, grueling months in Europe. The captain had miraculously cheated death in a plane crash. If they were both headed to the South Pacific for more fighting, that meant they were both *still* in danger. It was almost more than she could bear.

The question still haunted her the next day. In an effort to steer her mind another direction, she went to the post exchange to see if any sewing supplies had come in.

"Afternoon, miss." The clerk smiled at her. "We received only a hundred cases of Spam this time along with some dried applesauce, several cases of chocolate bars, and a pitchfork."

"Do you have any sewing supplies?" she asked, devoid of hope.

"Why, yes we do," the clerk piped.

After nearly fainting from surprise, Stella purchased some new thread, three yards of sage-green ribbon, and three yards of soft beige cotton. The pitchfork she had no use for. Thanks to Irving's help the previous night, the quilt top was nearly finished. Mama had scrounged a threadbare blanket from Mary, which they planned to use as batting. An old sheet she obtained from the hospital would serve as the backing. Once

587

they sewed it all together the quilt would be done.

She planned on giving it to Irving, but would he live long enough to enjoy it?

The following day she walked to the edge of the airfield. Irving didn't need to see her, she just needed to see him.

A large supply plane came in and landed. It frightened her to hear the plane's engine roaring. Would she ever hear one again without her stomach clenching with anxiety?

Then she watched the ground crew roll a staircase up to the plane's side. The door opened, and moments later, a thin, hunched-over man hobbled from the exit.

"Papa?"

"The supply plane has been unloaded and is out of your way," the air traffic controller said over the radio. "You're free to take off, Captain."

"Roger that," Irving replied. He taxied the B-17 across the tarmac and stopped at the beginning of the runway. Silent prayer for a safe mission.

"Max power!" he hollered.

"Max power," Jack repeated.

Irving gave the plane some gas and accelerated. Almost in slow motion, he guided the craft into the sky. If the mission went well, he'd be back soon to sew quilt blocks again with Stella.

In his right breast pocket he carried a small quilt square with her initials he'd sewn into it. He'd placed the rest of the quilt block in an envelope along with a letter he'd written. He'd given the envelope to the chaplain to give to Stella if he didn't come back.

But Irving didn't want to think of not coming back. For now, he had to focus on his mission. He worried about the two new crew members, turret gunner Private Worley and right waist gunner Private Ormond. This wasn't their first mission, but they were still green as an Irish shamrock.

"Where did the general say we were headed?" Ormond asked.

Irving detected a note of apprehension in the nineteen-year-old's voice.

"As far south as possible before refueling on the aircraft carrier and then heading farther south."

"Look alive out there, men," Jack called. "Remember to call out those fighters if you see any." Irving knew Jack wanted to keep morale up, but all Irving could think about was coming back safely.

The blue sky spread out as far as he could see; the ground below him disappeared

589

under a mass of cottony clouds as he maintained altitude.

Hours passed while the enlisted men told jokes. Jack poured a cup of coffee from his thermos and offered it to Irving. Irving gladly took the cup and sipped it, savoring the warmth. Sometimes they had to fly at such high altitudes frost gathered on the windows. So the coffee was a welcome treat.

"Zeroes, four o'clock low," the belly gunner called over the headset.

The gunners swung into action and peppered the Japanese plane with bullets. Another silver plane with a red circle painted on the side appeared and fired at them. Ormond yelled but returned fire. Bullets pinged off the left wing.

Irving pulled up, attempting to get into a mass of gray clouds before the strafing tore his plane apart.

"Flak jackets and helmets, boys!" Jack called.

No more Zeroes popped over the horizon, but it was still several tense minutes before the crew could take a deep breath. Irving placed a hand over his pocket. Every part of him yearned to get back to Stella as soon as the mission was over.

"Anybody hit?" Jack asked. The men did a roll call, and everyone was unhurt.

Irving focused on the dials and gauges before him. Something wasn't quite right. Then smoke began to pour from one of the engines on the left wing.

CHAPTER 8

Irving's plane had taken off that afternoon. It cut Stella to the bone, knowing he had been sent to the South Pacific. If only they could have spent more time together before he had to leave. Yes, he had to train for, and focus on, his mission, but there were so many things she wished they'd had time to talk about.

An ambulance had picked her father up from the airfield and taken him to the hospital. Stella ran home to get her mother, and together they rushed to see him. Mama cried and thanked the Lord at least a dozen times as they tended to her father's every anticipated need. Not that he spoke of his needs or much of anything else, for that matter.

Colleen interceded when visiting hours were over. Stella walked her mother home and spent a sleepless night worrying about both men she cared deeply for.

Mama rose early the next morning and, with a bounce in her step, was anxious to get back to her husband. Stella shoved pins into her hair without taking much time to see if it looked presentable.

After gulping a cup of coffee, Stella held her mother's hand as they strode back to the hospital.

The ward held fewer wounded men for Stella to visit, but the man resting beside the window was her father. She sat on one side of his bed, reading *The Grapes of Wrath,* but she knew Papa absorbed little of the words she read.

A much heavier version of him had gone off to war in Europe more than a year ago. Now all that remained was a thin, pale, shell-shocked soldier who rarely said anything.

Mama had perked up, though, at having her husband back from Europe. She occupied the other side of his bed and fed him a big bowl of beef stew that she'd scrounged from the kitchen. Afterward she covered him with an extra blanket.

"There you are, I hope this keeps you warm enough." Mama smiled through the tears glistening in her eyes. Stella was grateful her family was together again, but the wounds to her father's mind would heal much slower than the ones to his body. That is, if they healed at all.

Unable to watch her father in such a state, she rose and stepped to the front desk, which sat vacant. Stella wondered where Colleen might be.

Thinking her friend might have some ideas on how to help Papa, Stella tiptoed down the hallway. She really shouldn't be snooping around the places where only medical personnel were allowed, but she needed to see her friend.

Colleen strode around the corner.

Stella's heart pounded in her chest. "Goodness, Colleen, you scared me."

"You shouldn't be back here. If the doctor finds you near the operating room, he'll yell at me." Colleen craned her neck both directions. Then she said, "But I have something to tell you."

She pulled Stella into a linen closet near the operating room. She put a finger to her lips. "What's going on?" Stella hissed. "Why all the secrecy?"

"I received a telegram this morning."

Stella shivered. Telegrams usually meant bad news, that loved ones were missing, or worse, dead. Except her friend acted way too chipper to be a grieving widow.

"Relax, Stella, it was from my husband."

Colleen squeezed Stella's hands. "But you know Mr. Hapsock's son, the one who's missing in action?"

Stella nodded. She gulped and said a silent prayer for the Hapsock family. Knowing the answers were preferable to not knowing, but sometimes the answers produced as much pain as the unknown. She ached for her boss and for what the rest of the boy's family must be going through.

Colleen said excitedly, "He's not dead. My husband just operated on somebody who claims to be him. Officials are checking to be sure it's true."

"Oh, thank the Lord," Stella said. "Is he all right?"

"Yes, though my husband wasn't able to save the boy's left leg. It was badly infected after spending weeks in a POW camp."

A deep breath of relief flew out of Stella's lungs. "At least he's coming home. That's more than what some families have."

Colleen dropped her hands. "I have to go; they're doing surgery on a new private."

Stella frowned. "Surgery? Not for battle wounds, right? I would have heard about that."

"No, he put on a pair of roller skates he got from the post exchange and hung on to the back of a jeep as it raced around the base. Two sergeants bet him a week's pay he couldn't hang on for a mile. He held on for two miles and won the bet before he fell off and whacked his head good."

Stella asked, "Is he all right?"

"He will be, eventually. Right now he's got a broken nose and a broken jaw and needs stitches all over his fool head."

"Good gracious." Stella laid a hand on her chest. The idiotic things young men tried.

"I have to go. Don't say anything about the Hapsock boy until we know more for certain." Colleen exited the linen closet.

Stella stood there, thinking, and then remembered her father. She had to get back to him. She made her way to the cafeteria, hoping to find something to eat first. A tattered copy of *Stars and Stripes* sat on a counter beside a loaf of bread. She helped herself and went back to her father's bedside.

General Valens boasted his way into the room, followed by a news reporter for the *Adakian* and one from *Stars and Stripes* as well.

They stopped at her father's bedside, and the general stood ramrod straight and saluted. Then he pulled a small box from his pocket. "Major McGovern, I'm General

Valens. It is my honor to bestow upon you this Purple Heart."

Mama beamed, but Papa stared at the man and said nothing. The reporters snapped a few pictures and included Mama in one of them. Mama smiled at the camera but glared at the general. The man's reputation for pompousness preceded him.

Stella wondered if this was the homecoming Mr. Hapsock's son would receive when he returned. Her heart cinched tight in her chest, thinking of all the lives that had been changed by this war. And it wasn't over, not yet.

Her thoughts turned to Irving. Nobility wove its way through the man's character, but he didn't seek fame or flattery, by any stretch. Stella doubted he'd want his picture taken, especially for a newspaper article. Where was that man, anyway? She hadn't seen him since the night they'd sewn quilt blocks, when the enlisted man showed up with a message for him.

Panic shot through her heart.

"General," she said, not entirely certain she wanted the answer to the question she was about to ask. "Is there any word from Captain Morgenstern?"

The man stood rigid as a fresh-cut board. "The captain and his crew have been sent to the South Pacific, as you very well know. The rest of the details are classified."

Irving managed to shut down the damaged engine without too much difficulty. They could fly on three, but not too far. He placed his hand over his right breast pocket, the one that contained the remaining square to the nine-block in Stella's quilt. He might make it back to Dutch Harbor to sew with her again after all.

He worked the dials and gauges on his plane without any difficulty or pain from his hands. He flexed his fingers. Okay, maybe there was a small amount of pain, but it would heal with time, he was sure of it.

The putty-colored clouds parted and revealed a warm summer sun. It had to be past noon, but where over the Pacific were they? The water had gone from dark to light blue. When they stopped to refuel, the men could eat some lunch before returning to the air.

They were flying low over the water when three additional Japanese fighter planes flew into his field of vision. Gunfire echoed in his ears. The Zero's bullets made for a wicked pinging sound as they bounced off the side of his aircraft.

"Navigator and bombardier, take cover!" he shouted. They could hold out as long as they didn't lose another engine, or worse, get shot down.

The gunners returned fire and managed to shoot down one of the Zeroes. Irving watched it burst into flames and go down in a hail of bullets.

Flames erupted from somewhere.

"We've been hit," the bombardier hollered. "They ruptured our fuel tank."

Déjà vu?

Irving gripped the steering column to steady the aircraft. Had he survived the last plane crash only to crash-land again? This time in the ocean?

Images of Stella danced in his mind as the plane lost altitude and hovered over the vast blue water. He thought of the square of fabric in his pocket and prayed he'd return to give it to the woman he loved.

"Bombardier, make sure you get that life raft afloat. Everyone, get into your Mae Wests." It was the last thing he screamed before the plane plunged into the water.

CHAPTER 9

Sleep refused to cocoon Stella with a blessed semblance of peace as she tossed in her small bed. Fear, anguish, and hopelessness had haunted her with eerie whispers of "he's dead, he's dead," mocking her, tormenting her, throughout the darkest hours of night.

Regardless of what the voices tried to convince her of, she refused to believe her Irving was dead. MIA. That's what the other pilots had said the previous evening as they wound down the search for the night, but her heart stubbornly clung to a thread of hope. After all, they'd only been shot down yesterday afternoon. She reminded herself of the Hapsock boy and how long he'd been missing, and he came home alive. Yes, there was still hope, and surely there must be news by now.

Tossing the covers aside, she rose from her bed and quickly donned her clothes.

Prayers for Irving and his crew had flown

from her lips from the time she found out about his missing status. They continued through the night, and to that very moment.

She stepped outside to gather an armload of firewood. A faint pink colored the horizon to the east, announcing the dawning of a new day. In spite of the warm rays of sunshine lighting up the atmosphere, Stella was chilled to the core of her bones. She shivered and ducked back inside.

After stoking the fire so Mama would be warm when she awoke, Stella put on a pot of coffee. When it finished brewing, she took two sips before her stomach churned with anxiety. She rubbed her aching temples. Lack of sleep was likely the cause, but she could rest after Irving was found, alive and well.

Mama padded into the kitchen area. "Any word?"

Stella shook her head. "Here, Mama. I'm going to see if they found anything yet." Stella handed her mother the cup of steaming coffee.

"Will you meet me at the hospital later today to visit with your father?" Mama asked.

"Yes, of course." Stella donned her overcoat. "Give me just an hour at most at the airfield, and I'll meet you and Colleen at the hospital in time for Papa's breakfast."

Stella kissed her mother on the cheek. The color in Mama's face and her heartier appetite made Stella's heartache a little lighter as she stole out the front door.

She walked as fast as her shaky legs could carry her to the airfield. She had to find out if there was any word regarding Irving. Someone had said the odds were slim, but she refused to believe it. The pilots she'd spoken to had said they couldn't fly at night, but still, there might be some kind of news.

Perhaps a fishing boat had rescued them during the night.

For all she knew, Irving was sitting at the airfield joking with his crew about another close call with death.

Then again, maybe not. She pushed the troublesome thoughts from her mind.

The air was crisp that morning, almost savage, as if it too wished to torment Stella. She was strong enough to survive on her own, so why did the thought of living without Irving cinch her heart tight with raw pain?

The word *love* bounced off the walls of her heart, but she couldn't make herself say it aloud. Was it a means of shielding herself from heartbreak if he didn't come home? What if he came home in the same shell-

602

shocked condition as her father?

She passed by the blue house with the white shutters and flower boxes. Time and weather had peeled layers of paint from the shutters so that they weren't nearly as white as they once had been. A myriad of weeds had burst from the flower boxes and cascaded down the windowsill. For Stella to see her childhood home in such disrepair caused tears to brim in her eyes.

At one time she'd believed that once Papa came home he'd take care of her and Mama, and living in the blue house once again would be a real possibility. But her father's hospitalization and his state of mind caused her to toss the dream aside like a scoopful of well-used coffee grounds. Her family depended on her now, and with or without Irving, she needed to step up to the challenge.

With a waning glimmer of hope, she stepped into the office at the airfield. Several enlisted men hunched over typewriters. One, with a clipboard in hand and a pencil nestled behind his ear, stepped forward to greet her.

"Is there any news of the plane that went down yesterday afternoon? Have the patrols found any survivors?" Stella squared her shoulders and squelched her tears.

The man flipped through the pages on his clipboard, cleared his throat, and refused to look her in the eye when he spoke.

"I'm terribly sorry, miss. We've found pieces of wreckage miles from their charted course, but we've found no survivors."

Stella trembled, prayed her legs would support her.

"Wh—" Her voice wavered. "What's being done about it now? There are still patrols out looking for the men, aren't there?" She swallowed hard, a gritty, rock-sized lump in her throat. From somewhere within, she found the strength to continue. "Captain Morgenstern is the best B-17 bomber pilot in this outfit. You can't give up on him. You just can't."

The fear, despair, and anguish that had whispered to her all night now returned, only this time they shouted their evil taunts. Stella fought to keep them from shoving her into the abyss of hopelessness. Still, her voice cracked when she spoke. "You can't give up, please."

The man lowered his clipboard and looked at her with eyes full of sorrow. "Yes, we know that, and we're still looking. But even if they survived the crash, they've been out all night on the ocean, and even in the summer, it's cold. Even if they're in a life raft and have their Mae Wests on, it's still like looking for a needle in a haystack. I'm sorry, miss, but there really is little hope."

The voices screaming in her ears nearly deafened her. *He's dead, he's dead.*

Stella slapped her hands over her ears. "No!" she cried. She turned and prepared to flee the office, but General Valens stepped through the door.

"Miss McGovern, I've been meaning to find you."

This was the man who'd ordered Irving to go on his mission. The man seemed to care most about his own status, and his pompous air made her stomach roll. What could he possibly have to say to her?

"Captain Morgenstern asked the chaplain to give you this in the event he didn't return. The chaplain is busy writing letters of condolence, so I'm giving it to you now." He held out a plain white envelope.

She recognized Irving's handwriting. With a shaky hand she reached out and took the missive. "Thank you," she said.

The general saluted her and expounded on the virtues of the captain and his crew and the nobility of dying for one's country. Stella should have been more polite, but instead she bolted from the office. She sprinted toward the beach, the same rocky shore where she'd walked with Irving only a few nights ago. The same shore where they'd faced gunfire and survived. The same rocky beach where they'd nearly shared a tender kiss.

Bracing herself against a large boulder and gasping for breath, she allowed the tears to stream down her cheeks. She tore the envelope open. A quilt block fell from the pages of the letter. The block had only eight squares, and Irving's initials were embroidered into the upper-left hand square. The lower right square was missing.

She slowly read through the letter.

My darling Stella, if you are reading this, then something must have happened to me. I want you to know I grew to care a great deal for you the past few weeks. Our walk along the moonlit beach made my heart smile. I wish we could have spent a lifetime together, but God holds all our days in His hands, doesn't He?

I admire your virtue, your goodness, and your willingness to work with your hands. You extend your hand to the poor and needy. You watch over the ways of your household and you don't eat the bread of idleness. Don't blush at these compliments, my dear Stella. You are a woman who fears the Lord, and you deserve praise. You are everything a Proverbs 31 wife would be.

Someday, some man will be lucky to have you. Just make sure he's worthy of you. I wish I could have been that man. Take this quilt block to remember me by, and know that I'm carrying the missing square, with your initials, into eternity with me.

Please keep sewing quilts for the soldiers, and please take care of my Bible for me. It's in my footlocker. One last thing. Don't grieve my loss too much. I'm singing praises with Jesus.

Until we meet again in heaven,
All my love, Irving

The very core of Stella's soul writhed in an agony she'd never experienced before and prayed she'd never feel again. She dropped to her knees and emitted a primal cry of wretched pain.

Irving was gone.

The same fear, anguish, and hopelessness that had haunted her earlier now formed a circle around her heart as if she were a maypole, and then, instead of dancing in celebration, they stomped on her dreams, her hopes, and her soul.

In a high-pitched, whiny voice, they chanted their tormenting lyrics.

"He's dead, he's dead. He's dead."

And she had no strength left to fight them.

More than twenty-four hours adrift on the open ocean. An icy coldness seeped into Irving's very soul and threatened to freeze him solid. Never had he been so cold. Shivering accomplished little. Next to him in the life raft rested the young Private Worley. Jack occupied the other raft with a badly wounded Private Ormond. They had fished two Mae West life vests from the water and placed them on the enlisted men. In Jack's raft, which was tethered to Irving's, poor Ormond teetered on the verge of delirium.

The rest had gone down with the plane, God rest their souls. Should he say a few words, a scripture, perhaps, as some sort of memorial service?

Irving gripped the side of the raft and fought the urge to vomit. Hunger, seasickness, fear, all three? He knew the search planes wouldn't have looked for them during the darkness of night, but now a healthy shade of pink colored the eastern horizon with a promise of a warm summer sun. Irving refused to give up hope of being found alive.

Supplies held within the pockets of the life rafts included bars of chocolate, fishing hooks, a jackknife, and a compass. Several tins of water would help keep them alive.

A small wooden crate bumped against the raft. Irving tore into it and found, of all things, a can of Spam and two boxes of crackers. Four small tins of water were at the bottom of the crate. With icy hands that were stiff from cold, he opened one and gave each man a few sips. Next, he handed each man a small cracker. Lord only knew how long it would be before they were found. Best ration the meager supplies.

Waves battered the tiny boats, nearly swamping them. Irving led his men in the Lord's Prayer for the umpteenth time. He was just as frightened as they were, but he didn't want them to see his fear. He had to be strong for them.

They were close to Japanese territory. He half expected to see a Zero fly overhead and fill the life rafts, and the Americans, with bullets.

Sharks circled the rafts, likely hoping for a quick and easy meal. Freezing as they were in the tiny boat, it would be colder in the water. In the lifeboats, they had a chance. In the water, with the sharks, none.

Irving pulled the soggy quilt square from

his pocket. He ran his scarred fingers over Stella's initials. Would he ever see her again? The chaplain had probably given her his letter by now. What would she do with the unfinished quilt block he'd left her along with the letter?

"I'm cold." Ormond's voice was barely a croak. "And thirsty."

Jack tucked his coat around the man and said, "If we're not rescued soon, I'll see about giving you another few sips of water."

"And whatever you do, men," Irving added, "don't drink the seawater. It will make you sick."

A few minutes later, Irving heard an airplane. He strained his eyes to see if it had a bend in the wings like the American Corsairs, or straight wings like the Japanese Zeroes. It was much too high to tell, but that didn't stop them from yelling and waving their arms in hopes of being seen.

To their dismay, the airplane flew into the sunrise. There was no way to tell if it had seen them. Irving's heart sank like the wrecked fuselage of his plane.

Silence engulfed the men, and then Irving heard a quiet sob from Ormond. Unable to stand the hopelessness threatening to overtake them, he decided to sing.

Together they sang "The Star Spangled

Banner" and then "Amazing Grace." From there they pieced together some mismatched lyrics from three hymns, "The Old Rugged Cross," "How Great Thou Art," and "In the Garden." When Worley belted out a rowdy tune that would have burned Stella's ears, Irving had to chuckle.

Oh, the bawdiness of men.

The sun climbed higher in the sky, toward its zenith. As cold as it was at night, days proved to be baking hot. Thirst drove poor Ormond closer to madness, while Worley seemed to manage all right. This had to be rough on the new recruit.

Over time, Irving's skin burned, but there was no more sunscreen. He didn't care. He could survive a sunburn.

The outline of a gray ship emerged over the horizon.

"Help," Irving yelled. He waved his arms and did his best to attract attention without his movements overturning his raft. After everything they'd been through, the last thing he wanted was to become shark dinner.

Jack held a mirror in the air and flashed it back and forth.

Rescued! They were going to be rescued. They were going to make it. Irving fought the urge to cry. Twice now he'd cheated death. A laugh escaped his lips, and he would have cried real tears had he not been so dehydrated. The Lord must have something really big in store for him to be spared, not once, but twice.

The ship sailed toward them.

It finally got close enough for Irving to see it in more detail.

His heart lurched to a stop.

Attached to the highest mast of the vessel, a Japanese flag.

CHAPTER 10

Three days Irving's plane had been missing. Stella's mother and Colleen had brought her into the doctor's small office for privacy, to tell her of a recent discovery, one that could put a final end to her questions. She stared at Mama and her friend in sheer disbelief.

"I'm so sorry to be the one to tell you, really I am," Colleen said. "Maybe it's time to let him go."

The anguished faces of her mother and her friend told Stella they did care and would be there for her, but the heartache was too raw to process at the moment.

Everything in her field of vision blurred, from the medical books on the shelf to the stethoscope on the desk. She wailed and fled the room.

"Stella, wait!" Mama tried to run after her, but Stella wanted to be alone. The thought of Irving dead exploded in her soul like a mortar shell, creating deep, gaping craters. Wounds, she was sure, that would never heal. She wished she'd told him more often just how much she cared.

She burst through the hospital's exit doors and out into the warm early June sunshine.

"It's not true! It's not true!" The mantra hammered in her heart as she ran. Her lungs ached, but she compelled her feet to keep moving. Sickness roiled in her stomach. Tears streamed down her cheeks. But she had to know for sure, had to hear it for herself.

Minutes later, she pushed through the doors of the main office at the airfield. Two men looked up from their typewriters. The officer she'd talked to two days ago, the one with the clipboard, spun in his chair to face her.

Gasping, she sputtered, "I heard you, you found, found . . ." Bile once again rose from the depths of her stomach. She choked it back.

"Yes, ma'am," the officer said as he stood up. "We've recovered a few bodies, or, rather, what's left of the bodies. We believe they were local boys, but we're not sure. The doctor is trying to identify them as we speak."

Stella stood in disbelief and stared at him.

How could he be so matter-of-fact?

"You have to let me see them, please," Stella begged. She'd know if one of them was her Irving. Tall lanky frame, blond hair, scarred hands.

The officer shook his head. "We have to assume the rest have been eaten by crabs, fish, maybe even sharks."

One of the men bent over a typewriter coughed so loudly the noise bounced off the interior of the building. He shot a glare at the officer and then went back to typing.

The officer continued. "We've been ordered to call off the search. General Valens is speaking with the chaplain about funeral services with full military honors. They'll all be given medals."

Stella thought of Irving's family. How soon before they received one of those dreaded telegrams? Yes, Irving was a hero, and she prayed the medal would be a balm to their aching hearts, but no medal, full military honor, or commendation could take the place of him in person. Of course the family would want him buried in close proximity to their home. She couldn't begrudge them that, not that she wanted to, but she at least wanted to say goodbye.

"But please, if Irving Morgenstern is one of them" — she gulped — "let me see him,

615

to say goodbye, please?" She placed her hand in her pocket, the quilt block soft and smooth to the touch. The block hadn't left her hands since she'd discovered it in Irving's final letter to her. She ran her fingers over his initials sewn into the corner.

Is this the closest she would ever be to him again? She had fished his Bible out of his footlocker. She kept it on her nightstand during the day, but at night, she clutched it to herself. It was almost like holding him close. With the exception of his Bible, was this patch of material the only thing she'd have left to remember him by?

The officer cleared his throat. "Miss, I really don't think you should see him, or what's left of him, considering the condition he's in. Providing one of the bodies is really his."

Stella's middle twisted as she fought to maintain her composure. This was possibly her Irving the man spoke of. But maybe he had a point. Perhaps it was best if she remembered him the way he was, full of patriotism, compassion, and faith.

Trembling overtook her. She'd come back later when she could think more clearly. And she'd bring her mother or a friend for support. Lord knew, she'd need it.

Once again, Stella bolted from the airport

hangar office. Once again she raced down to the water's edge. She leaned against the same boulder where she'd read his last letter to her. A lone, silent tear of resignation meandered down her cheek.

She pulled the quilt block from her pocket and used it to dry her eyes. She would sew the block into the quilt they had worked on together, minus the section he'd taken with him. Rather than give it away, she vowed to keep it forever.

This time he was gone. Really gone. The mantra in her head switched cadence and played a mournful tune. Melancholy mixed with denial. Colleen's words echoed all around her.

Let him go.

From his earliest memories, Irving had prided himself in obeying the rules and being a law-abiding citizen. He'd never picked on other kids at school, never rebelled against his parents, and never received a parking ticket. He couldn't think of a time he'd so much as jaywalked. He reminded himself that being a POW was no crime, but still, staring at the world through bamboo bars was both a mystery and a shock to him.

The fact that Irving and his comrades

hadn't committed a crime didn't stop the Japanese from treating them all as if they were criminals. Not a day went by they didn't remind him of it. For the first five days he'd remained stoic as they'd pummeled him and, in broken English, shouted curses enough to make a seasoned sailor blush.

Now Irving gripped the small square of fabric he'd managed to hang on to. He'd been searched upon arriving at the camp, but he'd folded the four-inch square in half and in half again and placed it between his teeth and cheek. It was a wonder his captors hadn't discovered it. He still feared they would. The fabric reminded him of Stella and helped him hang on to his sanity while adrift in this desolate place.

Jack, who'd been caring for the wounded Ormond, interrupted Irving's thoughts.

"I'm sure his concussion has healed enough by now, but I'm afraid his badly busted leg is getting infected, and there's nothing I can do for him. The guards aren't exactly sending in their best doctors." Jack's voice brimmed with sarcasm.

Irving noted the anguish and frustration boiling under his copilot's skin. Then again, the hot summer sun was enough to boil anyone. Irving kept watch over the other enlisted man, Worley, who'd been captured with them. He seemed to be faring well, at least physically. Emotionally was another story.

One particularly cruel Japanese guard had beaten both Irving and Jack. The man had delivered repeated blows with a bamboo stick, first Irving, then Jack, then Irving again, and so on. The pummeling was severe enough to push Irving to the edge of unconsciousness. His head still hurt. He held his hands to his busted lip and bleeding temple and tried to extend forgiveness, but fell short.

The suffering endured by the POWs was not just physically difficult. The cruelty inflicted drove many to the brink of insanity.

Breakfast, lunch, and dinner consisted of the same fare, boiled rice and bugs, all in meager supply. There was never enough water to quench his ever-present thirst. The stench of the camp did nothing to whet his appetite anyway. Still, after five days he found himself dreaming of extravagant meals. Of his mother and sisters preparing ham dinners with mashed potatoes and gravy, roast beef, pasta dishes, and fried chicken with corn on the cob. For dessert, chocolate cake and a variety of fresh baked cookies.

What he wouldn't give for a can of Spam.

He'd lost track of the days, even though he tried to count the lines he'd scratched on the wall to mark the days he'd been in prison. The lines, like the days, blurred before him. Hunger, pain, and fatigue were ever-present companions.

At night, he pulled the quilt square from its hiding place and ran his fingers over her initials. He prayed for her, that she was safe, that her family was well, that she'd wait for him. His thoughts turned to the days he'd spent with her in the hospital, and those precious hours walking along the beach.

Was he listed as missing in action? If so, would she wait for him? Or had she been told he was dead? Any telegrams would be sent to his mother. He prayed for her and the rest of his family, that they wouldn't give up hope.

Rumor had it that Olympic runner Louis Zamporini was held captive somewhere within Japan. Although Irving didn't know where, he still took the time to pray for him, and all the other POWs.

Weeks into their captivity, Irving's prayers for Ormond were answered as the private slipped into eternity. Irving was grateful for the opportunity to lead the boy to Jesus before he drew his last breath on earth. At least he wasn't suffering anymore.

Heaven only knew what the guards did with the boy's body, but Irving decided to hold a service for him to honor his sacrifice.

That evening, during dinner, after they'd finished the day's workload, Irving began, " 'The Lord is my shepherd. . . .' " When he finished reciting the rest of the twenty-third Psalm, he led the twenty or so POWs in "Amazing Grace." Jack and Private Worley both wept bitterly.

Partway through the third stanza, the most brutal of the guards ran at them in a rage and began beating Irving and Jack once again. Irving fell to the ground and curled into the fetal position to protect his head from the onslaught of punches and kicks. Determined to remain conscious, he concentrated on the words of the hymn.

Moments later, he was only vaguely aware of being dragged into a dark, stone cell, roughly three-feet square. Why this particular guard hated him and Jack so much remained a mystery to Irving.

In the cell next to his, he heard Jack's sobs. Irving added a few of his own. He'd tried to be strong for so long, but each day sapped his strength like the hot sun evaporated water.

He almost welcomed the thought that came next, because it would mean an end to the pain, the hunger, the mind-twisting psychological torture.

What if he didn't live to see the end of the war?

CHAPTER 11

With bittersweetness flooding her heart, Stella stood in church on Monday evening, August 6, 1945. Her parents stood beside her, along with her friend Mary and Mary's family. In her hands she clutched Irving's Bible, the unfinished quilt block bookmarking her favorite passage.

The pastor had called a special service to pray for the people of Japan.

Stella didn't understand the science behind an atomic bomb. All she knew was that the Japanese people were suffering, and thus, she would pray. Tears slipped down her cheeks. As heartbreaking as the situation in Japan was, the end had to be near. She could feel it in the core of her being.

Papa had come home from the hospital. Mama proved to be a good nurse, and with gentle care, Papa emerged from his shell. After a few days of healthy food and an abundance of love, he regained his strength.

Then he and Mama chose to spend time at the hospital.

Mama worked on her sewing while listening to Papa read to the remaining soldiers, but Stella couldn't do that anymore. The one time she had gone back to read to the soldiers again, she found herself staring at Irving's bed, then fled the room in tears.

Three days after the church service, another bomb dropped on Nagasaki.

Five days later, Japan surrendered.

The war was over.

Mama said over dinner that night, "I ache for the poor souls in Japan, but at least your father won't have to go away again."

"Yes, Mama," Stella replied. "All the men will come home." All the men, that is, except her Irving. She learned that moving forward was a process. Most days she could manage all right, but then she'd hear an airplane overhead and think of him.

"You miss him, don't you?" Mama asked.

"Yes, I do," Stella said. "I hate being in limbo like this. Part of me hopes he'll come back, but another part of me wants to let him go and get on with my life. He'd want me to move on and be happy."

Papa smiled warmly at her. "You never were a patient thing. Give the Lord time to work."

Her father spoke the truth. In spite of the feeling of hanging in midair, there were happy moments. Local soldiers were coming home to happy families. Like the Hapsock boy.

Mr. Hapsock had stopped making parachutes and acquired funding to open a new fish processing plant. He'd been so impressed with Stella's work ethic as a seamstress that he hired her to work in the packing department. He even hired her father to be foreman. August was peak fishing season for halibut, rockfish, and salmon. Therefore Mr. Hapsock wanted the cannery up and running as quickly as possible.

And there was another miracle.

With the generous bonus Mr. Hapsock had given her, plus the security of Papa's new job, they were able to buy back the blue house. Elation had her smiling.

When moving day arrived for her small family, she was determined to be happy. She helped her mother carry their meager furnishings inside and place them next to the fireplace. Mr. Hapsock's son was there to help. He got around all right, considering he'd lost part of his left leg.

Stella lugged her things into her old bedroom, the one she'd vacated so long ago when the bank foreclosed on the house. She thanked God for bringing her, and her family, back home.

The following morning, a cool late-summer Sunday, she wore her new cream-colored blouse to church. A smart green ribbon adorned one of her mother's old hats that she'd worn during the Gilded Age. Stella didn't care that it might have gone out of fashion since then. She wore it with pride as she walked behind her parents on the way to church.

The Hapsock boy tipped his hat and greeted her. "You look really nice today, Miss McGovern."

"Thank you." Stella entered the sanctuary and found a seat next to Mary.

"That green ribbon on your hat matches your eyes," Mary said.

The young Mr. Hapsock moved to his seat and placed his crutches under the pew. He turned and smiled at Stella.

Mary giggled and leaned close. "I think he's sweet on you."

"What? Don't be absurd. He's much too young." Even so, warmth flooded Stella's cheeks. The minister stepped to the podium and thankfully saved her from the potential of further embarrassment.

Stella found it charming, the way he'd doted on her on moving day. He did have a handsome smile and was kind. But could she open her heart to another?

After uncountable days in the concrete box their captors liked to call a prison cell, Irving and Jack emerged into daylight.

"Aahh!" Irving shielded his eyes from the glaring sunshine. His lungs aching for air, he gasped at the fresh oxygen. His legs lost their ability to support him, and he fell to the ground.

Jack groaned. "Water, please."

A guard brought a bucket containing lukewarm water, but at least it was clean. They were allowed two dippers full, and then they were dragged back to the barracks. That evening at roll call, the cruel Japanese guard ranted about the weakness of those who surrender. The guard berated the men, especially Jack, Irving's copilot, his friend.

Irving could stand it no longer.

"Why don't you leave him alone?" he yelled at the guard. Irving worried for Jack's sanity. Not only was Irving in much better condition to take a beating than his friend, but as the superior officer he considered it his duty to protect his men however, and whenever, possible.

Rumor had it things were bad for the

Japanese Empire. While he'd been in his concrete cell, he'd heard Allied aircraft flying overhead during the day. It wasn't difficult to recognize the sounds of the B-17 bombers. Though he didn't know the reason for so many planes, he considered it a good sign.

It seemed only a matter of time before the empire crumbled, if it hadn't already. The frustration must be driving the guard to madness, hence the motivation for such frequent and unprovoked beatings.

The guard gave him a murderous glare. His chest heaved in and out with each breath. Still, he didn't say a word. Slowly, the man came toward Irving.

To fight back was folly, certain death. After months without adequate food, he didn't have the strength to fight back anyway. So Irving crouched into a ball and prepared for the hit. The blow landed across his forehead.

Stars!

More blows, accompanied with screams of incoherent rage.

Pain!

Screams continued as the bamboo stick broke and then the kicking commenced.

Irving's whole body ached. He was sure at least one of his ribs broke with the assault.

Unconsciousness beckoned him a half second before the beating stopped. Irving couldn't see much due to the blood streaming down his face, but he recognized the voice of the cook. It was mealtime. Literally, saved by the dinner bell.

Meals were down to two per day, each consisting of a small scoop of rice and bugs. His comrades resembled walking skeletons. His own limbs swam in his now oversized uniform, or what was left of it. It hung on him in tatters. Days ago he'd poked another hole in his belt to tighten it around his waist. Much more of the rice and bugs diet, and he'd be able to wrap it around his middle twice.

Irving opened his left eye and saw men hobbling toward a table in the center of camp. A guard stood by the table stirring a cooking pot of what had to be more rice and bugs. Only starvation could propel men forward for a meal of this poor caliber. But, starving and weakened as they were, even the sickest were pressed into slave labor. This told Irving how desperate the Japanese were for manpower.

That night when he lay down to sleep, Jack confronted him.

"You didn't have to do that."

"I know you're still grieving the loss of

Ormond. I was worried about you."

A sob erupted from his copilot, his friend. "I don't know how much more I can stand, Irving."

"I know," Irving muttered. He thought of praying, but his faith had grown weaker at witnessing such cruelty. He found himself questioning God. How the Lord must grieve such brutality. Irving had started out surviving day by day, but now, weakened by hunger and torture, he survived hour by hour.

Then came the day many of the guards made a hasty departure. Some prisoners whispered to themselves that Japan must have surrendered and the guards wandered off somewhere to end their lives. Irving didn't care to speculate. All he wanted was to go home.

A week later, an American plane dropped loads of supplies into the camp — crates of food, along with copies of *Stars and Stripes* and other newspapers, cigarettes, and to Irving and Jack's elation, a Bible. The war was over.

When reading a copy of the *New York Times* Irving learned of the terrible tragedy of the *USS Indianapolis.* The famous ship had been torpedoed while returning from a classified mission and sank. Three-quarters of the men had initially survived the ship-wreck, but after days in the water, only a quarter of the men were found alive.

Irving clutched the newspaper and shook his head. Such a heavy loss of life. It was heart-wrenching, but it made him determined to get word to his family, and Stella, as soon as possible.

The following days blurred together. American forces landed, liberating the camp. The rescuers rounded up the POWs and gave them medical treatment. The Americans were then placed on a ship bound for San Francisco. The rest of the POWs went back to their home countries of Great Britain and Australia.

While on the ship, Jack met with a psychologist and seemed to be doing better. Worley gorged himself on food and then vomited that night. Irving was content with chicken broth for the first few days. When the ship sailed under the Golden Gate Bridge, he couldn't contain his tears.

Home soil. America. He was home, and no longer under the threat of dying in the war. His first call had been to his family to let them know he was all right. But he wasn't ready to go back to the family farm, not yet. He needed time to get his strength back and to recover emotionally. And he needed to find out if Stella waited for him.

Thoughts of her had flooded his mind all those long lonely days on the raft and the torturous days of captivity. Now, in the hospital in San Francisco, he still thought of her. The quilt square had gotten dirty and tattered in the time he'd held on to it, but he couldn't bring himself to wash it. It served as a reminder of what he'd endured. He hoped she'd see it as a symbol of the hope he had of being with her.

Every day he called Fort Mears, trying to get word to her that he was alive. The telephone either went unanswered or, if someone did answer, Irving was transferred from one man to another before the call was cut off. On his last day in port, he got a call through to a frazzled enlisted man who took a message. Irving prayed the news of his survival would get to Stella. If she still cared for him and she thought he was dead, and then he suddenly showed up, it might give her an unhealthy shock. Or worse, in Irving's mind, had she believed he was dead and fallen in love with someone else? He hoped either case wouldn't become a reality.

Irving's guess was that most of the men had shipped out, gone home, and left Fort Mears low on manpower. It occurred to him that Stella and her mother might have moved away too. A mix of worry and anxiety filled him and propelled him to leave San Francisco.

The moment the doctors let him out of the hospital, he took a cab straight to the airport. There, he booked the first flight to Dutch Harbor, hoping, praying, that Stella hadn't thought him dead and moved on with her life.

CHAPTER 12

By the middle of September, most of the soldiers who'd occupied Fort Mears had been shipped back to the States. Some agreed to keep in touch with Stella. Some decided to stay in Dutch Harbor. Colleen Gardner's husband, Luke, had come home from the hospital ship, and together they'd found permanent work at the hospital on base.

Stella and her parents were all settled in their new home. Fires blazed in the fireplaces, and Mama was putting on weight. Papa performed well at his new job. Stella had more time to sew, but doing so made her think of Irving.

Sitting in the parlor of their new home before a roaring fire, Stella folded the quilt block, the one Irving had given her, and placed it in his Bible. There were times she doubted she'd ever get past missing him. She dropped her sewing into her lap.

"Mama, I'm going for a walk."

Her mother nodded and went back to her embroidery. Papa ruffled his newspaper and puffed on his pipe. Life had settled into a semicomfortable routine. As comfortable as could be without the man she still loved.

Stella donned her coat and slipped out the front door.

In a few moments she stood on the beach looking out over the waves. Every day there were reports of soldiers who were missing in action who had been thought dead. The days of summer had come to a close, and the cooler days of autumn would soon give way to winter. In spite of the cold, dark days lingering on the horizon, she still found herself clinging to a weakening thread of hope that Irving would come back to her.

A tear tickled in the corner of her eye. She had to face the fact that he might be dead. And if he was alive, would he be the same man she remembered from their walks? Or would he be maimed or mentally wounded after experiencing Lord knew what?

She choked back her tears and accepted things as they were. He was gone. At least she had his Bible. Even now, she held the worn book close to her heart, bookmarked with the quilt block that she would cherish to her dying day.

The moon peeked over the eastern horizon as twilight settled. It was time for Stella to get home. She pushed off from the boulder she'd been leaning against and tightened her scarf around her head to keep off the chilly wind.

A man hobbled toward her. A skinny man, but she couldn't quite tell who in the semidarkness. The Hapsock boy hobbled, but not this fast. A flicker of recognition . . . ?

Could it be?

Her heart lurched to a stop. Seemed to stop beating for a few seconds. Then beat again to the rhythm of his name.

"Irving!"

It took only three leaping steps to be in his arms. He embraced her so tightly her breaths came in gasps. She couldn't seem to get enough air into her lungs.

"You're alive, and you're here," she managed to sob. Irving held her close, and she nearly melted like an iceberg in the summer sun.

"Yes, I'm here. I was a Japanese POW for a few months. It was brutal, but I had it so much easier than most of the men held captive."

"It must have been awful." Stella noted

the angry red scar running across his forehead, the sunken cheeks, and his pale complexion. "How did you find me?"

"Well, first thing when I arrived in San Francisco, I called my folks and let them know I was all right. Then I tried to place several calls to the base here, but there was always a long line of soldiers behind me who wanted to use the phone too. They weren't very patient. I did leave one message, but apparently it didn't make its way to you. I'm sorry."

He tucked a stray strand of her hair under her scarf. "As soon as my plane landed, I checked at the hospital with your friend Colleen," he said. "She told me you and your family moved back into your childhood home, and how happy that had made you."

"Yes, it's made my folks very happy." Stella laughed. She could hardly believe the man she loved had come back to her. So much had happened in his absence, she wanted to tell him everything, but decided to let him speak first.

"I went to your home and spoke with your parents. Your mother recognized me right off. She introduced me to your father. He said you might be strolling along the beach. So, here I am."

"I'm so glad you're home safe, that you

came to find me." Stella leaned her head against his chest. She was surprised to feel his ribs through the sleeves of her coat. A shudder swept over her, imagining what he'd been through.

He smiled. "I have a few things to give you." He pulled a dirty, worn quilt square from his pocket. She recognized it as the one missing from the quilt block. She pulled the block from his Bible, and they held the pieces together. The forces of evil had tried unsuccessfully to keep them apart, but God had been merciful and allowed them to come together once again. It was a blessing and a gift Stella vowed to be thankful for, forever.

"And I wanted to give you this." He pulled a small box from his pocket and got down on one knee. "Stella McGovern, will you marry me?"

Tears of joy streamed down Stella's cheeks. "Yes, Irving, I will marry you."

Irving jumped up with more vigor than she thought possible from a POW survivor. He twirled her around. Then he grimaced, groaned, and quickly lowered her back to earth.

"I kinda need to take it easy until I get my strength back."

She laughed.

"I have one last thing for you," he said. "If I may?"

"What?" Stella asked. A quiet moment elapsed.

"This." Irving took her in his arms, and under the new moonlight he laid a tender kiss on her lips.

Across the country, soldiers were coming home from the war. They reminded her of worn, ragged remnants of scrap material. Frayed edges, hanging threads, a mishmash of odd shapes and sizes, but within the tatters there was something of worth, something hauntingly beautiful, something with amazing potential. And sure enough, over time, and with constant care and the help of God, those tattered pieces, those men and women of the Greatest Generation, would bring wisdom, courage, and hope to a world in need of all three.

ABOUT THE AUTHOR

Debby Lee was raised in the cozy little town of Toledo, Washington. She has been writing since she was a small child, and has written several novels, but never forgets home. The Northwest Christian Writers Association and Romance Writers of America are two organizations that Debby enjoys being a part of. As a self-professed nature lover and an avid listener of 1960s folk music, Debby can't help but feel like a hippie child who wasn't born soon enough to attend Woodstock. She wishes she could run barefoot all year long, but often does anyway in the grass and on the beaches in her hamlet that is the cold and rainy southwest Washington. During football season, Debby cheers on the Seattle Seahawks along with legions of other devoted fans. She's also filled with wanderlust and dreams of visiting Denmark, Italy, and Morocco someday. Debby loves connecting with her readers

through her website at www.booksbydebby
lee.com.

The employees of Thorndike Press hope you have enjoyed this Large Print book. All our Thorndike, Wheeler, and Kennebec Large Print titles are designed for easy reading, and all our books are made to last. Other Thorndike Press Large Print books are available at your library, through selected bookstores, or directly from us.

For information about titles, please call:
  (800) 223-1244

or visit our website at:
  gale.com/thorndike

To share your comments, please write:
  Publisher
  Thorndike Press
  10 Water St., Suite 310
  Waterville, ME 04901